FATED

3/16 Ingram 15⁰⁰

BY SARAH FINE

SERVANTS OF FATE
Marked
Claimed
Fated

GUARDS OF THE SHADOWLANDS
Sanctum
Fractured
Chaos
Captive: A Guard's Tale from Malachi's Perspective
Vigilante: A Guard's Tale from Ana's Perspective
Stories from the Shadowlands

FATED

SARAH FINE

47NORTH

Text copyright © 2015 Sarah Fine

Published by 47North, Seattle

www.apub.com

Amazon, the Amazon logo, and 47North are trademarks of Amazon.com, Inc., or its affiliates.

ISBN-13: 9781503947184
ISBN-10: 1503947181

Cover design by Cliff Nielsen

Printed in the United States of America

For Sue, my strong, clever friend.
Keep vanquishing your enemies, my dear.

FATED

CHAPTER ONE

Moros might have been born of darkness, but that didn't mean he shied away from the light. As he sat on the rocks outside the entrance to the cave, he closed his eyes and lifted his chin, enjoying the brilliant afternoon sun on his face. The breeze carried a faintly bitter, metallic tang—fumes that wafted from the sprawling slums and makeshift factories of Beirut, now a megacity with edges that butted up against the long-dry bed of the Al-Kalb River at the base of this peak. Beggars and refugees had pitched their tents on every flat piece of earth along the winding trail up the hillside, poverty spreading up from the metropolis like a fungus. Only here at the highest point did the crowd thin and the noise fade. The last time he sat in this spot, forest had carpeted the slope that now stretched bleak and dusty for miles. The air had carried only the scents of leaves and wood smoke and the wool of nearby grazing sheep.

Then again, that had been centuries ago. He laughed softly, remembering how he'd once believed he had made time his slave. He'd mistakenly thought he would only need to fight each battle once to enjoy victories that stretched long and unending into the future. Now every minute seemed precious.

"Who comes for the grim reaper at the end?" he muttered as he glanced at the dark cave, the earth's waiting mouth. He stood up and dusted his hands off on his trousers, already knowing the answer. He wasn't ready to give up yet, though. He might be the personification of doom and the leader of a vast army of Kere, the bringers of death, but he was not prepared to surrender his own life. He had fought too hard for it—and now he was searching for the weapon that would bring him the ultimate victory.

He felt a familiar pricking deep within him. Usually, when Atropos cut the thread of someone's life, signaling it was time to reap the soul, Moros passed along the duty to one of his Kere with the ease of a fleeting thought. But this time, there was every reason to do the job himself. He sensed the soul nearby, and he wasn't eager for anyone to know he was here—he had been betrayed so many times that he had no idea who he could trust. He closed his eyes and let the face of the doomed human rise in his mind, one with olive skin and black hair much like his own, unlined and youthful. He could feel the man approaching, his footsteps light and agile on the rocky spill above the cave's entrance. "I'll return for you soon," he whispered.

Moros envisioned his destination—the cavern nestled deep within this peak, down in the earth where the heat alone would have killed any human. Unlike them, he had been created in that heat and pushed into this realm to serve fate, cut from the soul of Night herself.

Now it was time to pay Nyx a little visit—his mother was the key to finding what he needed. The mist beaded on his skin as he stepped through the Veil and into the depths of the cave. Though the darkness was complete, Moros knew he was standing on the shore of an underground lake, its black waters lapping at the rocks beneath his feet. He inhaled the dank air.

"I never expected you to return." The voice came from everywhere at once, the blackness made sound.

"You told me not to," he replied, regret surging inside him for leaving her alone. "How are you?"

He could feel her in the air around him. "I am as I always have been."

He sighed. "I don't think so. The last time we were together, you had obsidian hair and eyes like stars. I kissed your cheek and wiped your tears. And now . . ." He waved his arm through empty space.

"There is less pain like this," she said. "Less loneliness. Within a physical body, with walls of flesh to contain the poison, all kinds of things can fester." Her voice echoed within the cave, and he felt it sliding along his arms and up his neck, coaxing a shiver from him that felt painfully mortal. "Now I am no longer contained." In the distance, something pearlescent and white glittered, reflected in the ebony water of the lake. An orb, small enough to fit in the palm of his hand, was floating toward him. "This is all that is left of me now."

The orb came to a stop, hovering a few yards away, flickering and pulsing. Divinity in its purest form, the night rolling out from it like a wave, making the darkness around it even thicker. Despite its beauty, the sight made his heart ache. He would never look upon his mother's face again. He drew himself up straight. Later he would grieve. For now . . . "I need answers," he said. "And help."

"And why do you think I could offer either?"

"Because you are everywhere, and see everything."

"Untrue. The Veil is vast. There are realms within realms."

His eyes narrowed. "Three of your daughters, the Fates, are in one of those realms, and that is not enough to keep them safe from what is happening. *Someone* is trying to destroy us."

"You speak as if you think I already know who."

"Don't you? The last time we spoke, you told me 'Eris is gone.' I comforted you as you wept over her, over Nemesis and Apate, too."

The orb dimmed as the air around Moros roiled and the darkness pressed too close, oily and heavy. "Can you blame me for accepting the same fate?" she asked.

"It is a choice we all have," he said. "But apparently it is possible to undo." *Or you lied to me,* he thought.

Nyx became quiet, the kind of quiet that is never possible in the light.

Her nothingness made him keenly aware of his own body, his skin slick with mist, his muscles tense with wariness and anger. "Eris has returned, Mother. I saw her myself. Did you know?"

Silence.

"Not only has she returned, but she is working against me. Against order. She has managed to use some of my Kere for her own purposes." Losing Mandy had been irritating. Losing Trevor? Painful. And nearly losing Eli . . . disastrous. "Somehow she's controlling them—there are times when they aren't under my influence. And with their help, she is responsible for scores of unauthorized human deaths. I have been called before the Keepers to explain."

"You've already shown that you can deal with them."

"The treaty that made the Ferrys mediators between me and the Keepers has stood for two thousand years. I have respected it. But because of Eris's actions, I am being accused of violating that treaty, the penalty for which is surrendering myself to the ministrations of the Keeper of Hell." His stomach turned at the thought. "And I suspect he has long been waiting for this opportunity to punish me."

"I have confidence you can convince the Keepers of your innocence."

Her indifference stung. "Even if I can, Eris has another aim. She is trying to awaken Chaos."

He waited for her outrage to flare as he named her ancient enemy, but the orb was not only silent, but dimmed, now barely visible in the darkness. "You gave birth to me—to the Fates—to bring order to the world," he continued. "If Chaos awakens, we will all fade, just as our birth forced him into everlasting slumber."

"It was the beginning of the end," she whispered.

"It was the beginning of human civilization! Before that, nothing could thrive. Advancement was not possible."

"Look at this world, my son. To what end have humans advanced?" The orb floated out over the water, sinking deeper into darkness. "They have destroyed themselves! Their progress was so swift and thoughtless that it has brought this world to the brink of destruction."

"But there is a predestined rhythm. The Lucinae bring souls into the world, and *we* reap each one at the chosen time. I serve fate, not humans."

"For a price."

"My fight with the Keepers was one you championed, as I recall, and it was about more than petty gold." His eyes were glowing with anger; he could see their ruby reflection in the water. "You told me you didn't want any child of yours to be a slave."

"It was true," she said, her tone softening. "And you have enjoyed your freedom, I think. You've done well."

"So well that my own sibling is working against me. Is she the only one, Mother? Or are Nemesis and Apate helping her?" He doubted they'd be able to resist—Nemesis was made of vengeance and jealousy, and Apate was the original liar.

They had once been his allies. All three of them had cheered him on as he challenged the Keepers two thousand years ago. They had been the devils on his shoulder. They had been a family. "I never should have accepted their help," he muttered.

"They never forgave you for turning your back on them."

"I had no choice. Violating the treaty would have been a death sentence for me. And if I had continued to fight with the Keepers, it would have further damaged the fabric of fate, something I could not risk. I was treading a knife's edge."

"And now they seek to cut you with it."

"Are you truly indifferent? Some of your children are trying to wake your ancient enemy, at the cost of your other children, of me, and Clotho, Atropos, and Lachesis. Should I tell them you've abandoned them?"

From deep in the blackness came a rumble, almost like a growl. "Would you have me take your side and stand against Eris? You are both my children."

"Eris has brought war to my doorstep. And she has help—I know she does." Someone who had figured out how to turn Rylan Ferry into a Ker, or something very much like one.

"As I recall, you are fond of war."

"Being good at something isn't the same as being fond of it." He looked about, catching ruby shards of light in the dripping cave walls nearby—his crimson eyes reflected back at him.

"How close is he to waking?" Nyx asked.

"Chaos? He only requires the destruction of the fabric of fate, which is now unraveling at a catastrophic rate. Eris has gone after the one thread linked to all others. If she were to eliminate this human, the scientist Galena Margolis, that would be enough. But Eris's destructive efforts are taking a toll anyway. If she wants a war, I will give her one. And if Chaos awakens, one of us will kill the other."

"Be careful, my son. The weapon you need to vanquish him is equally deadly to you."

It was a risk he had to take. "Where can I find it?"

"I am sure it has long since crumbled to dust."

"Please tell me where you've hidden it." He believed she was lying. He had spent the last three days—ever since Rylan Ferry had revealed Eris's intention to awaken Chaos—consulting every ancient text in his archives, but he needed confirmation of its location from the one who had last wielded it.

"When I gave up my physical form, I gave up all connection to material things, including the Blade of Life. It is lost to us all."

"It was dipped in the Spring of Life itself, Mother. Is it in Kailash? I know that's where you fought him." The ancient peak, tucked away in the Himalayas, was sacred in at least four religions, and that was no accident. It had been the birthplace of hope, of myth and meaning. "Did you hide it there?"

Her sigh pushed against him, a wall of disinterest. "Why seek something that could annihilate you?"

"When the alternative is so dire, I have no other choice."

"Stay with me, Moros," Nyx said abruptly. The glassy water reflecting his red eyes rippled, and the orb reappeared, far across the lake. "You have had your time. You made the Keepers meet you as an equal, and you changed the world. But nothing lasts forever, not even order and fate. Stay with me here. Humans will continue to die whether you have a physical form or join me. Aren't you tired?"

He closed his eyes, his world a fog of crimson. "Yes." *Of so many things.*

"Then stay."

He shook his head. "I'm not ready, Mother."

"You have existed for thousands of years, son. You have witnessed the birth and death of empires. What is left to experience?"

A bitter chuckle escaped his throat. "What a question."

"Not a rhetorical one, either."

But one too painful to answer. "I will not simply give up."

"Then do what you wish. I will not take sides."

His throat tightened. If he relinquished his physical form and became nothing more than the glowing orb that held his divinity, would his emotions fade as well? Would it make him as unfeeling as she had become? "You have abandoned me," he said.

Nyx was a cold black breeze across his cheeks. "We all choose our own path."

Dejected, he willed himself into the Veil, burying himself in its gray embrace before appearing outside the cave once more. The last time he and his mother had been together, she had sent him away, his physical presence too cruel a reminder that Eris, Nemesis, and Apate had let themselves fade. And now she'd chosen the same fate, and she wanted him to join her.

Should he?

Or should he will himself deep into the heart of Mount Kailash and claim the blade that could defeat his enemy—but possibly kill him in the process?

Blunt metal jabbed him in the back of the head. "Now give me your money," said someone behind him.

Moros smiled. "Ah, my friend, is this really how you'd like it to go?" He spoke in Arabic, the man's language. He wanted him to understand every word. "I could make this easy—or spare you no pain. But please understand that I'm giving you a choice."

"Shut up and give me your wallet, or I'll shoot." The man prodded Moros again, pushing his head forward.

"We all choose our own path," the Lord of the Kere murmured as the need spiraled inside him, an instinctive, sweet pull impossible to deny. This was who he was, who he would always be. It was why people feared him, why they hated him. But he refused to feel ashamed—he was a servant of destiny.

"I'm afraid I have no money," he said. "So you'll have to shoot me. There's the barest chance it would give you a few more minutes to live." He raised his head, easily pushing back against the gun pressed to his skull. "But I don't think you're fast enough."

Moros disappeared into the Veil just as the bullet rocketed from the barrel of the gun. As he watched the young man's shadowy form looking around in confusion, he removed his gloves and stepped behind his victim, taking in the drop of sweat on the man's temple, the frantic ticking of his pulse, so desperate, so *alive.* The sight drove him over the edge. He reappeared in the real world, and his fingers closed over the man's arm, just for a moment, but it was enough.

The Mark glowed, visible only to Death himself. It was a lovely thing to behold.

The young man gasped and staggered back, his eyes round and his weapon already rising to shoot again—because Moros hadn't bothered to conceal his true form as he stepped from the Veil. His claws curled from the tips of his fingers, his teeth were long and jagged, and his eyes were crimson. A monster.

One moment, the man's heart beat hard and urgent and whole, and the next, it faltered, blood gushing through ragged holes. He collapsed to the dusty road, wheezing and pawing at the five puncture wounds in his chest.

Moros squatted next to him and casually wiped his claws on the man's shirt. "Where do you think you're headed next?" he crooned.

The man's mouth opened and closed, but he had already uttered his last words.

Moros leaned close. "I'll end the suspense. Please give my cordial regards to the Keeper of Hell." His own pulse thrummed as he watched the light fade from the man's brown eyes. As soon as it was gone, he willed himself back into the Veil.

Given the number of unauthorized Markings in the past weeks, he should've stayed to greet the Ferry called to shuttle his victim's soul, but he had neither the patience nor tolerance. It had felt good to sink his claws into that man's chest, and he ached to do it again, just to feel the release. One fearful, hateful look from some sanctimonious Ferry would bring out the worst in him and increase the tension between him and the Ferry clan. It was best to leave.

Moros appeared in his penthouse high above Boston, and the first thing he saw as he turned to the wall of windows was the soaring tower of Psychopomps Inc. He placed his hand on the glass and focused on his reflection, civilized once again. In this realm, he looked so human, his eyes gray, a smile like any other. His heart thumped, a pretend drumbeat but one that felt a part of him. He ran his fingertips across the back of his other hand, marveling at the deceptive fragility of his skin.

But he was not human. He could never be one of them, and most of the time, he had no interest anyway. Sometimes, though . . .

The loneliness sat there, a pit in his stomach. His mother was, for all intents and purposes, dead to him. The Fates had lost their faith and trust in him, wondering if he had allowed his Kere to rebel, if his weakness and inattentiveness had brought about this threat. His Kere owed their very existence to him, but the majority hadn't returned the favor with true loyalty. Most were motivated by gold or the suffering of others. And then there were the Ferrys, mired in their own politics, probably eager to negotiate their own deal, hoping the Keeper of Hell would take care of him for good.

There was no one to protect him, no one who cared if he disappeared or not.

Why was he still fighting?

Because I have a right to exist.

Because I bow to no one.

He leaned his forehead against the window. *And because, foolishly, I still hope for things I will never have.*

His eyes refocused on the Psychopomps tower, a lighted beacon in the sour, humid fog of the embattled city. Aislin Ferry was in there, he was certain. He imagined her standing in her office, her long platinum hair pulled atop her head, her suit perfectly tailored to her lithe body, her pale-blue eyes always assessing, weighing and measuring a man in the space of seconds. She was one of the few Ferrys who had never looked at him with fear. Suspicion, most certainly. Exasperation, definitely, which he found highly entertaining. And in their last meeting, there had been a moment when her icy gaze had melted, and he had felt her eyes on him like a touch. But the softness had disappeared before he could be sure it had been there at all, and in its place was her usual haughty stare. She was so determined to prove herself as Charon, to protect her empire, to lead the Ferrys through this crisis.

And he had left her with a decision to make.

Would they face the Keepers united, or would they lay traps for each other and wait to hear the snap? Would they go after the enemies of fate together, or would Moros fight them alone? Worse—would Aislin join her brother Rylan and help Eris bring him down?

And what would she do with the knowledge that there was a weapon that could kill him? Telling her of his quest might earn her trust—he was well aware that his habitual secrecy made her question his motives. But trusting her might be as dangerous as the Blade of Life itself.

"Which will it be, my dear?" he asked softly, staring at a lighted room in the distant tower. "Allies or enemies?"

He stepped back from the windows, the corner of his mouth curling in a slow smile.

It was time to hear the Charon's answer.

CHAPTER TWO

Aislin pressed her fingertips to her temples and took a deep breath, trying to slow the pounding of her heart. She felt like she was about to detonate, but, right now, she needed her composure more than she ever had.

She lowered her hands and raised her head. The conference room of her executive suite still bore Rylan's tastes, with blues and greens and way too much gold, which she found appallingly garish. She hadn't had time to redecorate, though. She'd been too busy defending her decisions to the board. This was the second meeting they'd called in twenty-four hours, and the fatigue was a seed of pain just behind her eyes threatening to spread. "As I have told you before, I am not completely sure who transformed Rylan, only that he now appears to be a Ker. He's not on our side."

There was silence at the long table, and the ten stony stares made her wish for a shield. She stood up a little straighter. "I am being transparent, as you have requested—Rylan appeared to me and told me that he is part of a group attempting to 'awaken Chaos' and vanquish Moros, and I—"

Hugh Ferry groaned, rubbing his hand over the receding silver hair high on his forehead. "'Awaken chaos?' What does that actually mean? With all due respect, it sounds like a distraction."

"I am trying to determine exactly what it means." She was still in the dark because Jason Moros was infuriatingly fond of keeping secrets—and hadn't been answering her calls since Rylan confronted them in her office a few days ago. "But if it is anything like it sounds, the Servants of Fate—those of us who care about destiny and order and complying with the ancient treaty—should pay attention."

"We are paying attention," said Ciara Ferry, a second cousin with fiery-red hair shot through with streaks of silver. "But maybe to things you wish we wouldn't."

Aislin bit back yet another angry reply and told herself, *Stay. Calm.* "You may attend to whichever of my leadership decisions you like. I have informed you of each one. The Lord of the Kere and I will go before the Keepers of the Afterlife in three days, and I will confirm that the Ferrys have never violated the treaty."

"And will you confirm that Moros has?" asked Hugh. "Or are you afraid of him?"

She gripped the table to keep from clenching her fists. "Afraid of him? His negotiating position is weaker than it has ever been." She paused, remembering Jason Moros as he had been the last time she saw him, his mouth hard as he told her war was imminent and demanded that she choose a side. He certainly hadn't looked weak. For an instant, she'd seen the warrior inside him, and part of her quaked at the thought. Not with fear, exactly, but . . . She cleared her throat. "I do not believe the Lord of the Kere has violated the treaty. It's not in his interest to do so, and he always acts according to his own interests."

Hugh smirked as the others grumbled. "And yet one of his Kere kidnapped Rylan. Another attacked Declan and caused him dire physical injury—"

"Declan is fully recovered, and that Ker was not in control of himself at the time. Now he is." In fact, Eli seemed as determined to stop Eris—and anyone helping her—as Moros was.

"But the fact remains that Moros has lost control of his monsters," said Brian Ferry, Hugh's son, who shared his father's brown eyes and prominent jaw. "We've had more unauthorized Markings and killings in the past few weeks than we've had in the last millennium."

"Moros has also joined in protecting Galena Margolis," said Aislin. "He dedicated two of his most experienced guards to the task."

A poisonous smile spread across Hugh's face. "If my information is correct, at least one of them also lost 'control of himself,' as you so tactfully put it."

Aislin's cheeks burned. "Nader, the Ker of which you speak, is also solidly back on our side, and Moros has informed me that there is no danger of him repeating his attack on Dr. Margolis." She'd seen Nader's soul herself, a slithering golden wraith with crimson streaks, tucked into a small silver case that Moros carried with him at all times.

"You believe you can trust anything the Lord of the Kere says, it seems," Ciara said.

Aislin let out a long, slow breath. "Jason Moros has worked collaboratively with all the Charons before me. By my father's report, he operated in good faith—"

"Forgive me, Aislin, but you are not your father," said Hugh, leaning back in his chair and steepling his fingers beneath his jutting chin. "What makes you think Moros isn't taking advantage of your inexperience?"

The question plucked at a thread of insecurity inside her. She wasn't sure what Moros thought of her, only that he'd known her since she was a child. The darkest part of her feared that he still thought of her as one. "He can try," she said in a low voice. "But if he's smart, and all of us know that he is, he will work with us to—"

"To what?" Brian blurted out. "We've spent millions to protect one person who threatens our long-term profits. We've tried to cooperate with the Boston authorities, who are putting the screws to us because of the damage caused by Dr. Margolis's enemies, only to have our efforts subverted by Declan. And we have to sit by and deal with all this because you allowed that woman to become a Ferry, and now we're stuck with her."

All of the board members were nodding now, even Aunt Rosaleen, who had always supported Aislin. "I was told today that you have requisitioned the entire fifteenth floor for use as Dr. Margolis's lab," Rosaleen said, the lines around her mouth deepened by disapproval. "Which is why I requested we meet again to discuss it."

"The lab is being funded by Declan personally," Aislin said.

Rosaleen shrugged the clarification away. "I was in favor of protecting the woman, Aislin, but now we're actively helping her achieve her goal to cut the death rate, dramatically, as soon as she possibly can."

Aislin met her aunt's gaze. "If that is what is fated, who are we to undermine her work?"

"If that is what is fated, shouldn't it happen without our help?" asked Hugh, looking around at his fellow board members for support. "Why are we investing in research that will negatively affect our earnings?"

Aislin rolled her eyes. "Please. If the death rate due to contagious disease drops, won't the birth rate rise? Eventually, all those people will die, and we will reap our profits then."

"But if it happens a hundred years from now, what are we expected to do in the meantime? We don't live forever," said Ennis, his white hair tufting about his ears. "And who's to say she'll stop when she finishes her work on this vaccine? Who's to say she won't find other ways of prolonging life, maybe indefinitely?"

"Again, if it's fated, who are we to interfere?" Aislin asked, her voice rising. "Since when are we responsible for increasing profits at the expense of our sacred mission? I am the CEO of this company, but I am first and foremost the Charon, pledged to uphold the treaty with the Keepers above all else. If there is a threat to our revenue stream, we will find other ways of offsetting that, through development of additional businesses—possibly including the manufacturing of this vaccine." She swallowed, wishing her mouth wasn't so dry. "Forgive me, but you all seem overly focused on factors outside of our control."

Hugh's dark eyes flared. "And forgive me, but you seem overly focused on everything but our profit margins, on which we depend to support our entire race! Tell me this, Aislin—if Rylan is determined to bring Moros down, and Moros currently represents the biggest threat to our ongoing existence, who's to say we *shouldn't* discuss aligning with your brother?"

Aislin's mouth dropped open. "You're talking about a man who plotted to assassinate his own father!"

"But perhaps the enemy of our enemy is our friend." Hugh's voice dripped condescension. "Though I suppose it all depends on what your priorities are."

"The ongoing strength and well-being of the Ferrys is my only priority," Aislin shouted, her temper breaking free for a moment before she stepped back and bowed her head. "I am the Charon," she said quietly, willing her voice into steadiness.

"Maybe that's the problem," Hugh retorted.

"Hear, hear," said Brian. "Now more than ever, we need strong leadership, and your branch of the family seems to have lost its way, cousin."

"So now I am to be blamed for my brother's crimes?"

"Haven't you committed enough of your own?" Hugh snarled. "The city is in an uproar. In this past week alone, Declan has defied you and made a fool out of us all by helping Dr. Margolis escape from prison."

"For a crime she did not commit," Aislin reminded him. "One for which she was framed. And the true culprit has since been arrested."

"We couldn't have allowed the legal process to run its course?" Rosaleen asked, leaning forward in her chair. "I always thought you respected the rule of law, Aislin."

"I respect principles over rules." Aislin was still ashamed for not supporting Declan from the beginning. If she had, he wouldn't have been forced to take action on his own to save Galena from bitter and dangerous injustice. Aislin should have honored the strength of his commitment and been brave enough to stand behind him. Instead, she'd bowed to her fear of losing control. "Sometimes principles dictate that rules be broken."

"And sometimes principles dictate the need for new leadership," said Hugh, rising from his chair. "I, for one, have lost confidence in this Charon's ability to manage the empire. She has neither the will nor the know-how to guide us through this crisis. I cannot in good conscience continue as a member of this board if she remains at the helm. Our summit with the Keepers looms, and nothing could carry higher stakes. If Moros is able to convince them that we are unnecessary or incompetent, they could withdraw all our privileges entirely, leaving us as regular mortals— with a host of Kere that would be happy to avenge years of imagined slights." Hugh's arms rose from his sides as his voice carried through the conference room. "We need authority and strength from our leader at a time like this." He gestured at Aislin. "And right now we have a Charon who can't even control her own little brother."

"I vote to remove Aislin Ferry from the position, and I nominate Hugh Ferry to replace her," said Brian, his smile triumphant.

"Seconded," said Ciara, "And I—" She gasped, staring over Aislin's shoulder.

Aislin whirled around, having felt the heat at her back. Terror surged inside her as she pictured Rylan, his eyes glowing red. But the eyes she found herself staring into weren't her brother's. "Jason," she whispered, too startled to find her full voice—or her formality.

The Lord of the Kere smirked at the assembled Ferrys. "Pardon me for interrupting."

"Oh, I'm thinking we're almost done," said Hugh, his nostrils flaring. "But perhaps you'd like to wait outside while we conclude our business."

Moros, dressed in an elegant black suit, his ebony hair slicked back and a small gold hoop glinting in his left ear, tilted his head. "And perhaps I wouldn't. I couldn't help but overhear a bit of your conversation." He glanced at Aislin before returning his focus to Hugh. "I think there are things you should know."

"I think we know all we need to," said Ciara, her eyes narrowed.

"Or just all you want to," replied Moros. "As it turns out, my dear Ferrys, my family is just as dysfunctional as yours." His tone was amused. His control made Aislin envious. "At least one of my sisters is working to bring about the end of the Servants of Fate. She is hoping, I think, that the Keepers will do it for her, but failing that, she will cause the return of Chaos himself. Please trust me when I say that this is an outcome you should try to avoid at all costs."

"And what is the cost?" Ennis said, banging his gnarled fist on the table. "You allowing your creatures to abuse and threaten us? You conspiring to remove us from power altogether?"

Moros took a step forward, so that he was standing right next to Aislin. She could feel the heat from his body against her cool skin, raising the tiny hairs along her arms. "I will do whatever is necessary to protect destiny and fate. It is the reason I exist." He stared Ennis down. "And if I sense the Ferrys are not my allies in this mission, you may rely on me to bring you low."

Ennis's eyes widened at the threat, and his wrinkled face turned a mottled purple. He jabbed a thick finger at Moros. "You see?" he said, his voice shrill. "I knew he wasn't on our side!"

"That's not what he said," Aislin replied, annoyed at Moros for stirring the pot.

"Thank you," Moros said smoothly. "I said I serve fate, which automatically aligns me with those who do the same. Based on my understanding of you esteemed people, there is currently only one Ferry I trust as a fit partner during this crisis, and she is standing right next to me."

Aislin blinked, then carefully controlled her expression as Moros continued.

"If the board decides to remove her from her position and impose new leadership, it will destabilize our alliance. I am sorry to say that the Keepers would not be pleased to hear of it." He laid his gloved palms on the table, and every single board member flinched. "I strongly suggest you postpone this ill-conceived action. Think of the future." His lips curled into a devastating half smile.

"I-I move that we meet again in twenty-four hours," said Rosaleen, her face pale.

"Seconded," muttered Ennis, leaving clammy handprints on the table as he pushed his chair back.

Hugh's high forehead shone beneath the overhead lights, an expanse of blotchy pink interrupted only by a deep widow's peak. "I suggest you all take the time to truly consider what you're committing to," he said, his voice trembling with rage. "The Lord of the Kere is clearly as good as his minions when it comes to intimidation."

"A convenient mischaracterization," said Moros. "But call it what you will. Again, I do apologize for interrupting your meeting."

As the other board members rose from their seats and rushed from the room, murmuring angrily among themselves, Aislin gritted her teeth. "Can I see you in my office, please?" she asked stiffly.

Then, without a backward glance, she turned and stalked toward her private elevator. She focused on walking steadily, on keeping her head high, even though her eyes stung with tears of humiliation. She jabbed the elevator button and stepped inside when the door opened, not waiting for Moros to follow.

She was not surprised to step out of the elevator and find him leaning against her desk, looking suave and smug and so distractingly handsome that she had the sudden and ridiculous urge to throw something at him. She closed her eyes for a moment, reminding herself that emotionality was the enemy. "In the future, I would appreciate it if you would not intrude on Psychopomps board meetings," she said.

"Even when it saves you from losing your job?" He reached up and loosened the knot in his scarlet tie. "Come now—I thought you respected results."

"Results? We have another meeting in twenty-four hours, and you just sent my board away to angrily conspire in the meantime. *Without consulting me first.*"

He waved away the complaint with a gloved hand. "They're easily manipulated, ready to turn on each other whenever it becomes convenient, just like they turned on you. I would have thought you'd be happy for the interruption."

"You undermined me."

His lazy smile faded. "I was trying to do the opposite."

"Because you didn't think more than one step ahead." She walked to her desk and glanced down at the screen embedded in its surface, currently streaming performance updates from financial markets around the world. "The board already believed me to be weak. You just bolstered that belief by swooping down to rescue me."

He chuckled, and the sound vibrated along her limbs, making her feel even more unsteady. "Are you in need of rescue, Aislin?"

"No," she said, hating the tremor in her voice.

He stood on the other side of her desk, and she fought to meet his eyes. "You underestimate your power," he said quietly.

"I've told you before—don't patronize me."

He sighed. "It's merely an observation, Aislin, informed by many years of working with your predecessors."

She almost laughed. *Many* years. More like two thousand. "I am realistic, Jason. And realism leads to caution. Do not mistake that for a lack of confidence." And then she betrayed herself by looking away, too afraid he would see exactly how uncertain she was.

"Very well." His voice was low, deep, and rich. "You don't underestimate yourself. You underestimate my need for your help."

She raised her head and found him staring out the window at the skyline of the city. "Has something happened?"

"Maybe." He gave her a sidelong glance. "First, I need to hear your answer. I need to know if we are to be allies."

Or enemies, she thought. She glanced at his hands, clad in black leather, so feared and notorious for the pain their simple touch could cause. He coaxed the future out of people; he could know their secrets with a brush of his fingers. Her little sister had been one of his victims but had somehow survived it. Aislin had heard stories, though, of those who weren't so lucky, those who had been driven mad as the weight of the years ahead crushed them. And if he could cause that much suffering with a mere touch, what else could he do? He was Death. He led an army of killers. If she were to turn against him, she would have to do it very, very carefully.

But as her gaze slid up his body and settled on his face, she felt moved to help him instead. "Make me understand the threat," she said slowly. "If you want me as an ally, I need to know everything you do."

That lazy smile returned, and Aislin huffed with exasperation. "Just tell me the basics, then, without the mocking commentary."

He laughed, his canines catching the light. "How well you know me."

She wasn't sure she did—but she couldn't remember a time when she hadn't been fascinated with him, first uncritically and then begrudgingly, and she couldn't recall a time when he'd looked as tired as he did now. "What is Chaos, really?" she asked.

"He is the enemy of fate." Moros strode to one of the couches in her sitting area and settled himself on it, gracefully unbuttoning his suit coat. Then he spread his arms along the back of the sofa and began tapping his fingers rhythmically.

As she took a seat across from him, she became keenly aware that his fingertips were striking the cushions in time with the beat of her heart. There was a full ten feet between them, but suddenly it felt much smaller. "Why had I never heard of Chaos before Rylan appeared in this office a few days ago to taunt us?"

"Because Chaos was vanquished ages ago—by my mother."

"Your mother . . . Nyx." Aislin's father had told her of Moros's origins, conceived from his mother's will alone, born fully grown. "How did she defeat him?"

Moros's stare was an intrusion she felt along her spine, deep in her belly. It was as if he were trying to dismantle her with his gaze, to unravel every secret thought. "She used an ancient weapon." His mouth opened, and it seemed like the words were poised on his tongue. But then he focused his attention on the darkness outside the window. "It is long since lost."

Frustration flared hot in her chest. "You're holding back."

He kept his attention on the night. "When the first of the Servants of Fate came into the world, our existence kept Chaos, one of the original, primordial gods, in deep sleep. He cannot rule while I walk the planet, while my sisters weave the fabric of destiny, while we keep watch over the order of things. But if we are defeated, he will rise, and he will bring total destruction in his wake. The bombings here in Boston over the last week would be just a tiny ripple compared to what he would inflict. Cities and countries would fall. Civilization would collapse. No one would be safe."

Aislin's stomach churned. "And us?"

"You could not hope to maintain your grip on power, not that it would matter anyway. If I perish, the Kere will be subject to the will of the first being to seize their souls. They could fall into the hands of the enemy."

"You said you had safeguarded their souls."

"I have done what I can, Aislin, but I am not all-powerful." For a moment, his face fell, and Aislin read the desolation in his unfocused stare.

She had the urge to kneel beside him and smooth his worry lines with her fingertip. The sensation was so sudden, so compelling, that it pulled her to the edge of her seat before she managed to stop herself. "Are you all right, Jason?" she asked quietly.

He turned from the window. "Am I . . . *all right*?"

She could feel the blush creeping up from her chest, threatening to stain her pale skin. "I-I just meant, well, since the fabric is unraveling, I wondered if you felt it. If it made you feel sick, or weak."

"Oh." He was silent just long enough to make her heart pound. "I am as strong as I need to be, as always." His cockiness disrupted whatever moment they might have shared.

"What do you propose we do next?" she asked. "We have seventy-two hours until our summit with the Keepers, my board is in rebellion, and your sister and my brother are off somewhere plotting to bring us down. Now might be the time to try to acquire that ancient weapon you mentioned."

He smiled, and it made her breath catch. It wasn't the calculating smile he so often wore, or the mocking one that made her blood boil. This was open and shocking in its beauty. "You make it sound very simple."

"If I focus on the magnitude of what we're facing, I'll collapse under its weight," she admitted.

His smile disappeared. "I believe I know what you mean." He was silent for a second, peering at her across the distance between them. Once again, Aislin wanted to reach out, to risk the fear that he wouldn't reach back, simply because it felt so truthful.

You can't understand him, her father had told her once. *He's beyond us. But he reveals his character in his actions, if you take the time to look.*

She was looking now. And having trouble looking away. "I've frozen Rylan's funds, for what it's worth. And I tried to warn the board of what he's become, in case he visits any of them."

"They don't hold the power, so they won't hold his interest. Make sure your personal security detail is alert, though, hmm?"

"I already have."

He stood up. "Well, I have a little errand to run. But first I need to check in with my sisters." He moved toward her, getting close enough for the temperature around her to rise. "Aislin, I believe Eris is not the only one of my siblings working against me. Apate—lies—and Nemesis—vengeance—are probably helping her."

"I'm sorry." She knew the sting of family betrayal.

"We've been playing defense since the beginning of this fight, and it's time to start playing offense."

"Agreed. What do you need me to do?"

"Decide which of your Ferrys you trust. Tell them what is happening and warn them of Rylan's betrayal. Have them keep you apprised of any unusual behavior from my Kere and let me know immediately if you have news. And do what you do best, my dear."

Her eyebrows rose.

He leaned forward. "Vanquish your enemies."

Aislin's heart skipped. He was right. She had a coalition to form and board members to corral. "I'll see to it."

His grin returned as he offered his hand. "Allies?"

This was it, her point of no return. If he was lulling her into providing her cooperation just so he could stab her in the back in front of the Keepers, she was stepping right into his trap. But she didn't believe it was a ruse; she'd seen the desperation and loneliness in those cold gray eyes.

But she also knew he wasn't telling her everything. And if he was planning to betray her, she would fight back with every ounce of cunning she possessed.

She slid her palm along his, only a thin layer of leather between them, their fingers curving, their grips tight. "Allies."

He squeezed her hand. "You'll see me again soon." And then he disappeared.

Aislin looked down at her fingers, still warm from his, hoping she hadn't just sealed her own doom. Then she pulled her phone from her pocket as it buzzed.

It was Cavan, the Ferrys' ambassador to the Lucinae, the beings responsible for transporting new souls from the Spring of Life into the human realm. His sculpted face appeared on her screen as she touched his name. "Aislin," he said in a tight voice. "Can I schedule a meeting with you for this week?"

"This week is rather inconvenient. Can't it wait until our monthly meeting?"

He shook his head, and from the way his eyes darted to the side, she could tell he wasn't alone. "I really have to talk to you about something."

Her heart knocked against her ribs as she tapped out a text, one she hoped his companion couldn't see. *Are you safe?*

As soon as he read it, he laughed, but it was strained. "Yes. That's not an issue." His eyes met hers again. "But I'd be grateful if you'd make time."

Cavan was so dependably tactful, so calm and courteous even under pressure, that she wondered what could make him this jittery. "I'll tell my assistant to make room on my schedule," she said. "He'll call you with a time."

Her ambassador gave her a relieved smile, even as his eyes flicked to the side once more. Aislin's fingers curled around the phone. "And will you be coming to this meeting alone?"

"Oh—yes. I'll be alone." His jaw tightened. "I should go. I don't want to take up more of your time. But I'll see you very soon—and thank you." His handsome face disappeared from her screen.

Aislin frowned as she slipped the phone back into her pocket. One more thing to add to her list of worries. Maybe it was good they would be meeting in the next few days—she could tell Cavan about Moros's siblings, a warning he could take to the Lucinae. But she would also be on her guard; after what had happened with Trevor, the Ker who infiltrated Psychopomps and helped Rylan escape, she needed to be ready for anything.

"Ms. Ferry?"

Aislin turned to see the wide-eyed face of one of her guards, a distant cousin, peering at her from the Veil through the circular window of his Scope. "What's wrong?"

He opened his mouth to speak, then let out a wrenching scream, his Scope falling from his hands and landing, still open, on the floor.

Aislin staggered back as Rylan appeared in front of her, his fingers dripping with blood. He leaned over, picked up the guard's Scope, compacted it, and tossed it. The disk landed on her desk and spun on its edge.

"Hello, Aislin," her brother said, wiping his bloody hands on the upholstery of a nearby chair. "I thought it was time we had a talk, just the two of us."

CHAPTER THREE

The moment Moros stepped through the Veil and into his sisters' domain, he knew he was running out of time. The fabric of fate hung from its massive frame, yawning rips and tears scattered along its shimmering expanse, millions of stray threads dangling loose, a few sections dangling to the travertine floor as if carelessly sliced away.

"Welcome back, brother," said a hard voice. "I hope you've been off having fun."

Moros turned to see Atropos glaring at him, her black hair dull beneath the glittering complexity of the fabric above her head. She held her curved sickle in one hand, the tool she used to cut the threads of life that turned gray, the souls whose time had come.

"Not exactly. I went to visit Mother."

"You didn't tell us you were going to see her."

"It was a spontaneous decision." One he'd made out of desperation and hope—the two things fueling him right now. "She has faded to abstraction, I'm afraid."

"Something we all should probably have done centuries ago," Atropos said bitterly. "It would have saved us from this."

Maybe it would have, but he couldn't bring himself to agree. "At least this way we can greet our enemies with weapons in our hands."

"What weapons?" she snapped, waving her sickle. "This? It will do me little good against what's coming for us."

"I plan to be holding the weapon Mother used to defeat Chaos in the first place." He watched Atropos closely, waiting for her reaction to the news.

Her lip curled in disgust, and she turned away. "Best of luck with that—another ridiculous waste of time."

His brow furrowed. "The Blade of Life could save us, even if Chaos were to stride into this domain and try to dismantle the loom himself."

"And who would wield it—you?"

"Of course."

"So like always, you'll follow your futile quests, leaving us to do the real work. Have you ever thought about what it's like for us here, brother? Locked away, toiling, with only each other for company, while you come and go as you please?" Atropos rolled her eyes, which were ringed by dark circles. "Go talk to Lachesis and Clotho. I have a job to do."

He took a step back, regret and sorrow twisting inside. There had been a time when he and Atropos had adored each other. She was the sickle and he was the reaper, clearly the more bloodthirsty of all the siblings—and the fiercest. But sometime over the last many years, the fondness had faded, replaced by resentment. "Atropos, I'm trying to save us. I'll make this better—I promise."

The sickle of death caught light from above as she lunged forward and edged it up under his chin. He felt the nip, but it was like that of a friendly animal, one that knew its master, as he met her dark gaze. "Save your promises for someone who has faith in you," she said. Then she turned and stalked away, pausing only to grab a graying thread and brutally cut it away.

Moros flinched as he felt the sting. He pushed the hurt away, willing one of his Kere to reap the soul, and headed for the loom, frowning at the clanking coming from the other side. When he peeked around the edge of the fabric, he saw Lachesis, her short blonde hair standing on end, kicking the grand loom. She was disheveled, her suit jacket hanging open to reveal a sweat-stained shirt beneath. "Has it malfunctioned?" he asked.

Her head jerked up at the sound of his voice. "Moros," she said softly, her face crumpling.

He rushed forward, his arms open, desperate to offer her comfort and push back the helplessness threatening to choke him.

She stumbled into his embrace, and he shushed her as she sobbed. "She was here," she said. "She walked right in to gloat."

"Eris, here?" he murmured. He gritted his teeth as she nodded. "Atropos didn't mention it."

"Atropos was standing right here when Eris appeared. We all were."

"How did they find you?" He felt sick as he thought of his trunk of souls. He had moved it from his private sanctuary after what happened with Nader, Eli, and Trevor, creating a new realm in which to hide it, but before then, Eris might have found a way to enter his quarters unnoticed.

"I have no idea," said Lachesis. "But Eris wanted to know where you were."

And that was why he hadn't told anyone where he was going. He'd hoped their mother would come to his aid, and he hadn't wanted to tip his hand. "Was she alone?"

Lachesis shook her head, her fingers curling into Moros's lapels. "Apate and Nemesis were at her side, as you predicted." She hiccupped and sniffled. "I don't know why they hate us so much."

"Because it's what they were created to do," he said softly. It was a fact he had ignored when their rage suited his purposes, when he'd had a rebellion against the Keepers to wage. They had stirred up enough pain and mayhem to force the Keepers to deal with him, to stop treating him and his Kere like dogs. But when the negotiations had ended, his siblings' thirst for inflicting pain on hapless humans had not, and Moros had distanced himself from Strife, Vengeance, and Lies. Yes, they were his brother and sisters, but the Kere were his children. "And it's my fault they've focused on us," he told Lachesis. "My fault they're hurting you." His fingers curled into her hair, the soft strands tickling. "I'm so sorry."

She looked up at him. "Aren't they targeting you, too?"

"They're trying. But I swear, Lachesis, I'm going to stop them." He kissed her brow. "I'm going after the Blade of Life."

"Atropos suspected you might." Her grip on him tightened, her hands shaking. "You know where it is?"

"I think so. I've consulted every ancient text I possess, and there were enough clues to give me a solid idea of where it might be hidden. Mother didn't deny it was there. I'm going after it now."

She wiped tears from her face and stepped back. "You should hurry, then. Because, yes, the loom *is* malfunctioning. It keeps tangling the threads, and no matter how hard I try, I can't measure out some of the lengths. They get away from me. I . . ." She pressed her lips together as her tears sprang to the surface again. "Clotho has it the worst, though."

Moros looked toward the barnlike structure that housed the great wheel from which Clotho spun the thread of life. "Is she still working?"

"I think so," Lachesis said, running her finger along the edge of her ruler, which was lying at the edge of the loom. "You know how I love order. I really do love it. It's been so hard to let it go . . ." Her voice broke over the words.

"Don't let go. And don't give up," he said, reaching to touch her shoulder. His hand fell short as she moved away. She trudged up the length of the loom, her fingers trailing along the snarled threads, her ruler forgotten.

Rage coursing through him, he strode into the spinning room to find Clotho sitting on the dirt floor, her hands buried in the bottomless basket of fleece that she fed into the wheel to create the thread. "It won't hold together," she said with a moan. Her brown hair hung lank and snarled down her back. "We're going to run out of thread." She gestured weakly at the pile of stout bobbins stacked against the wall, the thread waiting to be measured and incorporated into the fabric of fate.

"How long?" he asked.

She turned, revealing bloodshot eyes. "I don't know. A week, perhaps? Maybe less."

It only confirmed what he'd suspected. "I have to find our siblings. I have to take the fight to them."

"You'd need years to search the Veil," she said wearily. "They could be anywhere."

"They found this place somehow. And they must have been here before."

"It makes me wonder," she murmured. "Do you trust Atropos?"

He glanced back toward the loom, the tattered tapestry of fate, beneath which Atropos prowled for souls to reap, threads to cut. "I'm not sure."

She reached out and touched his hand. "Me neither. But I know you're trying to save us, Moros. I know you are."

Determination crystallized inside him. "I'll return with the means to protect you, or not at all." Gathering every ounce of concentration, he willed himself back into the cold and gray, to where mountains still stood majestic and unchanged while the rest of the world had faltered. The north face of Mount Kailash was striped with snow and dark with challenge as he paused at its base to gaze at its peak. It was said that Shiva the destroyer lived at its summit—but then again, it was also said that Buddha made this place his home.

The reality was far more frightening. This mountain symbolized the divine because the truth slept, vanquished, deep inside. But Moros could feel Chaos even now, a vague muddiness ebbing his will, an uncertainty chipping away at his resolve, a confusion pricking at his sense of mission—the Blade of Life waited within, he hoped, and that was what he had come for. It was the only reason he would ever venture so near the resting place of this ancient enemy.

"I'd best get this over with," he muttered, appearing briefly in the real world to let the wind whip his hair. He'd changed into a plain T-shirt and leather pants, all the easier for scrambling over rocks. He closed his eyes and pictured an image drawn in one of his faded scrolls, a door carved into a rock face, etched with ancient symbols—the entrance to the old battleground where his mother had finally cornered Chaos and bent him to her will. Before long, he stood in front of it, his thoughts having carried him through miles of solid rock to where the gods had hollowed it out.

He laid his palm against the damp, cool stone, running his fingers along an image of his mother, her eyes blazing and her mouth set, wielding a thin blade against the god who had subjugated the world, kept it from being what it was meant to be. As in the ancient texts, here Chaos was half man, half monster, horns jutting from his massive head like a bull's, several sets of arms sprouting from his body, all with massive hands reaching out to crush the goddess determined to slay him.

Because no text included images of what lay behind the door, Moros couldn't simply will himself inside, so he stepped into the Veil and pushed his way through the barrier of rock. It was thick and suffocating, crushing him in an unwelcome embrace. But a moment later he stumbled out the other side to find a massive, soaring tomb. In the always-gray Veil, he could easily make out the sheer face of rock split down the middle, rising as high as a mountain itself, with a small plateau about several hundred feet up.

He could also easily feel the evil presence within. Even safe within the Veil, he could hear it breathing, and with every intake of air, Moros felt his thoughts scattering, as if Chaos were sucking away his reason, his memory. Raw fear ran through him. Could Chaos sense him here? Was the god already growing stronger as the fabric of fate frayed?

Not wanting to spend one extra moment here, he staggered toward the ancient tomb. He had to reach that high plateau—because sitting on its edge, barring the entrance, was a carved stone casket. It probably held the weapon he'd come for. His mother had pulled a curtain of rock closed and left the Blade of Life there, ready to be used again if the need ever arose.

Moros imagined plunging it into Eris's chest, and savage joy quickened his steps. With the Blade, he could kill all of them. And even if they succeeded in awakening the sleeping god in his mountain tomb, Moros would have a chance of defeating him. He then reached the edge of the Veil, for this tomb existed in one of those hidden pockets, a realm within the realm that could never be reached from the real world. He ran his palm along the dull, slippery surface and then stepped through, right at the base of the rock face. The soaring chamber was filled with an eerie green glow, emanating from somewhere deep in the mountain above him.

Stale air rushed past him like it was trying to pull him up the cliff, toward the crack in the rock and then through it, right into the jaws of his enemy. Steeling himself, Moros began to climb the sheer, rough rock, his mind focused on the Blade. His bare fingers found every handhold as he pulled himself higher, his breath rushing sure and strong from his lungs. He weathered every echoing inhalation from the monster buried within the thick wall of rock, reminding himself that he had nothing to fear—although tattered, the fabric of fate was still intact, and while it was, Chaos would not wake.

And Moros would make sure he never did. He heaved himself onto the plateau halfway up the cliff and found himself on his knees before the stone casket. Into its surface was stamped the silhouette of a blade, elegant and long, deceptively thin. Panting but grinning with triumph, he hooked his fingers into the groove of the lid and wrenched it upward. The lid fell away, clattering onto the rocky path that led to the sinister crack in the rock, only steps away. Moros barely felt the deadly pull of Chaos now—he was too elated. Eager to claim his prize, he leaned over the casket.

And his sense of triumph shattered, along with his hope.

Though the imprint of a sword could still be seen inside, the stone casket was empty.

Someone had beaten him to it.

CHAPTER FOUR

Aislin's hand was halfway to her silent alarm when Rylan laughed. "Are you sure you want to do that? Killian and Timothy are both lying in the Veil, dealing with fairly nasty gut wounds right now. I'd hate to have to do that to another of our cousins."

Aislin silently willed her guards to live, but she let her hands fall to her sides and faced her brother. He looked dapper in a business suit and tie, his dark hair swept back, his broad shoulders square. For so long, she'd been envious of his imposing presence, of his easy confidence. Now she knew they masked a deep insecurity. "You've given up pretending you're anything but a bully, obviously."

He smirked. "Can you blame me for enjoying my new powers? Aislin, you really have to try it. Our Scopes are nothing. Now I can travel with a simple thought." He raised his eyebrows. "I think you'd enjoy it."

"You're wasting my time," she snapped. She could practically feel the suffering of her guards, who had been hurt because she'd asked them to protect her. "What do you want?"

Rylan flopped down in a chair, the very one Moros had occupied only minutes before. He looked down in mock surprise.

"My, this seat is warm. One would think you'd been consorting with a Ker."

"Were you spying on us?" she asked through gritted teeth.

"Only for a moment. You know, I always thought the Lord of the Kere knew everything, but it turns out he has some gaping blind spots." He grinned. "And my mistress is exploiting them to the fullest."

"I'll be sure to let him know."

Rylan's lip curled. "Have you really chosen him over me? You're dooming our family, Aislin. What does the board have to say about this?"

She glared at him. "I am well in control of the board. They'll comply with whatever I decide."

"Really?" He chuckled. "Does Hugh know that?"

Aislin could barely contain her rage. "You've been conspiring with him?" It made so much sense—Hugh had practically suggested the Ferrys join Rylan and whomever he was serving.

"And so what if I have visited him? I'm not a Ferry anymore—I'm not subject to your command. You made sure of that." Rylan ran his fingers along the arms of his chair.

Aislin could still see the blood of her guards under his fingernails. "You became a monster even before you were made a Ker."

His eyes narrowed. "Maybe I'm something else, Aislin. Something you can't understand, seeing as you're so blinded by your faith in the Lord of the Kere!" He shot up from his chair, so suddenly that Aislin gasped. "He leads an *army* of bullies who've intimidated us for centuries. Wouldn't you be glad to see his downfall?"

"Not if it came at the expense of our family." *Not even if it didn't,* her mind whispered. She couldn't help the thought that Moros was like her, determined to look after the people he was responsible for. "We serve fate, Rylan, and so does he."

"Screw fate!" he shouted. "In the end it's just another master. If we unleash Chaos, we'll be free of it."

"Or crushed. Who's telling you these lies?" But then she remembered—Moros had a brother who was the living personification of lies. "I am so sorry for what's happened to you," she said quietly. "And for my part in it."

"Don't you dare pity me." Rylan stalked forward until he towered over her, even in her four-inch heels. "I don't regret any of it," he said, his eyes taking on a crimson glow, heat pouring from him as his hands closed around her upper arms. "The Ferrys have always done the most work with the most risk while the Kere cause all the suffering and pain they can. We're the ones who planned for the future while they took pleasure in the moment. We're the ones who upheld the treaty. And Moros—the being you're aligning our great empire with? He's just a killer, and he has been for *millennia*. Do you wonder why his siblings hate him? Do you wonder why his own mother won't look him in the eye? He betrayed *all* of them. And he'll betray you, too."

She squirmed to get away from him, but his grip only tightened. "Are you too timid to challenge him, Aislin? Eris and the others have spent years gathering their strength to defeat him, years looking for the means to do it. Why not take advantage of their efforts?"

"Because doing so might end our entire race," she said unsteadily, the pain in her arms becoming unbearable. It felt like Rylan was about to snap her bones.

"He's filled your head with stories meant for cowards," Rylan snarled. "This is why you never should have been Charon. You have no vision and no strength. It's why Father picked me to lead."

"He chose me to lead, too," she said, remembering her father's last words to her. Wasn't that what he had meant? *The fate of the Ferrys rests with you.*

"Then lead," Rylan said, his breath hot on her face. "Have the guts to seize the opportunity you've been given. Join me and help Moros's sisters and brother end him. Without him getting in the way, we can take over. If we can capture the souls of the Kere, we'd have them at our beck and call. And even if we can't, we have enough businesses and gold to hold on to our empire if the worst happens. This isn't the time for clinging to the status quo." He looked her over, seeming to focus on the sweat that beaded her brow, the fear in her eyes. "Unless you're too weak to do anything else."

"Let me go," she whispered. The pain was so intense that she'd become light-headed. She drew in a sharp breath and forced authority into her voice. "Rylan, let me *go*."

He obeyed, stepping back and straightening his tie. "I'll leave you with this: my mistress will be generous with us if you help her and the others end Moros."

"Who is your mistress, Rylan?"

"Pledge to defeat Moros and I'll introduce you to her myself."

Aislin scoffed, even though her whole body pulsed with terror. "Would she turn me into a Ker, too?"

"Only if you're very lucky." Rylan winked. "It only hurts for a second."

"And does she keep your soul in a box, Rylan?"

Rylan frowned. "I'm not a slave, if that's what you're asking."

Aislin suspected that was exactly what he was, a tool that would eventually be discarded. "I'm just wondering why you ever believed destroying the order of things would be better than what you had. You were the *Charon*."

"I've been promised that once Moros is having his insides torn out by the Keeper of Hell, I'll have anything I want. Our family could rule the whole planet. We could do it together."

You're a fool. "I'll think about your offer."

He gave her a superior smile. "Do. I'm eager to hear your answer." He vanished.

Aislin grabbed the edge of her desk, trembling all over. Tears stung her eyes as she fought to draw reason around her like armor.

Rylan was wrong. Aislin wasn't weak. And she wasn't stupid. She knew evil when she looked it in the eye, and she also knew she'd never felt that way when she'd met Jason Moros's gaze.

But he didn't trust her. He'd held back in their last meeting; she could tell.

And if he didn't trust her, he could easily turn on her at the worst moment.

• • •

With Killian and Timothy now safe and being healed by the Ferrys' personal physician, Aislin called a car and told her driver to take her to the Chinatown EMS station. On her way there, she contacted Cacia to make sure she wasn't out on a call and was available to meet. Her younger sister sounded surprised but said she was about to take her break and would make time.

Aislin leaned her head back against the cushioned headrest and watched the filthy canal water splash against the windows of the amphibious limousine. Exhaustion threatened to pull her under even as she tried to summon the energy she needed to survive a meeting with Cacia. Somehow, they infuriated each other without meaning to, and it made her ache. She had adored her feisty little sister when Cacia had been a child. And she actually still did, as frustrated as she got when Cacia was rude and ill-mannered, when she didn't respect the politics and relationships required to run a large corporation full of walking egos who held on to every slight and wielded every grudge as a weapon.

Aislin had succeeded because she always knew what to say, how to act, where to push, and when to smile and let someone believe he was getting his way. "Too bad that won't help me now," she muttered as the limousine pulled to the curb outside the spare EMS station. She knew Declan wasn't here—he was at Psychopomps helping Galena supervise the setup of her new lab space.

Aislin told the driver to wait and got out. She tapped on the screen set into the door of the EMS station, and, a minute later, her sister's face appeared. "Hey," said Cacia. "Come on in."

The door clicked, and Aislin pulled it open to see Cacia coming down the hall. She was in uniform, her black hair in a high ponytail. She gestured toward an office, and Aislin followed her in, catching a glimpse of a few curious paramedics watching from the locker room.

"Have a seat," Cacia said, gesturing at a few metal chairs against the wall. She plopped down into the chair at the desk, upon which sat several computer monitors.

This was probably Declan's office. "Are you supposed to—?" Aislin pressed her lips shut.

Cacia rolled her eyes. "Were you about to ask if I'm allowed to be in Dec's office?"

"No." *Yes.*

Cacia crossed her arms over her chest. "Did you come over here just to criticize me, Aislin?" she asked, her voice sharp. "Because I've got shit to do in the garage, and a soul to ferry before my next call, which could come at any moment."

"No, Cacia, I'm sorry." Aislin leaned forward and planted her elbows on her knees, then rubbed at her eyes. "I needed to talk to you about something . . . personal. I need some advice."

Cacia let out a surprised laugh. "What?"

Aislin lifted her head. "I guess I've never said that to you, have I?"

"Not even close." Cacia's brows drew together as her gaze traced over Aislin's face and clothing. "Hey—what the hell happened to you?"

Aislin looked down at herself, realizing there were bloodstains on her gray skirt, red smudges on the cuffs of her suit jacket. Self-consciously, she tucked a loose wisp of hair behind her ear. "Rylan came to my office. He got through my guards—"

"Jesus, Aislin, what the fuck? Does Dec know?"

"It's fine. I made sure the guards received the care they needed, and—"

"I have no doubt, but are *you* okay?"

Aislin met her sister's eyes. "I'm not sure," she admitted. "I think I need to sleep soon."

Cacia dropped from her chair and squatted at Aislin's feet, looking up at her face. "You look like you need a lot more than a nap. Did he hurt you?" She put a hand on Aislin's arm, tender and gentle.

"Only a little," Aislin said in a choked voice. "But it's all right. It's good, actually." She cleared her throat. "It was helpful. I know what I need to do, and that's why I'm here."

"Rylan wanted you to help him take Moros down, didn't he?"

Aislin nodded. "Aligning with Moros is the only way forward. But he doesn't trust me, and I need him to." She looked down at her hands, open and helpless in her lap. "So what I need to know is . . . what happened when he touched you?"

Cacia's hand fell away from Aislin's arm. "What? Why? You can't be serious. You're actually thinking of letting him touch you?"

"Maybe. That's why I need to know what it's like. I want to be prepared."

Cacia swallowed and lowered herself all the way to the floor, sitting cross-legged, like a child. She rubbed her palms on the legs of her pants. "It's . . . um . . ." She let out a weak chuckle. "Well, it pretty much sucks."

"Did you see your future?"

Cacia's face crumpled, and Aislin immediately regretted asking. But her little sister pulled herself together quickly, scrubbing her hands over her face before raising her head. "Yes. I saw what was supposed to be my future. Of course, it didn't turn out that way." She glanced toward the hallway, perhaps thinking of Eli and what he'd become. "It was like all the years of my life splashing and crunching inside my brain all at once. Agony is the only way to describe it. And when it was over, I thought my life was over, too. It felt like it had already been lived, like there was nothing left."

"But clearly there was. You kept living. You seem sane."

Cacia's eyes narrowed.

"All right. You *are* sane. And you have endured tremendous hardship since then and managed to emerge intact—with Eli at your side."

"Eli is a big part of *why* I'm intact," Cacia said quietly. "He came to me and put me back together right when I needed it. But Moros's touch . . . it leaves a scar, okay? You might not be able to see it, but it's always there."

Hesitantly, Aislin reached out and ran her hand over Cacia's soft hair. "You must have been very determined, if you let him do that."

"I was trying to protect Galena and Eli," Cacia whispered. "Moros said he could feel not only how much I wanted to save them, but how desperate I was to protect what was meant to be. He told me that it made him even more determined to do the same."

Aislin stared at her sister, admiring the raw resolve that drove her—so powerful that it had even influenced the Lord of the Kere. Aislin hoped she had even half as much resolve, considering the stakes. "And *I* need to protect our entire family from whatever's coming. This is our best chance."

Cacia interlaced her fingers with Aislin's. "Moros can see your future, too, when he touches you. He'll know who you love and what you want. He'll know *everything*."

Aislin's stomach tensed. Allowing anyone to know that much about her, let alone a man like Moros, was terrifying. But she had no choice. "So he'd know whether I was going to betray him."

Cacia looked thoughtful. "Theoretically."

"And if he knew I wasn't going to, he'd trust me."

"How do you know what he's going to see? You can't really, Aislin. You're messing with something out of your control."

Aislin threw her head back and laughed. "I feel like that's my new hobby."

"But this is . . . *inside* you." Cacia looked haunted at the memory, her turquoise eyes wide and shining. "You're letting him in your head. And I think he gets off on it."

Aislin sat back, her cheeks heating and her breath quickening as a thousand confusing thoughts and sensations cascaded through her body. "Oh," was all she could say.

Cacia arched an eyebrow. "Or . . . maybe you wouldn't mind that so much."

"Of course I would!" Wouldn't she? The thought of Jason Moros with his hands on her sister made her want to slap him. But the thought of his hands on her own skin? She was ashamed to admit this wasn't the first time she'd thought about it. "It just seems like the quickest way to show him I'm serious about being allies. The summit with the Keepers is in less than three days, and if we go before them divided, I have a feeling they're going to choose one side or the other—and we might lose."

Cacia squeezed her hand. "Just be sure, okay? I know you're a dedicated Charon, Aislin. And I know everybody wants you on their side. I saw how awful you felt about what happened with Dec and Galena. I know this is hard, and you want to do the right thing. But . . . be careful."

Aislin looked into her little sister's eyes. "Thank you," she whispered.

Cacia gave her a pained smile. "You're my sister, Aislin. I don't want anyone to hurt you. And Moros? Sometimes I wonder if he enjoys causing pain." She rose on her knees and slid her arms around Aislin.

Aislin stiffened with surprise but let her sister enfold her, slowly leaning forward to hug her back. Her arms ached from where Rylan had squeezed them, but the bruises would be gone by the time she got home. Her head throbbed, and she knew sleep would ambush her at some point. She needed to be strong enough to handle her next meeting with Moros. She needed to be ready.

She let herself enjoy being hugged by her sister for another long moment, realizing that this was something she had missed, for so long. "I'm proud of you, Cacia," she said quietly.

Cacia sniffled, her head buried against Aislin's shoulder. "I'm proud of you, too, Aislin."

They broke their hug, both swiping at tears with their sleeves. "I guess I'd better get back to work," Cacia said, rising from the floor and turning away, giving Aislin a moment to compose herself.

Aislin stood up. "Thanks for meeting with me." She placed her hand on Cacia's shoulder for a moment before stepping out of the office and heading back down the hall, toward her waiting car. As soon as she slid onto the seat and the driver had closed the door, Aislin pulled out her phone. She stared at the screen for a long time.

And then she dialed Jason Moros's number.

CHAPTER FIVE

Moros appeared outside Aislin Ferry's door and paused. The last few hours had been a maelstrom of rage and helplessness. He was willing to bet his existence that Eris had found a way to claim the Blade, and now she had the means to destroy him, if she dared to get close enough. But he knew her—she was no warrior. She enjoyed causing pain, but through manipulation, not direct confrontation. With Nemesis and Apate's help, she would find a way to divide any coalition Moros tried to build. She would go after every ally he had.

And now he was standing outside the Charon's apartment door, wondering if her invitation was a trap, if perhaps hers was the hand Eris would use to strike. He bowed his head and chuckled. If that was the case, at least the blow would come from a beautiful woman. It would be a pity to destroy her, but he'd do it if he had to.

He reached up and tapped the screen, and the door clicked open immediately. She'd been waiting. He pushed the door ajar and waited, on guard.

She pulled it wide, and her eyes met his. Her platinum hair fell in loose waves down her back, and instead of her usual suit, she wore a pair of slacks and a cashmere tunic. Casual, but still undeniably stately. "Thank you for coming," she said, gesturing him inside.

He pushed down his surprise at the change in her appearance. Barefoot, she seemed so much smaller than in her usual heels that made her nearly as tall as he was. Now she looked soft and vulnerable, two things he would have thought she'd try hard to avoid in a meeting with him. He took her in, including her hands and slender fingers, and saw no weapons. He looked around, wondering where she might have stashed the Blade.

"I was intrigued," he said, adopting a casual tone. "Not everyone gets an invitation to the Charon's home."

She glanced at her surroundings as if wondering what he might notice. It was as tidy as a pin, and he would have expected no less. The decor was elegant and modern but not frilly or fanciful: simple cream-colored couches and chairs, cushions that provided hints of color, paintings and knickknacks that spoke of her years dealing with business partners all over the world. Everything flowed, streamlined and organized but still beautiful, like Aislin herself. "I didn't really feel safe at Psychopomps," she said quietly.

His eyes snapped back to her as she closed the door. Her hands were trembling, just the slightest bit, but he felt the unsteadiness in his gut. "What happened?"

She turned to him. "Rylan assaulted my guards and appeared in my office." She folded her arms, looking so vulnerable that Moros had the sudden urge to move close and shield her from the specter of her brother.

Which might be exactly what she wanted—it would be an excellent opportunity to slide a blade between his ribs. He stayed where he was. "Did he hurt you?"

She shook her head, but he could tell she was lying. And he couldn't stop himself from indulging in a momentary fantasy of tearing Rylan Ferry's head from his neck. The former Charon had caused Moros so much irritation over the years, intruding on his meetings with Patrick Ferry, constantly complaining about the Kere, suggesting a new rule every week to "manage" the Kere's money. He'd never liked Rylan. But now?

Now he craved the man's blood on his hands.

Still, that didn't mean he could trust Aislin. "So it was a social call," Moros said, making sure to sound indifferent. Unconcerned.

Her eyes met his, and he read the pain there. "He wants me to join him."

"Not surprising at all, my dear. Did you call me here to renege on our agreement?" He'd actually dared to hope Aislin would be steadfast in her commitment to fate. And to him.

"No," she said, straightening and letting her hands fall to her sides. "I invited you here to cement our alliance."

He gave her a close-lipped smile. "Haven't we already done that?"

Her eyes narrowed. "I don't think so. We might have shaken hands, but you're still keeping secrets. I know you don't trust me."

"I don't trust anyone," he admitted. "To do so would be rather naive, don't you think?"

To his surprise, she nodded instead of arguing. Then again, Aislin was one of the few beings able to surprise him.

She was staring at him, those ice-blue eyes riveted on his face. "How can we work together if I don't know what you're trying to accomplish?" she asked, taking a step closer to him. He let her come, but had to restrain the urge to strip off his gloves. She tilted her head as she noted his tension. "You look like you think I'm going to attack you, Jason."

He smiled. "You're the only one apart from my sisters who calls me that." And even with them, it was rare.

"Isn't it your name?"

It was the name he'd chosen as he'd joined the modern world, not the one he'd been born with. "Perhaps, but others prefer to use the name of myth, the one that makes clear they know what I am."

He watched her as she took another step closer. He could smell her now, a hint of spring violets tempered by honey, and the scent made his blood run hot. His fingers twitched. "But you, my dear, I suspect you prefer to think of me as human."

She smiled. "I've never once thought of you as human. But would you prefer I call you Moros?"

"No," he said, caught off guard by his own honesty. "I suppose I wouldn't. But I would like to know what you're up to."

"I need you to trust me. And I want to trust you."

"I wouldn't be standing in front of you if I didn't trust you at least a little."

She took another step forward. She was now only a foot away. He could hear her heart beating inside her chest, could feel the tension in her body—

"You're lying," she whispered. "I don't think you trust me at all."

He could feel his eyes sparking with crimson as hers traced his face. "Just tell me what you want," he said.

"I want you to touch me."

He blinked at her, unable to contain his shock. "What?"

Her fingers rose to his face, but he stepped out of her reach just in time. "Do you have any idea what would happen to you if our skin touched?" he asked, wishing his heart would slow.

"I talked to Cacia. I know exactly what would happen."

"And did she explain the toll?" His fists clenched. The mere idea of touching Aislin had awakened a shaky hunger inside him, but also an anger. No one had the right to affect him like this. He set the tempo. He was the one in control. "Did she tell you what I took from her?"

Aislin bowed her head, and her hair slid over her shoulder, finely spun platinum catching the light. "She did. But I've decided it would be worth it. I think you need to see my future. You need to see that I'm not going to betray you."

He shook his head. "You have no idea what I'll see." And neither did he, oddly enough. He edged to the side, so that one of her couches was between them. Usually, he caught wisps of people's destinies if they were near him, but he couldn't sense Aislin's. That might be a result of her distracting him, though, or his own lack of concentration after failing to retrieve the Blade. "You can't know your own future, Aislin."

"Don't my intentions matter? Doesn't my will?"

He wished she'd stay still and give him a moment to think, but she was already moving around the couch, closing the distance between them again. Determined and unstoppable, like he'd always known her to be. "It will change everything," he warned, his voice strangely deep and unsteady.

Her hand slipped along the upholstery of the couch. "I know," she murmured. "It's a sacrifice I'm willing to make for the sake of the Ferrys."

A sacrifice. Suddenly, he wanted to roar with frustration. Allowing him to touch her skin was a sacrifice, an unwanted burden. But she was so close, and so enticing, and she was offering something he rarely refused.

A touch, skin to skin. A taste of life, of destiny. Both at once.

And with Aislin, it came with an added benefit. If the Charon was going to betray him, he would know. Servant of Fate or not, he would be ready for her to try, and ready to destroy her. She wouldn't be able to get the best of him. His brow furrowed. Either way, touching her would give him what he needed. Certainty. He raised his hands and tugged at the fingers of his gloves, deliberate and unhurried. He wanted her to see every movement.

Aislin's heart raced. He could hear it, addictive and frantic, ticking away the seconds of her life. It made his mouth water, and for more than just a taste of her future. "You'll do it?" she asked as he pocketed his gloves.

"Oh, yes," he said, keenly aware of the stirring inside him. He needed to push that away and focus on what he might see, but it was driving him now, rushing through his veins, awakening buried cravings. "How could I turn down such an offer?"

Her pupils dilated, possibly with fear. "Should . . . should I sit down?"

"No, my dear," he said quietly as he moved closer. It took all his restraint not to yank her into his arms and crush her against him. Her chest rose and fell to the rapid cadence of her breathing, drawing his gaze to her breasts. "I'll be holding you up."

Her fingers curled into the soft cushion of the couch. It looked like she was trying to keep herself from running away. He almost wanted her to, because now the hunter in him had been loosed, and he longed for a chase. But Aislin merely widened her stance and waited for him to approach.

Brave. And dangerous, his thoughts whispered. *But so tempting.*

She held out her arm, as if to shake hands. "I'm ready."

He smirked. "That's not how this is going to happen." With one step, he brought himself so close that her palm was on his chest. His hands were at his sides, clenched into tight fists. The feel of her filled him with raw desire. "We can't go back after I do this."

She looked up at him, her pale eyes fathomless. "I know. So let's move forward instead."

Her palms slid from his chest to his ribs, and he had to suppress a sudden shiver that coursed straight down his back. Her face was inches from his, her lips soft and pink. He closed his eyes to keep himself from leaning down to taste them. He would have to be gentle. And alert. He couldn't allow his desire for her body to interfere. Slowly, he slid an arm around her waist, nearly groaning as he felt her temperature rise—from fear or need, it barely mattered. He spread his fingers across the soft cashmere of her sweater, feeling the smooth expanse of her back, only a thin layer of fabric keeping them apart. As soon as his fingers brushed her skin, she would lose control, and he mustn't allow her to fall. He pulled her even closer, eager to see what she would look like, helpless under his hands. But the moment her lithe frame settled against him, her hips to his and her breasts pressed to his chest, he stopped breathing. Sweet heaven, nothing had ever felt so blindingly delicious. He let out a breath and opened his eyes to find her staring at him, her lips parted.

He gritted his teeth. If he didn't dive in now, he was going to kiss her, and that would be disastrous. "Let's begin."

She pressed her lips together and closed her eyes as his hand rose, as he held her tightly, as he laid his palm on her cool, smooth cheek.

Moros gasped as the room disappeared, along with everything in it. The floor vanished beneath his feet, plunging him into a bottomless abyss. With Aislin still snug in his arms and his eyes wide open, he fought the wash of darkness filling his mind. His heart pounded as if he were running for his life. His body screamed for air as his hand slid down her face and curled around her neck. Deep inside the roaring silence in his mind, he could faintly hear her voice, but he couldn't make out what she was saying, couldn't tell if it was now or in the future, couldn't catch a single word even though the sound was louder with each passing second.

"Jason!"

He jerked away from her, nearly stumbling over the end of the couch.

"Jason?"

He lifted his head to find Aislin, arms out, as if she had been trying to steady him. His chest heaved. This . . . didn't make sense. It made no sense at all. Slowly he straightened, his heart still galloping.

"What did you see?" she asked.

He shook his head. "Did you—?" He rubbed his hands over his face and tried again. "Did *you* see anything?"

"No. Did you do it right?"

The laugh burst from him, broken and astonished. "There's no other way to do it."

"Should we try again?"

He held his hand up to ward her off, then jammed it in his pocket as she reached for it. "No!" He was reeling with what he'd seen—or rather, what he hadn't. Sorrow was squeezing at his chest, realization making it harder and harder to breathe. "Aislin . . . I . . ."

"Just tell me what you saw," she said, her voice small. "Did you see me betraying you?"

"No," he replied, certainty strangling him. He swallowed hard and met her eyes. "I saw nothing at all."

Her eyebrows rose. "What does that mean?"

Disbelief and defiance pushed back the constricted feeling in his chest. "Give me your hand."

"But you just said—"

"I know what I said," he snapped. "Just do it." He couldn't accept this. It had to be a mistake.

Her hand shook only a little as she placed it in his. The blackness hit him again, but this time he was ready. He didn't fight it, merely welcomed it like a rushing stream, letting it flow over him, past him, taking the blindness with it. Slowly, his vision cleared and sharpened, and he found himself looking at Aislin's pale face, her high cheekbones and blue eyes. So fragile. So temporary. Unbidden sadness coiled around him once more, tightening like a noose.

"Do you see anything now?" she asked, looking utterly confused. "I don't feel anything except . . ."

"What?"

"You're squeezing my hand very hard."

He opened his fingers and looked down at hers, red with the heat and tension of his grip. But instead of letting her pull away, his fingers closed over hers again. "I didn't mean to hurt you."

"It doesn't hurt," she murmured. "But you've worried me. I don't know why this didn't work."

"I do," he said in a hollow voice. "I know exactly what it means." He forced himself to let go of her hand as a bitter taste rose in his mouth. "It means you're going to die."

CHAPTER SIX

As soon as she closed the door behind Moros, all the strength she'd held on to in the last few moments evaporated, and her legs gave out. She hit the floor hard enough to knock the wind out of herself. A sudden stab of sorrow pierced her straight through, leaving her clutching her stomach and hunching over in pain.

She'd expected to feel something like this after Moros touched her, but not for this reason. She'd thought she would be dizzy and reeling beneath the weight of her future. Instead, she'd discovered she didn't have one.

She wouldn't have believed it, but Moros's reaction had left no room for doubt. For some reason, he'd looked as stricken as she'd felt. He'd gone from smug to smoldering as soon as he'd pulled her close. She'd been almost sure he was about to kiss her, and she was embarrassed and surprised at how badly she'd wanted him to. But as soon as he touched her, all of that desire had fallen away, replaced by shock.

She hadn't wanted the pity of the Lord of the Kere. She'd wanted the moment before, when his red-flecked pupils had dilated with need, when his breath had been hot on her cheek, when she'd felt the unmistakable arousal of his body. For a few seconds, she'd pretended that they were two normal people about to become lovers, a secret fantasy she'd had to suppress too many times to count. She'd felt alive, every nerve thrumming and ready.

Maybe that was how impending death felt. Like an overdose of life. Like everything hazy had suddenly come into sharp focus.

"Focus," she muttered. "That's what you need to do." Moros had told her that he didn't know how much time she had left, but it couldn't be long. Somehow, she would be stripped of her Charon's Scope, and then she'd be mortal. She couldn't bring herself to think of what would happen after that, but she could only hope the Keeper of Heaven would welcome her in. It hadn't been how she expected their first meeting to go.

She clumsily got to her feet, walked to her home office, and slid her finger across the screen on her desk, bringing up dossiers on every one of the board members, as well as several Ferrys who held powerful positions within the company. She was guessing the board was going to vote her out, and their next meeting was about twelve hours from now. Plenty of time to make calls and gather allies. She'd start with Rosaleen. Though her aunt's support had wavered, it seemed possible to win her back. She'd been Aislin's biggest advocate as she maneuvered to oust Rylan as Charon, and she was the only board member Aislin felt could take her place once she was gone. She also needed to call Cavan. His political acumen would come in handy, and the support of the Lucinae would make all the difference, no matter what happened.

Her plan forming in her mind, she got out her phone just as she felt the pull of a soul in the Veil. More powerful than usual, it was like a sharp tug from a rope wrapped around her spine. She dropped the phone and grasped the edge of her desk to steady herself. Then it happened again, harder this time.

Her phone began to ring. It was a general Psychopomps number. But just as she reached to answer, it stopped. And she felt another tug. Alarm growing, she pulled her Scope from her neck.

She paused. Was this it? Whatever was happening—was this the beginning of the end?

Stop it, she thought. *That's no excuse to stand still. Do your duty and stop thinking about yourself.* She slipped a pair of flats on her feet, opened her Scope, and stepped into the Veil. Concentrating on the insistent tugs, she flipped the Scope and opened a portal to the soul calling to her.

What she saw on the other side was absolute mayhem. Here in the Veil, at least a dozen dead were rising from their fallen bodies, which were scattered in the real world outside the Psychopomps tower, some floating in the canal, some sprawled across the sidewalk. Stunned, Aislin stepped through the portal at the same time Declan came out of one nearby. Her brother cursed as he watched one of their human guards rise from his shadowy, headless body. "What the hell is going on?" he asked as Cacia stepped out of yet another portal several yards away.

Aislin squinted into the real world, because humans there appeared only as transparent apparitions to people in the Veil. Marked corpses lay everywhere, and fast-moving hunched shapes ran among them. As Aislin watched, one leaped toward a human getting out of an amphibious taxi and sank its teeth into her neck.

"Those are Shades," Declan shouted. "They've escaped from the Veil!"

Galena stepped out of her Scope's portal right next to him, and her green eyes went round as she took in the carnage. The Shades—and there were several of them—had already killed all the human Psychopomps guards and at least a dozen pedestrians. "How is this possible?" she asked as she opened a portal to Heaven for one of the dead guards. She pulled her Scope over his head even as she watched the Shades kill another shadowy man only steps away. "Don't people have to be Marked to die?"

"They are Marked," Cacia said in a high, uncertain voice, pointing to the Mark of death glowing orange on the man. "But where are the Kere?"

"Oh my God," said Declan, grasping Aislin's arm and pointing. "Look at that."

Aislin obeyed, her eyes shifting to the Shade attacking a woman getting out of the taxi. With its arm wrapped around her neck, it slapped her chest, and when its skeletal hand fell away, there was a Mark, glowing stark and clear in the Veil. It examined its handiwork for a moment before wrenching the woman's head from her body.

"The Shades," Aislin said, disbelief making her numb, slowing everything down. "Someone's turned them into Kere."

"How is that possible?" Galena asked, moving aside so Declan could use his Scope to guide another guard to Heaven.

"Someone reached into their chests and took their souls," Aislin explained. "That's how a Ker is made."

"We have to stop them," said Declan.

Aislin looked over to see her brother open a portal to the real world. "Dec—"

"No, Aislin. I know someone might see us coming out of our Scopes, but—"

"Declan," said Aislin. "I just wanted to say that I'm going with you."

Declan shot her a look, and Aislin knew exactly what he was thinking. Her younger brother had always been a brawler, keenly physical in every way. Cacia was the same, never shying away from a fight. And Aislin was standing here in her cashmere sweater and tailored slacks, looking like she'd never gotten her hands dirty in her life.

"You don't think I've ever chased a Shade through the Veil?" she asked. "I've been doing this since before you were born."

Declan smiled and flung his Scope even wider, gesturing for her to step through, but he touched her arm as she moved forward. "Be careful."

She squeezed his hand. *I'm already doomed,* she thought. "Thanks."

The clamor of the real world filled her ears, screams and sirens and vehicles crashing as panicked drivers tried to stop their amphibious vehicles in the canal. The Shade-Kere, skin peeling from their rotting skulls, clothes in greasy tatters, leaped onto roofs and clawed at hatches, trying to reach their intended victims. In the Veil, the Scopes had been their targets, escape their only motivation to attack. Now, these creatures were driven by pure bloodlust, making them even more vicious.

"Galena, get back into the Veil," shouted Declan as his wife stepped through her own Scope.

"I'm covered," she said, pointing at Tamasin and Nader, who had appeared on either side of her looking like they wished she'd stayed in her lab.

Declan ran his hand through his ebony hair. Aislin could tell that he wanted to protect the woman he loved, but that he also had to respect her determination to do her duty. "Stay close to her," Declan said quietly to Nader. Galena focused her attention on a Shade-Ker that was loping along the canal wall.

Nader nodded curtly, and Declan charged forward, pulling open a portal to Hell and attempting to loop it over the head of one of the creatures before it saw him coming. But it turned at the last minute and, instead of dodging, disappeared into thin air, then reappeared behind Declan. Tamasin, still standing next to Galena, whirled and delivered a side kick that sent the thing flying into the canal.

"They have all the powers of the Kere," Aislin yelled as several other Ferrys stepped through their own Scopes, including Killian and Timothy, her personal guards, who Rylan had attacked. They were healed now, but she'd given them the night off so she could meet with Moros privately.

Both men moved close to her, Killian giving her a worried look. "You sure you want to be out here?" he asked her. "It might be safer in the Veil."

Timothy let out a weak chuckle and ran his hand over his stomach. "You sure about that?"

Killian blanched, probably thinking of Rylan's claws.

"These Shades can enter and leave the Veil easier than we can, so it doesn't matter," Aislin yelled as she ran toward a couple just pushing a stroller around the corner at the end of the block, two women chatting and cooing at their baby. When they realized they had walked into a war zone, they screamed, drawing the attention of two nearby Shade-Kere that had been finishing off their latest victims. "If they touch them, they'll be Marked!"

Aislin picked up speed, desperate to stop the monsters before they reached the women and the child. "Hey," she barked, trying to draw the Shades' attention. She scooped a phone from the ground, its owner lying with his throat torn out just steps away. With strength born of desperation, she hurled the thing at one of the Shade-Kere, managing to hit it in the back. It snarled and spun around, glaring at her with oozing eyes.

Out of breath, Aislin stopped, even as Killian ran past her, pulling an electroshock baton from his belt and racing toward one of the monsters still pursuing the couple. Timothy was struggling with another off to her right, jabbing at it with his baton and trying to keep it from clawing him. Aislin stared down the beast she had clocked with the phone, her thumb pressed to her Scope and her teeth gritted. The world disappeared around her, narrowing as the Shade-Ker let out a rending wail and charged her. She forced herself to stay still, her hands at her sides, until the thing was only three steps away. And then, with experience drawn from years of corralling Shades in the Veil, she threw her Scope wide at the very last moment and stepped to the side as it dove for her. It flew head-first into a fiery portal to Hell.

Smoke filled the air as the thing screamed, an eerie sound that carried across their battlefield, echoing off the edifices of the buildings around them. The nearby Shade-Kere paused, staring at the portal as Aislin closed it tight around the beast, trapping it inside. Taking advantage of the distraction, Cacia threw her Scope open and got another Shade-Ker that had been hunched over a bleeding woman on the sidewalk.

All of the Shade-Kere yowled with anger.

And then they disappeared.

Aislin flipped her Scope and tore it open, peering anxiously into the Veil. The Shade-Kere weren't there, but several Ferrys were, guiding the dozens of doomed, the unsanctioned victims who weren't meant to be Marked today.

A hand closed over her shoulder. It was Declan, with Galena at his side. "I've never seen anything like it," he said in a low voice, looking over the bodies strewn along the block, all dead. "This is a fucking disaster."

"I know," Aislin said, breathing hard, her eyes stinging as they focused on one young woman, possibly not even eighteen years old, sprawled on the sidewalk, one of her fingers still hooked over the handle of her shopping bag, her reddish hair drenched in her own blood, her blue eyes empty. Rage pulled tight inside Aislin. "It's an abomination."

A commotion behind her brought her around in time to see Hugh and his son Brian push their way through the revolving doors of the Psychopomps tower, both too late to be of any use. "My God," Hugh said. Brian made a gagging sound and retched on the sidewalk.

Hugh patted the young man's back and turned to glare at Aislin. "I want an explanation," he said.

Aislin put a hand on Declan's arm as she felt him tense beside her. "I will do my best to provide one," she said in a steady voice. "*After* I help clean this up." And with that, she opened her Scope and stepped into the Veil, because if she stayed there another moment, she would tell Hugh what a coward he was. He'd felt the pull of all these dying people, she was sure. No Ferry inside Psychopomps wouldn't have. But he'd stayed safely inside the building until the Shade-Kere were gone, then dared to come out and act shocked. Her fury burned so hot it was making her sweat.

The cool air of the Veil was a relief. So was the crowd of Ferrys already at work. Her family members were compassionately guiding souls to Heaven despite their own ashen faces and trembling hands. Aislin tucked a loose lock of her long hair behind her ear and walked forward to help, suspicion rising like a tide. Someone had turned all these Shades into Kere, probably the same being who was controlling Rylan. And the more she thought about it, the more she wondered if it was one of the Fates. They were the only ones who, like Moros, served destiny. He'd said he didn't believe Eris or his other siblings were capable of this. But if not them, who else could create beasts who Marked people for death?

Her mind was a swirling frenzy of thoughts, about her Ferrys, about what would happen now, about how very much the scene in front of her looked like pure chaos.

She shuddered. Chaos. Was this what it would be like? She desperately hoped Moros was strong enough to defeat him, to defeat all of them, to survive and triumph. Then she remembered she wouldn't be around to witness what happened—and realized she might never see him again. She had sent him away without saying good-bye.

Her eyes shut as despair licked at the edges of her mind, threatening to close her in. But then her usual resolve pushed it away. Until the very last moment, she would do everything she could to beat back the threat, to ensure that what was *meant to be* actually happened. No time for pity. She would fight until her heart stopped.

Judging from the carnage all around her, the battle had only just begun.

CHAPTER SEVEN

Moros arrived in the weaving room, both hungry for answers and full of dread. He wished he was wrong about Aislin, but he'd felt the nothingness before, so many times. And most often, he sought the feeling out. He chose the doomed carefully, women whose souls were ready to be reaped, who appealed to him physically, who were alone. Once every few years, he found the perfect woman. He appeared to her, her personal angel of death, to Mark her with the very first seductive touch. For those who were willing—and nearly all were—he gave them a simple one-night stand that always ended the same way. He could touch them without hurting them, give them ecstasy without pain, take his own pleasure from their willing bodies. Of course, they had no idea that making love with him would be the last thing they ever did, and he never told them. What good would it do to steal their last minutes of happiness?

He always killed them quickly and painlessly—a sudden and devastating heart attack, a catastrophic burst aneurysm. Before they even knew they were dead, their spirits were sliding from their bodies in the Veil to greet their final fate.

He had expected Aislin to cry when he told her the news. Or to fight, to rage against the sheer wrongness of it. Instead, she'd escorted him to her door with a polite good-bye, eerily calm. She'd seemed more willing to accept the idea of her doom than he was. But how could a Charon meet her fate so abruptly? How could her death be anything but a violation of what was meant to be? Would it be the Keepers? Eris? Rylan? Someone on her own board? Whoever would be responsible, however it would come, he wouldn't be able to save her. Her fate had been foretold.

Why hadn't he sensed this before? Not even caught a hint of it? He meant to find out.

"Lachesis!" he called as soon as he materialized, glancing up the vast length of the massive loom for his sister. Where was she? "Lachesis?"

"Here," came a weak voice. Lachesis came trudging out of her private quarters, ghastly pale and clutching her stomach. "I haven't been feeling quite right, I'm afraid."

He met her in the middle, grasping her elbow to support her. "Worse than before?"

She nodded, then gave him a curious look. "I didn't expect to see you back so soon."

"I need to consult you and Atropos."

Her eyebrows rose. "Why?"

He began to guide her toward the loom. "I need to look at the life thread of Aislin Ferry."

"Oh," said Lachesis, her voice unmistakably hollow. "The Charon?"

He nodded as he led her to the edge of the fraying tapestry of fate. That tight feeling was back in his chest as they stepped beneath the fabric, held up by stout timbers over the travertine cutting floor. Atropos was many yards distant, coming toward them unsteadily, her steps faltering. "What do you want?" she snapped hoarsely.

"Aislin Ferry," he said, then cleared his throat. "I mean, I want to look at her thread."

"Why?" Atropos looked up at the fabric, at the gaping holes and missed stitches, and sliced a gray thread above her head.

Moros felt the sting and pushed the feeling outward, where it would find one of his Kere. "I touched her," he said simply. "And I was surprised by what I saw."

Atropos let out a ragged laugh. "With the fabric unraveling, you're still arrogant enough to believe your future-sight is trustworthy?"

Moros thought about that. Ever since Patrick Ferry's Marking, there had been holes in his sight, blank spots where he'd previously seen the future clearly. But this was different. "I didn't believe she was fated to die. I would have seen it." If not now, then years ago. He always knew the *when* of someone's death—unless that death wasn't meant to be. But he couldn't recall ever sensing anything about Aislin. He'd always assumed it was because he'd found her distracting, and he'd worked hard to push her—that face, those eyes, that voice—out of his mind. "Just show me her thread."

"You don't know which one it is?" Atropos asked, her tone mocking.

Moros's fists clenched. Usually, he could easily feel which thread went with a particular soul, but none of the threads brought her beautiful face to mind, no matter how closely he looked at them. He recognized Galena's, and Declan's, and Cacia's, and so many of the other Ferrys', but not the Charon herself, when she should have been prominent and shimmering and easy to spot. "I feel nothing." How he wished that were true.

"You sound like it matters to you," Atropos replied.

"Of course it matters," he barked. "She's the Charon. And she's—" He gritted his teeth. *Necessary.* When had she become so necessary? He could work with any Charon, couldn't he? "I just need to see where she is."

Lachesis leaned into him. "You don't usually care so much," she whispered, her breath tickling his ear. "But I can tell something has changed."

"Nothing has changed." He blinked. If that were true, why was the thought of Aislin's death eating at him this way? He'd spent only a handful of hours alone with her over the last eighty years, and though he'd always been amused by her, always admiring, and definitely intrigued, that didn't explain this need he had to see a future for her, this inability to accept that she didn't have one. "We're meeting with the Keepers in less than three days, and I wanted to examine her thread before we appear in front of them together."

"Spare us your excuses. The current Charon is right—" Atropos's mouth dropped open. "She was here." She slid her finger along a split in the fabric, not that far from Galena Margolis's sparkling tangled thread. Many of the threads that had been connected to the scientist's were now separated from it by that long tear, which looked like it had been made with a scalpel . . . or a sickle.

"What have you done?" Lachesis asked her sister, gaping at the neat slice, which traveled from the base of the loom, up onto the frame, and into the far distance. "Her thread is gone. Did you cut it from the cloth?"

"N-no," stammered Atropos. "Why would I do such a thing?"

"I don't know," said Lachesis, her voice taking on an edge. "But I'd love to hear an explanation."

The accusation was clear, but Moros could see the shock on Atropos's face. It looked genuine. "The thread disappeared?" he asked, staring at the tapestry and willing Aislin's thread to appear again. "How is that possible if it wasn't cut?"

"It's not possible," croaked Atropos, looking ill. Her usually neat black hair tumbled over her face as she looked down at her sickle.

He glanced around, a terrible possibility dawning on him. "What happened to Rylan Ferry's thread when someone took possession of his soul? Did it disappear like this?" He imagined Aislin with glowing red eyes, glaring at him with hatred, eager for his destruction. Was that her destiny now?

Atropos shook her head. "It turned gray, and I cut it from the fabric, just like all those you turn into Kere."

"I didn't turn him, though."

"Then who did?" asked Lachesis. "Could one of our other siblings have done it?"

"They don't serve fate," said Atropos. "They couldn't create something like a Ker, that wields the power of death."

Moros wasn't actually sure Rylan *could* Mark humans for death. "He was killed before his soul was taken—you're sure?"

Atropos nodded, her dark gaze on him defiant and sullen. Moros stared back, wondering if she was lying. He cut his eyes toward Lachesis, who was glowering at their sister with clear suspicion. "I would have thought you'd have mentioned slicing away someone so important," Lachesis said quietly. "But you didn't. I learned of Rylan Ferry's demise from our brother."

Atropos waved her sickle between them, looking like she wanted to cut their throats. "I—" She let out a choked noise just as a rending pain tore through Moros's chest. Lachesis wailed as gray threads began to rain down around them, pulling from the fabric and dangling like paralyzed limbs from the tapestry above.

The burn inside him drove him to his hands and knees as dozens of threads landed on the floor around him. He raised his head to see his sisters in similar positions, both staring with wide eyes at the fraying cloth. Moros forced himself to his feet, pushing the pain away. The dangling and severed filaments were clustered around the tear where Aislin's thread had once been, and horror washed over him. He'd known something was coming for her, but he'd left her alone, so disoriented by his feelings about her impending doom that he couldn't bear to be near her another moment.

But had she already died? Would he even know if she was gone? "I have to get back," he said.

"You're leaving us? Like *this*?" cried Lachesis, her hair grayed by threads that had tangled with her short blonde locks.

"I have to." He *needed* to. "I can't do anything here. I should never have left. Whatever this is," he said, motioning to the gray threads, "it's happening in Boston, so that's where I need to be if I'm going to stop it."

"But whatever's happening . . . this could be the end," Lachesis said quietly, her eyes burning as they met his.

He couldn't explain it, only that he was desperate to know if Aislin was still walking the Earth.

"Then go," Atropos said, her voice thick with pain. "But if you leave now, don't bother coming back. Ever."

Moros looked at his sisters, feeling like a lash their resentment and anger at being left behind. Lachesis, usually loving and understanding, looked just as angry as Atropos. There was nothing he could do for them, though, except to find Eris and take her on. And he was certain she was behind whatever had caused all these unsanctioned deaths. There was no one else it could be. He couldn't help a pang of suspicion, though . . . "Hold on for as long as you can," he said to them.

He closed his eyes and willed himself back to Boston, dreading what he would find when he arrived.

CHAPTER EIGHT

Aislin entered the lobby of Psychopomps to find several Ferrys lying maimed and bleeding on the marble floor, their corporate physician frantically attending to broken bones and torn flesh so they would heal properly, administering massive doses of pain meds to keep the process from hurting too much. Their Scopes had protected them from being Marked by the Shades, but they hadn't protected them from the creatures' rotting teeth and freakish strength.

Hugh had come back inside as well and was near the elevator banks, talking into his phone as he watched his relatives suffer. He looked perfectly calm, and it made Aislin want to rip the phone from his hand and crush it beneath her heel. She'd just spent several long minutes in the Veil guiding several of her human employees to Heaven—and one of them to Hell. All dead before their time, Marked without any regard for what was meant to be. The Shades had acted mindlessly, controlled by whoever had taken their souls.

She'd put Declan in charge of liaising with the human authorities in the real world. In her gut, she knew it was only a matter of time before the Shade-Kere attacked again. Aislin had done whatever she could to keep everyone calm, telling them that she and Moros would control the threat as soon as possible—assuming she could find the man. She'd tried to reach him on his phone, but as was so often the case, it went straight to voice mail. Technology didn't work in the Veil, and that was most likely where Jason Moros was.

She fought the inexplicable desire to have him by her side right now. It wasn't that she couldn't face this latest challenge alone, but she would have appreciated his confident presence. He was rarely rattled and never, ever afraid.

Right now, though, her own rage was overcoming her fear at what had happened, and what it meant. She stalked toward Hugh, who had shed his suit jacket and tie. His tailored white shirt looked pressed and neat, especially in contrast to Aislin's blood-smeared cashmere, sullied as she'd helped move wounded Ferrys from the sidewalk outside to the lobby, where they could heal out of the view of the public. Before she was halfway to him, Hugh turned his back to her and stepped into the elevator, still absorbed in his phone conversation as the doors slid shut.

Propelled by suspicion, Aislin tried to be patient as she fielded a frantic call from her media liaison, who needed to know what story to feed to the press, then summoned an elevator. Her last moments with Moros beat in her head like a pulse. She had no future to speak of, nothing but blackness. And that meant that somehow, her Charon's Scope was going to be stripped from her. Maybe by Hugh and his allies. Even now, he might be finalizing his plans.

The elevator finally arrived, and she took it to the floor that housed a warren of executive offices, including for the board members. It had been her home for two decades when she'd worked as vice president of foreign exchange. Her office had been down the hall from Hugh's then, so she marched in that direction, unsurprised at how quiet it was—the sun was still an hour or so from rising, and with the exception of the finance floor, which remained busy twenty-four-seven as the Ferrys traded on the world markets, Psychopomps wouldn't open for business until eight.

Her shoes were silent on the carpet as she treaded down the hall. At the sound of a quiet moan, she stilled, her stomach tightening. She had just begun to creep forward again when another low cry reached her. The noises were coming from Hugh's office. His door was slightly ajar; he thought he had the floor to himself.

Well, to himself and whoever was moaning in his office.

Disgust roiled inside Aislin. She pushed the door wide and stepped inside. Sure enough, Hugh was with someone. He was on his knees, his head buried between the legs of a woman lying on his desk, her black dress hiked up her thighs, her back arched, her hands threaded through his silver hair.

At the sound of Aislin's intrusion, the woman shoved him away, and Hugh ended up on his backside next to his desk. Furiously wiping his mouth, he scrambled to his feet as his partner unhurriedly slid from his desk and tugged her skirt back into place. Her golden hair fell around her face in tousled curls, and when her eyes met Aislin's, her eyebrow arched in keen assessment. "This is her, isn't it, baby?"

"Get the hell out of my office," Hugh rasped, glaring at Aislin.

"Two dozen of our family members lie wounded in our lobby," said Aislin. "Thirty innocent people have been slaughtered. And you—" She gestured at the erection tenting Hugh's pants. "You're up here with yet another plaything." Hugh was known for his office liaisons, one more reason Aislin disliked him.

The woman chuckled. "Oh, darling, I'm anything but a toy." She reached over and took Hugh's hand.

"I'm actually glad you're here then, Aislin, because I have something to tell you," he snarled. His face twisted with hatred. "I have the votes locked in. When we meet later this morning, you're out." He took a jerky step forward, his face turning a mottled pink.

"And when I'm Charon, I'm going to strip you of your status as a Ferry. No one will have the time or will to stop me."

"The board members don't know what's happened yet," Aislin said in a hard voice, but as Hugh advanced on her, his fingers still tightly laced with the blonde's, she couldn't help but retreat. He looked murderous. "And you heard what Moros said about working with me—"

"Moros will soon be at the mercy of the Keeper of Hell," Hugh shouted, spittle spraying from his lips. "I'm going to make sure of it. This latest attack proves he's completely lost control."

Aislin opened her mouth to respond but was struck by the shining eagerness in the blonde's slate-gray eyes. There was something about her features that was strangely familiar, but Aislin couldn't place her. "Who are you?" she asked, pausing in the doorframe.

But she never got an answer. Hugh lunged forward and shoved her out into the hallway, slamming his office door in her face. "Better get your affairs in order, Charon," he yelled from the other side. "You're going to suffer for what you've done—I will make sure of it!"

As Aislin stood, stunned, she heard the silky lilt of the blonde's voice, then a low groan from Hugh. Her mouth dropped open. As Hugh's grunts became rhythmic, she strode back down the hall, her thoughts a hum of possibilities—and worry.

"Is this how it's going to happen?" she whispered to herself as she got on the elevator. Hugh had indicated he had the votes to unseat her as Charon, but he'd also revealed his plan to strip her of her status as a Ferry as well.

And if he did that, it would be so easy to kill her.

Her fingers dipped into the pocket of her slacks as the elevator began to descend, and she pulled out her phone. "Please answer," she whispered as she touched Moros's icon—the ancient Theta symbol of death.

The sound of ringing startled her, and she looked up to find Moros standing right in front of her, his gray eyes sparking with crimson. He reached back and hit the elevator "Stop" button, bringing them to a halt between floors.

"What happened?" he asked, his voice rough. His hair was tousled, and he was breathing hard and clutching his side, looking startlingly human.

"Are you hurt?" she asked. It wasn't the answer to his question, but it was the first thought that sprang from her mind.

He didn't reply. Instead, he took her by the arms, looking her up and down. "Which Ker did it? Were you there?" His grip tightened as he noticed the bloodstains on her sweater. "Are *you* hurt?"

Her hands rose to cup his elbows. "I'm not hurt, but I was there. It wasn't one of your Kere, though. A horde of Shades have been transformed—someone has taken their souls. They can Mark people for death, and they attacked right outside this building less than an hour ago. They killed over two dozen humans and injured several of my—"

Aislin felt a rush of cold, then hot, air. She clung to Moros's arms as she found herself tugged through the Veil. They arrived in a stone room, much like she imagined would be in a medieval castle, complete with a grand fireplace, a thick wool rug, and a large ornately carved trunk against the wall. "Where are we?"

"My new domain." Moros let her go and rushed over to the trunk, lifting the lid to reveal what she assumed must be the souls of his Kere, brilliant snakelike apparitions of all colors. He stared at them for a minute, then his tense shoulders relaxed slightly. "They're all here," he muttered. "They couldn't have done it."

"I didn't see any Kere at the scene, apart from Tamasin and Nader, who were protecting Galena."

He straightened and turned to her. "She shouldn't have been there, and neither should you. You could have been—"

She smirked and folded her arms over her chest. "Are you actually suggesting that I should be protecting myself? There's really no point in keeping my head down, is there?"

He shook his head, brushing a stray lock of ebony hair out of his eyes. "I don't believe that's your fate. You're not supposed to die, just like none of those poor souls outside of Psychopomps were fated to perish."

"Even if that's true, it's going to happen anyway," she said in a small voice. "You said it yourself." She watched as he drew nearer, relishing the heat that rolled from him as it warmed her Veil-chilled skin. "Plus, I've just been informed by Hugh that he has the votes to oust me as Charon. He said he would take my Scope—and my status."

Moros's eyes narrowed. "He won't allow you to remain a Ferry?"

"I found him in flagrante delicto with some woman in his office, and he was enraged at my intrusion."

Moros looked skeptical. "But I know Hugh. He's been on the board a long time, and he isn't stupid. If he stripped you of your status, he'd have to deal with the rage of all those loyal to you, a waste of energy and time as he tries to gain power."

She clasped her hands together. "I need to get back to Psychopomps to try to stop him. I don't know exactly how many votes he has, only that he says he has the majority he needs. If I can reach . . ." But even as she thought about it, she knew the truth. She remembered how each of the board members looked last night. Not a one of them was on her side, not even Rosaleen, not anymore. She raised her head and met Moros's eyes. "I won't be Charon for much longer," she said, her voice breaking.

Her fingers rose to clutch her Charon's Scope. "My father . . . He told me the fate of the Ferrys rested with me." She bowed her head as her exhaustion and fear finally broke loose, exploding through her veins like the deadliest poison. "He would be so disappointed in me," she said, swallowing back a sob.

Warm, strong arms wrapped around her in an instant, and Aislin stiffened, shocked, as they gently pulled her close. But instead of flinching away, she relaxed into the embrace, laying her head on Moros's shoulder as he stroked her back. She needed this.

"You're so wrong, Aislin. Your father took such pride in you," he said, his voice uncharacteristically soft.

A tear slipped from Aislin's eye as she wrapped her arms around Moros's waist, craving his steady strength. "But I've failed. I've presided over the collapse of order, the destruction of the city, and dozens of unsanctioned deaths with no end in sight. I'm leaving my family with a catastrophe, one that's worse for my leadership." She gritted her teeth and squeezed her eyes shut, holding in a scream. She had worked so hard, for so many years. "I never expected it to end like this."

"This is not the end, Aislin," Moros said. She looked up to find him glaring down at her with steely eyes. "You're forgetting who you are."

"I know who I am. And what I am." *A failure.*

"You're dead on your feet. You've been through a hellish ordeal. And you're facing the biggest challenge of your life. None of that changes who you are." His gaze softened as he focused on her face. "And I, for one, am very thankful for that."

She looked into his eyes, marveling at the cut of his cheekbones, the strong line of his jaw. She'd never believed touching the Lord of the Kere's bare skin was possible, but now . . . Tentatively, her fingertips rose, and she bit her lip as they brushed his cheek, keenly aware of the burst of heat low in her belly. He closed his eyes, and she pulled back. "Is it unpleasant?"

"No, just a flash of black," he murmured, "but it passes quickly if I'm expecting it. And now . . ."

"Now?"

He took her arm, his thumb caressing the inside of her wrist. Slowly, he guided her hand to his neck and held it there. His pulse ticked steady and powerful against her palm, and his lips parted as he tilted his head back. "Now I don't want it to end."

It was as if she'd shifted on her axis, and now he was true north, the only certain thing in a world that was falling apart. He inhaled sharply as her lips touched his throat, his hand sliding up her back to the nape of her neck. His fingers curled and tangled in her hair, then he pulled her face away. She felt a flash of disappointment—

Aislin gasped as his hot tongue swept along her bottom lip before plunging into her mouth. Moros anchored her against his body as he controlled the kiss, and Aislin welcomed it, an invasion she had secretly wished for during a thousand forbidden fantasies. Beads of sweat pricked at her temples as she ran her hands along his ribs to his hard chest. Being so near him was like sitting too close to a fire; getting burned was a definite possibility but one she was willing to risk for a taste of what he could offer.

She met each thrust of his tongue with her own, matching his violence with passion. As her arms slid around his neck, his hands traveled to her hips, holding her flush against his growing arousal and sending a zing of pleasure up her spine. She smiled against his mouth, triumph singing in her veins. His hands were addictive, spreading heat as they skimmed up under her sweater to meet her bare skin. With his fingers slipping higher, with her breaths halting and hurried, Aislin found it easy to forget all the misery and defeat that awaited her in Boston. This was all there was, and it was more than enough.

She was in the arms of death himself, and she'd never felt more alive.

He pulled away from her mouth and touched his forehead to hers, his eyes tightly closed, conflict etched across the planes of his handsome face. But when she lifted her chin and touched his lips with her own, he began the invasion anew, moaning as her breasts pressed to his chest, as she rolled her hips so he could feel the curves of her body. Suddenly her clothes felt thick and heavy, an unwanted barrier between them. She wanted more of him, more of his taste, his heat, his hard grip and commanding kiss. If she had to die, this would be an exceedingly pleasant way to go.

One of his hands curled around the back of her neck while the other cupped her backside, and Aislin felt his thick erection against her abdomen. She made a choked sound as his tongue trailed down her neck, as the sharp edges of his canines scraped against her sensitive flesh.

Harder. The word was about to roll off her tongue when he pushed her away, his chest heaving and his eyes glowing crimson.

"This is a mistake," he muttered, turning away from her and running his hands through his hair.

Aislin shivered. This gray stone room, its high windows black with a starless night, or maybe deep within the Veil, was unheated and cold, something she hadn't noticed with his body so close to hers. She stared at his back, at his strong fingers laced behind his head, waiting for him to say more. But he remained silent, staring at the unlit fireplace. "Jason—"

"Don't fool yourself into thinking I'm something I am not." He cursed. "This is a ridiculous game we're playing, Aislin. It's a distraction neither of us can afford."

I may have only hours to live, she almost said, but then realized how pathetic that sounded. Did she really want him to kiss her because he pitied her? He thought she was a distraction, for God's sake. Humiliation crystallized inside her, hard and brilliant as a diamond. Of course he had a different perspective. He was thousands of years old and had seen so much. Compared to him, she was a fleeting presence in this world, especially now.

She drew herself up and took a step back. "Agreed," she said evenly, adopting the tone she used to speak to employees who disappointed her. "And perhaps, considering everything that's happening in Boston, you shouldn't have brought me here."

Really, she should be thanking him. Less than an hour ago, she'd been scolding Hugh for trysting while everything was falling apart, and now she had done the same thing. It had been a moment of weakness she shouldn't have indulged.

Moros looked over his shoulder at her, and for a moment she could have sworn she saw a glint of pain in his eyes. "You're right," he said. "It was impulsive, but fortunately, easily rectified."

His hand shot out and closed around her wrist, and Aislin fought to stay upright as he yanked her into the Veil, through space, across the world. She had no idea how far they traveled, only that a moment later they appeared in her office. He let go of her immediately and stepped back. His dark, slashing brows were low, his mouth hard. Was he angry at her? Their attraction had been mutual—hadn't it been?

She crossed her arms over her chest. "Now what?"

"Now I deal with the Shade-Kere, and you deal with your board. Then we meet with the Keepers and ask for their aid in dealing with the threat. Even if they refuse, we may be able to buy enough time to find Eris and the others before they can reach their goal."

A quiet laugh escaped from her, despite the ache inside. "This time, you're the one making it sound simple."

"At the moment, simple is the best I can do." He paused, his arms hanging loose at his sides, elegant and dangerous. "Aislin, I regret blurring the boundaries of our business relationship. You have my apologies."

"I apologize as well. I suppose the stress got to me momentarily, as you so helpfully pointed out."

He looked away. "I will update you when we've dealt with the threat to the city."

By then, I might not be Charon anymore. He might be giving his updates to Hugh. She might be mortal. She might be *dead.* Suddenly, she wanted to be in his arms again, to ask him to carry some of this burden of fear and worry. But he clearly had no interest in doing any such thing, and he had more than enough to deal with already. "Very well. Good luck."

"Luck is for mortals," he said, vanishing.

She turned away, furious at the sting of tears in her eyes. He was right—what a ridiculous distraction. She couldn't waste whatever time she had left fantasizing about Jason Moros, his devastating kisses, and his fiery hands as they slid across her skin. She had to try to bring some of the board members back to her side. She needed to call Cavan and ask him to be ready to bring the voice and favor of the Lucinae to the table. She had to be at her best, even though fatigue was making her head swim. She hadn't slept in nearly two days.

"I'll sleep when I'm dead," she whispered, then jumped at the sound of sharp laughter.

It hadn't come from her.

She looked over at her desk to find Rylan sitting there, feet up. "Your guards are still busy downstairs, lucky for them." He gave her a bland smile. "You look so tired, Aislin. Rough day?"

Hatred boiled up, hot enough to pour strength into her muscles and keep her upright. "Father would be so ashamed of you. I know I am."

"But he always respected people who got things done. How do you think he'd feel about what you've accomplished today? Humans meant to live long lives are being slaughtered in the streets, and you're about to be voted out, a disgrace. I think he would be ashamed of *you.*"

She looked away before she could stop herself, and Rylan laughed. "You always cared so much about what he thought of you."

"You say that as if it's a bad thing." She tensed as she heard his shoes moving along the floor toward her. She'd never been afraid of Rylan . . . until now.

"It's a weakness to care what anyone thinks of you," he said. "And it's always been one of yours. It's held you back in so many ways. It's the reason why I always beat you."

That brought her eyes back to his. "Did you?" she snapped. "Are you sure?"

He grimaced and took a step closer. "Any victory you might have claimed was pathetically temporary. And look at us now. Who would you say has the upper hand?"

Her fingers rose to her Scope. "Morally or physically?"

"Morally?" Rylan chuckled. "Oh, Aislin." His eyes flashed red before he disappeared—and reappeared right in front of her.

She forced herself not to take a step back. "Get out of my office."

He grinned. "As you wish." He grabbed her arm and jerked her into the Veil, buffeting her with frigid air and burning wind before throwing her down roughly.

Aislin landed on her hands and knees on rocky ground, cutting her palms on sharp stones. Wincing, she raised her head to find herself in a massive cavern lit with hundreds of torches. Rylan stood smirking a few feet away, next to a dark-haired young woman wearing a dress more appropriate for a rooftop party than spelunking. Lounging on the rocks around them were two other people, one a stocky, bald young man in a T-shirt and jeans, and the other . . .

The blonde from Hugh's office waved at her. "Told you I wasn't a toy," she said silkily.

The dark-haired woman next to Rylan clucked her tongue. "Nemesis, this woman is a guest. Be polite." She took a step forward and bent low so she could speak right in Aislin's face. "Hi there," she said softly. "I'm so glad you took the time out of your busy schedule to come visit us."

Aislin sat back on her knees. "You must be Eris." She was out of breath from pain and fear but unwilling to cower. "Your brother is looking for you."

Eris grinned, revealing her shiny white teeth. "Aw, does he miss me? I've certainly missed him. That's why I'm going to send him a present." She moved a little closer. "Rylan tells me Moros is quite fond of you," she crooned. "So what better way to hurt him?" She gestured to Rylan, who strode over and squatted in front of her.

"Good luck, Aislin," he told her as Eris ran her fingers through his hair, petting him like a dog. "Oh, and you won't be needing this."

His hand rose so quickly that Aislin couldn't stop him from tearing her Scope from the chain at her throat. She cried out in pain and lunged as he stood up with the Scope of the Charon in his hand.

"Is that what this was about?" Aislin asked, her voice rising. "All of this destruction just so you could be Charon again?"

Rylan chuckled and slid his arm around Eris's waist. "I don't give a fuck about being Charon anymore, Aislin."

Eris got on her tiptoes and kissed his cheek. "Get going."

Rylan grinned down at her, then disappeared. Eris returned her attention to Aislin. "Shall we get better acquainted?" Her nostrils flared as she inhaled deeply. "Because I can smell my brother all over you, and I've got to say, that makes me curious."

"Moros won't rest until he stops you, no matter what you do to me." *He knows I'm already doomed.*

Eris rolled her eyes. "I don't want to hurt his *feelings*, darling. I want to see him on his knees, with a sword rammed through his gut." Her lips curved in a fond, cheerful smile, and she gestured toward the stocky young man, who brandished a sword, its blade thin and razor-sharp, emanating a warm yellow glow. "*That* sword, to be precise. And you're going to make that happen."

"I'll never help you hurt him," Aislin said in a hollow voice, struck with horror at the image of Moros on his knees, vulnerable and defeated.

Nemesis appeared at her sister's side, twisting a blonde lock of hair around one of her fingers. "Oh, honey, trust me. When we're done with you, you'll want to kill him more than we do, and that's *really* saying something."

With that, Eris and Nemesis reached out, each taking one of Aislin's hands. The moment their skin touched hers, her mind exploded with hate.

CHAPTER NINE

Moros stood in the Veil, on the roof of a tenement at the edge of what had once been Boston Common, now a lawless swamp. Aching with throbbing, unsated need, and a violent anger, he looked toward the gray half-circle of sun rising in the east, peeking between the massive skyscrapers of downtown. He shuddered as he considered the magnitude of the mistake he'd just made.

Aislin's taste was still in his mouth. Her scent was on his hands, his clothes—a delicate violet that made his heart race. Her face was in his mind—her creamy skin flushed with desire, her full lips swollen from the force of his kiss, her gaze sliding over him like a curious caress. It was all he could do to stop himself from going straight back to her.

No one had ever affected him like this. No woman had ever embedded herself in his thoughts as she had. The impending betrayal by Hugh, the specter of her life ending . . . fury tore through him, lengthening his claws and turning his world crimson. How had she become this important?

You've been intrigued by her for years, his thoughts whispered.

But this was different. More dangerous. Now his head was full of relentless fantasy, of the need to feel her beneath him, panting and willing. He raked his hands through his hair. "Stop," he said and focused on his Kere.

He took a deep breath and let it out, and then began to call each of his subjects to mind, one by one, soul by soul. He kept his eyes closed as he heard them materializing around him, concentrating on the next and the next and the next. The first he summoned were his most experienced, and they remained silent as their brethren appeared around them. He could feel their heat, their power, and he smiled.

When he was certain he had enough, he called one more—and opened his eyes as Eli Margolis appeared right in front of him, fangs bared. "Can't this wait?" he snarled.

Moros arched an eyebrow. "I'm sure Cacia can do without you for a few minutes."

Eli's angular face contorted with frustration. "Not when she's fighting a horde of Shade-Kere trying to kill everyone in the North End!"

"That's why I've gathered you here." Moros raised his arms, turning to the group of Kere he had called to him, summoned from every corner of the world. Some of them were hundreds of years old. He felt a pang of sadness as he realized Trevor would be standing here, too, if his soul hadn't been stolen by enemies. But he couldn't focus on his losses—he still had his most loyal Kere with him, and he needed them now more than ever. "We are going to war, my friends," he told them. "And make no mistake, to lose is to face extermination."

Hai, his black hair pulled back, his wiry body taut with readiness, scowled. He was one of the ancient ones, his loyalty stretching all the way back to the rebellion two thousand years ago. "Is that a threat?"

"Not from me," Moros told him. "Some of my sisters and my brother are determined to awaken an ancient enemy who could destroy us all. They have created an army of their own by stealing the souls of Shades here in the Veil and turning the creatures loose in the real world to wreak havoc. As Eli said, they're Marking and killing innocents who were never meant to die, and it is fraying the fabric of fate at an alarming rate."

Eli turned to look at the others, who were crowded on the roof, crouching on the solar panels, perched on the half walls that bounded the space. "They disappear as soon as they're really challenged. It's made it impossible to keep up with them. They're as strong as we are and hard to take down. The Ferrys have gotten a few through portals to Hell, but they're suffering because of it." Eli's fingers were curled into fists. It was clear he was desperate to get back.

"You will crush them," Moros said. "Before this day is over, I want all of them dead."

"How many of them are there?" asked Parinda, another ancient comrade, her upturned cat-eyes focused on Eli.

"No idea," said Eli. "But it seems like there are more every time we catch up with them." He turned back to Moros and gestured at the others. "Maybe more than this number can deal with."

Moros grinned. "No matter. Each of you catch one." He ran his tongue along his fangs, ready to let the animal inside him loose, eager to slake his thirst for violence. "And bring them to me." He spread his fingers. "I'll do the rest."

His eyes met Eli's. "Take us to them."

Eli gave him a curt nod and disappeared. The rest of the Kere looked to Moros, awaiting a signal. "Can you feel him?" he asked them. They nodded. "Then let's go. Do not disappoint me."

He focused on the trace of Eli, the subtle essence of the man. He imagined his fingers hooking around that thread and letting it pull him forward through the Veil.

He emerged into absolute mayhem: burning vehicles floating in the canal, shattered glass everywhere, and bodies lying on the sidewalk, a few of them injured Ferrys. The air was filled with the scent of decaying flesh. Skeletal monsters in rotting clothes, skin sagging from their bony fingers, stalked the living. Screams and shouts echoed in the air, and down the block, Eli was calling Cacia's name, searching for his mate in the chaos. As his Kere appeared around him, Moros saw one of the Shades drag a woman through the shattered window of an amphibious bus even as another creature landed on the vehicle's hood. Inside, the terrified driver cowered.

"Bring them to me!" Moros roared.

The Kere charged. Moros willed himself through space and reappeared on the roof of the bus. The Shade-Ker dropped the lifeless woman it had just strangled into the canal and climbed onto the roof, its oozing eyes on Moros. "Where is your master?" he asked the thing.

It snarled and charged, senseless and brainless and driven by a thirst for death. But Moros *was* death. He caught the Shade around the throat, and it exploded in a flurry of greasy dust. Moros vanished and reentered the real world down the block, where Eli was still searching for Cacia. Moros could sense her nearby as well but couldn't see her. He willed himself into the Veil, and Eli appeared next to him, cursing as they both saw Cacia struggling with two Shade-Kere who had her by the arms. Her left leg was bent at a terribly wrong angle, and her lovely face was scratched and bleeding, but she was fighting fiercely to keep the Shades from stealing her Scope.

With a growl, Eli leaped forward, tearing the head off one of the Shades with curt brutality. He glanced over his shoulder and tossed the head at Moros, who caught it and rendered it to ash with a mere thought. Cacia fell to the ground as they dispatched the other one the same way. Her wheezing gasps told Moros she was hurt far more severely than her obvious injuries. Eli bowed over her, murmuring in her ear, his rage and violence tamed by the petite bleeding woman gathered in his arms.

The Lord of the Kere pushed down the longing he felt at the sight of their intimacy. "There are more to be found."

Eli looked up at Moros, his eyes pleading. "Let me get her out of here. Please. You can't ask me to leave her like this."

"Eli, I'll be fine," Cacia said weakly, her breath halting. Her fingers rose to touch his face.

The memory of Aislin's fingertips against his cheek nearly knocked Moros to the ground. "Take her," he snapped, needing both of them out of his sight. "I'll summon you back if I need to."

As Eli vanished, taking Cacia with him, Hai appeared before Moros, holding a struggling Shade-Ker by the neck—and the thing's head in his other hand. "It keeps trying to disappear," Hai said with a huff.

But it couldn't; Hai was a stronger being. "Another," Moros roared as he dispatched the Shade-Ker. As soon as Hai was off again, Moros willed himself back into battle, losing himself in the joy of killing. It had been so long since he'd struck with abandon, stealing life and existence with a mere stroke of his fingers, sucking the will from a living being's limbs, the fight from its very cells. Because the Shade-Kere were soulless, nothing remained once they were destroyed. The Ferrys could send them to Hell, which would accept them for the abominations they were, but Moros couldn't help but delight in removing them from existence entirely.

It was satisfying, like scratching an itch. He could have spent his entire day in the dusty haze. His Kere brought him victim after victim, monster after monster, but Moros didn't wait for them to find him. He stalked through the North End, hunting the creatures himself, following them as they tried to disappear into the Veil.

He had just terminated a particularly muscular Shade-Ker when Eli appeared once more—his fingers wrapped around the wrist of Declan Ferry. Aislin's brother had eyes the same icy shade as hers, and it brought her immediately and painfully to mind.

"What is it?" Moros asked, brushing a few bits of ash from his sleeve. "Another attack?"

Declan shook his head. "I just went to check in with Aislin."

Moros tensed. "And?"

"She's not in her office, and she's not answering her phone. I called Eli to help me find her."

Eli let go of Declan's wrist. "Moros, I can't sense her at all."

Everything inside Moros went still. He'd been so desperate to push Aislin out of his thoughts that he hadn't dared turn his consciousness toward her, but now he did with all the concentration he had.

He felt nothing. And then he felt too many things to name—horror and fear and need and worry, all jagged edges rubbing up against each other inside his chest, shearing away anything else. Aislin was *gone*.

His heart thrumming, he grabbed Declan's shoulder and dragged him through the Veil, straight to Aislin's office. His first breath brought her scent back to him, awakening the ache. He stalked to her desk and turned, taking in the room. One of her shoes lay on its side near the desk. He had left her here a few hours ago, too jumbled and lost in his desire to be near her for another moment, and now . . . "Where are her guards?"

"They were involved in the first Shade-Kere attack, and when they came back to reconnect with her, she wasn't here." Declan looked around, his black hair standing on end, lines of worry bracketing his mouth. "When they weren't able to find her or reach her, they called me. You can't trace her, figure out where she went?"

"Where she was taken, you mean." Moros pointed at the lost shoe. "No, but I know who has her." Rylan could have transported her anywhere, though. Moros's hand rose to rub his breastbone as he pictured a hand punching through Aislin's chest, tearing out her brilliant, shining soul.

Eli appeared in the office with Cacia leaning against him. Her face was still healing, red gashes fading across her cheek, and she was keeping the weight off her left leg, but she still managed to look defiant. Eli, on the other hand, looked irritated as he steadied her. "You should be horizontal," he said to her.

"Was it Rylan?" Cacia asked, her turquoise eyes on Moros. "Did he come back?"

When Declan's eyebrows shot up, Moros explained. "Your brother came to threaten her earlier. He wants her on his side, aligned with my siblings against me."

Declan frowned. "Do you think she might have agreed to that?"

Moros paused, caught by the suspicion on Declan's face. "Do you have so little faith in your sister?"

Declan looked away. "She nearly stripped me of my status a few days ago for defying her."

"She relented when she knew you were in mortal peril."

"But Aislin's got her own way of doing things, and she likes to win." The implication hung in the air between them: Declan thought Moros might lose.

Moros chuckled. "You really think her desires are so simple, that she would choose to win for the sake of winning, even if the world around her crumbled?" Didn't they see what he saw? Aislin was stronger than that. Smarter, as well. Certainly, she was fallible and frustrated at times, but she always seemed to find her way.

Declan stood up straight, his muscular arms at his sides. "That's not what I'm saying at all. My sister's just . . ." He sighed impatiently and ran his hands through his hair. "If she thought it would protect our family, I think she'd do just about anything. Even at the expense of everyone else."

"Wait," said Cacia, her breath whistling. Eli had been correct when he said she shouldn't be here. Any ordinary human would have died from the injuries she'd sustained. Her eyes burned as she stared at Moros. "Did you touch her?"

"*What?*" Declan snapped. "Why would he do that?" His eyes narrowed as he glared at Moros.

"She told me she was going to ask you to touch her," Cacia said quietly, looking haunted. Moros felt a flash of guilt at how he'd callously sifted through Cacia's intended future, taking advantage of her desperation to save the man she loved. "She wanted you to trust her. She needed you to know she wouldn't betray you."

Moros leaned back against Aislin's desk, considering that. She was so brave, full of steely courage with a ruthless edge. She'd been willing to sacrifice herself to forward her cause and protect her family. She would make a powerful enemy. But when he'd held her in his arms, her surrender had been anything but calculated. It had been soft and needy in a way that had made him want to crush her against the wall and claim her completely.

Declan poked him in the shoulder, pulling him from the fantasy. "Well? Did you touch my sister?" He looked as if he wanted to hammer one of his fists through Moros's skull.

Moros sighed. "It is no business of yours."

Declan was in his face in an instant, his hands fisted in Moros's shirt. "The hell it is. From everything I've heard, your touch is virtual torture, and if you did that to Aislin—"

Moros put his hands up, though he easily could have shoved Declan away. "She asked me to, as Cacia said," he replied. "I acquiesced."

"And?" Cacia asked, her voice a bit stronger this time.

His eyes met hers. "And I saw nothing."

"What the fuck does that mean?" Declan snapped.

It felt like someone had carved his chest hollow. "It means Aislin has no future."

"Wait," said Cacia, frowning. "You told me my future disappeared after Eli was killed, and that was because my fate was still wrapped up with his, but he had become a Ker, right? You can't see the futures of your Kere. What if that's what's happening here?"

"No . . . this felt . . . different." Darker. Denser. Utterly blinding and all-encompassing.

"Are you saying she's going to die?" Cacia asked in a small voice.

He nodded. "I cannot say exactly when, but it will be soon."

Cacia stood up straighter. "How did she react?" The shadow of her own memories darkened her eyes. "Was she okay after you touched her?"

More okay than I was, it seemed. "She was unharmed," Moros said.

"But now you know she won't betray you, right?"

"I did not see whether she would betray me or not." He turned away from them, his thoughts of her far too private to share. "But I think I do trust her," he finally said, trying to gather enough logic to offer an explanation more intelligent than how devastatingly perfect it felt to have her near, how wrong it felt not to be able to sense her now. "She understands that the threat of Chaos would affect the Ferrys along with every other being on the planet. She wouldn't bow to Rylan's coercion." He looked over his shoulder at her sister and brother and spoke the terrible truth. "And that means she is in grave danger right now." They could hurt her in so many different ways. The sharp urgency of it flayed him.

"Would Ry—or whoever controls him—turn her into a Ker?" Declan asked.

"They could do anything." The idea of Aislin's precious soul in the hateful hands of one of his siblings kindled a rage inside Moros like nothing he'd ever felt. "I have to find her."

Eli frowned. "How, if you can't sense her?"

Moros grinned, though in his present state, it probably looked more like he was baring his teeth. "I know someone who might be able to help . . . if I apply the right kind of pressure."

As his vision sparked crimson, the Lord of the Kere willed himself straight into the Psychopomps boardroom.

CHAPTER TEN

The faces crowded her, sneering. Their eyes raked over her like knives, cutting into her marrow. Declan. Rylan. Hugh. Rosaleen. Each of them had taken a turn.

Now it was her father's.

He looked up from his desk as she stalked into his office. "My darling. To what do I owe this pleasure?"

She was so angry she could barely get the words out. "You canceled my gold exchange initiative without even consulting me." She'd been in the position of vice president of foreign exchange for only two months, and this was her first major move to control the markets. "I'm not breaking any laws!"

He gave her a small sad smile that she suddenly wanted to slap off his face. "Not technically," he said gently. "But though China and the US would have profited, it would have bankrupted several smaller countries."

Her fists clenched. "Those countries shouldn't even be trading!"

"But they do, and the last thing they can afford would be for you to flood the market. It would collapse their currencies. Think of the suffering that would cause."

"Who cares about places like Senegal and Hungary, for God's sake?" Her entire body was quaking. "I'll have to explain this to my

team." She'd promised them so much profit that each of them could buy Senegal or Hungary if they wanted to, and she'd reveled in the way they'd looked at her, with admiration and awe. She had felt invincible. Loved. And now . . .

Her father stood up, his blue eyes meeting hers. His black hair was flecked with gray, but he was still vital, still sure he knew everything. "Then you'd better explain it to them. And perhaps you'd like to spend some time thinking about the difference between what is expedient and what is right, hmm? People who like you only for what you can give them are rarely steadfast friends, and not often worth what you sacrifice to keep them."

Humiliation was a noose around her neck. "They'll hate me!" She'd worked her whole department to the bone for the last two months preparing this strategy, and now everything had come crashing down. Because of her father.

He smiled, and she was certain he was thinking of how her employees would turn on her, whisper behind her back, sullenly defy her, fail to defend her when Rylan dipped his smarmy fingers into her business. She'd thought she could match her brother. She'd wanted to beat him. This embarrassment would delight him. As it delighted her father. What a wretched, hateful man. She wanted to scratch his eyes out, to throw him off a balcony, to—

She fell to the ground, gasping as nausea tangled her guts. Eris and Nemesis smiled down at her. "That was beautiful, Aislin. You're doing so well."

Aislin pressed her cheek against the cold rock and shut her eyes tightly. *That wasn't how it went. He wasn't hateful. He wanted me to become something better, something he could be proud of—*

"Oh, no," said Eris, clucking her tongue. "We can't have that." She reached down and wrapped her fingers around the back of Aislin's neck, and Aislin was sucked down into the flood of memory once again. All of them were laughing at her. None of them understood how hard she had worked to get to her position. None of them liked her. Their resentment was so bitter that she retched, her body desperate to empty itself of the poison. But nothing would come—nothing but more memories.

Cacia stepped out of the elevator, her mouth set with defiance. Cavan glanced at her, then turned back to Aislin. They'd been in the middle of discussing how to reassure the Mother, the leader of the Lucinae, that order would remain despite Patrick Ferry's untimely death. Cavan arched an eyebrow. "I assume this was your two o'clock?"

Heat spread from Aislin's neck to her cheeks. Defied by her own baby sister. "I expected you half an hour ago," she snapped as Cacia approached her conference table.

Cacia stopped in her tracks. "Did you expect me to get here by magic?"

Aislin glared at her. Declan had informed her that Cacia had used her Scope for unofficial purposes, an act that had put her very life in danger. What if she'd been attacked by a Shade and left for dead? Cacia was so selfish that she had no idea what it would do to her family if she got hurt.

"I expected you to take my summons seriously," Aislin said in a cool voice, determined to project control in front of her most important ambassador. The last thing she needed was more gossip about her.

Cacia rolled her eyes. "Look, I'm here," she said tartly. "Did you want to complain about what Father left you in his will or something?"

The insult burned all the way down her spine and straight into her blood. She'd worked for her father for years. She'd done everything he'd asked. And yet, when it came down to picking a trusted executor for his will, he'd chosen Cacia—who had rejected Psychopomps and a position Aislin had created just for her, in her own department. Aislin had been hopeful that she and her sister would be closer once the young woman came to work at the company, and she'd *entertained fond thoughts of them spending more time together. But no—Cacia had spit on the job and everything that came with it, including Aislin, in favor of riding around in an ambulance all day.*

And even after that, their father had chosen Cacia. Her little sister loved to rub salt in the open wound, the vast grief that was eating Aislin up. Cacia wanted to hurt her. She wanted to make sure Aislin suffered. She wanted to humiliate her in front of her ambassador. She had planned this whole thing to make Aislin look bad.

Aislin raised her head and imagined slamming Cacia's face onto the desk, then pulling the chain of her Scope tight and strangling her with it, watching her sister's face turn pink then red then purple then blue, willing her to die in pain knowing how much Aislin hated her—

Aislin arched back, her hands twisting in her hair, her toes pointed and curling as the violent images faded for a moment. Every part of her was alight with caustic hatred. For her father, for Cacia, for . . .

It's not real. Cacia never wanted to hurt you. She was trying to do the right thing.

Her vision focused slightly as Nemesis stroked Aislin's hair back from her sweaty forehead. "Your little sister is such a bitch," she whispered. "Haven't you ever wished a Shade would tear her head off?"

"Yes." *No! No. She's my sister, always.*

"She's still fighting it," said a male voice. The stocky, bald young man leaned over her, gazing at her with the same gray eyes as Moros's, so cold when they wanted to be. "Let me have a go." He dropped to his knees, bracing himself with his palms on either side of her head. "How well do you know my brother, princess?" he asked, his voice gentle.

Aislin stared into his eyes, looking for shards of crimson. "I . . . have watched him for years," she said in a broken voice. This man was Apate, the personification of lies—so how was he able to draw the truth out of her? "I've been fascinated by him for as long as I can remember."

Apate nodded, like she'd done a good job. His approval felt like a beacon inside her chest, glowing and warm. When he smiled, it was pure seduction. She wanted to tell him everything; she knew he would understand and sympathize. "You've imagined yourself with him, haven't you, Aislin?"

"Seriously?" said Nemesis. *"Ew."*

Apate cut his sister a nasty look. "Shut the hell up and let me work." He turned back to Aislin, his handsome face pleasant once again. He had blond stubble on his chin, and a strong jaw, just like Moros's. She stared up at him, breathless and entranced, her head buzzing with a mishmash of the past and the present. Apate laid his palm on her hip and slid it up slowly until it reached her waist. She squirmed to escape him, but he shushed her like one might a child. "Don't fight. Think of Moros. You've envisioned his hands on you. Just . . . like . . . this." His fingers burrowed under her sweater to find her skin.

Moros gazed down at her, his wavy black hair hanging over his forehead. His gray eyes traced her face, down the column of her throat, to her breasts. She was naked before him, bare and vulnerable. His warm hand was at her waist, and she was desperate for it to move between her legs, where she needed it most. She held her breath as she watched him look her over. Did he like what he saw? Did he care about her at all? Did he have any idea how much she craved him, each flash of his eyes, every hint of the awesome power he wielded?

He leaned down, so slowly it made her throb with need. "Here I am, darling." His voice was a caress. "Tell me what you want. Tell me *everything.*"

"I want you inside me," she whispered, her hands rising to touch his face. It felt so good, to finally admit this to him. "I want to feel you." She spread her legs and tried to pull him down, but he was so strong that she couldn't budge him. "Please," she begged. "I've waited for so long."

The beauty of his lazy smile made her want to cry. "You are nothing to me, did you know that?" he crooned.

She blinked up at him. "What?"

"You're a plaything. A ridiculous, vapid distraction." He sighed. "Barely a distraction, at that. You're actually quite boring."

Aislin's eyes stung with tears. "Then why . . . ?" He had kissed her. It had looked like he was fighting to keep himself from doing more. She could have sworn she'd read desperation in his eyes when he'd noticed her bloodstained sweater. She'd been sure he cared, at least a little.

"Why have I pretended to want you?" He sat back and tilted his head, the charade over, and Aislin crossed her legs and covered her chest with her arms, her body coursing with sudden chills. "Because it kept you from working against my interests, and when we appear before the Keepers, it will be easy to convince them that you're useless." He leaned down and brushed his lips over her forehead, and when she tried to turn away, he pinned her shoulders to the rock. "Because you are."

She struggled then, all the hurt and rage and rejection splintering, embedding needle-sharp shards in her heart. He'd fooled her, just as she'd feared all along. Of course he hadn't wanted her. Of course it had been a game. He was a god, for goodness' sake. She was powerless.

I am far from powerless.

A laugh snapped her back into reality. "Oh, I went too far there." Apate was smiling as he tugged Aislin's shirt down and looked up at his sisters. "This only works if she's bought in to the lie, at least a little bit. She pushed back on that one."

Aislin thrashed, desperate to cover herself. She was naked and—no, wait. She was wearing a sweater and slacks. She was in a cave. Moros wasn't here. *That wasn't real. It's not real it's not real it's not real . . .*

"Ugh. So annoying. Let's give her a double shot, then," said Eris, her gray eyes lit with eagerness. She knelt by her brother, her dress fanned around her knees.

Apate caught Aislin's wrist as she jerked her arm up to slap at his sister, his broad fingers folding over her sleeve. With his other hand, he slowly lifted the edge of her sweater again, revealing a swath of her stomach. Aislin tried to twist away from him, tears starting in her eyes. "Don't touch me," she said between gasping breaths.

"But you were begging for it a moment ago," he said. "Didn't you want me inside you? We all heard you quite clearly." Nemesis and Eris giggled as his brow furrowed in an expression of mock hurt. "Wait, were you thinking I was someone else?"

She shut her eyes tightly, telling herself to stay anchored to reality. But then Eris laid her palm on Aislin's cheek as Apate stroked the skin just above the waist of her slacks. The cave disappeared.

She fell to her knees in a grand throne room, barely catching herself before her forehead collided with marble. A chuckle brought her head up. Moros stood next to her, dressed in a suit that was obviously custom-made for his chiseled frame. Diamond cuff links sparkled against his crisp white shirt, and his hair was neatly slicked back, revealing the aristocratic sweep of his brow, the square set of his jaw. He looked down at her, his eyes glowing red. "You're late, my dear. We were just discussing the childish pettiness of Ferry politics, something you know more about than anyone."

Aislin slowly turned her head toward the dais several yards in front of them, upon which sat two thrones. One was so heavily cloaked in shadow that she couldn't see its occupant, and the other so bathed in light that the result was the same.

Their voices, however, were unmistakable. "This is the Charon? She's a little young," said a female voice, sparkling and brilliant as cut glass. It was coming from the beam of light enveloping the throne on the left.

"Pathetic," said a deep male voice emanating from the throne on the right. "Is this the best they can do?"

"She's typical of her kind," said Moros. "Did you expect something more from them? They are only human, after all." He looked straight at the beam of blinding light and offered a smile full of intrigue and promise.

"This is a waste of time," said the rumbling male voice. "I hate to say it, Moros, but you were right."

Moros bowed. "I'm glad you understand now. The Ferrys were never necessary."

"Proceed," said the deep voice, sounding bored. "I have no objection."

"I won't interfere," said the bright female voice.

"But we *are* necessary," Aislin said, her voice suddenly thin and raspy, as if a hand were wrapped around her throat. "We-we—"

And then she realized someone *did* have her by the throat. Moros slammed her to the ground with merciless force. The cold marble at her back told her she was naked once again, unable to hide. The Lord of the Kere's face hovered right above hers, twisted into a monstrous grimace. "Oh, now you're *finally* turning me on," he said as his grip on her tightened, crushing her airway as she pawed feebly at his sleeves.

He placed his forehead on hers, pressing so hard it felt like her skull was going to cave in. "I told you that you were going to die, Aislin," he murmured. "But perhaps I should have mentioned that I would be the one to kill you."

Aislin surfaced all at once, coughing and flailing like a rag doll, shuddering from head to toe. Above her, dim silhouettes hovered, but her vision wouldn't focus. Where was she? With fumbling fingers, she reached up to touch the Scope of the Charon at her throat, needing its comforting weight . . . and remembered that Rylan had taken it.

"I've got to go help make another batch of minions," Eris was saying. "I'll be back later. Are you going to work on her some more?"

"She's had enough for now," said Apate. "If we scramble her too much, she won't be able to follow basic instructions."

"Fine," Nemesis said in a whiny voice. "But I get first dibs when we come back."

The silhouettes disappeared, leaving Aislin in the massive cavern, the sound of trickling water somewhere nearby. A low sob escaped her, and she rolled to her side and pulled her knees to her chest, so thankful to be clothed again, to be alone.

Everybody hated her. Everyone wanted her dead. And they would all be glad that she was gone.

Stop it. They're trying to break you.

Moros was scheming against her. He didn't care about her. It was an act, one she had fallen for completely because she so badly wanted it to be true, especially now when she had so little time left. He would use her vulnerability to destroy her. He was a monster.

Cold stone rubbed against her cheek, and she was grateful for the rough feel of it. It was real. She was sure of it. As sure as she was that Moros needed to be destroyed.

Think about who they are. Think about what they're doing.

They were going to use her as the weapon of his destruction.

She smiled, imagining plunging the sword through his stomach, watching his face go slack with shock, all the smugness gone. His gray eyes would shine with pain.

Misgiving swirled through her. *I don't want to . . .*

His mouth would drop open, but he wouldn't have any breath to tell her how little she meant to him. Blood would trickle from the corner of his mouth. She would wipe it away with her thumb, then smear it on his pressed white shirt. *Hurts, doesn't it? Good.*

"No," she said with a moan. "I won't let you control me." Her voice echoed in the dimly lit cavern, and for a moment she watched the torchlight dancing on wet stone as an idea licked at the edges of the chaos in her mind.

She was fated to die. That part hadn't been a lie.

She was the Charon, at least until the board officially awarded her Scope to someone else and Moros approved it. If any Ferry was mortally injured, a mere thought from her was the difference between life and death. She still held their lives in the palm of her hand.

And her own.

She could take herself out of the equation forever. It was better than being controlled and used.

New energy crackled up her arms, allowing her to push herself up and look around. The cavern was huge, and she was on a platform of sorts, a flat expanse of stone near one of the walls. In the distance, across the rocky terrain of the cave floor, there was a sumptuous silk tent, but she knew she didn't have the strength to get herself there.

So what could she use to get this done? She imagined trying to bash her own head in with one of the loose stones at the edge of the platform, but she wasn't sure she was powerful enough to strike a deathblow. She looked down at herself. At some point, she'd lost one of her shoes. Her slacks were smeared with dirt. The bottom edge of her bloodstained sweater was torn. Hope quickened her thoughts. If she could tear a strip from it, she could wrap it around her neck and . . .

Her eyes blurred with tears. She didn't really want to go this way, but she'd heard Apate, Nemesis, and Eris. They were coming back soon, and when they did, they would pack her head full of deception once again, and then use her to hurt people she cared about.

She'd wouldn't allow them to steal any more from her than they already had. With shaking hands, she reached down and began to tug at the tattered sweater.

CHAPTER ELEVEN

Ten startled faces turned toward Moros as he appeared in the boardroom. The heat poured from his body, warping the air. "Greetings, Ferrys." He took a mock look around. "I believe you're missing your Charon."

Hugh Ferry stood at the opposite end of the table, his lips tight. His silver hair was combed back, revealing his severe widow's peak, and his chin jutted out in defiance. "This is a scheduled board meeting," he said. "And we were just discussing the fact that Aislin hasn't bothered to show up. Apparently she's abdicated her position."

"What?"

Hugh reached into his pocket and lifted out the Charon's Scope.

Moros's throat constricted. "Where did you get that?" he asked in a low voice.

Hugh's eyes widened in innocent surprise. "It was delivered to my office a few hours ago, along with her letter of resignation."

Rosaleen Ferry, who had been a board member for decades, frowned at the sight of the Scope. "You didn't mention that, Hugh. Why would she do such a thing?"

"I didn't have a chance to tell you before we were so rudely interrupted," Hugh explained, holding the ornate platinum disk in his palm. That Scope belonged around Aislin's neck, and without it, she was fearfully vulnerable. "And as for why she would do it," Hugh continued, "perhaps she realized she wasn't up to the job."

Brian Ferry, the same age as Aislin but full of hubris instead of her tempered wisdom, folded his arms across his chest. "Once again, I nominate Hugh Ferry as Charon. It's time we had some stability, and Patrick Ferry's branch of the family has proven unfit for leadership."

Hugh Ferry's fingers closed over Aislin's Scope. Moros stared at the man, feeling a strong desire for blood.

"Seconded," said Ennis Ferry, giving Moros a nervous glance.

Brian grinned. "All in favor—"

"I object," Moros said evenly, a dangerous smile pulling at his lips. He tugged off his gloves and pocketed them. "I don't believe I know you well enough, Hugh." He willed himself across the room, appearing right next to the would-be Charon. "Let's go someplace and have a talk."

He grabbed Hugh's sleeve and dragged him into the Veil, where they appeared on a high plain somewhere in Wyoming, open space for miles. Spluttering and shivering, Hugh staggered back. "How dare you!"

Moros felt his fangs pressing against his lips, turning his smile grisly. "But I am the Lord of the Kere, Hugh. I must approve every Charon. It is my right."

"You could have done that in Boston!"

"No, and I won't do it here, either. Because Aislin didn't resign, did she? Not of her own free will."

Hugh took an unsteady step back as Moros moved closer to him. "Of course she did. I received her letter—"

"You're lying, or you've been duped. Which is it?"

Hugh couldn't meet Moros's crimson eyes. "I thought for certain it was from her. It bore her electronic signature. You think it was fake?"

"I know it was," Moros said softly. "She's missing. Someone took her." The memory of her shoe, lying abandoned by her desk, was one he'd never forget. "And you haven't questioned it. You've made no effort to find her."

"But how do you know she didn't just run away?" asked Hugh.

"Because Aislin Ferry never runs from anything."

Hugh's watery eyes narrowed. "How would you know? Or are you just into her looks? Are you really letting that frigid bitch give you a case of blue balls?"

"How utterly disrespectful." He was only a few feet away from Hugh now, and his calm was slipping away with each second. The man was emanating fear and hatred, but also a scent that Moros hadn't smelled in ages. The moment it hit his consciousness, his entire body reacted, tensing in readiness for an attack. "Hugh," he murmured, his ears roaring. "Who have you been spending time with?"

His hand shot out, and his fingers wrapped around Hugh's throat. The moment their skin met, a face appeared in Moros's mind, one he hadn't seen in nearly two thousand years. Her curly blonde hair bounced around her face, and she bit her lip coyly. Hugh's thoughts were saturated with her venom—images of the Charon's Scope around his own neck, visions of Aislin lying in the Veil, bleeding and dying as Shade-Kere closed in . . .

Moros could feel the man thrashing in his grip, clawing at his arms, kicking frantically, but none of it reached him. Bile rose in his throat as Nemesis coiled herself around Hugh. Together they watched Aislin being torn apart, her body mortal and fragile, the light in her eyes fading. And Hugh felt nothing but joy at the sight. No remorse, no pain.

Moros's claws cut into Hugh's neck, and the man's scream finally penetrated his consciousness. With the visions still pulsing in his skull, Moros opened his eyes and focused on his victim, this man who dreamed of seeing Aislin suffer. "You certainly have colorful fantasies," he hissed.

He kicked Hugh's legs out from under him, and the Ferry collapsed to the ground and slid away, his blood painting the Veil red. "You can't do this," Hugh shrieked, clutching at the wounds on either side of his neck. "You're violating the treaty! We have to appear before the Keepers tomorrow night, and I'll tell them what you've done!"

Moros laughed, sharp as a blade. "You're foolish to believe that I would ever allow you to stand next to me before the Keepers."

"I'll make sure they know you attacked me!"

"How will you do that, Hugh?" He walked slowly after his quarry, who was scrambling back, designer shoes slipping on the soft ground of the Veil. He was still hungering to hear Hugh scream again, but reason reined him in for a moment—the man was the key to finding Aislin. He had to clear away the fog of horror and *think*.

Hugh's face was purple. "The board witnessed you kidnapping me. If I don't return, everyone will know you did something."

"You still seem to believe I'm concerned about what they think," Moros said, vanishing and then appearing behind Hugh, halting his backward progress. "And that I care about the treaty right now."

Because he didn't, he realized. Aislin was the only thing that mattered, even if the Keepers slaughtered him for this. He grabbed Hugh by the shoulders and hoisted him up, forcing the man to look him in the eye. "Where is she?" he asked, then he touched Hugh's cheek and closed his eyes.

Flashes of Hugh's future sprang forward, but Moros suppressed them. He didn't want the man to panic and become uncooperative.

With merciless control, Moros sifted through Hugh's intentions and wants, his past actions and motives, the company he kept and the things he'd done. He saw Nemesis, her head thrown back as Hugh did his best to pleasure her. He saw Aislin, her gaze cold and detached, leaving Hugh with a simmering rage and a desire for vengeance that Nemesis had fed with delight.

And he saw Rylan Ferry handing Hugh the Scope. Hugh wasn't as innocent as he claimed.

Moros dug deeper into the man's brain, searching for any clue as to where Aislin had been taken. Nemesis would know, but she had appeared to Hugh only in Boston—in his apartment and his office, in some of the finer restaurants in the city, too. She'd been manipulating him for some time, filling him with the desire to punish Aislin for her arrogance, her unwillingness to listen to Hugh's suggestions and advice. But through all that, Nemesis had never shared who she really was, had never taken Hugh out of the realm of the real world. She'd driven him to seek vengeance and get rid of Aislin, but he had no idea he was doing these things because of Nemesis's deadly touch.

Moros latched on to a vision of his sister's face. "Who is she to you?" he demanded as Hugh whimpered.

"Who?" Hugh asked in a strangled voice.

Moros brought the image of his sister's face to the fore—her gray eyes, her poisonous grin—making sure Hugh could see it, too.

"That's . . . that's Nina," Hugh said. "She's my . . ." He cleared his throat. "Why are you interested in her?"

Moros had no patience for explanations. "I'm going to find her and destroy her."

"Wh-what?" Hugh stammered. "B-but she's just a human!"

Nothing could be further from the truth. "I think she's been a bad influence on you."

Hugh's veins stood out stark on his temples. "She's been supportive of me!" he said in a shrill voice. "She loves me!"

Moros didn't know whether to feel pity or disdain. "I'm sure she does. But I'll have to take her for myself, I'm afraid."

The man's eyes were practically bugging out of his head now. "She'd never want you! You're a monster!"

"So they tell me." Moros's eyes glowed crimson as a new strategy came to him all at once. He let Hugh go. The Ferry's neck was still bleeding, but the wounds weren't too deep. A few minutes in the real world and he would be good as new. "I think it's time we get back."

Hugh gaped at him. "You're letting me go?"

"Yes," Moros promised. "I'm letting you go. I have other people to deal with."

"Like Nina?" he squeaked. "Is she fated to die?"

"That's not the worst thing I can do. Death is preferable to certain kinds of pain." He couldn't help but bare his fangs, especially as he considered what Aislin might be going through at that very moment. "Perhaps I just want to have a little fun."

Moros willed them out of the Veil, transporting them back to Hugh's apartment. He'd never been there, but he'd seen it all from Hugh's perspective, making it easy to appear within the space. He stepped back. "I'm glad we got to talk. And I'm sorry about your mistress." He rubbed his hands together in mock eagerness. "I hope you weren't that attached to her."

Hugh's mouth opened and closed with shock, and Moros fought a smile. Maybe this trick would work. "If it's any consolation," he continued, "I'll let you keep the Charon's Scope. Perhaps I was too hasty in judging you. Have a lovely afternoon."

He willed himself into the Veil. And waited.

Hugh, a mere apparition from Moros's vantage point in the gray between-realm, poked at the wounds in his neck, which were rapidly healing. Moros stepped behind a wall as Hugh opened the Charon's Scope. He felt the warmth of that portal to the real world and waited until it closed again, then looked around the corner to see Hugh, apparently satisfied that Moros was gone, pocket the Scope. Then the man pulled out his phone and made a call, hopefully the one Moros needed him to make.

Every second felt like an hour. A year. A century. All filled with fears of how he would find Aislin, whether he'd ever feel her pale-blue gaze on him again.

But then he sensed it, like a static shock on his skin, a sour tang in the back of his throat. He smiled despite the discomfort and willed himself into the real world. He arrived in the private lobby outside Hugh's apartment—just as Nemesis appeared.

"Hello," he said quietly.

Her eyes wide, she staggered back against Hugh's door. "Moros."

"Nemesis. It's been so long. You're a vision." He smiled at his younger sister. And then he pounced.

CHAPTER TWELVE

Aislin's fingers wouldn't work properly. Her hands were shaking both from weakness and the chill of the cavern, but she finally managed to tear a strip from the bottom of her sweater. It was long enough to do the job. She sat on the cold stone platform and stared at it, smeared with blood and dirt, seemingly harmless.

She'd spent her whole life surrounded by death, serving fate, but somehow, she'd never spent much time thinking about her own demise. She'd always thought it would be centuries into the future. She'd never imagined it would come so soon, so strangely and abruptly. Twenty-four hours ago, she wouldn't have believed she'd be sitting in some secret pocket in the Veil, planning her suicide.

She took a moment to think about what she'd miss. The satisfaction of knowing she'd taken care of business, the luxury of a rare evening spent in bed with a glass of excellent wine and a well-written novel, the few fragile moments of closeness she'd shared with her siblings. And Moros. Missing him was different, though, more like a gash than an ache, and it wasn't about the past at all.

Until today she'd never believed they could touch each other. She'd never thought they would be anything other than business partners, and she'd accepted that despite the throb of fascination and excitement she always felt when they were in the same room together. She'd had many lovers in the past, but none had ever touched her heart. They were always too intimidated by or resentful of her power for her to truly open herself to them. But now, with Moros's touch, with his taste, he'd managed to create a home for himself inside of her. He'd carved out vast amounts of empty space . . . and the hope that she could fill them with new experiences and thrilling moments, all still to come.

She would experience none of those moments, though. And she shouldn't even allow herself to think of them. He had told her she had no future. It had been the only reason he could touch her in the first place. The same thing that had created the hope had dashed it to bits.

Maybe he had been toying with her all along. How very like him.

Stop. She pressed her fingertips to her temples, still trying to sort out the real from the imagined. She wouldn't last under another assault from Strife, Vengeance, and Lies. She wasn't that strong. Her gaze dropped to the strip of cloth in her hands. This was her only escape.

She shuddered with the thought of losing herself, maybe becoming a Shade, but would that be so different from what was happening now? Yes. Now, she could be used by the enemies of fate to destroy the one person strong enough to stop them. Suicide was the better choice. The only choice.

She wrapped the strip around her throat, determination giving her strength.

"I can't let you do that," came a deep, familiar voice. She pivoted to see Trevor sitting on a rock behind her, his muscular arms folded over his chest, his smooth brown skin lush against the gray stone. Declan had brought the Ker to a few Psychopomps events, and Aislin had always found him polite, if a bit rough around the edges—a perfect best friend for her brother. But now he just looked . . . tired. There were circles beneath his dark-brown eyes and a slump to his posture as he got up and came toward her. She stared up at him as he gently unwrapped the cloth from around her neck with his large warm hands.

"Trevor," she said quietly. "How long have you been sitting there?"

"Awhile," he admitted. "You were pretty absorbed in your own thoughts."

She gave him a weak smile. "Are you my enemy now?"

He tossed the hard-won strip of fabric off the edge of the platform, and it spiraled through the air, landing out of easy reach. "Depends on whose side you're on."

"What if I don't want to be on a side?"

"Killing yourself isn't the same thing as not choosing a side."

He settled himself on the platform beside her, his warmth reaching her an instant later. She fought the urge to lean toward it just to chase some of the chill from her bones. "But I'm fated to die."

His eyebrows rose. "How do you know that?"

"Moros." It hurt to say his name.

Trevor's jaw tightened at the sound of it. "How do you know he wasn't messing with you?"

Because it looked like it had hurt him. "What good would it do to toy with me like that? He wanted me on his side." No one else was, after all. Everyone had abandoned him.

He deserves it. He was trying to use you.

Aislin shuddered, and Trevor placed his hot hand on her back. "I know it's hard to tell what's real from what's not," he said quietly.

She looked up at him. "They did it to you, too?"

"Just Eris. But she got me good enough to do a lot of damage."

Aislin thought back. Trevor had been responsible for the slaughter of Galena Margolis's lab assistants and research subjects. He'd also been the one to kidnap Rylan, right out of Psychopomps headquarters. "Declan knew you were being controlled."

Trevor's hand slipped from her back, and he bowed his head. "I was too weak to stop it, and now look at me."

"Do they have your soul?" she whispered.

He gave her a sidelong glance. "I'm not allowed to say who has it."

"But you have to obey whoever does."

Trevor nodded. "And that means I can't allow you to hurt yourself."

Aislin looked toward the large tent on the opposite side of the cavern. "They knew I might try to commit suicide."

He bumped her shoulder with his. "You were fighting pretty hard. They know they haven't won you over yet, so they'll work harder next time."

Aislin tried to push down a swell of nausea, needing to rid herself of the memory of Moros slamming her against stone, his hand around her throat, telling her she was useless, that he'd only been pretending to care. "It feels like a memory," she said in a choked voice. "But it never happened."

Trevor sighed. "You won't know the difference soon."

Tears stung her eyes. She had always prided herself on her control, and having it stolen from her like this was almost more than she could bear. "Why are you being kind to me?"

"They didn't tell me I had to be cruel."

"And they told you not to allow me to hurt myself." Her thoughts whirred. "But did they tell you that *you* couldn't hurt me?" She turned to him, new hope taking root. "If you were to . . . I don't know . . . strangle me, could you do that? I could will myself to die and . . ."

But he was already shaking his head. "I can't. Even if I was willing to do that to you, I couldn't. They were very thorough. When they come back, you have to be alive—or I won't be."

She sagged, hopelessness and dread weighing so heavily she could barely hold herself up. "Do you have to keep me here?"

"Yes."

"Can you take a message to someone for me?"

"No."

"But you can talk to me. You can sit next to me."

A faint smile appeared on his face. "What's six inches long, has a head—and is something I like to blow from time to time?"

Aislin stared at him.

"Money. See? I can tell dirty jokes, too, but I don't think that'll help you much."

A weary chuckle escaped her. "Money. Very amusing."

Trevor snorted. "Dec thought it was funny."

"Of course he did." Her chest ached suddenly, missing her brother. "I hope he's not too upset," she whispered, and then her face crumpled as she realized a bigger fear—that he wouldn't be upset at all. She could barely blame him, after what she'd done.

Trevor caught her and held her up as she began to collapse onto the platform. "Dec doesn't give up easy," he said. "It's one of the best and worst things about him."

"He didn't give up on you. We all thought you had gone willingly, that you'd fooled Declan and infiltrated Psychopomps on purpose, but he insisted your confession was sincere, that someone took control of you again once you were inside."

"He was right," Trevor said in a hollow voice.

"He still hopes he'll get you back."

"I don't think so," Trevor muttered.

"But you seem to be yourself. You don't seem—"

"Evil?" His eyes glowed red. "How about now?"

"I'm afraid I've grown a bit fond of red eyes of late," she admitted.

He looked surprised for a moment but apparently decided to let her comment slide. "Are you going to keep fighting them?"

She nodded. "Now that you've given me no other choice." Her brow furrowed. "Why haven't they made me a Ker? They apparently have the ability—that's what they did to Rylan."

"They might," he said. "Not all of them can do it, though."

"Which of them can?"

He shook his head.

"Got it. You're not allowed to tell me. Can you tell me which of them *can't* do it?"

He chuckled, deep and rumbling. "They're not stupid."

She shrugged. "Well, you can't blame me for trying."

Trevor grinned, his white teeth gleaming. "You're all right, Aislin. You know that?"

Despite everything, she found herself smiling back. "Thank you. Tell Declan and Cacia that, if you see them again?"

Trevor's grin dimmed with sadness. "They know it already, Aislin. Dec does, at least."

She winced. "I've made so many mistakes with both of them." Her throat tightened mercilessly. "I wish they knew how much I love them. I wish I'd been able to tell them."

"Maybe they know, Aislin. Both of them tend to cut through the bullshit."

She covered her face, thinking of her brawling, salty-mouthed siblings, of their good hearts and unwavering sense of right and wrong. "I hope they don't think I abandoned them."

"They're smart enough to figure it out."

"But what if I, I don't know, what if I do something terrible?"

Trevor's dark eyes were hard on her face. "You can join the club."

"If you could choose, would you go back to Moros?" she asked suddenly.

Trevor sighed. "If I did, he'd probably dust me before I had a chance to explain."

Moros had promised to do exactly that, actually, but that was before it had become clear Trevor hadn't gone rogue—he'd been commandeered, used by Moros's enemies. "I don't think he would."

"He was a decent boss," Trevor said. "Now that my head has cleared, I can see that. And I'll keep seeing it until Eris and Nemesis work on me again. But then?" His fingers flared, as if he were letting his understanding of Moros blow away in the wind.

She stared at his fingers, wondering if, with enough torture, her own feelings for Moros would be so fleeting, so easy to lose her grasp on. "We could help each other," she said in a low voice.

"I told you—I can't help you escape," he said, annoyance creeping into his voice.

"But what if I could help *you*?"

He went still, and she took his silence for interest. It was a dangerous gamble—he could easily be a spy for Eris and her siblings, but what did Aislin have to lose? If she did nothing, she was doomed anyway. "Do you know where your soul is being kept?"

Trevor's gaze darted to the tent and then back to her in a sheer instant. "Why?"

Aislin forced herself not to look at the tent, but eagerness made her heart beat faster. "I bet they've forbidden you from taking it back."

"Yep."

"But if I could get a hold of it?"

He blinked at her, looking stunned. "You serious?"

"Did they tell you to stop me from going into that tent?"

He nodded.

"Did they tell you not to *carry* me into the tent?"

His eyebrows shot up. "But they'll destroy me if they catch me."

Aislin paused. "Then I suppose it's your choice." And for a man who'd had his soul taken, who hadn't been truly free for as long as Aislin had been alive, she knew he had to be the one to make it.

Trevor stared at her for a long, breathless moment, his mouth set. Then he stood up abruptly, leaving Aislin sitting on the rock, wondering if she was strong enough to stand. She was bracing her palms on the stone when Trevor reached down and pulled her up, letting her lean against his powerful body. He was strikingly tall—the top of her head only made it to his shoulder—but he leaned closer as they took their first step. "Thank you," he murmured.

"For what?" The perky voice sent a hard shiver right down Aislin's spine. Eris had appeared right in front of them, her hands on her waist, her skirt fluttering.

Trevor stiffened. "For giving me a choice."

He couldn't lie to his master. She knew that about Moros's Kere. They had to tell him the truth. "It was—" Aislin began, desperate to protect Trevor. "I gave him the choice—either he could take me someplace private where I could relieve myself, or I was going to empty my bladder right here."

Eris snorted. "Humans." She waved toward a far corner of the cavern. "Take her over there, but then bring her back. Apate is right behind me, and Nemesis should be here any minute, and we've got a really fun evening planned."

Trevor's fingers spread along Aislin's ribs, almost as if he wished he could shield her from what was coming. "I'll be right back, then."

He transported Aislin across the cavern to the place Eris had pointed, and stood with his back to her as she pretended to relieve herself. Her body was empty, though—she hadn't had anything to eat or drink in at least a day, she realized. "Perhaps I'm going to die of dehydration," she whispered, and to her surprise, Trevor let out a low chuckle.

She took as long as she could, but eventually he said, "I have to take you now. They'll know something's up if I don't."

Dread stabbed through her. *I won't let them win. I won't let them make me forget who I am. I won't—*

Trevor turned around and his eyes met hers. "It has to be now. I'm sorry."

She stood up. "Okay." She closed her eyes as he took her hand, and when she opened them, she was inside the silk walls of the tent. There were pillows everywhere, along with a tray of olives and fruit and a pitcher of wine. Aislin's eyes streaked around the space, looking for a hint of where Trevor's soul might be hidden.

Eris leaned in front of her. "Nice, huh? I did the decorating myself."

Aislin stared at her, hatred pulsing behind her eyes. But Eris only smiled. She looked so young, so innocent—it was difficult to believe the woman was thousands of years old, made of conflict and feuds and bitter rancor. "It's a bit gaudy for my tastes," Aislin said coldly.

The corner of Eris's mouth twitched. "Trevor, tell her she's rude."

"That was rude, Aislin," he said woodenly. He'd stationed himself at the opposite side of the tent, and he wasn't looking at her—he was looking past her. Staring hard, in fact. But when Eris turned to him, his gaze immediately flicked away from the spot to land on his mistress. "How was that?" he asked.

"I could use more enthusiasm next time," Eris said blandly.

Apate materialized inside the tent and looked Aislin up and down. "Oh my," he said, eyeing the bottom of her torn sweater. "What have you been up to?"

When no one answered, Eris turned to Trevor. "Well?"

His nostrils flared. "She was going to kill herself. I stopped her."

Apate gave Aislin a hurt look. "Aislin, that would have made me very sad."

"Liar," Aislin whispered, glancing over his shoulder to see what Trevor had been staring at—a stack of small wooden boxes, resting on a footstool. Trevor's soul had to be in one of them.

Apate grinned. "Are we ready to get started again? I've got some good stuff lined up, but I could use Nemesis's help. When is she going to be back?"

Eris shrugged. "She got a call from that geezer she's been fucking—Hugh Ferry. He's about to be named the Charon, just like we planned. She went to ensure that he's ready for the summit, but she should be back soon."

Aislin put her hand to her stomach—was she not the Charon anymore? She hadn't felt a thing. Had she been stripped of her status as a Ferry, too? Was she mortal now?

Apate pressed his face into her hair, pulling her from her thoughts. "Are you ready, my dear?" he asked softly, his voice morphing into a painful imitation of Moros's.

She tried to take a step back, but his arm snaked around her waist, and he pulled her against him. And when Aislin looked up, she was gazing into a different face, one with olive skin and a dark-stubbled jaw, his black hair swept back, his gray eyes glinting with shards of ruby. They were in a ballroom, a massive chandelier glittering above their heads, couples waltzing in slow circles around them. "Let's have one last dance," he said, his mouth against her ear, sending chills rippling along her skin.

It's a lie, Aislin told herself. *This isn't real.* She focused so hard on the thought that it felt like her head might explode. But when his lips touched hers, it shattered her resistance. The kiss was soft and seductive, making Aislin's legs weak.

When he pulled back, they were surrounded by Kere. Eli was there, and Nader and Tamasin. Hai and Parinda, two centuries-old beings she'd met only once or twice, as well as Luke and a crowd of Kere who frequented Boston. Their eyes glowed as they grinned at her, as their fangs lengthened even as she watched and their claws curled at the ends of their fingers. Moros spun her around and pinned her arms behind her back. Again, she realized she was naked, her breasts and belly exposed.

It had been a trap. "But the treaty," she said in a broken voice. "You're violating the treaty."

"But you're not a Ferry anymore, my dear," he said, his hot breath tickling her neck. "And that means you're fair game, just like your father was."

A horrible realization sliced through her heart. "But you said—"

"I know I said I had nothing to do with his death, but I *lied.*"

Lies. Lies . . . Her thoughts caught for a moment, like fabric snagged on a nail.

"I helped Rylan do it," he continued, dragging her mind back under his authority as his hard body pressed against her back. "Because your father was a nuisance. Just like you."

His grip on her wrists was so tight she was sure her bones were about to shatter. "Have at her," he told his Kere. "But don't touch her face. That's mine to ruin."

He tilted her head up, his claws digging into her cheek. His breathtaking smile was the last thing she saw before her world turned red with agony.

CHAPTER THIRTEEN

Moros's fingers closed around his sister's throat, and he jerked her deep into the Veil. She snarled and struggled, her fingernails digging into his arms. But he was stronger than she was. He was made to dominate. She might be Vengeance, but he was Death. And no one was immune.

"Come now," he murmured as he straddled her, using both hands to pin her to the soft ground. "Tell me where she is, and we can be done with this."

Nemesis tried to spit in his face but didn't have enough air. He leaned down. "Help me take my revenge on Eris, and I'll forgive you anything."

Something stirred behind her gray eyes, ancient and hungry. The possibility of vengeance was a drug to her. He loosened his grip on her throat to allow her to speak. "You'll let me live?"

"If you side with me." He stroked her curls back from her face. "You're my sister. I've never forgotten that."

She gave him a wary look as he swung his leg off her and allowed her to sit up. He captured her wrist and held on to prevent her from disappearing, but she'd stopped struggling. He'd whetted her appetite, and now she only needed a target. She was what she had been made to be, just as he was. Neither of them could resist their natures. "Is that all you want?" she said. "To get vengeance?"

No. I want Aislin, more than I've ever wanted anything. "Can you blame me?"

She bit her plump pink lip. "But we've been working on this plan for so long. And we're winning."

He couldn't argue with that. "Do you want it to end so soon, though? Where's the fun in that? Revenge is a dish best served cold, hmm?"

"It took us five hundred years to regain our physical forms, and another hundred to become strong enough to challenge you," she said in a flat voice. "Pretty damn cold."

"Indeed. But worth dying for?" He leaned forward, baring his fangs. "Tell me where she is right now, or I'll make it happen."

Nemesis's eyes narrowed, and her mouth quirked into a calculating smile. "And which *she* are we talking about, brother?"

He went still. "Eris, of course."

"And not Aislin Ferry? Because she craves your touch. Did you know that?" She giggled. "She was so desperate for your affection that she made a total fool of herself. Apate had marvelous fun with her."

The fury was like a tidal wave, rising so high he couldn't see past it. Apate was a snake, a smooth-talking deceiver who could take on any form, who could draw the truth out of people while filling their head with lies. Moros drew in a tight breath, trying to control the searing ache inside. Aislin had truly wanted him, and it had made her vulnerable. The tragedy of it was overwhelming—he would have preferred that she'd hated him, that she'd wanted him dead, because it would have kept her safe. "Take me to her now," Moros said with a growl, every word deep and guttural.

Nemesis squirmed in his grasp, but there was no way she could escape. Moros forced his way into her thoughts, sifting through stomach-churning images of her in Hugh's embrace, visions of

Moros himself dead with the Blade of Life through his chest and then of Aislin, her arms spread wide, her back arched and her head thrown back, held tightly by both Apate and Eris. She was in a vast stone cavern, stalactites descending like blades from its roof, darkness beaten back by hundreds of torches positioned around its rough walls and all along the paths across its rocky floor.

Moros imposed his will, twisting around his sister's defiance and crushing it to dust, driving her to pull him all the way to the border between the gray world and this domain tucked away inside it. They arrived just at the edge, where Moros could see into the cave through the elastic barrier that marked the edge of the Veil. Nemesis lay at his feet, panting, her mind thoroughly pillaged. He looked down at her through the prism of his crimson rage, and all he could think was that she would enjoy seeing his thoughts right now.

He knelt next to her and took her hand. "Consider this my final gift to you." And he showed her his contorted face as he leaned over her, his craving for her blood and pain, his need to see her suffer for what she had done. She screamed once before he clapped a hand over her mouth. The images poured from his brain into hers, shattering her will, her desires, leaving her with nothing but his revenge. Her skin split and smoked as she thrashed, trying to escape the inexorable grip of death.

But there was no escape, not even for her. She fell apart, flesh and bone collapsing, burning. She was a pile of ash by the time Moros got to his feet, and his need for pain hadn't abated. "I suppose you'll live on in me," he said softly. "And I'll let the Keepers decide what to do with your divinity." She would appear before them now, he knew. He was willing to bet that very shortly she'd be at the mercy of the Keeper of Hell.

He placed his hands against the barrier between the Veil and his siblings' domain, peering inside. There was a tent on his far right, a frivolous confection made of colorful silk. Lanterns blazed within, casting shadows against its billowy walls. He couldn't see anyone else in the rest of the cavern, so he silently stepped through the squishy wall, appearing in the chilly space. He had to hurry; they would sense him soon, but—

He staggered as his awareness of Aislin returned. She was inside the tent. Relief roared through him—she was alive. But, like acid on his skin, he could also sense Eris and Apate with her. A faint cry echoed through the cave, a sound full of suffering and fear. He was charging along the path toward the tent when a gasp from inside it brought him to a halt.

"He's here," snapped Apate.

Moros ripped the tent flap aside an instant later, in time to see his brother disappear, leaving Aislin, who had been in his arms, stumbling backward. Eris had her by the wrist, and Trevor stood against the back wall, a looming presence. "Apate, you fucking coward!" shouted Eris, her cheeks suffusing with pink.

Moros froze as Eris steadied Aislin. Her long blonde hair was tangled, and there were tearstains on her pale face. Her eyes were wide but unfocused, her pupils so dilated that only a thin ring of pale blue could be seen around the edges.

"Let her go," Moros said quietly.

"Come any closer and I'll end her," Eris replied. "What have you done with Nemesis?"

"I'll be happy to show you," Moros snarled.

"You won't." She arched an eyebrow. "Because I know something you don't." She stroked Aislin's hair, and Aislin blinked frantically, like she was trying to come back to herself. "You might serve fate, but, brother, it doesn't serve you. She's proof of that."

Uncertainty prickled inside him. "What?"

Eris grinned. "Never mind." She leaned in and spoke in Aislin's ear. "He's right here, sweetie. Don't you have a few things to say to him?"

Aislin grimaced and shook her head, but then their eyes met. For a moment, they stared at one another, and Moros willed her to understand, to fight whatever venom Eris had projected into her mind.

Aislin's stance widened, and she peeled herself from Eris's side, seemingly determined to stand on her own. "You bastard," she whispered, glaring at him. "I trusted you. And look what you've done!" Her voice cracked as she gestured down her body. She seemed unhurt—physically, at least—but obviously that wasn't what she was seeing.

She gave him a look drenched in hatred. "I believed every word you said. About my father, about your intentions with the Keepers . . . but you lied about all of it, didn't you? You were always serving yourself at the expense of everyone I love."

Eris shushed her, though her keen eyes were on Moros the whole time. Trevor shifted behind him, and Moros hoped he wouldn't attack—he couldn't afford the distraction.

"Aislin," Moros said gently. "Think about where you are. Think about who you are." He didn't know what else to say to bring her back, if that was even possible. She was strong, but she'd been in their clutches for hours, and each one must have felt like a decade.

"I know who I am—or who I was. But thanks to you, I'm nothing now." Her lovely face radiated agony as she looked down at herself once again. "I'm a bloody corpse. I'm a Shade. I'm dust. Because you betrayed me." Her expression crumpled. "Because I trusted you. Because I thought you were worthy of it."

"I thought I was worthy of it, too," he admitted. More than anything right now, he needed to pull away, to be cold and detached and merciless, but her pain held him where he was. "But I failed you."

Again, her eyes snapped to his, and for the briefest moment, he saw something there, a sharp flash of awareness and cunning. But then she looked away. "You didn't just fail me. You destroyed me."

Eris let go of Aislin, watching her carefully, and grinned when the bitter hatred in Aislin's voice remained as she said, "I am ashamed to have fallen for your lies. The day you writhe in chains at the mercy of the Keeper of Hell will be the day I'm free."

Eris took a step back, delight making her glow. "See? She knows your true nature. How you use people, then abandon and betray them. And it didn't take her even half as long as it took me." Eris reached behind her, where a wooden table sat, and opened its long drawer.

Moros tensed as she drew out a blade, softly glowing with life. He'd suspected she'd been the one to steal it, but in his desperation to get to Aislin, he'd overlooked the danger.

Aislin stepped between them. "Have you come to finish the job?" she said to him in a hard voice. "Is that why you followed me here?"

Moros inched to the side, keeping his eye on Eris and the Blade of Life. "Aislin," he said evenly, "this isn't your fight."

Her eyes blazed with defiance. "The hell it isn't," she snapped.

And then she turned and dove under Eris's arm, colliding with a stack of small wooden boxes atop a footstool. They clattered to the ground, a few of them popping open and spilling their contents—*souls*. Eris shrieked and drew the Blade back to stab her, but Moros lunged for his sister, forcing her to dodge out of the way.

"Trevor, stop her!" Eris barked at the Ker, slashing the Blade through the air and forcing Moros back.

Aislin was busy gathering the souls to her chest as Trevor stalked forward. The Ker looked like he was trying to hold himself back while Aislin grabbed for the wriggling, colorful strips of human essence. "None of those are mine," Trevor said.

"Kill her!" Eris screamed as Aislin dropped the souls to the floor.

Moros dodged another strike from his sister, barely avoiding the bite of the sword, while Aislin ripped open the lid of the smallest box. Just as Trevor crouched, preparing to leap on her, she reached inside and came up with a pale-green wraith with threads of brilliant blue. At the sight of it, Trevor let out a wrenching sound of longing, but it was nearly drowned out by Eris's squeal of rage. Ignoring Moros, she charged Aislin. Moros threw himself between them just as the Blade descended. Pain seared itself along his upper arm, but he ignored it, reaching out to grab Aislin, who now had Trevor's soul clasped against her chest.

"Trevor!" Moros shouted, and in an instant, the Ker was at his side. He kicked Eris away, and she hit the ground.

Her eyes flashed red as she spat blood on the pillows beneath her and scooped up a few of the lost, writhing souls from the ground. "At least I've still got Rylan," she said in a deadly voice.

And then she disappeared, taking the Blade with her.

Moros pulled Aislin to her feet, gently taking Trevor's soul from her. He reached into his pocket and pulled out the container he carried, no bigger than a cigar case. He slipped Trevor's soul inside and turned to the Ker. "Mine again."

"Yours again," Trevor said, his expression inscrutable until he looked down at Aislin. "But also hers. Aislin, thank you."

"I told you I would help you," she whispered wearily. Her eyes were closed, and her forehead lolled against Moros's neck. He could almost feel the fight still going on inside her.

Trevor turned to Moros. "Your arm . . ."

Moros glanced at his left arm. The slice of the sword had torn his sleeve and cut through his flesh, leaving a deep gash. "I'll be fine." At least, he thought he would be. He'd never been wounded before.

"Will you destroy me now?" Trevor asked.

Moros shook his head. If he'd had the time, he would have explained how glad he was to have Trevor back. But Aislin was sagging in his arms, any strength she'd summoned in the last few minutes rapidly fading. "Go to Declan Ferry," he told Trevor. "Tell him what's happened, and that Aislin is with me. I'll update him as soon as I can."

Trevor gave Aislin a concerned look. "Moros, I couldn't stop them. What they did to her, well, it was bad, man."

Moros closed his eyes and wrapped his arms tight around her, ignoring the fiery pain of his wound. "I understand. Go now. I need to get her back to Boston."

Trevor nodded sadly and disappeared. With dread coursing through his veins, Moros tilted Aislin's chin up so he could see her face. "You are the bravest person I've ever known," he murmured.

"Jason?" she whispered, blinking up at him. "You-you—" Tears filled her eyes.

His hand closed around the back of her neck, leaning her head against his shoulder. "Shhh. I won't hurt you."

"You *did* hurt me," she said in a choked voice.

He didn't want to imagine what Apate's version of him had done to her, but it made bile rise in his throat. "None of it was real, darling." He willed himself back to Boston with Aislin, straight to his penthouse, where he would be able to take care of her human needs.

He held her steady as she lifted her head and looked around. When she saw the silhouette of the Psychopomps tower through his windows, she sighed, as if the sight of it gave her strength. "Are we really here?"

"We're really here," he said, fighting his sadness at the uncertain quaver in her voice. "Do you want to lie down?"

She looked down at herself again, but this time, she squinted like she was trying to discern the lie from the truth. "I'd like to take a shower."

He took her hand and led her to the bathroom, but when they reached the door, he couldn't let her go. She looked too unsteady on her feet to take care of herself. "When was the last time you slept, or ate?"

"I don't remember."

His stomach tightened. He didn't even know if she was still immortal, or if the board had stripped her of her status. She suddenly felt very fragile in his arms. "Will you let me take care of you?"

She gave him a wary, fearful look. "I can manage by myself." Her palms pushed against his chest, creating distance between them. "Please." She looked away, like she couldn't bear the sight of him.

It hurt worse than the gash in his arm. "As you wish." He released her and let her close the door in his face. He turned around and leaned against it, then slowly slid to the floor, propping his arms on his bent knees and bowing his head into his hands.

The water in the shower switched on, and he pictured her stepping into the spray, rinsing the dirt and dried blood from her skin.

No matter how hard he wished it, he knew the lies that had been forced on her wouldn't wash away so easily, especially when he heard her start to sob, a sound so drenched with defeat that it sent shocks of anger straight down his spine. Was he really going to sit here and surrender, allowing her to put up a wall between them? Was he going to allow his siblings to win?

"Remember who you are," he muttered to himself. "Remember who *she* is."

Because he knew exactly who she was—someone he wouldn't let go without a fight.

CHAPTER FOURTEEN

Her head jerked up as she felt a wave of heat wash over her. She'd curled up, still fully clothed, next to the tiled shower, where steam billowed from the top of the shower curtain. As much as she'd craved it, the water seemed too far from reach, clean and fresh when all she felt was ruined and torn. And now a monster was descending on her, his eyes blazing and his hands hard as he hoisted her from the floor.

She struggled, instant hatred welling up inside. This was the man who'd killed her father, the one who'd convinced her siblings to turn against her, the one who'd clawed her face and left her a wreck.

Are you sure that was real?

She was sure. Wasn't she?

Moros pulled her close as she kicked at him. "Is this how you want it to end, with you in a huddle on the floor? Have you given up?" His eyes sparked with ruby as he wrenched her sweater off her shoulder, the cashmere tearing like tissue.

She yelped and grasped at the fabric as he stripped her down, yanking the shredded garment from her body before deftly unfastening her pants. Before she could blink, she was down to her bra and panties, but those were gone in an instant as well, ripped apart by his merciless hands. His jaw was set as he tugged the shower curtain open and curled his hand around the back of her neck. "You're going to get cleaned up, and then we're going to talk."

"Let go of me, you bastard!" she shrieked. Why was she even surprised he was treating her so callously? He'd told her she meant nothing to him, that she was merely a pawn in his plan to eliminate the Ferrys.

Did he really? Are you sure?

She spluttered as he plunged her face in front of the spray. Her feet slipped on the wet tile, but his arm was around her instantly, keeping her from falling. "You were kidnapped by your brother Rylan," he said in a razor-edged voice as he held her in the stream of hot water. It splashed over her hair and ran down her naked body, washing away the blood from all her injuries.

She glanced down at her breasts and belly. She'd been sure they'd been torn open, that the Kere had eviscerated her at Moros's command, that he'd laughed while they'd smeared her blood down their faces. But she was untouched. Her palm ran down her side, smooth and unmarred. "I-I'm not hurt."

He flinched, but his grip remained unrelenting. "Your body is whole. Your mind is a different matter."

"My mind is fine," she snapped.

He let out a harsh laugh. "Prove it."

"Let me go."

"Not a chance."

She rammed her elbow into his hard stomach, but it didn't budge him. If anything, he only held her tighter, his arm an iron bar around her waist. She could barely breathe for the steam and the closeness. His shirt and slacks were soaked, and he was still wearing his shoes, but he didn't seem to care as he grabbed the shampoo and dumped a generous dollop on her head, then began to scrub at her head with rough fingers. "I can do that," she said irritably.

"Be my guest."

His hand moved from her hair to her hip, and she shuddered, remembering how that hand had slid up to her waist, how beautiful his lazy smile had been, how silky his voice before he'd stomped on her heart. "Is this the part where you tell me I mean nothing to you? Because I got the message the first time."

"No, this is the part where we rinse your hair." He shouldered her forward, forcing her head into the spray again. Shampoo suds stung her eyes and ran down her face, but the smell, clean and fresh, was comforting in a way that brought strength to her aching limbs. Water dripped in sheets from her blonde hair, and for a moment she just stared, caught by how normal it was.

Well, not quite. A fully clothed man was holding her up—and was now briskly soaping her back. "I can do this myself!"

"Really? Because all you seem able to do is whine."

Rage zinged through her, and she stomped her foot onto his toes, which accomplished nothing at all except making her feel like a petulant toddler. She rolled her eyes and twisted to grab the soap from him. A flash of dark red in her periphery drew her eyes down, and she froze. "You're hurt."

"How astute," he said cordially, though she could detect the tightness in his voice. "And would you like to know how it happened?"

She stared at the gash in the fabric, beneath which lay a wound nearly as long as her hand, deep as the muscle. "Who hurt you? Did I do that?" She looked up at him, reminding herself not to be fooled by his gorgeous smile and lethal charm.

"No, you didn't do it. Unless you consider that I was protecting you at the time."

Her fingers closed over his sleeve. "You were protecting me . . . I was . . ." Where had she been? "From your Kere? You told them to attack me!"

Pain flashed across his face. "Aislin, I would destroy any Ker who laid so much as a finger on you. Do you remember being in the tent with Eris? With Apate? I came for you." He pulled her against his chest. "I would never have left you there. I should never have left your side in the first place."

She was panting, trying to sort out the confusing barrage of memories. How much of it was real? She remembered fighting for her life, but she also remembered knowing she was in the grip of the original liar himself. She had fought as hard as she could. And she'd been determined to help someone . . . Was *that* real? "Was Trevor there?"

Moros nodded. "You defied Eris and grabbed his soul—and it nearly got you killed." He chuckled. "When I saw you come up with it in your hands, I was sure you had fooled us all, that your hatred for me was just a ruse." His jaw tightened, and he looked away.

The hot spray of the shower fanned across her shoulder blades as she watched him. His fingers were spread over her waist, skin to skin. She wanted this touch . . . or did she? She was naked now, and that always happened right before he struck, before he slammed her to the stone, before he bared her for all to see, before he humiliated her. She clamped her eyes shut and bowed her head. Was this just another trap?

Beneath her fingers, his heart beat, solid and fast. "When was the last time we were together?" she asked.

"In your office. I believe I apologized for blurring the boundaries of our business relationship." Amusement had crept into his voice.

She glanced down at her breasts pressed to his soaked button-down, keenly aware of his warm hand resting on her hip, his arm clasped around her waist. "But then you . . . you came to me and . . ." Then she'd made a fool of herself, begging for him when he'd had no interest in her at all.

He leaned down, his black hair tumbling across his brow. "Aislin. I left you in your office, and I didn't see you again until I stopped Apate and Eris from torturing you. Whatever you remember, it's not real." He touched his forehead to hers. "However you think I hurt you, I didn't. Whatever cruel words you think I said, you're wrong. If you find me guilty of anything, it's of not protecting you well enough. And for that, you can punish me as severely as you like." His eyes bored into hers. "But I refuse to surrender you to Lies."

"So I didn't . . ."

His eyebrows rose. "Didn't what?"

Her cheeks burned as she thought about what she'd done, spreading her legs for him, begging him to be inside her, her body aching to feel his weight. "Nothing."

He froze. "I'll kill him," he muttered.

"What are you talking about?"

"My brother. He exploits every hidden vulnerability. He twists until the truth is so mangled that it can't be distinguished from a lie. And Nemesis told me he'd done exactly that to you."

"Knowing that she told you only makes it worse. I made such an idiot of myself." She let out a breath. If she was going to move forward, she couldn't hide from it now.

"You have feelings for me. And they used them against you."

"Yes," she whispered. "And you didn't return them."

He took her face in his hands, the hard edge of his jaw softening as he looked down at her. "Lies," he said simply. Then his mouth was on hers, unrelenting and hot. She melted under the heat, parting her lips to allow him entrance, rising on her tiptoes to meet force with force. This wasn't the soft, seductive kiss from the betrayer who'd given her up to his Kere. It was jagged and frantic, teeth and tongues, a challenge, a plea. His fingers burrowed in her wet hair, and she tilted her head back, exposing her throat.

If he wanted to tear it out, there had never been a better time. His mouth slid down the column of her neck, and she felt the hard edges of his teeth, the stroke of his tongue. His hand slid up across her ribs to palm one of her breasts, his thumb toying with her pearled nipple as she tugged at the buttons on his shirt. Water dripped from his ebony hair as he drew at her neck, hard enough to bruise but not to harm. It felt real. It felt true. It felt necessary.

It was also terrifying. Every second was like dancing on the edge of a blade. Water poured down on them, drenching their kisses. Her body was alight with desire for him, but her mind was a storm of fear. Would this be the moment he pulled back and laughed? She clung to him, her hands shaking as she finally managed to unfasten his top button. As soon as her fingertips caressed his collarbone, Moros pulled back and yanked at his shirt, abruptly tearing it open. Buttons ricocheted off her belly, the floor, the walls. His hand slid around her back to press her bare chest to his, and as their skin met, his head fell back and he moaned. It was the opposite of cold and detached.

She wanted more of that sound, animal and full of need. Vulnerable and hungry. For *her*. Her fingers followed the trail of dark hair down the center of his taut stomach to his belt, and then further down to explore the thick erection beneath the fabric of his slacks. But as soon as she touched him, he spun her around and pressed her against the shower tiles, his chest heaving against her back. "What are you after, darling?" he whispered between breaths, his arousal pressed against her backside.

She felt savage and desperate, a beast caught in a trap. She prized her ability to think through every possibility, but now she wasn't even sure of her own mind, of her own reality. And so she surrendered to instinct. She wriggled against him, needing his unsteadiness to steady her. His hand slapped onto her hip, holding her still. She could feel his heartbeat thumping against her back as he leaned against the wall and captured her wrists, trapping her. The ragged sound of his breath made her smile.

She wasn't sure whether she wanted to conquer him or submit to him. Perhaps both at the same time. But either way, as she looked over her shoulder and found him staring at her, his half-lidded eyes laced with pure lust, she knew they were in for a collision that would change everything.

CHAPTER FIFTEEN

He was teetering on a high precipice, seconds from diving over the edge. Being in a shower with a naked woman was a temptation he should be able to bear. But it was *her*. The Mark of the Ferry spread across her back, the wings of the raven shifting as she undulated against him. Her platinum hair and pale, smooth skin were soft and shining. And when she looked over her shoulder at him, the fierce challenge in her eyes set his blood on fire.

Walk away.

She wanted this for all the wrong reasons, he was sure. Her mind had been violated and ransacked, and he couldn't blame her for trying to regain her sense of control—but this? There was no tenderness in her eyes. Suddenly he wanted to reach straight into her chest and pull that tenderness out, much as he would a soul. He had wanted her to ask him for comfort, to let him help. He'd spent the last several hours wild with worry for her—it felt as if he'd been with her the whole time, suffering at her side. It had sanded away all his control and patience, and now he wanted her to meet him in the middle, to offer him part of herself because he had already given more than he ever had. He'd never felt so off-balance.

Fury flowed hot over his skin. How dare she make him feel this way? Weak and confused and wanting. His fingers dug into the swell of her hip, and she gasped and pushed back against him. Teasing him.

The gash in his arm blazed pain from his shoulder to his elbow, but he ignored it, a new urgency seizing him—the need to punish her for making him care so damn much. His hand traveled down the flat of her stomach until his fingertips met the apex of her thighs.

"Be careful what you ask for," he said in a low voice. "Because I might just give it to you." And then he slid his fingers between her legs. He clenched his teeth at the sound of her moan, at the way she widened her stance to give him access to the softest, most sensitive part of her. His body throbbed with need as he toyed with her, circling her clit before caressing the delicate folds of skin around the entrance to her body. She was slick with desire and whimpered at his touch, and it turned his vision red. He held her wrists above her head with one hand and slid two fingers inside her tight, silky channel. Even with his hips pressed against her ass, it wasn't even close to being enough.

This is a mistake. Stop now.

He wouldn't. He couldn't. He pulled his hand from her body and had his pants undone a moment later, freeing his aching cock. Here he was, dripping wet, his shirt hanging open in tatters, his arm flayed and bleeding, his pants slipping down his hips to his thighs, his custom-made shoes soggy and squeaking. He had to be inside her.

He took himself in hand and stroked the head of his erection between her delectable mounds of flesh. With her wrists still trapped, all she could do was writhe as he probed at her wet pink slit, teasing her. "Do you feel in control now, my dear?" he asked in a rough voice. "Is this what you want?"

She *laughed.*

Frustration seared through him. He grabbed her by the shoulders and turned her around, wanting to shout at her, planning to stop this farce. But instead of looking him in the eyes, she dropped to her knees and flashed him a defiant, cool look as she ran her hands up his thighs. His cock jerked as he felt her breath on his skin. Before he could summon the will to step back, her fingers encircled him, and she ran her tongue up his shaft. The sight of her lips stretching around the head nearly shut his brain down, except for one stinging thought—she was on her knees, his cock in her mouth, and somehow she *still* had the advantage.

His fingers raked through her hair, his intention to pull her off him, but then he felt the flutter of her tongue, the pressure of her mouth, and his body refused to obey. *Just another second,* his thoughts whispered. *One more second, and then I'll end this.* But then that second passed, and he was more caught, more addicted. Her fingers tightened on his hips and then slid around, her fingernails digging into his ass. The pleasure and the pain twisted inside him as she sucked and licked, each firm stroke of her tongue and fingers pulling him a little closer to release. She welcomed each little flex of his hips with a soft noise that he longed to hear again and again. His breath caught as he looked down at her, so exquisite, so fragile. Something black and deadly inside him wanted to break her—he wanted her to submit completely.

And the rest of him wanted her to cut him open and take out his heart.

He let out a ragged groan and pulled her up, his grip so tight it would bruise. Heavy tingling spread from his groin up into his lower back and belly. Being able to touch her was both a miracle and a curse, and in this moment he was sure it would destroy him. Her lips were swollen but cast in a mischievous smile, and his mouth crashed down on hers, taking ruthless possession. His fingers dipped between her legs again, stroking until she whimpered with need. And as his hand fisted in the hair at the nape of her neck, keeping their kiss deep, he stroked her thigh and lifted it, anchoring it against his hip. The length of his erection nestled against the slick flesh between her legs.

Point of no return. Even through the haze of rage and confusion and need, he knew this. Nothing would be the same after he'd been inside her.

Just this one time, and then the novelty will be gone. She won't affect me anymore.

He pulled back from her mouth and set his forehead on hers. Her back was against the wall of the shower, and she was pinned against him. There was no escape unless she begged for it.

And there was no way he could stop unless she did.

Instead, she reached down and guided the head of his cock to her waiting entrance. She dragged it through the slippery evidence of her desire, but the veiled look in her eyes didn't make it feel like an offering—it felt like another challenge. Driven by animal lust, unable to fight the endless desire that rushed through his veins, he flexed his hips and entered, making her cry out. Her hands settled on his waist as he pushed himself farther inside her. He reveled at the tight resistance, the press of her breasts to his bare chest, the way she buried her face in his neck as he pulled back and thrust again, hard and unrelenting. Her breath puffed against his skin as her hands dipped lower, guiding his hips, urging him on. The two of them were tangled, dripping, bucking, and gasping. Fighting. Struggling. Refusing to give in.

But her body was rapidly undoing him. With one palm braced against the tile and the other holding her leg to his hip, Moros was lost in Aislin, the hot, heady scent of her skin, the flush on her cheeks, the way her eyes squeezed shut as she felt him moving inside her. He ground against her, and she clutched at him, clawing at his back. He smiled as he did it again and felt her clench around him. He wanted her screaming; he wanted her mindless. He wanted her to know he'd gotten to her.

He needed her to come before he did, dammit.

Aislin's fingers wound in his hair and pulled as he invaded her, crushing her against the wall. All his good intentions had been burned away along with his gentleness. Anger hardened his thrusts. Her whimpers became cries, rising in pitch, drawing his insides tight, threatening to finish him. But, oh, then every part of her went stiff and her inner muscles contracted around him, squeezing rhythmically as she stifled a scream against his shoulder. It was too much to bear, too much like surrender, and it stabbed through him in one final slice of ecstasy. He let go, burying himself to the hilt as his entire body throbbed.

For one moment, caught in blinding pleasure, everything was perfect. The fog of negative emotion cleared, revealing what could only be the truth. They were part of each other, and nothing could separate them. This was right. He held her impossibly close, and her arms were wrapped around him like she couldn't let go. It seemed obvious—they belonged with each other, bound by heart and mind. He'd been stupid to try to shield his heart when it had been rightfully hers all along. She was his match in every way, and together they were unstoppable. The feeling was as brilliant and honest as any future vision he'd ever had. He was going to love her forever.

But then he collapsed against her, panting, as the elation swirled away like so much water down the drain. He slipped out of her body and they were separate once more, two beings with a vast canyon of mistrust between them. No longer entwined with Aislin, those fleeting thoughts of safety and sacrifice, of offering himself to her because he trusted that she'd accept him and then offer herself in return, faded, leaving him edgy and strangely tired. What had felt like fate was nothing more than a foolish, euphoric notion. He looked down at Aislin, needing to read the expression in her eyes, but she was leaning against him, her muscles going slack, her arms hanging uselessly at her sides.

He realized she was losing consciousness just in time, and caught her before she could fall to the tile. Clutching her against himself, he turned off the water and hoisted her into his arms, panic eating at the edges of his sanity. "Aislin?"

Her head lolled against his neck. She was as limp as a rag doll. He kicked off his ruined shoes and stepped out of his pants, then carried her into his bedroom and laid her on the bed, naked and dripping. He closed his eyes and focused, listening for her heartbeat. It was steady and solid. Her chest rose on a breath, and her skin was still rosy and flushed from exertion.

She was fast asleep. He bowed his head and chuckled. Ferrys and their odd sleep needs—he should have guessed. For one dumbstruck moment, he'd thought that this tryst had ended like all his others had, with the woman dead in his arms. Aislin *was* fated to die, after all; it was somewhat of a shock that she was still alive, especially after what she'd been through. But Aislin seemed healthy and exquisitely alive. She'd merely succumbed to her body's demands.

He leaned over her, brushing her wet hair away from her face. "You didn't even have the decency to stay awake long enough to tell me I won," he said, unwanted affection seeping into his chest as his eyes traced over her lips, her nose, the pink tinge on her cheeks. Then he looked away as the truth broke the surface.

He hadn't won. He had barely held his own. Now was the time to walk away, to keep his heart behind a wall. If he could do that, victory was his. She wouldn't be able to hurt him or distract him from what he had to do. Their summit was looming, and Eris and Apate were still on the loose. They had the Blade of Life and an unknown number of Shade-Kere at their command. Kidnapping Aislin had pulled her away from Boston at exactly the wrong time, and Moros's desperation to save her had kept him from eliminating Hugh and grabbing the Charon's Scope for safekeeping.

He had work to do.

He allowed himself the luxury of kissing Aislin's forehead, letting his lips linger against her skin, listening to her breathing. "You are not special to me," he whispered. "Not at all."

The lie was like acid inside him, and it reminded him of his brother. He could lie to everyone else, but he shouldn't lie to himself: he felt something for Aislin, and it was primal. Fundamental. But whatever Aislin had felt for him before had been stripped away by Moros's brother and sisters, replaced with something hard and cold. And while it still turned him on, infuriatingly so, it wasn't what he wanted from her.

He shouldn't want *anything* from her, though. He needed to crush this longing beneath his heel and move on.

He pushed back from the bed, his arm throbbing with new intensity. The pain was so foreign and yet so intimate, winding along his bones, whispering danger, the threat of losing his physical form here in the real world and appearing weak and vulnerable before the Keeper of Hell. The thought of it sent a chill down his back, so he once again let his eyes stroke over Aislin's sleeping body, knowing it would warm him. Protectiveness surged inside him as he watched goose bumps roll across her skin, and he gently lifted her once more and tucked her beneath the blankets.

"You have to stop this," he muttered, then pivoted on his heel and walked into his closet, where he shed his ruined shirt and donned a new pair of slacks. He pressed the torn shirt to his arm and stifled a groan. The wound would heal in its own time—mortal time. Too slowly for his liking. Fortunately, it didn't seem that deep. But it was still bleeding, and it would slow him down. It would also be a signal to his enemies that he was weak, and that was something he couldn't afford.

He closed his eyes and called one of his Kere to him, the one he needed most right now. Then he headed out to his patio overlooking the city. From here the canals were actually pretty, the water glinting beneath the moonlight, darkness concealing the disorder and violence. What would happen to it if Chaos reigned?

"If you brought me here because you changed your mind about executing me, I'm gonna be pretty disappointed," Trevor said as he materialized next to Moros's chair. Then he saw Moros holding his bloodstained shirt to the gash on his arm. "Oh."

Moros cleared his throat. "I was actually hoping you could provide me with some medical assistance."

Trevor blinked. "Why isn't that healing?"

Moros fixed his eyes on the Psychopomps tower. "The weapon Eris was wielding is an ancient one, and it has been dipped in the Spring of Life. Let's just say I'm allergic to it."

Trevor's eyebrows shot up. "No wonder they wanted it so bad."

"They didn't tell you why?"

The look on Trevor's face was pained. "I-I can't really remember. It's a little hazy."

Moros leaned back in his chair, wincing as his wound pulled. "They probably told you to forget."

"They could do that?"

"If they possessed your soul, they could make you do anything."

Trevor stared at him. "Have you ever done anything like that to me?"

"No. I expect my Kere to obey me, and to know there are consequences for defiance. But I have never controlled your minds. All of you are warriors. Fighters. You have my respect. I might own your souls, but I won't steal anything else."

Trevor ran his hand over his short black hair. "Shit. You make me feel like an asshole for ever resenting you."

"You may resent me all you like, Trevor. I've got your soul in my pocket. That makes our relationship, shall we say, uneven."

Trevor nodded. "Now—want me to take a look at that arm?"

"Please."

Trevor knelt next to him and peeled back the shirt, then grimaced when he saw the wound. "You need more than a bandage. I have to go get some supplies. I'll be right back."

After he vanished, Moros looked up at the stars, wondering where Eris and Apate were right now, and when they would strike next. Would they dare face him, knowing he'd already destroyed Nemesis, or would they attack somewhere else? Should he go to the Fates and try to move them someplace safer, even though it would leave the loom unattended?

Either way, he was of little good like this. He never slept, had never needed to, but this heavy feeling in his muscles could only be fatigue. With the fabric of fate fraying so dramatically, his own strength and health had been diminished. He was weaker than he'd ever been in his entire existence. But he would still fight.

"I'm back," Trevor said as he appeared in front of Moros, a med kit in his hands. "But—"

"I decided to invite myself over," said a hard voice to his right. Declan Ferry climbed out of his Scope, wearing his paramedic uniform and looking characteristically pissed off. "Where the fuck is my sister?"

CHAPTER SIXTEEN

Aislin awoke with a start to the angry sound of her brother's voice. She sat up quickly, looking around. She was in a dark bedroom, the sheets soft and fragrant against her bare skin. She ran her hand over her body, feeling weak with hunger but otherwise fine . . . except for the fact that she wasn't wearing a stitch of clothing.

She closed her eyes at the sudden memory of Jason's body against hers, of the way they'd come undone together. It had been euphoric, triumphant. She'd never felt so powerful as when the Lord of the Kere pulsed inside her. His moan had infiltrated her bones as pure pleasure. For one moment, everything had been clear. They belonged together. They understood one another so perfectly. He was what she'd been missing all along, and she had felt in that moment that she couldn't be complete unless she offered him her heart. So simple, so true.

"So ridiculous." She slid out of bed and padded to the open doorway of his expansive walk-in closet, smiling at the rows of designer suits, the stacks of folded shirts, the rack of ties. The man certainly knew how to look good. She grabbed a button-down and slipped it on, even as she heard Declan's words: "If you don't let me see her, I swear to God I will find a way to fucking end you."

Aislin felt inexplicably warmed. Declan cared, in his own rough kind of way. She poked her head into the hallway to see Trevor, Declan, and Moros on the patio, the glass door half-open. Trevor was kneeling at Moros's side. The Lord of the Kere was shirtless, and there was a pile of bloody fabric at the base of the chair he was sitting in. His posture was lazy and relaxed, but Aislin could see the taut lines of his muscles, the hard edge of his jaw as he looked up at Declan. "You can try if you wish, Declan, but as I told you, Aislin is sleeping. I will not allow her to be disturbed."

Declan's thickly muscled arms were folded over his chest as he glared at Moros. "Forgive me if I don't take your word for it. Trev said she was in bad shape. I just want to see her."

"And so you shall, when she is ready to be seen," Moros said mildly.

"What the fuck are you hiding?" Declan snarled.

"Dec, back off," said Trevor, who was wearing gloves and peering at what Aislin realized was the gash across Moros's biceps. "If it weren't for Moros, Aislin would be gone, man. They weren't going to let up until they owned her mind for good."

Declan took a step back. "Thanks for saving her, then," he said brusquely, looking out over the city. "But I still need to know she's okay."

Moros had saved her. That was real. Aislin shook her head, hating the jumble of images inside, still feeling the edge of what Apate had done to her. She'd been so desperate to regain control that she'd thrown herself at Moros, and he'd given her exactly what she wanted. His hands on her skin had been electric, forceful but frenzied. Ravenous. And she'd needed that, to see him lose his usual amused detachment. But now what?

Aislin looked down at herself. Had he actually been protecting her dignity when he told Declan he couldn't come back and see her? Her cheeks heated. Given the way Declan looked right now, it seemed better to reassure him than to hide. Tucking a loose lock of hair behind her ear, she stepped into the hallway, her bare feet cold on the marble floor, and strode through the living room to the patio. Declan saw her first, his face lighting up. But then his eyes went wide as he took in her bare legs and her chosen attire—a very nice pale-blue button-down, the sleeves of which hung to her knuckles, the hem tickling her thighs. Trevor leaned to see her, then quickly averted his eyes, and that was when Moros turned.

His eyes took her in slowly, from her head to her toes, and Aislin's heart sped. She hadn't taken the time to consider how things would be between them after what they'd done, and she had no time to ponder it now. Declan slid the glass door all the way open. "Hey," he said, stepping inside. "You okay?"

"I'm fine," she said. "My clothes were damaged during the rescue."

Behind Declan, Trevor arched an eyebrow but remained silent, and Moros smirked. There it was, that sense of amused detachment. Aislin tensed. Very well.

Now she knew where she stood.

Declan came forward, his arms rising from his sides, and she walked into them, so grateful for his love.

"I really thought you might have been gone for good," he said hoarsely.

She closed her eyes. "I almost was." A twisted memory of Declan defying her just to undermine her power tried to rise in her mind, but now she was able to turn it on its head, to remind herself that he had been willing to sacrifice everything for the woman he loved. "I'm so glad to be back," she whispered.

"You want me to take you home?" he asked, his head bowed over hers.

"Not quite yet." She pulled out of his embrace and headed to the patio, strengthened by the knowledge that she was in control of her mind once more.

Moros was still lounging in his chair, but he had returned his attention to his wound. "Will this take much longer?" he asked Trevor.

Aislin stepped behind them and looked down to see that Trevor had packed the wound with some kind of compound and was now aiming a laser stylus at the top edge of the wound. He looked up at her and then back down to the gash. "This'll activate the compound and seal it. Won't take more than another few minutes."

Moros sighed and tilted his head back until he was gazing up at her. "And how did you sleep, my dear?"

She braced for him to make a callous remark about what had happened before she'd passed out, but it didn't come. "I slept well. And thank you for the loan." She lifted her arms—but not too high. She wasn't wearing anything under the shirt.

"Of course." The corner of his mouth curved as his fingers began to tap the arm of his chair, keeping eerie time with her thrumming pulse. "But although you look predictably lovely this way, I'm sure you'd like to change as soon as possible."

Now that he mentioned it, she was rather enjoying the smell of the shirt, a deep woody scent with a hint of lavender that made her recall hours spent staring at Moros in meetings, watching every movement of his fingers, his mouth. She blinked and stepped back out of his line of sight. "Yes. I would. But I thought perhaps this was a good time to discuss next steps."

"The Shade-Kere have disappeared," said Declan. "I left Galena at Psychopomps with her guards while I've been coordinating the emergency response, but Eli came in around eight and said they couldn't find any more in the city. It's been quiet for the last few hours, which is good. I've made nice with Police and Fire." He rubbed at a smear of something on his sleeve. "It's given us a chance to pick up the pieces." He glanced at Trevor and smiled, and Aislin could read relief there. Declan had his best friend back at his side.

"Where would the Shades have gone?" Trevor asked, sitting back and examining Moros's wound, then reaching for a beige cuff that must have been some sort of bandage.

"I'll have to check with the others," said Moros. "They might know if the monsters have merely transported themselves to some other city to wreak havoc."

"My Ferrys will know more quickly than that," said Aislin. "They'll sense souls in the Veil. I'd better get back to Psychopomps and coordinate communication."

Declan gave her an anxious glance. "Um, I'm not sure that's the best idea."

"And why not? It's my job, isn't it?" Her fingers rose to touch her Charon's Scope, and her eyes went wide as she realized she wasn't wearing a Scope at all. "What—?" Then she remembered. "Rylan stole my Scope."

"And gave it to Hugh Ferry," Moros said quietly.

"He's been named interim Charon," said Declan, looking wary, as if he expected Aislin to explode.

It was tempting. She looked down at Moros, but his head was bowed as Trevor fastened the bandage tightly over his arm. She stared at the back of his neck, his smooth skin and thick ebony hair, his bare muscular shoulders. He was perfectly made—and deceptive. He still wasn't telling her everything. "You knew, when you came to get me, that he had my Scope? That he was claiming to be Charon?"

"It seemed, quite frankly, the least urgent of the problems at hand."

"So while I was gone, my board completed a coup."

"I wouldn't say it is complete, my dear."

Aislin thought about that. Even before Rylan had kidnapped her, the board had turned against her. They thought she was weak, unable to get things under control. The attack of the Shade-Kere might have cemented that notion in their minds. They also thought she was blindly loyal to Jason Moros, of whom they were all endlessly suspicious. If she went back to them to reclaim her position, she needed to be able to offer something—a plan, a strategy for victory. She couldn't beg for her job back. She had to make them beg her to take it.

She looked down at the bloody shirt at her feet. "The blade that Eris used to hurt you—you called it the Blade of Life."

Moros got to his feet, and Aislin looked away from his bare torso, the trail of hair down his flat belly that, even now, her fingers itched to trace. *It was a one-time tryst, something to clear your head—and then forget.* She forced herself to look into his eyes, refusing to let him see the way he was affecting her. "Where did the Blade come from?"

"I told you—my mother used it to vanquish Chaos. She buried it near his tomb. But Eris found it."

Aislin shook her head. "But why is it called the Blade of Life?"

"It has been dipped into the Spring."

"In the Lucinae realm?" she asked, her eyes wide.

Moros nodded. "They allowed my mother to coat the metal with its water, the source of all new souls."

"And it can hurt you," Trevor said simply.

Moros rolled his shoulder, wincing at the movement of his arm. "Obviously. But it is also deadly to Chaos, which doesn't help us at the moment, because my sister and brother are trying to raise him, not hurt him."

"Would any sword do, as long as it was dipped into the Spring?" Aislin asked. "Could we make another one?"

His eyes met hers. "Theoretically, but the Lucinae despise me with the fire of a thousand suns, so somehow I doubt they would be eager to help."

"Don't they serve fate, like we do?" she asked.

"Not like we do at all. They can bring new life into the world whether or not those lives have a destiny. And remember—they might live for a very long time, but they are mortal creatures, through and through. They abhor and fear death in any shape or form, no matter how charming." He gestured expansively at himself.

She fought the urge to smile. "They might despise you—but they don't despise me."

"Even though you usher those precious souls into the Afterlife?"

"Even though. And that might have something to do with the fact that a year after I took over Foreign Exchange, I reached out to them with an offer." When she'd told her father, she'd delighted in the glow of pride on his face. "We provide them with a share of our commissions. We have for the past two decades."

"We have?" said Declan.

Aislin nodded. "It's part of your banking fee. Don't you ever look at your account statements?"

Declan shrugged. "I look at the total. That's about it."

Her mouth dropped open. "Really, how have you survived?"

He chuckled. "Good thing you're in charge, right?"

She stood up a little straighter. "Anyway. I created the ambassador position to furnish them with updates regarding any shifts in policy or outlook, and we manage their money."

Moros looked puzzled. "Why would they need money?"

Aislin shrugged. "They might inhabit their own realm, but they spend time in this one, just as your Kere do. They do enjoy the finer things." She'd always known instinctively that solid relations with the Lucinae might come in handy, though she'd always imagined it would be in the context of a conflict with the Kere, not an alliance with them.

"So what are you proposing?" Moros asked.

"I should go to them," she said. "I'll explain the threat and ask for the favor. My ambassador, Cavan, will help with any negotiations. I'll create another blade, or perhaps several, and then we'll have a fair fight."

Moros stared at her, and in his gray eyes she saw something stir, wary but admiring. "You are quite something, aren't you?"

She folded her arms over her chest, hoping none of them would notice how her body was responding. "Don't say that quite yet. Before I go, I need to go to the office and get my Charon's Scope back. I can't travel to the Lucinae realm without it."

"I'll go with you to Psychopomps," he said. "They can't appoint a new Charon without me, no matter how badly they wish otherwise. And if they want any representative before the Keepers, it will be you." His eyes caught and held hers, and she wished she could translate what lay in their depths.

Trevor cleared his throat. "Uh, can we go? Dec, you ready?"

Declan was looking back and forth between Moros and Aislin, a distinct glint of suspicion in his eyes. "Sure," he said, drawing the word out. "I'll just . . . go now." He looked at Aislin. "If you're okay with that."

"All is well, Declan. Thank you for your concern." She touched his arm. "Really," she added quietly.

He smiled as Trevor's hand settled on his shoulder and they both disappeared. Slowly, Aislin turned back to Moros, uncertain once again. Part of her wanted to go to him, to wrap her arms around his waist and lay her head on his warm shoulder, to feel his skin against hers one more time. But the rest of her remembered how hard and desperate their coupling had been, how even while he was inside her, it had been a battle of wills.

And now the softness in his eyes was disappearing behind a wall, the smirk returning to his face. "I assume you'd like to return to your apartment and clothe yourself for battle." He looked her up and down. "Or would you prefer to appear before your board au naturel?"

The mocking condescension in his voice confirmed that the old Moros was back. "One guess," she said.

"Your wish is my command." He reached out and touched her cheek, just his fingertips making contact, but the moment he did, she was yanked into the Veil in a burst of hot and cold air. Her apartment materialized an instant later, and she grasped the back of her sofa to keep from staggering.

By the time she'd straightened up, trying to remain dignified in the face of what she was sure would be yet another flip comment . . . he was gone.

CHAPTER SEVENTEEN

Moros stood next to his bed, looking down at the place Aislin had slept. Before he could stop himself, he lowered his face to the sheets and inhaled her delicate violet scent. And then he shoved himself up and walked into his closet. He gritted his teeth as he dressed himself, furious at the feel of the bandage against his skin, the ache of his wound, the fact that he could be hurt at all.

Including by Aislin. He refused to allow it. She'd seemed herself just now, composed and coherent, so sharp and clever that he'd wanted to scoop her into his arms and laugh. She'd made creating a new Blade of Life sound so easy, so possible, so utterly and obviously logical that it was impossible to argue. He wasn't used to depending on anyone but himself to take action, but if anyone could accomplish this task, Aislin could.

He pushed away the swell of admiration for her, because it came along with a dangerous side effect—adoration. Desire. Not just for her body, though his had hardened at the sight of her wearing his shirt and nothing else. Her sense of herself, her confidence, her power—they all turned him on, too. And now he needed to get a grip. She'd gotten what she needed from him, and everything was back to how it had been. He had to trust her in matters of business, but that didn't mean he had to hand over anything else, including his heart.

He put on a gray suit with a pale-blue tie, musing at its color, the similarity it bore to the color of her eyes. Then he sighed, slipped on a pair of gloves, and traveled through the Veil and into the Psychopomps tower, arriving in the waiting area of Aislin's office suite. Her door was open, but as he took a step toward it, her voice was not the one he heard. Hugh Ferry strode out, wearing the Scope of the Charon, furiously dressing down a cowering assistant, a fleshy young man with freckles and curly red hair. "When did she say she would get here?" he snapped.

"M-m-momentarily," the assistant stammered, then pulled up short with round eyes as he spotted Moros.

"Moros," Hugh said, surprise in his tone. "To what do we owe this honor?"

Moros adjusted his tie. "I was made aware that Aislin Ferry has called an emergency board meeting. And as this involves my interests, I decided it would be worth my while to attend." He grinned at Hugh, showing his teeth. "I know I left our last encounter abruptly, but as you know, I had something important to attend to."

Hugh swallowed and looked away, and Moros felt a shocking surge of anger on behalf of his sister. During their last meeting, Moros had made a clear lethal threat against "Nina," as Nemesis had called herself. Hugh hadn't heard from her since—Moros had made sure of that—and now the man was acting as if none of it had ever happened. Was he willing to forget his feelings so easily? Suddenly Moros couldn't blame Nemesis for her cynicism about the world. Some people deserved to suffer.

"Well, I'm pleased you could make the time to attend," said Hugh, sounding jittery. "Though Aislin doesn't have the power to convene the board, they wanted to hear what she had to say before they finalize their decision." He gave Moros a tentative smile and smoothed his hand over his widow's peak. "It will be good if you're there. Now that Aislin's safe and sound, we can settle on her replacement. Then you and I can discuss how we'll manage those Keepers, man to man, eh?"

Moros chuckled and slung his arm around Hugh's shoulders, enjoying how the Ferry stiffened with fear. "Indeed, my friend. Shall we go?"

Laughing nervously, Hugh led the way to the elevator. Moros and the fleshy assistant followed. Every few steps, Hugh looked over his shoulder, as if he worried what Moros might be doing behind his back. *Wise,* Moros thought. They rode up together to the boardroom, and as they entered, Moros caught sight of Aislin standing by the long row of windows. She wore a pale-pink suit, and her platinum hair was drawn up in a neat twist. She looked breathtaking, though Moros would have expected no less. This was her armor, and no one wore it better. She was in conversation with Rosaleen—her aunt, if Moros remembered correctly—and the woman was listening intently as Aislin spoke.

Hugh strode to the head of the table, his hands fluttering at his sides until he clasped them together. "I think we're all here, aren't we?" he asked.

His son, Brian, gave Moros a suspicious look as he seated himself at the table. "Are these meetings open now?"

"Only if you plan to have a Charon at the end of it," Moros said, settling himself into a chair and unbuttoning his suit coat. "But please. Proceed."

Aislin stood at the opposite end of the table from Hugh as everyone else took a seat. Her icy gaze was riveted with a predator's concentration on the ornate Scope of the Charon around Hugh's neck. It only made Moros want her more.

Hugh gestured at Aislin. "We are grateful that you've returned," he said to her. "When I received your letter of resignation, I was puzzled as to why you'd do something so impulsive."

Aislin gave him a condescending smile. "I would have been puzzled, too, if I had been in your shoes. And I would have immediately assumed foul play."

Hugh tugged at his collar. "Your letter of resignation was very clear."

"But without a verifiable biostamp on the signature," she said patiently. "I'm sure you checked."

Hugh's nostrils flared. "What did you come here to say, cousin?"

She gave him a look of mock surprise. "I've come to tell you where I was, of course, since you didn't bother to search for me."

"Are you saying you were kidnapped?"

"By Rylan," she said. "He took my Scope. But I'm sure you had no idea he would ever do such a thing, did you?" She stared at him, calm and collected, and Moros smiled.

Hugh's mouth dropped open as a few of the other board members looked at him with new suspicion. "You think I colluded with Rylan to steal your Scope? You must be joking."

"Yes, given my habit of joking about completely serious things." She looked at Rosaleen. "I was taken by Moros's sisters, Eris and Nemesis, and his brother, Apate, the personifications of Strife, Vengeance, and Lies respectively. As you can imagine, they were happy to attempt to coerce me into using a very dangerous weapon against our colleague here." She waved a hand at Moros but didn't look at him.

"So you were to be the key to their nefarious plans?" Hugh bowed his head and chuckled, and it made Moros want to rip his throat out. "And where did they take you exactly?"

"I cannot tell you a precise location, as they are able to move through the Veil like Kere, but it appeared to be a large cavern."

"But you can't actually say where, and none of us has ever seen any of these immortals for ourselves," Brian said. "That's convenient."

Hugh shushed his son. "Now Brian, Aislin has been through a trauma. It does funny things to a person."

Aislin's eyes blazed with cold fire. "Indeed it does, Hugh," she said quietly. "I am fortunate to be alive and in my right mind." Her gaze flitted to Moros for a moment, but then she went back to ignoring him.

"But how do we know you're in your right mind now, Aislin?" asked Ciara Ferry, her red-and-silver hair messy. She looked like she'd been caught napping when she was summoned.

"If you wish to examine my mental status, you may, but I'd prefer to discuss our next steps, now that we know a bit more about how our enemies plan to strike."

"Is there really a weapon that could kill the Lord of the Kere?" asked Ennis Ferry.

"Don't look so eager, old friend," Moros said with a tight smile. "It could kill you just as easily."

Ennis slid back a few inches, glowering at Moros, with his hands laid protectively over his round belly.

"It's a sword," said Aislin, drawing everyone's attention back to her, commanding the room. "Not only can it be used against Moros, but also Chaos, should he rise. And, I assume, it would also be lethal to Eris, Apate, and Nemesis?"

Moros nodded. "Though Nemesis is no longer a threat. I have eliminated her." He turned to Hugh. "My condolences, dear Hugh. But I'm sure you're happy to be back in *your* right mind now that I've reduced her to dust."

"What?" he sputtered. "I have no idea what you're talking about."

Moros tilted his head. "Don't you? Blonde curls, gray eyes, enviably lovely, with a fondness for synthetic leather . . . No? Nothing?"

Ennis's bushy white eyebrows were nearly at his hairline. "Was that the woman I saw you with at Lombo's the day before Patrick was killed?"

"Didn't I see her in your office last *week*?" asked Ciara.

Aislin arched an eyebrow. "I'm afraid I also interrupted Hugh with her just yesterday. At a highly embarrassing moment."

Brian set his elbows on the table and covered his face with his hands. "Not again, Father," he said with a groan.

Hugh was shaking his head, but then he glanced at Moros and realization suddenly kicked in. "Nina?" he whispered.

"Oh, yes," said Moros. "Your lady mistress was the personification of Vengeance. You were so fully primed, though, that you made her job easy, didn't you?"

Every gaze in the room was on Hugh, whose face was getting paler by the minute. "But I . . ."

"Plotted against our Charon?" Rosaleen asked. "From where I sit, it's sounding more likely by the second."

"But I-I only—"

"Did you share our confidential dealings with that . . . *creature*?" Ennis barked. "Once again, boy, you let the smaller of your two heads lead the way." He gestured contemptuously at Hugh's pants. "Someone strip that Scope off his neck. He's not fit to wear it. He's not fit to be on the board, for that matter."

Moros wanted to laugh. These Ferrys were quick to turn on each other, but in this case, it was completely justified.

"None of you should be so hasty to judge him," Aislin said gently, interrupting the low, angry muttering of the board.

Moros swiveled in his chair to stare at her, stunned. She'd been so close to victory, and suddenly she was laying down her sword?

"The moment she touched you, it was all so compelling, wasn't it?" she continued, sounding haunted. "All the ways I hurt or slighted you, all the things I have that were rightfully yours, how your skill and intelligence has never been recognized. She brought it all to the surface and then showed you how you could bring me down."

"How . . . how did you know?" Hugh asked, his fingers gripping the table.

"Because they did it to me, too, while they had me in their clutches. It was like torture."

Hugh nodded eagerly. "You're right," he said, staring at her gratefully. "It *was* like torture."

Moros nearly scoffed. He'd seen the memories in Hugh's head, and the only thing that had resembled torture had been Hugh's fantasies of Aislin being torn apart by Shade-Kere.

And here she was—showing mercy to this piece of human garbage?

"Now that you're free of it, you see things clearly, don't you?" she asked Hugh with a soft smile.

"I do," he said, looking around at the rest of the board. "I definitely do. I'm no longer under her terrible influence."

Aislin slowly walked around the table, her fingertips trailing along the back of each board member's chair. Her face seemed lit from within, ethereal and lovely. "I know, Hugh. I know. I'm so glad to have you back." Aislin reached her cousin and placed her hand on his arm. "Especially now that you realize you never should have challenged my position, particularly not at this crucial time."

Hugh froze midnod.

"You understand that I have a job to do," she said. "One that I am well prepared for. You understand that I have the support of the Lord of the Kere." She looked over briefly and gave Moros a small knowing smile that sent his blood rushing south. "And you understand that the best thing to do now is to allow me to get on with it, don't you?"

She held out her palm.

Hugh blinked down at her hand, looking like he'd been clubbed over the head. Moros couldn't blame him in the slightest; he felt the same way.

"Get on with it, Hugh," said Ennis impatiently. "We have work to do."

His hands trembling slightly, Hugh unfastened the Charon's Scope from the chain around his neck and handed it to Aislin. She patted his arm. "Thank you for keeping it safe for me," she said, her voice lilting and kind.

"Of course," Hugh replied. "It was an honor."

"I know." She pulled a delicate chain from under her collar and clipped the Scope to its setting. Moros grinned. She'd anticipated this outcome all along.

She was now standing next to Hugh at the head of the table, and even though her cousin was several inches taller, he seemed to fade into the background as she addressed the board. "I have reports that the Shade-Kere have, for the time being, left the city. Declan is leading the emergency response and coordinating with law enforcement."

"Who created those things?" Ennis asked.

Aislin gave Moros an uneasy look. "Eris and her allies. I have instructed my assistant to send a message to all Ferrys in the field, to let us know if they reappear anywhere else in the world. We need to respond rapidly to any additional attacks to keep the fabric of fate from unraveling further."

"It feels like we're just waiting for the other shoe to drop," said Ciara.

Aislin nodded. "I agree, but I have a plan to change that." She explained her intention to go to the Lucinae realm and negotiate with them for access to the Spring of Life, so that new weapons could be created. "With such weapons, we could eliminate the Shade-Kere, which right now can only be disabled—until they are killed by Moros directly."

Moros nodded, though he couldn't quite imagine the Mother, the leader of the Lucinae, would allow them to build an actual arsenal, and maybe that was good. More blades might help—but it also might result in more death—including his death—if they fell into the wrong hands.

"I'll leave tonight," Aislin announced. "As soon as the arrangements have been made with Cavan. I will return in time for our meeting with the Keepers, and in the meantime, I would like Aunt Rosaleen to manage business, with particular attention to maintaining order both within the city and the world markets. Does anyone have an objection to the plan?" She stared at Brian, who put up his hands and shook his head. Everyone else was doing the same, including Hugh, standing impotently at her side. Next to him, she was luminous. A goddess.

The thought of her being taken from this world was unbearable.

A slow, triumphant smile spread across Aislin's face. "Very well then," she said. "I think we're done here."

CHAPTER EIGHTEEN

Sitting on her bed, Aislin ran her fingers down the slope of her neck as she stared at her phone, wishing her body didn't heal supernaturally fast. There was no trace of what Moros had done to her, no bruises, no soreness, though he had claimed her body so thoroughly. She'd wanted them, at least for a little while, keepsakes to remind her that it had really happened.

She refocused on her phone, pushing that sense of longing away. It was impractical and pointless. She hadn't bothered to tell her board that she was going to die soon, and she certainly hadn't talked it over further with Moros, but that didn't mean she'd forgotten. In fact, she was a bit surprised she was still breathing, considering the fight with the Shade-Kere and her subsequent kidnapping. Perhaps it meant she had something to do before she went, some final contribution to the fight, something that would save the fabric of fate. *And Jason,* she couldn't help thinking.

What had happened between them was in the past, a one-time release, a mind-bending loss of control after years of fascination and the realization that she was living the last hours of her life. She'd tossed caution out the window and taken what she wanted, and she'd been rewarded with his hands all over her, his body against hers, inside hers. His inability to resist had been delicious.

But now he was back in control, detached and superior, focused on the fight ahead, and she needed to be the same.

Her incoming call light blinked, and she tapped to open the chat. "Thank you for leaving the realm long enough to talk," she said to Cavan as his face appeared on the screen, his dark hair neatly styled, looking only slightly less edgy than he had the last time they'd spoken.

"It's always easier when the Mother is out of the realm," he said. "She likes to deliver souls herself from time to time, particularly if she senses something special in them."

Aislin understood that. She guided souls regularly even though she was the Charon; it was simply part of being a Ferry and not something she wanted to lose touch with as she'd moved up the chain of command. "I know you wanted to meet, and as it happens, I need to arrange a visit to the realm," she said. "We are in need of a great favor from the Lucinae." She explained what she wanted and watched Cavan's hazel eyes go wide.

"You want to dip a *weapon* into the Spring of Life and give it to the Lord of the Kere?" he asked, his usually refined voice rising in pitch. "Something he will then use to kill living beings?"

"I know it is an affront to their sensibilities—"

"With all due respect, it's more than an affront."

"But we need it," Aislin said firmly. "Cavan, our existence is at risk. I need you to understand the stakes."

He sighed. "Do you want me to raise the topic with the Mother before you arrive?"

"I want you to make sure she understands what we're facing. This could be a disaster of apocalyptic proportions, and it is naive to think that any of us would escape unscathed, including the Lucinae."

"They've been going about business as usual, though," said Cavan.

"But I think the Mother can understand. She need only con-sult their ancient texts. One of her ancestors must have recognized the danger Chaos presents, as she negotiated with Nyx to create the original Blade of Life."

"But that was Nyx. Now you're asking her to make one for the Lord of Death."

"No one else is powerful enough to win this fight, Cavan. From what I understand, Moros's mere presence on the battlefield would help keep Chaos in check." She wouldn't let herself think about what that kind of proximity might do to Moros himself.

"This Chaos being hasn't risen, though, has he?" Cavan asked. "How do we know it's not just a false alarm?"

"I don't think it is," Aislin said. "And that should be enough for you."

"I will explain the threat and encourage the Mother to exam-ine their archives," he said, still sounding unconvinced.

"Please inform her that I am requesting an audience as well."

Cavan blew out a breath through pursed lips. "And you'll be the one to tell her of your proposed solution?" He looked like he'd rather have his fingernails yanked out than to propose it himself.

"I will. But Cavan, I need to arrive no later than tonight." It was now the middle of the afternoon, and she could feel time slipping away. "My summit with Moros and the Keepers is tomorrow at midnight, and if we don't present them with a plan to overcome this threat, I'm not sure what they'll do."

"Understood." He smiled. "I must say, this challenge agrees with you. You look positively invigorated."

"Don't flatter me," she said, but she returned his smile. "Thank you for being so reliable. And—we can talk about whatever you needed to tell me once the negotiations are completed."

His smile faltered, and he cleared his throat. "Thank you," he said, then ended the connection. Wondering what could possibly be on Cavan's mind, Aislin set her phone down and walked to her closet to select her wardrobe. She'd need something appropriately formal for the audience with the Mother, as well as traveling clothes. The trip was short, but it felt ridiculous to do it while wearing a floor-length gown.

Just as she had selected a coral-colored silk number that had a simple modest neckline but an open back that would show her raven mark, something she rarely did in public, her door buzzed. She looked at the monitor and was surprised to see Cacia standing there, but she immediately unlocked the door and went to meet her.

Cacia tugged at her paramedic uniform as she walked into Aislin's apartment, her face bearing the strain of worry.

"You look like you've had a very long day," Aislin said.

Cacia nodded. "The Shade-Kere are gone, though. Dec said he told you."

"Perhaps you should be home resting, then." But Aislin couldn't help but be glad to see her. She stared hungrily at Cacia's face, forcing herself to reject sneering images of her little sister's open defiance, her happiness at Aislin's downfall. None of that had been real. She was . . . almost sure of it.

"I'm definitely going to pass out soon, but I needed to see you first," Cacia mumbled. She had her arms folded over her chest as if she expected Aislin to dismiss her.

"I'm grateful for your concern," she replied quietly.

Cacia's eyes searched her face. "Are you okay?"

Aislin smiled and shrugged. "I think I am. It's been a strange twenty-four hours." What an understatement.

"Trevor told me Moros busted into his brother and sisters' hiding place to get you."

"That's a fairly accurate way of describing it."

"He also said you rescued his soul and gave it back to Moros." Cacia's eyes were shining. "He was amazed you did that for him, after what you'd been through."

"Trevor was kind to me while I was in captivity. Besides, helping him helped me. If he had still been under Eris's control, it would have been harder to escape."

"Stop pretending like you're not a decent person. You helped him because it was the right thing to do."

Aislin chuckled. "I only wish I'd been able to recapture Rylan's soul."

Cacia frowned. "Me too."

"Would you like to sit down?" Aislin gestured toward her sitting area.

Cacia shook her head. "I'd get crud all over your furniture." She wrinkled her nose as she looked down at herself. "I don't even know what I've got on me."

Some of it smelled like canal water, but Aislin wasn't about to mention it. "How's Eli?" she asked. "Was he with you last night?"

"He wouldn't leave my side after the first fight with the Shade-Kere."

"It sounds like things are better between you two." Aislin had been well aware of Eli's despair after he'd hurt Declan so badly. She'd been relieved to know that Moros had chosen to keep his soul, along with Tamasin's and Nader's, on his person at all times.

Cacia looked away. "Things are better, but he's still conflicted. Being a Ker hasn't been easy on him. He's still adjusting. I know we can get through this if we have the chance, though. I'd rather be struggling beside Eli than living easy with anyone else." She laughed quietly to herself. "I can't believe I'm talking to you about this."

"You can talk to me about anything," Aislin said. "That's something I've wanted for years." She braced for a harsh comeback. Lord knows, she deserved it.

Cacia gave her a cautious look. "That's not how it's felt to me."

Aislin's throat went tight. "I know. I've made many mistakes where you're concerned, but I've always wished we were closer."

A hesitant smile pulled at Cacia's lips. "I'm good with starting now, if you want to."

Aislin turned away quickly, heading for her wine rack while trying to regain her composure. "Of course we can start now," she whispered, wondering if she was being selfish. She would be dead soon, and she didn't want to hurt her little sister more than she had to. But this—she'd wanted this for so long. She whirled around with a bottle of her finest Barolo. "Let's drink to it."

Cacia smiled and walked to the large island in Aislin's kitchen, sliding onto a stool. "You look a lot better than I thought you would after being kidnapped and . . . whatever they did to you."

Aislin set down two glasses and opened the wine, then gave them each a generous pour. "I think I'm quite lucky. I was very confused at first."

"How did you recover so quickly?" Cacia asked, drinking Aislin's finest red as if it were cheap beer. "It took Eli a full day or two before he felt like he was in control of himself again."

Aislin swirled the wine in her glass to open it up. She closed her eyes and inhaled faint hints of truffle and marzipan. "Like I said, I was lucky."

She opened her eyes to see Cacia staring at her. "Trevor also might have mentioned that Moros took you back to his apartment. And that you were still there a few hours later." She took another gulp of her wine. "And that you were wearing Moros's shirt. *Only* Moros's shirt."

Aislin nearly choked on her first sip. "Trevor is quite the gossip."

Cacia snorted. "It's one of his hobbies. But seriously . . . Declan saw it, too. He's worried about you."

"Is that why you're here? Did he ask you to come?"

Cacia shook her head. "I wanted to come. But, Aislin, are you up to something with Moros?"

A sudden memory of Jason in the shower, water dripping from his ebony hair, his jaw tense as he jerked his hips against her, filling her so completely that she couldn't tell where he ended and she began, invaded Aislin's mind. Her cheeks grew hot. "I—" She cleared her throat. "He was helpful."

Cacia whistled low. "Be careful, Aislin."

"There's nothing to be careful about, Cacia. We are business associates. He has his priorities and I have mine, and at present, our interests are aligned."

"He's also pretty damn sexy when he wants to be."

Aislin pressed her fingers to her heated skin. "He certainly is," she admitted softly.

Cacia's eyes went wide. "No way. No fucking way."

"He can touch me without hurting me. He says it's because I'm fated to die soon."

"Moros told us." Cacia reached up and peeled Aislin's hand from her face, then held on tight, locking their fingers. "But if anyone can figure a way around that, it's you."

Aislin laughed. "You vastly overestimate me. I'm doing what I can, though."

"And Moros?" Cacia asked. "He looked a little frantic before he went off to find you."

"He did?"

"Well, as frantic as Moros gets."

Aislin bowed her head, thinking of the look on his face as she took him in her mouth, his eyes blazing, his fingers clutching at her hair. She shivered as pleasure shimmied down her back. "He doesn't lose his composure often."

"So it seemed like kind of a big deal," Cacia commented. "I think he has a crush on you."

"A crush?" A giggle burst from Aislin unbidden, and she slapped her hand over her mouth to stifle it. "That seems a bit beneath his dignity."

"Bullshit." Cacia grinned. "I think you've got one on him, too."

"Even if either of us had time for that, we wouldn't—"

"It makes a weird kind of sense." Cacia squeezed Aislin's fingers. "I'm just saying."

Aislin looked down at their joined hands. "You can't be serious."

"It doesn't matter if I'm serious or not—you get to decide what to do. As long as, you know, the world doesn't end and stuff." She tossed back the rest of her wine in a single gulp and set the glass on the table. "I need to get home to Eli."

Aislin walked her to the door. It felt like Cacia had just dumped out Aislin's neatly arranged thoughts about Moros and thoroughly shuffled them. She didn't know whether to feel grateful or angry about it.

Cacia threw her arms around Aislin, who turned her face away, grimacing at the smell of the city at its worst. But she hugged her sister back, unwilling to sacrifice this new, strange closeness.

"Be careful on your trip," said Cacia, her brow furrowing. "Are you sure you have to go, with Moros's prediction and everything?"

"Of my impending doom?" Aislin pulled away to look Cacia in the eye. "I can't curl into a ball and wait for the end to come. Bad things are happening, and our family is in danger. If I am meant to die while trying to save them, I'll do it happily, as long as I know I've given you all a better chance of surviving. Do you understand?"

Cacia's eyes filled with tears that she blinked away quickly. "Yeah," she said hoarsely. "I get it. But do me a favor."

"What is it?"

"Keep kicking ass, sis. I'm so proud of you." She stood on her tiptoes to kiss Aislin's cheek, then turned and walked out the door, jogging for the elevator.

Aislin closed her front door, bemused and smelling like canal water. This miracle had come too late, but she was grateful for it all the same. She walked back to her room just as she heard her phone buzzing. When she reached it, she saw that she'd missed three calls, all from Cavan. And he was calling back now. She quickly opened the line. "Cavan?"

Cavan closed his eyes in relief when he saw her face on the screen. "Aislin," he said, out of breath. As she looked closer, she could see the sheen of tears in his eyes. "The Mother . . ." He grimaced and looked away.

"Tell me now," she commanded.

"The Mother was delivering a soul, and she was attacked. We don't know what did it. The description made it sound like Shades, but—"

"Shade-Kere. I sent a message about them."

He swallowed hard. "I just read it. That must have been what this was."

Aislin's heart was pounding. "Cavan, focus. What happened to the Mother? Where is she now?"

Cavan's sculpted face twisted into an expression of sheer desperation. "She's dead, Aislin. They killed her."

CHAPTER NINETEEN

Moros was standing on his patio overlooking the city when the pain burst in his chest, causing him to stagger back. Gasping, he fell to his knees, arms curled protectively over his ribs, his forehead touching the ground. Several seconds passed before he could bear to raise his head, moments in which the certainty grew like a cancer inside him. Something terrible had happened.

He closed his eyes and willed himself into the Veil, all the way to his sisters' domain. Usually he appeared in the weaving room, but this time, he hovered just outside, preparing himself to meet any threat. What he saw instead brought him through the soft barrier between worlds, and he ran toward the prone form lying beneath millions of dangling threads, and millions more scattered across the floor, still vibrant but completely unraveled. "Atropos," he barked as he neared his sister. "Did someone attack?"

"No," she said with a moan. He turned her over and held her in his arms. Her face was ghastly pale, and he suspected his looked much the same. She gazed up at him, looking resigned and weary. "I felt it, though. Did you?"

He nodded. "A mass killing?"

She shook her head. "It didn't affect the fabric. But Clotho . . . I heard her screaming."

Moros picked up Atropos, and it was a testament to how bad she felt that she didn't try to kick him, or even to insult him. So many times, he'd asked himself if she might be willing to betray him. But seeing the pain in her eyes now drove those suspicions underground. "I've killed Nemesis," he told her as he walked toward the massive loom where Lachesis did her work. "Eris and Apate fled from me. But I'll find them."

"Eris hasn't returned here," she said as she leaned her head on his shoulder. "Which is a good thing. The more the fabric shreds, the worse we feel."

"I feel it, too," he said. "Not as severely, but I do feel it." Searing pain was coursing down his arm as he reached the end of the fabric and stepped around the loom to the other side. "And just now I felt—"

"It was terrible," she said in a choked voice. "I thought it would kill me."

He set her down gently with her back leaning against the loom and ran to the spinning room. Clotho lay curled into a ball, surrounded by a mass of stinking, singed wool. "What happened?"

"It caught on fire," she whispered, her knees hugged against her chest. "And then it went out. I don't know how."

Raw fear rose like bile in his throat. "Where is Lachesis? She wasn't at the loom."

"I don't know," Clotho said as Moros helped her to sit. Her thick brown hair was matted and greasy, and her skin was sallow. She almost looked like a Shade. "She's been ill, like the rest of us. I haven't left this room in a very long while, and I haven't heard her voice, either."

"I'll find her. Atropos was affected, too, and she's resting now. You do the same."

She nodded, looking too drained to speak again. Moros got up and headed back out into the larger weaving room. "Lachesis!" he called, looking down the length of the loom.

She stumbled out of her private quarters, and when she saw him, she fell to her knees, looking relieved. "You came back. Have you found the Blade?"

Moros had never felt like a failure, but suddenly the feeling was crushing him. "I haven't yet. Eris escaped me with the Blade in her grasp. But I intend to make another." And he planned to run Eris through with it at his earliest convenience.

Lachesis slowly got to her feet, accepting Moros's offered arm. "How will you do that? You're death. The Lucinae hate you."

"I have an ambassador," he said, and for the first time since he'd left the Psychopomps boardroom, he smiled. "I have every confidence in her."

"One of your Kere?" she asked, smoothing down a messy sprig of pale-blonde hair. "I can't see how that would be better."

"It's the Charon, actually." He couldn't help the way his voice softened at the mention of her. "Aislin Ferry."

Lachesis's eyes widened in surprise, but then she bowed her head and leaned against him as they started to walk toward Atropos. "Of course," she said. "The one whose thread has disappeared."

"She's still alive, and she's helped me reacquire Trevor, one of my Kere whose soul was stolen." He looked down at her. "I still can't figure out how Eris managed to take souls from my trunk. She would have had to sneak in here multiple times, right under your noses."

Lachesis sighed. "We've been preoccupied. And ill."

"I know," he murmured. "I'm sorry." Worry was carving at him as he looked at Atropos and Clotho. He wasn't sure how much longer they would last. "By tomorrow, I should have a new blade. I'll draw them out and end this."

"Hurry," she whispered as he lowered her down to sit next to Atropos, whose sickle hung idle at her belt. They were too weak to do their jobs, and humans would pay the price. Everything was falling apart.

"I swear to you, I'll make this right," he told them, then willed himself back to the real world. As soon as he did, his phone began to beep, signaling a message. He thumbed the screen to open it, and Aislin's face appeared.

"I'm about to leave for the Lucinae realm, but something has happened," she said, her eyes so focused that it looked like she was about to step through the screen and into his penthouse. "The Lucinae Mother has been killed by Shade-Kere. The funeral is taking place right now, but the coronation of a new Mother will happen tonight, and I will be there. I'll bargain with the successor for the Blade, but I don't know who she is or whether she'll cooperate." Aislin's mouth tightened for a moment, but then she continued. "I know you're depending on this. And I'll do my best. Just in case I don't see you before I go, be careful. Protect yourself." Her brow furrowed, and she looked like she regretted what she'd said. "I'll call you when I get back."

His screen went dark again, and he checked the time the message had been left—only a few minutes before. That pain he'd felt, the way Clotho's wool had caught on fire then gone out—the death of the Mother had to be the cause. He willed himself into the Veil, his senses immediately reaching out to find her. But when he looked up, he was greeted with two sets of glowing red eyes. Hai and Parinda were standing on his patio with the washed-out gray cityscape behind them. "We heard you were wounded," said Hai, his crimson eyes sweeping over Moros.

"And were you worried about me?" Moros asked with an amused smile. "How charming."

Parinda shook her head in disbelief, her long dark hair swishing across her shoulders. "It sounds like you should be more worried than you are."

He was more worried than he'd ever been, and he hated the feeling. "Or I could spend my energy on something more productive, like destroying Eris and Apate before they end the world as we know it."

Hai stepped forward. "Tell us how to help you. Wherever you're going, let us come, too."

For a moment, Moros wished he'd never taken their souls. Then he wouldn't have to deal with disappointing them now. These two had been with him almost from the beginning, during the rebellion, and had been loyal ever since. "You can't come where I'm going. But when I return, we will fight side by side."

"Where are you going?" asked Parinda.

Moros smiled. "I'll be accompanying the Charon to an event, it seems."

Hai's mouth dropped open. "Please tell me you're joking."

"Not remotely. Of course, that event is taking place in the realm of the Lucinae, which is why you're not coming. Our kind aren't exactly welcome there."

"Why the hell would you set foot in that domain?" Parinda said, her smooth voice growing jagged. "You've told us to avoid the Lucinae on pain of death!"

"True, but I have every reason for going to them now."

"Why can't the Charon go by herself?"

Moros shook his head. "Too dangerous."

Hai threw his arms up. "Who cares what happens to a Ferry, Moros? If she's maimed or lost, they'll just elect another. Why risk yourself? What if she's laying a trap for you?"

"She would never do that," Moros said simply. "It's insulting to even suggest it." Though a few weeks ago, he would probably have thought the same thing himself. How had he come to trust her like this?

Because she'd asked him to touch her, just to prove she wouldn't betray him. Knowing it would hurt, knowing he could take action against her if he saw something he didn't like.

How could he *not* trust her after that? And further—how could he not admire her bravery?

Parinda's upturned eyes narrowed. "This Charon is special to you?"

He met her gaze. "No." Apate would be proud. "I am merely protecting our interests."

"Don't get killed for those interests," Hai said angrily.

"I don't plan to," said Moros. "Go hunt the Shade-Kere, and call all of your brothers and sisters in death to help you—"

"While you go run off with a Ferry?" snapped Parinda.

"Go. Hunt. Them." Moros bared his fangs. "I'll summon you when I return." He didn't wait for them to vanish—he was gone before they could. He focused on Aislin, following his sense of her through the Veil until he appeared in a vast desert. She was standing there, alone, a garment bag slung over her shoulder, looking down at her Scope.

"I'm not too late, then," he said, bringing her whirling around.

"What are you doing here?" she asked. She'd changed into a different suit, slim pants and a simple jacket, all black.

"I assumed you'd need an escort to the coronation festivities," he replied.

She glanced over her shoulder at the empty miles of sand. "I can handle this."

He searched her face, wondering if that was concern flickering in her eyes—or irritation. "I know you can handle it, Aislin. However, you left a message telling me that Shade-Kere had attacked and killed the Mother. Forgive me if I'm not willing to lose the Charon as well."

She slid her garment bag from her shoulder. "I'll be inside the realm," she said. "It's not a place you want to go."

He couldn't explain the jagged feeling inside his chest as he watched her thumb stroke over her Scope. She was right—he didn't want to enter the Lucinae realm. He'd already felt the pain of the

Blade of Life cutting across his flesh. He couldn't imagine what it would feel like to be so close to the Spring. But at the same time, he remembered Hugh's visions of Aislin being torn apart by Shade-Kere, and he couldn't get them out of his head. "You're not going without me," he said, seeing his red eyes reflected in her blue ones.

"This is ridiculous." She tilted her head. "Isn't it more important to find your siblings?"

He was in front of her in two strides, his fingers wrapping around her upper arms. Their eyes met, and he reveled in how startled she looked, how vulnerable. He wanted to throw her down and claim her right there in the sand. He wanted to make her beg for him.

He just wanted *her*. Safe and whole and exquisite, always. "There is nothing more important," he said in a low voice, his gaze dropping to her mouth as his body roared. "Absolutely nothing."

Her hands came to rest on his chest, and she pushed him back gently. "All right," she murmured. "We'll go together."

He let her go and she turned away, but an instant before she did, he was certain he saw her smile. It dulled the pain in his arm and chest, and for a moment, he felt hope.

Then he remembered she'd be gone soon, and any hope where she was concerned was nothing short of insanity.

Aislin had turned back to the endless desert and was concentrating on her Scope, muttering a plea in a language long-since dead. Then she raised her head, and the air in front of her warped, a massive oasis taking shape behind a filmy bubble. Palm trees sprouted, succulents bloomed, and spreading across the sand before them was a shimmering stream leading to a lake, around which sat numerous tents and huts. At the opposite shore of the lake rose a stately sandstone palace, home of the Mother, queen of the Lucinae.

Moros shuddered, but then Aislin slipped her hand into his. She wasn't looking at him; her gaze was on the realm of the

Lucinae, on the shimmering Spring of Life. "Together," she said quietly. Her fingers tangled with his were cool and reassuring, a healing balm that shocked him with its effectiveness.

"Together," he replied. Hand in hand, they walked through the barrier. He took a careful breath, grimacing at the cloying taste settling in his mouth.

"Are you all right?" Aislin asked, releasing him and looking around.

"If I wasn't, I'd say you need a new protector." He looked away and swallowed back the strangest feeling, as if his stomach were trying to turn itself inside out.

"As long as you're sure," she said, "but I—" She gave a stifled cry.

Moros turned, prepared to tear her attacker's head off. But before he could see what had happened to her, he felt the sting of a blade at his throat, lifting his chin. He gazed into yellow eyes, like those of a tiger, lit with murderous hatred.

CHAPTER TWENTY

I know exactly what you are," said the woman holding a machete against Moros's throat. She wore flowing pants, a golden belt, and a collar of beads and baubles that barely covered her small breasts. Her dark-brown hair was in two braids that hung over her shoulders, and her olive skin gleamed with health and life—much like the weapon she was wielding.

There was an arm around Aislin's waist; she had the impression of dark-umber skin and the tangy scent of male sweat tempered by the sweetness of almonds and figs. She'd stopped her instinctive struggling the moment she saw that Moros was being threatened, but her captor didn't release her.

"We come as friends," Aislin said as the humid, warm air of the oasis raised beads of sweat across her brow. "I am the—"

"I know who you are, Ferry," the woman said as she jerked her chin toward Aislin's Scope. "And I know this one is an abomination. He desecrates our realm with his presence." She raised the handle of her machete, flexing her lean, muscular arm.

"Perhaps you could do us the favor of saying who *you* are, my dear," Moros said with a charming smile. His voice was steady, but Aislin could tell he was in pain.

"Magda," said the woman. "That's Zayed." She waggled her elbow at the man who had Aislin's back pulled snug against his hard-muscled chest.

Aislin smiled at Magda. "Unless I am mistaken, the Mother's youngest daughter bears the name of Magda," she said gently. "My condolences on her loss. We've come to pay our respects."

Magda's eyes shone with tears, which overflowed as she gritted her teeth. "If you wanted to be respectful, you would have stayed away. Why would we want two servants of death in our midst?"

"My ambassador said he would arrange it," Aislin said.

Magda pulled her blade away from Moros's throat, but only by a fraction of an inch. "Cavan is an idiot," she said.

"I'm sure they'll be expecting us," Aislin added. "One of your older sisters will be assuming the throne?"

Magda let out a frustrated growl. "Baheera." She grumbled something under her breath, and Moros looked at Aislin, as if wondering if she had caught what the young woman had said. Then Magda swished her machete through the air, and Zayed released Aislin.

She looked over her shoulder to see a tall young man, his body oiled and rippling with muscles. Zayed had curly black hair and was wearing loose pants and cloth boots. He carried no obvious weapons, but his grin was lethal as he flashed it at Aislin. "Your sweat smells like syrup," he said to her, his brown eyes skimming up her body.

Aislin smoothed her hand down her wrinkled blazer and gave Zayed a polite smile. Cavan had told her that the Lucinae were earthy and instinctual, valuing pleasure over protocol. "Thank you," she said, unable to stop herself from glancing at Moros, who was calmly staring at Zayed.

Magda rolled her eyes. "Save it for the party," she snapped at Zayed, then began to slash her way through the vegetation at the edge of the barrier between the Veil and their realm, heading for a sandy path that led to the palace. It meandered along the shore of the glittering waters of the lake, and as they got closer, a lovely cool breeze blew across Aislin's face, drying her sweat and making her skin tingle. She had the sudden urge to raise her face to the sun above and laugh out loud. Everything was so vibrant: the green of the palm fronds, the crystalline yellow of the sand beneath her feet, the glow of the water, the feel of the sunlight, the sound of laughter in the distance.

Next to her, Moros shuddered again. "You're having a party? I was expecting a slightly different response to the death of your Mother," he said to Magda.

"Which proves you don't understand us. You're a creature of death, and you don't know a thing about life."

Zayed, walking a step behind Aislin, chuckled. "We've celebrated the life of our Mother, and we've returned her to the earth. Tonight we will worship our new Mother and have a feast. We refuse to dwell on death."

"Have all the Lucinae been warned of the threat?" asked Aislin. "My understanding is that the Mother was attacked in the real world while delivering a soul." In some ways, Lucinae were as mortal as Ferrys without Scopes. The more time they spent in the realm of the Lucinae, the slower they aged. But they could be killed as easily as a regular human. "Your messengers should be careful."

Magda pointed her machete at the spot along the shore where the lake was fed by a stream. Two Lucinae, their dark hair braided, their tanned skin healthy and smooth, were capturing a glowing wraith in a net and hoisting it into the air. It was pink with streaks of amber, and the two women cooed at it, laughing as it wriggled. "Everyone's been warned," she said, her lip curling in disgust as she looked Moros over. "Cavan has convinced my sister that it would be bad for the servants of fate if deliveries were halted completely, though. Not that I give one heaping pile of camel dung for any of you."

Aislin gave Moros a sidelong glance. His skin tone was usually quite similar to Magda's, a lustrous olive that looked as warm as it had felt beneath her hands. But now he was a shade paler, and the black hair at his temples was damp with sweat. His gaze was directed away from the lake, and Aislin wondered if it hurt his eyes to look at it. And he hadn't vanished and reappeared elsewhere when threatened with that blade—Aislin wondered if he couldn't quite manage it here.

Once again, she wished he hadn't been so stubborn about coming. She understood how badly he needed the blades and wished he had trusted her to fetch them alone. At the same time, she hadn't been able to help the way her insides had melted as soon as he'd taken her by the arms, at the strain in his voice as he'd said this was important. Despite his monstrous appearance in the Veil, she'd wanted him to kiss her so badly, but she'd needed to keep a clear head. Her feelings for him were too messy to sort out, and further tangled by the way he switched back and forth between warm tenderness and utter detachment. She couldn't tell which was the real Moros, whether he cared about her or just needed her as an ally.

But as she watched him swipe his sleeve across his sweaty forehead and wince, probably as it pulled at his still-healing wound, she desperately wanted to take his hand again, to offer him whatever comfort her touch could provide. However, the presence of the two Lucinae guards who flanked them kept her hands at her sides.

The palace loomed on a stepped hillside leading down to the lake, bedecked with purple and pink succulents as well as several naked Lucinae, their bodies shimmering with crystal droplets as they sunned themselves at the very edge of the water.

"You swim in it?" Aislin asked. She'd always assumed the water was sacred.

Zayed's fingers trailed down her arm, and he pointed back to the mouth of the stream. "When a soul is ready, it travels up from the Spring. We capture them before they enter the lake and take them to their bodies in the real world. What is left is pure life." He ran a hand down his chest. "There is nothing like plunging into it, feeling it surround you. 'Invigorating' is not a strong enough description. And if your swimming companion is beautiful, and willing"—he grinned at Aislin—"you have never experienced such an intense pleasure."

Aislin's body flashed hot as she remembered her moments in the shower with Moros, hard and frenzied, ecstasy heightened by the slightest taste of pain, by longing so deep and fierce it could never be sated. "If you say so," she said quietly.

Zayed leaned down. "Tonight," he said in a low voice. "During the celebrations. We can—"

"Save it," snapped Magda, tromping up a staircase that had been carved into the broad steps leading up the hill to the palace.

"Yes, save it," muttered Moros, following her.

Zayed gave Aislin a mischievous smile. "Holding out only makes the release more powerful, don't you agree?"

Aislin let out a jittery chuckle and followed Moros up the steps, knowing that Zayed's eyes were on her body as she climbed. The palace was a vision, burnished golden sandstone, the facade intricately carved. The entrance was set back, leaving room for a large courtyard strung with colorful lanterns.

"This is where we will celebrate tonight," Zayed told her. "The view is magnificent, isn't it?"

She turned to look down the stepped expanse, across the lake. Tents dotted the banks, adobe huts interspersed along the wide sandy strip between lake and jungle. It was paradise, a place where it seemed nothing bad could ever happen. She greatly hoped that was true.

As they strode through the courtyard, several Lucinae who were decorating and setting out platters of fruit raised their heads to watch. When they spotted Moros, they scowled, muttering angrily to each other. Magda smirked as she held a door open for them to enter the palace. "You disgust us," she hissed as Moros passed.

His shoulders were stiff as he walked by, but he said nothing. Aislin looked at Magda coolly. "I met your Mother once. She was a great lady, and a gracious one. It would be a shame to disgrace her memory."

Magda's face twisted with hatred. "We can kill, you know," she said in a low voice, gripping her machete. "If the enemy is death, we can kill."

Aislin refused to look away from the young woman's fiery eyes. "Then learn to recognize your true enemy." She turned and walked past Magda, into the entryway of the palace, where Moros was staring up at a mosaic portraying the first Mother rising, fully formed, from the Spring. He seemed riveted by it, but before Aislin could ask him what he was thinking, Zayed stepped between them.

"The throne room is this way," he said, striding toward another set of arched doors. "Baheera has been communing with the Mother's spirit, but I'm sure she'll grant you an audience."

"Only if Baheera can take her eyes off Cavan's ass for that long," Magda muttered from behind.

Aislin's eyes went wide, and she whirled around to look at the woman, who merely offered a suggestive wink in return. It was enough to plant a seed of suspicion, probably exactly what Magda had wanted.

Aislin pressed her lips together, realizing the hypocrisy. Here she was, half her thoughts consumed by the Lord of the Kere and whether he truly cared or had merely screwed her. Perhaps she should wait to judge until she knew the whole story.

She kept her head high as she entered the throne room, the floor of which was scattered with sumptuous rugs, each one a work of art. The walls glittered with a rainbow of glass tiles, and the sun shone through, casting splashes of color everywhere. On a small dais sat a chaise longue laid out with silk pillows.

Magda shoved past Moros and glared at Aislin. "I'll go tell Baheera you're here. Zayed, you know what to do."

Zayed moved a step closer to Aislin. "I always know what to do," he said, seduction dripping from every word. "And who to do it with."

Moros calmly looked down at his hands, then began to remove his gloves. Her heart beating with alarm, Aislin sidestepped Zayed and put her hand on Moros's arm. "Jason," she said softly, nodding at his now-bare left hand.

"Of course. How careless of me." He put the glove back on.

Aislin glanced at the door through which Magda had exited. Raised voices emanated from within, the loudest belonging to Magda. "Does it seem like Magda is eager for a fight?" she whispered.

Moros stared at the door, but he didn't have the chance to reply before Magda and Cavan entered the room. She looked livid, and he looked harried.

"Aislin," he said, straightening his vest as he walked toward them. He had changed into traditional Lucinae garb, the flowing pants and cloth boots—and no shirt. Beneath the vest, his pale chest stood out like carved marble. His hazel eyes were lined, the black paint smudged slightly at the corners. He held out his hands to her, and she accepted them. "I've just been informed of Magda's behavior. I'm sorry you weren't welcomed properly."

Magda's mouth crimped with displeasure, like she was trying to keep all her angry words inside. Cavan looked down at her, and Aislin could see an uncharacteristic anxiety swirling within. "She's been through a lot today. They all have. I hope you can forgive her disrespect."

"I certainly understand and forgive her behavior, especially today," Aislin said, glancing toward Moros, who stood off to the side, silent and brooding, letting her deal with the diplomacy.

Cavan gave her a pained smile and tossed Magda a cautious look, but the young woman merely glared at him, her fingers wrapped around the hilt of the machete. Suspicion once again rose inside Aislin—she'd been fooled before. Eris had influenced Rylan, and Nemesis had sunk her claws into Hugh, and she'd never suspected a thing. Could Eris have gotten to Magda as well?

Cavan's fingers tightened around hers, bringing her attention back to him. "I'm afraid Baheera isn't ready to receive visitors yet." His grip was clammy. What was he so worried about? "But she asked that you attend her coronation and the feast afterward. She said she'd be pleased to meet with you as the sun rises."

Aislin gave Moros an anxious glance of her own. "Perhaps we should leave and come back." It looked like this place was rapidly siphoning Moros's strength and health.

Cavan shook his head and leaned down to speak in her ear. "These things matter to Baheera, and she would be insulted if you skipped her coronation." He looked over at Moros and spoke loudly. "She was intrigued by your presence here, Moros. She said she'd be honored to have you as a guest as well."

"You could have mentioned you were the actual Lord of the Kere a little earlier," Magda said peevishly.

"Would it have made a difference?" Moros asked, giving her a close-lipped smile.

Magda drew her machete. "Yeah. I might have cut your throat immediately, just to see the diplomatic dance Cavan here would have had to do. That's a situation even he couldn't worm his way out of."

Cavan closed his eyes as if praying for patience. "Magda—"

She put her hands up. "Like you said. It's been a rough day." Her voice cracked, and she turned on her heel and stalked away down a corridor leading further within the palace.

Zayed whistled low, but the sound cut out as Cavan nailed him with a stern glare. "Not a word, Zayed," he said. "Not a single word."

Zayed ran a finger down the crest of his beaked nose, amusement tugging at his lips. "Shall I show them to the guest quarters, Your Excellency?" he asked, making the honorific sound like a taunt.

"Please." Cavan looked at Aislin. "I'll come to fetch you once you've had a chance to change."

Zayed slid his fingers down the strap of Aislin's garment bag and tugged it from her shoulder. "I'll take this for you."

He led Aislin and Moros to the same corridor through which Magda had fled, but stopped only a few rooms down. Aislin peeked through one doorway to see an open space strewn with cushions, complete with a patio leading to the steps outside. A soft-looking mattress adorned with fragrant flower petals sat atop a wide platform bed.

"I trust this is to your liking?" Zayed asked, leaning against the wall as he watched her take it in.

"It's lovely." She looked over at Moros, who was also watching her, his gaze speculative. For a moment, Aislin imagined the two of them on that bed, tangled and panting. But then Zayed pushed open the door across the hallway.

"And this is your room . . . What am I to call you? Lord? Mr. Kere?" He grinned.

"How about 'the agonizing death you won't see coming until it's too late'?" Moros suggested. He smiled as Zayed's eyes widened. "I'm joking, my friend. You can call me Moros."

"I suggest you don't leave your room without an escort," Zayed said to Moros. "As you've seen, you're not exactly welcome." He gave Moros an assessing look, taking in his typically elegant slacks and button-down, and his expression became one of amusement and mild contempt. "I'll have some appropriate clothing brought to your quarters." He turned to Aislin. "And as for you, you could look good in absolutely anything—or nothing at all. But if you require wardrobe assistance, ring the bell. An attendant will see to you."

Moros backed into his room, his eyes on Aislin. She offered Zayed a polite thank-you and good-bye, to which he responded by taking her hand and lifting it to his mouth. His thumbs brushed over her knuckles, and his lips caressed her wrist. "Until tonight," he whispered, then straightened up and strode away, his gait cocky and assured.

Rattled, Aislin scrambled into her room and closed the door, forcing herself not to check to see if Moros was still watching. She spent the next half hour or so getting ready, freshening up, and changing into her dress—black and modest, perfect for a funeral—but then she realized how inappropriate it was. She had planned for a somber occasion, but it was clear the evening would not be a subdued affair.

She rang for an attendant, who came bouncing in with an armload of colorful garments for Aislin to choose from. After trying on several skirts and rejecting them because they didn't come with any sort of covering for the upper half of her body, she selected a dress that actually did cover her breasts—mostly—but left most of her stomach bare. It was flowing and long, made of a silky purple material that fluttered around her legs as she walked. Once the attendant was gone, Aislin pulled her long hair into a loose twist, allowing a few tendrils to settle around her face. She secured the whole thing with a few wooden sticks and tucked a pale-pink orchid with a deep-purple center into the back. She smudged a tiny bit of kohl on her lids and some pink stain on her lips, and decided to forgo jewels—the outfit itself was decoration enough, far more flamboyant and risqué than her usual.

When Aislin rang again to request shoes, the attendant looked at her as if she'd asked for a bolt gun and a laser cannon. Aislin looked discontentedly at her feet—she always felt more powerful wearing four-inch heels.

From outside, there came music and rising laughter. Aislin had expected to find the Lucinae reeling with grief, but the force of life was too strong in this place for that emotion to survive for very long. She wasn't sure how she felt about it.

And she wasn't sure how she felt about Magda, either. The woman was armed with a machete that had clearly been dipped into the Spring of Life. Her threat against Moros hadn't sounded idle. He was here to protect Aislin, but could he protect himself? Especially if his sister and brother had already infiltrated, leaving their poisonous influence festering inside their chosen pawns.

"You're stunning," came a voice only a few feet behind her. She turned to see Moros standing next to the bed. He had his gloves on as usual, but he was wearing a Lucinae garment, the flowing pants tied with a sash to his lean hips, a vest in place of a shirt. The bandage Trevor had placed on his arm matched his skin color so closely that it was easy to miss, but Aislin could tell that he held that arm more stiffly than the other. His cloth boots were silent on the stone-tiled floor as he came nearer.

"You're quite a vision yourself," she said honestly, wishing things were less complicated between them, wishing she could see into his mind. "How are you feeling?"

His expression hardened. "Don't ask me that. For the rest of the time we're here, please don't."

"I'm sorry."

He waved away the apology and lowered his voice. "Do you harbor any suspicions about Magda?"

"Did you sense that Eris had influenced her?"

He shook his head. "But"—he sighed—"I feel as though my head's been stuffed with wool, so I'm not sure I would pick it up."

"She could be dangerous."

He nodded in agreement. "Which is why I'm here, actually. My door was open, and I saw Cavan walk by." He looked back toward the corridor. "And then I heard arguing."

Aislin's eyebrows shot up. "Should we go listen?"

Moros grinned. "I was hoping you'd say that."

They padded out into the hallway, then pressed into an alcove when they heard someone coming out of a room down the hall. Moros's nose grazed Aislin's temple, and he smiled against her skin.

"What is it?"

"I hate to say it, but that bastard was right."

She looked up at him.

He tilted his head so his mouth was against her ear, making delicious chills spread through her body. "Your sweat does smell rather sweet."

Does it make you hungry? The question almost made it out of her mouth, but then she heard Magda's voice coming from a few doors down. They crept closer, and Aislin prayed that no one would see them slinking along. As they neared a doorway, two slightly muffled voices reached them. And as Aislin listened, she felt her blood go cold.

"If you don't want to do it, I will!" Magda said, her voice cracking.

"I told you I'd take care of it as soon as I could," Cavan replied. "But given what's happened, I just don't think now is the time." He muttered something Aislin couldn't decipher.

She looked back at Moros, who was staring at the door, frowning. "I couldn't catch it," he said. "But I wonder if you're right about her."

"You're a coward," Magda spat. "I guess you've always been a coward. But I'm not."

"Magda," Cavan began.

"Don't!" she shrieked. "You can't stop me, and if you try, I swear you'll regret it! I thought we were in this together, but now I'm past caring what you think. Now I'll take pleasure in watching you deal with the aftermath."

"Oh my God," Aislin whispered. "Jason." She reached back to touch him, but at that moment, Magda swung open the door and burst into the hallway.

CHAPTER TWENTY-ONE

Aislin staggered back, and Moros took an instinctive, protective step in front of her. But before either of them could do a thing, Cavan plowed into the corridor and hooked Magda around the waist, clamping a hand over her mouth and dragging her back into the room from which they'd emerged. He gave Aislin a sharp sidelong glance. "If you heard any of that, you'd better come in."

"Not if she's got that machete within reach," Aislin said, moving to stand beside Moros, somehow managing to be both stately and seductive in flowing purple that bared her taut stomach and hugged her hips and breasts. The mere sight of it made Moros want to stop time and peel every scrap of it off, tasting each revealed inch of her smooth skin.

She poked him in the side. "If she stabs me, I'll heal," she murmured, refocusing him on the danger at hand. "You're used to being invincible, but I'm safer here than you are." There was something like concern in her eyes, and he was ashamed by how much he craved it.

"She's unarmed," called Cavan. "Baheera insisted all the blades be put away."

That was both a relief and painfully disappointing. The longer he was here, the more he'd begun to contemplate stealing one

of the blades and making a run for it, damn the political consequences. Every hour in this place made him feel weaker. But if the
Lucinae complained to the Keepers that he was a thief, it would be
one more excuse to condemn him. Besides, he was not about to
leave Aislin's side.

They stepped inside the room to find Magda weeping on the
bed and Cavan standing over her, looking miserable. "I have to
talk to you," Cavan said to Aislin, giving Moros a nervous look.

Aislin's eyebrows rose. "Is this what you called me about?"

Cavan nodded. "But I'd really prefer it be a private conversation."

"Oh, just tell them," Magda wailed. "Or are you too ashamed
of me to do even that?"

"It's not that!" Cavan said, his own voice rising. He closed his
eyes and let out a breath, seemingly on the bleeding edge of losing
his diplomatic cool.

"Then tell us what you two are up to," Moros replied, looking
back and forth between them, not sensing even a whiff of Eris in
the air, or a sour tang on his tongue. But then again, he couldn't rid
himself of the cloying sweetness of this place.

Cavan and Magda exchanged glances, and in that second,
Moros felt the pull between them, a thread of connection so taut it
seemed he could reach out and strum it with his fingertip.

"What are you planning?" asked Aislin, clearly not sensing it.
"Cavan, I warn you now, if you've been working against our official
interests, I will not only strip you of your position and Scope, I'll
strip you of your status and feed you to a Shade myself."

Cavan's mouth dropped open. "But I . . . I didn't think . . . I
hoped you might understand?"

Aislin stepped forward, looking like a vengeful goddess. "You
thought I might understand a plot to kill Moros and subvert fate?"

Something warm and nourishing stirred within Moros's
chest. Was she angry because she felt protective of him—or just
of fate in general? Either way, Cavan and Magda had obviously

been planning a completely different kind of intrigue than the one Aislin was thinking. "Aislin," Moros began, his voice soft.

She put up a hand. "No. I've been too trusting, it seems." The betrayal was clear on her lovely face, in the tightness of her mouth and the clench of her fists.

Cavan fell to his knees before her, his expression creased with torment. "I knew it was wrong, but I couldn't help it. Please!"

Magda gasped as she saw Aislin reaching to snatch Cavan's Scope from his neck. "Don't touch him!" she shrieked, diving in front of Cavan with her arms out.

Moros caught Aislin's wrist and held it tight. "You're being too hasty," he said. "Look. Really look at the two of them."

Aislin glared down at Cavan and then at Magda. Tears running down her face, the young woman turned and threw her arms around Cavan. "I'm so sorry, my love," she said between sobs.

"Oh, for heaven's sake," Aislin said, throwing her arms up in exasperation.

Cavan folded Magda against his chest, still on his knees as he looked up at Aislin. "I never meant this to happen. But I can't help the way I feel about her." He bowed his head and pressed his face to her hair. "And you're right," he whispered to Magda. "I have been a coward."

"No," she said. "I had no respect for the pressures you face."

"How sweet," said Moros. "So the thing you're fighting over is whether to go public with this little affair?"

Cavan's cheeks darkened as he raised his head. He kept his gaze on Aislin, like Moros wasn't even there. "This is a sensitive time." His hazel eyes were intense, like he was begging her not to make him explain.

Aislin folded her arms over her chest. "If you're so in love, explain all your angry remarks about Cavan on the hike to the palace," she said to Magda. "Explain your comment about how your sister couldn't take her eyes off . . ." Her eyes went wide. "Good Lord." She took a step back. "That does complicate things."

"What is it?" Moros asked.

"Baheera is in love with Cavan, too, isn't she?"

Cavan bowed his head again. "I've tried to be clear with her, but, well, you have to meet her. She's—"

"A cow," mumbled Magda, her face pressed to his shoulder.

Cavan squeezed her. "Stop that." His eyes met Aislin's. "I was going to tell you in our meeting," he said.

"Now is the time," Aislin said firmly, every line of her emanating an authority that made Moros ravenous with want. "Join me outside."

She strode out to the patio, where the sun draped her in golden light. That was where she belonged, in the sun. Brilliant and shining.

Cavan extricated himself from Magda's arms, murmuring gently to her and helping her to sit on the edge of the bed. "I'll be by your side as soon as I can," he said. "I promise." He walked quickly out to join his Charon.

"Now I understand why this day was even more difficult for you than it was for others," Moros said casually to Magda, who was wiping her nose on the bedspread.

"He won't stand up to my sister," she replied, apparently too distraught and drained to hate Moros properly. "He's been too afraid to offend anyone to stand up for me. For us."

Moros sighed and sat down next to her, though he kept a safe distance between them. The girl seemed rather unpredictable. "Or perhaps he was too afraid of losing you to risk it."

Magda's tiger eyes narrowed with suspicion. "Too afraid of losing me to actually be with me? That's stupid. If you want to be with someone, you go be with them. Easy. Done."

Moros chuckled. "If only."

"What does the Lord of Death know about love?" she snapped. "I don't even know why I'm talking to you."

"I'm not sure, either," he said, his gaze drifting back out to the patio, where Aislin was deep in conversation with her distressed ambassador. "And to answer your question, the Lord of Death knows very little about love, and less about how to keep it."

He tore his gaze from Aislin to find Magda staring at him with shrewd comprehension. "To answer a question you didn't bother to ask," she said, "I know a lot about love, or some parts of it, at least. Enough to recognize it when I see it."

He leaned back on his hands, glad she wasn't sharp enough to hear the hammering of his heart. "I'm sure I don't know what you're talking about."

Magda sniffled and swiped her hands across her face, and then rose from the bed. She looked out to the patio. "Tonight at the feast, Zayed is going to offer his body to the Charon, as an instrument for her pleasure," she said simply. "Thought you'd like to know."

Then she walked to the door. "I'll be in my room, if Cavan asks," she called over her shoulder, then she disappeared into the corridor, leaving Moros alone, staring at the woman he craved with a passion that burned him from the inside out.

• • •

Moros stood at Aislin's side, ignoring the hate-filled, suspicious glares of all the Lucinae gathered for their new Mother's coronation. They were in the wide courtyard overlooking the massive lake fed by the Spring of Life. The sun was setting over the water, nearly blinding Moros with its poisonous brightness. His head was pounding, a foreign, unwelcome sensation that made him want to bury his head beneath a pillow, just to block out the light for a while.

Aislin's shoulder brushed his, the silky cloth tickling his bare skin. Everyone else gave him a wide berth—once they had learned who he really was, no one got within six feet of him. But Aislin held her head high and remained near, as if daring anyone to challenge Moros's presence. Caught in the misery of this realm, Moros had the urge to take his glove off and tangle his fingers with hers, to anchor himself to something strong and real. He'd never had such a desire, but here it was, and it made him feel even more pathetic. He was the Lord of the Kere. He shouldn't need anyone. Shouldn't trust, shouldn't depend upon, and shouldn't seek out anyone, let alone love them.

I don't love anyone but my sisters, he reminded himself. *Anything else is folly.*

A cool breeze blew strands of Aislin's platinum hair against his face, and he inhaled, nearly moaning at the scent of her. But then a stream of notes issued forth from the musicians on the far side of the courtyard, and a row of shirtless courtiers strode out from the palace. The Lucinae cheered, and Moros took Aislin and Cavan's cue and clapped politely. From beneath the grand arch of the palace walked a naked woman wearing an elaborate headdress. Her black hair flowed down her back, and her skin was fine and olive, much like her sister's, for this was clearly Baheera, the new Mother of the Lucinae. She smiled at the adulation of her subjects, her arms raised as she moved to the center of the courtyard, beneath several garlands of flowers and lanterns. She turned in place, stopping momentarily as she faced Cavan. Her gaze flared with challenge, but then she continued to move until she faced the lake.

"My children," she said in a high, clear voice. "We face a loss today, but we cannot dwell on the past, only the future that we represent. Together we will continue our work, without which the world would cease to turn. I will lead you and nurture you always. You are orphans no longer, for I am your Mother!"

The Lucinae were giddy with joy, wailing and calling her name, each peal of sound like an ice pick to Moros's head. The louder they got, the dizzier he felt. Then the courtiers began to dance around Baheera, their feet stamping in the dust-strewn courtyard, their oiled skin shining in the rays of the setting sun. Moros closed his eyes, pushing down another strange sensation, one he had experienced so rarely in his entire existence—fear. He'd never felt this way, his body betraying him. But the last thing he could afford was to show weakness. He forced himself to stand up straight and open his eyes again. He glanced over to find Aislin's gaze focused on the courtiers, one of which was Zayed, who was dancing and leaping as if springs had been attached to his feet.

"The Mother will choose her partner for the night!" shouted one woman, her large breasts bobbling as she rose to her tiptoes and swept her arms toward Baheera, who had been swaying to the music.

On Aislin's other side, Cavan stiffened and muttered something to his Charon, who whispered something back. Ever since their tête-à-tête on the patio, things had been tense between the two, but there hadn't been time for Moros to ask Aislin what had passed between them. Now, as Baheera strutted among the courtiers, who had stopped their dancing to preen for the new Mother, each obviously hoping to be chosen by her, Moros wondered—had Aislin asked Cavan to use Baheera's reported desire for him? It would smooth things over politically, but it had been obvious the boy was besotted with the fiery, semiferal Magda. Normally Moros would have found it amusing—the two were opposites in every way, and their youthful desperation might have once made him chuckle. But somehow, in the last many days, that detachment had been peeled away.

If Cavan offered himself to please Baheera, it might make it easier for Moros to get what he needed—a Mother who would give him a Blade of Life, if not an arsenal of them.

But the thought of that sacrifice, for some bizarre reason, made Moros ache for the poor lovers. To put one's heart on the chopping block . . .

Baheera ran her hands down her body as she wound her way leisurely through the throng of would-be "partners," offering each a suggestive smile. But she kept moving toward the spot where the foreign dignitaries stood, and with each step, Moros felt the tension rise. Finally, Baheera's eyes met Moros's, and she arched an eyebrow. "You are far finer than I expected from a creature of death."

Moros gave her a half smile. "I'm not so much the creature as the creator, darling."

Her gaze flared with intrigue. "You want something from me."

"True, but you should want it, too, if you desire to live free of the threat that took your dear Mother away from you this very morning."

Baheera rolled her eyes. "We can protect ourselves easily enough." Her full lips stretched into a brilliant smile as she gestured toward the lake, filled with pure life, as Zayed had told them. "We'll be prepared when we venture out to deliver souls. And here we are safe."

"Are you so sure?" he asked quietly.

She nodded, never taking her gaze from his. He had no doubt she was aware that every single one of her subjects was riveted to their exchange, though, because her voice rose as she said, "The sanctity of our realm has never been breached."

"Such confidence."

"Well earned," she retorted, tracing her fingertips up the center of her chest. She was trying to toy with him in the same way she did her courtiers, probably accustomed to being desired by every male she encountered.

It wasn't working in the slightest. "Ah, but sometimes hubris and self-assurance are indistinguishable," Moros said before he could stop himself.

Aislin elbowed him in the side. "But in this case, it is confidence, of course," she said quickly. "We're honored to be witnessing your ascendance."

Baheera ignored Aislin, which sent a bolt of anger through Moros. "I hope you're comfortable here, my lord," she said in a mocking voice that made Moros's stomach turn.

"Very," he gritted out.

"I've instructed that all our blades be locked away." She leaned forward, her eyes keen and knowing. "For your safety."

"You are the soul of compassion."

She took a step closer to him, her gaze drifting down to his gloves. "Is it true, the things I've heard about your touch? Because you look *very* touchable."

Aislin stiffened, and everyone in the courtyard gaped, the shock and outrage palpable.

Moros looked down at his hands and chuckled. "Best not to test it, hmm?"

She gave his body a lingering once-over, then shrugged. "I suppose not. Sorry."

Sorry? He almost laughed. "My poor heart." He couldn't suppress a grin.

Baheera might have been full of herself, but she was also observant. Her expression hardened when she realized he wasn't properly stricken with lust, and she took a quick step away, giving Aislin a dismissive wave as she passed. "Thank you for being here, Charon."

"My condolences on the loss of your Mother," Aislin said politely. "We're grateful you were willing to grant us an audience despite this tragedy."

Baheera's attention had already drifted to Cavan. "You have a very . . . *persuasive* ambassador," she purred.

Magda, standing several feet behind Moros, made a strangled sound. Cavan gave Baheera a slight bow. "Thank you, Mother," he said, his tone formal. "I am honored to serve."

"Are you?" she asked. "Is your whole self devoted to your duty?"

"I am committed to facilitating relations between our two peoples."

He sounded robotic. Like his brain had disconnected from his heart. Moros looked at Aislin. She had the power to demand this sacrifice of Cavan, to disregard his feelings and force him to comply for the good of all involved, except the poor ambassador and his lover.

Baheera inched closer to the man and put her hand on his cheek. "Then I choose you," she said, "for I can think of no better way to honor your commitment."

A choked sob came from Magda, followed by the sounds of her bare feet slapping the stones of the courtyard as she fled. It made Moros's throat go tight, especially when he caught sight of Baheera's triumphant smile. He was willing to bet she wasn't so much in love with Cavan as unwilling to accept that not every man would be fixated on her, unwilling to allow her sister to enjoy the attention of a handsome man. Her ego had to be fed, and Cavan would be her meal tonight.

But then Aislin sighed. "I'm sorry, Mother, but I must object."

Baheera's hand dropped away from Cavan's cheek. "What?"

Her voice was like a lash, but Aislin didn't flinch. "I know Cavan would be delighted to accept your invitation, and he will probably hate me for saying this, but one night with you would make him unable to do his job." Aislin smiled as she stroked her gaze up the length of Baheera's naked body, a look ten times as seductive as the new Mother could manage on her best day. (Of course, Moros realized, he might not be the most objective observer.) "You are so compellingly lovely that he would be unable to remember the Ferrys' interests."

Baheera's mouth tightened with suspicion. "I'm sure he could manage it."

"I beg you," said Aislin. "Don't cast your spell on him. It would be more than he could bear, and I fear he would be nothing but your slave from then on. I'm afraid I would have to appoint a new ambassador, one who would be less vulnerable to your obvious charms."

Baheera frowned as she glanced back and forth between Aislin and Cavan. Her subjects were all rapt, many of the males looking resentful that she would even consider a Ferry over one of them. But Moros was overwhelmed by Aislin's brilliance, especially when Cavan said, "Please, Charon, it is only for one night."

"No, Cavan, I'm afraid I can't even consider it," Aislin said. "Your mind must be clear."

Moros knew the two of them had sufficiently sated Baheera's ego when the woman nodded generously. "I understand," she said, casting a sullen look over Cavan's body. "I wouldn't want you to lose yourself."

Cavan put his hand on his heart, bowing his head so Baheera couldn't see his relieved grin. "You have my eternal gratitude, Mother," he said.

Baheera moved on, choosing a thickly muscled courtier with long black hair, and as she did, Aislin's posture loosened. Moros felt an unexpected surge of happiness in knowing that she wasn't willing to sacrifice her ambassador for the sake of politics, along with another wave of admiration for the woman by his side. Was there anything she couldn't manage?

Baheera locked hands with her partner and raised them into the air. "Let the revelry begin!"

A whoop went up from the crowd, and to Moros's shock, Aislin joined in the cheering.

"That was masterful, my dear," Moros said quietly to Aislin as Cavan turned on his heel and raced off into the palace, probably desperate to comfort Magda.

Aislin grinned. "Why, thank you." She glanced toward the dance floor and then up at him. "I don't suppose you would care to—"

Zayed suddenly appeared and bowed low in front of Aislin. "Would you honor me with a dance, Charon?"

"Oh." She tossed Moros a regretful, apologetic look. "Of course."

Zayed grabbed her hand and practically wrenched her onto the dance floor, and had Moros not been wrestling his own murderous impulses, he would have found the shell-shocked look on Aislin's face comical. She was elegant and graceful no matter what she did, but the foot-stomping aggressive undulations of the Lucinae were clearly not what she was used to. Despite that, she gamely tried to match Zayed's moves, probably eager to kindle as much good feeling from the Lucinae as possible, given the daring subterfuge she'd just pulled off with Baheera. She knew her mission—to obtain a Blade of Life—and she was focused on it.

For him. For his survival and that of the servants of fate. Moros thought there couldn't possibly be a person better suited for the job than she was, as hard as it was to watch her in the arms of another man. As Zayed's large hands skimmed over her bare stomach, as he pressed his hips to her ass and moved her in a wild circle with a look of sheer pleasure on his face, jealousy flared in Moros's chest.

As other courtiers noticed her beauty, they, too, lined up for a turn, each showing off his moves as she laughed and played along, looking delighted by the music and the dancing and the wild revels of the Lucinae. Many of them were twined around each other, thrusting and writhing as the musicians played on. Baheera had long since disappeared with her chosen lover into a hut down by the lake to swim and make love all night, but many of her subjects didn't bother to seek privacy as their dancing turned to something far more intimate. Moros could smell the sex in the air, hear the pounding beat of lust and the cries of pleasure. He kept his eyes on the Charon as the vibrations traveled up from the ground and through the soles of his feet, winding his body tighter with every passing second.

When Zayed approached Aislin for a second time, Moros gritted his teeth. The young man's gaze lingered on the swell of her breasts as he stroked his fingers down Aislin's arm and took her hand, and Magda's warning from this afternoon rang in his head. Zayed was about to ask for more than a dance.

Every inch of Moros's body rebelled against the idea of another man making love to Aislin. She belonged with *him*. Another moment of denying it might kill him. Suddenly, everything was clear, the string around his heart, connecting him to this woman, the knowledge that if it were cut, his existence would not be worth having.

He was taking a step toward the two of them, ready to confess everything, when Aislin laid her hand on Zayed's bare chest and gave him a radiant smile. "I'm afraid I haven't danced with everyone else quite yet," she said to him.

And then she turned to look straight into Moros's eyes. The string connecting their hearts shortened, pulling him toward her before he realized he was moving his feet. She met him in the middle, and the entire miserable, bright, loud, cloying realm vanished. The only thing he was aware of was Aislin as her hand rose to grasp his. The leather of his glove was an unacceptable barrier between them, but as he looked down at it, her grip tightened. "Don't remove it," she said quietly. "People will be suspicious if they see you touching me. There will be talk, and it could derail what we've come here to do."

Moros glanced over her shoulder to see Zayed watching them with a look of unbridled disgust on his face, as if he couldn't imagine why she would consider offering the Lord of Death a dance. He tugged her a little closer. "But you want me to."

Her lips parted as he moved within a few inches of her, the scent of her skin making his blood roar. "Now who's full of hubris?" she asked, slightly breathless.

"I'm too old for that," he replied, his body throbbing for her. If he pulled her against him now, she would feel every inch of his craving—his loose pants barely concealed it.

But her flimsy garment betrayed her as well—her pearled nipples were easily visible. "I'm merely being polite," she said. "Diplomatic."

"Is that so, my dear?" He skimmed a gloved finger down her stomach before settling his hand on her hip. "Or do you want this as badly as I do?"

"No idea what you're talking about," she whispered, her pupils dilating as she stared at his mouth.

"I'm talking about me, inside you. Right now." The thought of it had made him so hard that it was tempting to make the fantasy a reality right here in the courtyard.

She swallowed. "I think you've been affected by the festive atmosphere."

"I can smell your arousal from here." It was making him crazy. He wanted to sink his teeth into her shoulder as he pounded into her. If she touched his bare skin, nothing would hold him back.

Her cheeks were tinged with pink. "Jason," she murmured.

"What would the diplomatic cost be," he asked, "if I were to take you back to my room right now and fuck you until you're screaming that name?"

"Potentially high. A dance is one thing. A night together is another matter entirely." Her eyes met his, and the silence stretched between them. His ancient heart pounded, fueled by a need so powerful that he was ready to die for it. And then she whispered, "But I'm having trouble caring."

They had just turned and taken their first steps toward the palace when the horde of Shade-Kere burst from the jungle and began their charge.

CHAPTER TWENTY-TWO

The Shade-Kere poured from the forest on both sides, their rotting flesh and oozing eyes gruesomely at odds with the verdant surroundings. Screams filled the air as the Lucinae realized they were under attack, and many started up the stepped hillside, seeking the shelter of the palace. The monsters raced to cut them off.

"Run for the lake," Moros roared, ripping his gloves from his hands as he sprinted forward. "You'll be safe in the water!"

Aislin cried out in helpless horror as two Shade-Kere ran along one of the steps and caught a fleeing female Lucinae by her flowing hair. One of the creatures raked its jagged fingernails across her stomach while the other sank its teeth into her arm. The light in the girl's eyes brightened, then faded as her blood flowed onto the steps. That scene was replaying itself over and over on the hillside below them as frantic Lucinae scrambled in all directions, totally unprepared to deal with the threat.

From the shore of the lake, Aislin heard one shrill voice cry for help above the rest—

"Baheera is down there!"

Moros shoved Aislin back as the first Shade-Ker reached him. As the creature lunged, the Lord of the Kere slammed his fist into the creature's face, and it exploded in a haze of dust. "Get inside the palace," he said with a grunt, hooking another creature around the neck as it charged at Aislin.

"But—"

Moros's eyes glowed red as he finished off the Shade and turned to her. "Inside *now*," he shouted. When she didn't move fast enough, he grabbed her upper arm and shoved her toward the palace. "I can't be everywhere at once. Please."

Her first impulse was to argue with him—what did protecting herself matter if she was doomed anyway? But as the Shade-Kere continued to charge from the forest, she knew she was being self-ish. Moros was the only one who could kill them easily, and he was already depleted from being in this realm. His first priority had to be Baheera.

"Be careful," she said quietly as he leaped onto the steps that led down to the lake. Then she pulled her Scope from her neck and ran for the palace, her voluminous skirt billowing behind her.

As she reached the entrance to the palace, she heard a scream, followed by the slap of greasy feet against the courtyard stones. With her thumb pressed to the cold surface of her Scope, she whirled around to see a Shade-Ker coming for her, its muscles hanging from its bones in wiry ropes, the cavity of its chest a gaping, empty hole. She dodged its first mindless lunge, pivoting around a column and letting the Shade collide with a wall. And as it came for her again, its eyes glowing red like one of Moros's Kere, she flung her Scope wide and swung the portal forward, capturing the creature in a whoosh of acrid smoke.

She closed her Scope quickly, knowing there would be no coin flying forth from the fiery pits in exchange for a dead soul. She'd given the Keeper of Hell yet another soulless abomination to deal with, and tomorrow she would stand before him during the sum-mit and hope he could forgive the intrusion.

As the slaughter continued behind her, Aislin entered the palace. She had no intention of hiding out of sight until this was over. Cavan and Magda hadn't emerged, and they might not be aware of the danger. More than that, they might know where Baheera had locked away the weapons, all of which had been dipped in the Spring of Life. They needed them now more than ever.

As she entered the grand hall at the front of the palace, crashes and shrieks echoed toward her. Some of the Shade-Kere had already gained entrance. She grabbed a heavy ceramic vase as she passed a table, heading for the corridor where she and Moros had overheard Cavan and Magda arguing earlier. Her heart was thumping fiercely, and she could not help but think how vital it felt, how right. "I will not die today," she whispered as she peeked around the corner.

Three Shade-Kere were bashing themselves against Cavan's door, probably sensing the life inside. Like Moros, they didn't seem able to vanish and reappear at will here, but it was a small mercy at this moment, as Aislin could hear the wooden door beginning to splinter. A scream came from within—Magda. Was Cavan with her? The Shade-Kere were probably on their patio, too, closing in from both sides.

"Hey!" she shouted, her fingers clasped tightly around the rim of the vase.

The Shades paused for a moment, and as Aislin stepped into the corridor, they turned to her, their empty chests heaving with phantom breaths. Her muscles trembled, fighting terror as all three of them charged at once. *I won't die. I won't die.* She thought it over and over as they came after her, and when they were close enough, she crunched the vase into the side of a Shade's head, sending it staggering. But just as she began to open her Scope, the second one hit her, and the platinum disk flew from her hand.

As fingernails clawed at her skirt, she swung the vase upward with both hands, catching one attacker at the base of the chin and sending its skull peeling backward—she'd snapped its spine. It stumbled, its head hanging from the back of its neck. Aislin kicked at a second one and dove for her Scope, her fingers raking at it in desperation. It was a few feet from her, but the third Shade had caught hold of her ankle and was trying to yank her away. Then its friend grabbed her other ankle, and they wrenched her toward them. One of them fell on top of her, going for her throat. She could feel its hands burning—it was trying to Mark her, but it couldn't. She was a Ferry, and as long as she bore the Scope, surely she would remain immortal. *I won't die today.*

It didn't mean they couldn't hurt her, though. It didn't mean they couldn't tear her to shreds. She squirmed frantically, barely avoiding the creature's snapping, rotting teeth. Its partner was still pulling on her ankles, its ragged fingernails tearing her skin. Her nose filled with the scent of putrid flesh as she jerked her hip up and threw the monster off, then elbowed it in the side of the head, cracking its skull. Something hard bounced off her side, and she realized the stolen vase was on the ground next to her. As the thing lunged for her throat again, she slammed the vase into its forehead, again and again, until there was nothing left of its skull but a broken, empty bowl of bone.

It didn't stop it, only made it more confused and clumsy. She was able to roll it off her just in time to get her legs up and kick the third Shade-Ker away. Her limbs felt electric, surging with the will to live. She flipped over and threw herself at her Scope, and this time she was able to scoop it from the floor. As the Shade leaped at her, she whipped open a portal to Hell that swallowed her enemy whole. Blood from her torn skin seeping down her ankles and making the floor slippery at her feet, she stalked down the hallway toward the two Shades she had disabled, sending them to Hell with quick slashes of her Scope through the air.

"Cavan!" she called.

He opened the door and poked his head out, his eyes round. "Aislin? My God, I had no idea it was you out here—"

She held up her hand. "Magda?"

"Here," the girl said, appearing next to Cavan, her olive skin ashen. "We were hiding. They're on the patio—"

"Do you know where your sister hid the weapons? We need them now." She could barely hold on to her patience. Moros had been heading off to save Baheera, but it would put him in dangerous proximity to the water.

Magda's expression hardened. "She didn't tell me where she put them."

"I think I know where they might be," said Cavan, looking away from Magda as her eyes narrowed in suspicion. "There's a secret chamber attached to her bedroom."

"Take me there," Aislin said. Cavan hesitated as they heard the shrieking roar of a Shade-Ker somewhere nearby. Aislin grabbed his arm, patience gone. "*Are* you a coward?" She gestured to the Scope around his neck. "There is your weapon. Use it like you were born to wield it, because you were. Magda can be killed by these creatures, but you can't."

She could tell by the fear on his face that he was thinking of all the stories of how Shades had mauled Ferrys in the Veil, leaving them injured and helpless, but at the mention of Magda, his fog of terror seemed to clear a bit. He reached back and took the Lucinae princess's hand, his jaw set. "It's this way."

They ran, keeping Magda between them. Aislin took the front, meeting each attack with her Scope open and swinging. The bitter haze of smoke clung to her hair and skin, but to her it smelled like victory as they made their way across the palace to Baheera's quarters. Once there, Cavan pulled a key from beneath a pillow and used it to open a small chamber concealed by a hanging tapestry. Throughout, Magda watched with hurt shock as her lover demonstrated his familiarity with her sister's private sanctum.

Cavan avoided her gaze as he opened the door to the chamber to reveal exactly what he promised—about a dozen machetes and daggers, a spear, and one sword. Aislin gathered up as many as she could carry, sliding three blades between layers of fabric at her waist, a makeshift sheath, and keeping a long dagger in one hand and her Scope in the other. She wasn't exactly an expert at wielding knives and such, but she knew how to shove the pointy ends into oncoming monsters, and she figured that would be enough. Cavan had the sword, and Magda had the spear.

"We'll have to fight our way down to the lake," Aislin said. "Moros told your people to run there—they'll be safe in the water."

Magda nodded, though Aislin could tell by the look on the girl's face that the horror of what was happening was just sinking in. Her world had been so small, focused on Cavan and her anxious jealousy of her sister, and now she was probably realizing the survival of her entire people was in question. To her credit, she gripped the spear with resolve.

Together, they ran through the palace toward the front, taking out at least ten Shades on the way. The things were everywhere, looking for prey, and Lucinae bodies lay scattered in their wake. As supernatural beings, they lived outside of fate—they couldn't be Marked, but they could be killed. And once they were dead, they were gone forever. Seeing such beautiful, vibrant creatures destroyed so pitilessly made Aislin's heart ache—but also race with apprehension. Would the Keepers hold Aislin and Moros responsible for the slaughter?

With new urgency, Aislin burst into the courtyard to find more devastation, Lucinae who hadn't fled fast enough lying wounded or broken, all around. Magda cried out at the sight but kept moving forward, following as Aislin and Cavan charged toward the steps that led to the lake. The sounds of fighting and carnage were shrill as the bright moon shone down on the crystal waters below, and when Aislin reached the edge of the steps, she could see everything clearly.

Moros and a few Lucinae were fighting to keep at least thirty Shade-Kere away from the entrance to the hut containing Baheera and her lover. They were surrounded. Moros was destroying Shade after Shade, but they were so closely packed that he couldn't keep them off him entirely. His arms were marred by claw marks and bruises, and his face was a mask of rage. Aislin perched on the edge of the steep steps, ready to leap, but Cavan grabbed her arm and led her to a shallower set of stairs. She couldn't get to Moros fast enough, because even as she barreled toward him, the Shades kicked his legs out from under him, and he disappeared beneath the mob.

Rage exploded through her, quickening her pace. It was almost a relief to plunge her dagger into the back of a Shade at the rear of the attacking group. It collapsed in a heap as if she'd hit its off switch. Magda and Cavan were fighting by her side, killing Shades left and right, and for a few minutes, Aislin couldn't see more than a few feet in front of her, so intent was she on destroying every Shade that stood between her and Moros. But a shout from about twenty feet away brought her head up.

A group of Shades had hoisted Moros from the ground, holding him by the vest. His usually sharp, observant eyes were unfocused. Blood flowed from a wound at his temple, striping his handsome face and flowing down his neck. His arms were limp at his sides as they began to drag him toward the water.

"Cavan, they're going to throw him into the lake," she shouted, slashing her blade with absolute ferocity, neatly slicing a Shade's head from its neck.

Without waiting to see if her ambassador was following, Aislin kept her Scope nestled in her palm and drew a second blade. Her blood roared in her ears, each beat of her heart like a crash of clarity. She couldn't lose him like this. They belonged together.

Without him, she'd be only halfway complete. Each thought came with a slice of her blades. She was dimly aware of the creatures clawing at her, tearing her skirt, but she was all motion and action, zero hesitation. They were only steps from the lake. Moros was struggling weakly, trying to raise his head, but he didn't seem to realize how close he was to the deadly shore.

"Jason!"

At the sound of her voice, his head lurched up, and his eyes glowed red. Aislin surged forward, shoving her blade into the back of one of the Shades holding on to Moros's vest. It tumbled toward the water, which sizzled as the creature fell in. Within a second, it was nothing but bleached bones. Would that be what happened to Moros if he touched the lake? The sight shocked her into stillness for a second too long, and a Shade hit her from behind, wrapping its wiry arms around hers and taking her to the ground.

Aislin rolled over, gasping in agony as one of her own blades sliced along her ribs. But she ignored the pain and kept the momentum, rolling with her attacker straight into the water. As soon as she touched it, the strangest sensation streaked along her bones, tingling and cool and all-consuming. The Shade that had attacked her dissolved in an instant, leaving her by herself in the shallow water with golden, glinting sand beneath her palms, her hair dripping, her heart racing. She rose to her feet on suddenly rock-steady legs, looking down to see her torn dress hanging to her ankles, which had instantly healed as soon as they touched the water. Her skin sparkled under the moonlight as she walked forward and picked up her blade.

Moros was sitting by himself, a few feet from the shore, staring at her. He was covered in a fine film of dust, which had stuck to his eyelashes and the blood streaming from his wound. She glanced around. Cavan and Magda were standing next to a field of Shade-Kere bodies strewn between the shore and Baheera's hut. Cavan waved his arms. "They fled," he called out. "They're gone."

Aislin nodded, then returned her attention to Moros. As much as it hurt her to see him injured, he was alive. Unspeakable happiness filled her chest, bringing a bright smile to her face as she walked forward to help him up.

But at the sight of her reaching for him, he scrambled back, his eyes wide and his hands out to ward her off. "Don't touch me!"

She looked down at her palms, still shimmering with water, and her cheeks burned. Hastily wiping her hands on her soaked skirt, she took a step back. "I'm sorry. I just wanted to—"

Moros sank onto his back, staring up at the moon. "Thank you for rescuing me."

His voice was so weary that it made her eyes sting. "What can I do to help?"

"Just leave me be for now," he said quietly. "See to the Mother."

Although she wanted to stay with him, she trudged to the door of the hut and knocked. "Baheera? It's safe."

The door swung open, and a naked, warm body dove into Aislin's arms. Baheera clung to her, sobbing and hysterical, and Aislin found herself stroking the new Mother's hair, shushing her like a child, frustration building with every passing moment. "Your people need you," Aislin finally said softly into the woman's ear. "They need to see you being strong. If you're scared and helpless, they'll feel that way, too. If you're brave and confident, it will bolster their courage."

"But th-those things," stammered Baheera, tears still streaming from her face. "Was that what killed my Mother?"

Aislin nodded. "I'm so sorry they invaded your realm."

"But how did they get in? How did they find us?" Baheera gulped for air as she stared at the bodies scattered along the shore of the lake and the steep steps up the hillside to the palace, Shade-Kere and Lucinae, joined in death. "They killed all of us!"

"No, they didn't." Even now, hundreds of Lucinae were swimming to the shores of the lake. Moros's orders had saved most of them. "And the survivors need their Mother now." Aislin grasped the young woman by her bare shoulders, looking into her puffy red-rimmed eyes. "Be their Mother, Baheera. This is your chance to lead."

She wiped the girl's tears with a strip of her torn skirt, which was still soaked with the water from the lake. At the feel of the life-saturated substance, Baheera seemed to brighten a bit. She sniffled and nodded, her chin rising as if in defiance. "You're right. They need me now." She pulled out of Aislin's grip and walked toward Magda, who was helping her fellow Lucinae out of the water, giving each one a warm hug as they emerged.

Aislin turned back to Moros, but he was gone. She scanned the shoreline for him, worry pulsing inside her. And then she saw him, trudging slowly up the steps toward the palace.

They'd won. They'd killed the Shade-Kere that threatened the realm and saved most of the Lucinae. Moros himself had ensured that Baheera, the new Mother, survived the onslaught. It was a victory. But as Aislin watched the exhausted slump of Moros's shoulders while he walked away from her, it felt for all the world like a defeat.

CHAPTER TWENTY-THREE

Moros collapsed on the bed in his quarters, wondering if there was a single part of him that didn't hurt. His throat and eyes burned from the acid fumes of that wretched lake. His head throbbed from the blows he had taken. His muscles ached—it felt like his limbs had been pulled out of joint. And he wasn't healing. He couldn't possibly heal, not in a miserable place like this. The very air was like poison to him, seeping into his blood and spreading weakness. This feeling . . . it was enough to make him crave the abstraction Nyx had chosen, having no physical form at all.

He had to get out of here.

But he wouldn't. Not until he'd gotten what he came for. And now, after he'd ensured that the Lucinae didn't lose a second Mother in a single day, it seemed like his best chance. He just had to gather the strength to go before Baheera and ask for it—too bad the thought of asking that petulant woman-child for anything was more painful than his head wound.

Aislin had made it through the battle. He let out a weak chuckle. She'd more than made it through—she'd come storming out of the palace, her shredded gown swirling around her legs, her shining hair the color of moonlight, blades in her hands and murder in her eyes. She'd cut through her enemies like he'd always known she could.

She'd saved him.

And then she'd almost killed him, coming wet and gorgeous from that lake, her smile so radiant that it felt like she'd wrapped her fingers around his heart. So alive. So alive that it *hurt*.

As she'd reached for him, he'd nearly been strangled by all the threads of his feelings. Desire for her. Fear of losing her. Certainty that he would; it was only a matter of hours, surely. Tenderness and adoration . . . the mere sight of her did that to him. And shame. He'd never felt this weak, and he was determined not to let her see it.

But she had. The anxious pity that flashed in her eyes before she'd gone off to comfort Baheera had made him want to retch.

A knock at the door pulled him from his brooding. "Jason?"

He closed his eyes as she said his name. "Aislin," he whispered, knowing she couldn't hear him. "What are you doing to me?" She was the only person he would truly miss if he let himself fade—an idea that was becoming more attractive with each passing second.

"I'm coming in," she said.

Curse these Lucinae for not putting locks on their doors. He pushed himself up to sit on the bed but had to squeeze his eyes shut as the room spun around him. Shade dust gritted between his teeth, making him crave water he couldn't have.

"Oh God," Aislin muttered.

He peered at her standing at the foot of his bed. "Indeed. But you don't have to be so formal, my dear."

She snorted, a surprisingly uncivilized noise from such a stately woman. She had changed her clothes and was now wearing a new Lucinae garment, this one a shimmering green skirt and a beaded top that hugged the swells of her breasts. He wondered if she realized how sheer the fabric was. And then he realized—not *every* part of him hurt.

"We have to get you back into the real world, as far from here as possible," she said.

"We need to meet with Baheera first. I believe I deserve a reward for my heroics, don't you?" He tried to sound confident and nonchalant, but nothing could cover the hoarse rasp in his voice.

She sat at the end of his bed. "Yes. I've asked her for that audience, and she's agreed to it, as soon as all her people are accounted for and the wounded are healed in the lake. She said they'd gather in her throne room."

"Well, I'd ask to clean myself off first, but I'm afraid that if I tried to take a shower, all you'd find afterward is a pile of bones."

She didn't laugh at his joke. "You don't have to pretend to be strong."

Annoyance streaked through him, and he swung his legs off the side of the bed and stood up, tensing against the dizziness that made him sway. "I'm in a realm where everyone believes me to be an abomination. No one would have been sorry to see me fall into that lake—"

"Wrong," she said softly.

He sighed and leaned against the wall, the cool stone a relief against his burning skin. His determination had been worn paperthin, and it was all that was keeping him from begging her to take him in her arms, to spread her body over his, to welcome him inside. He wanted her kisses and the silk of her touch. He wanted her softness, the lilt of her voice, the graceful flex of her limbs. He wanted her to comfort him, to make all of this all right.

He wanted her to love him.

"Weak," he whispered, his fingers curling into the cracks between the stones.

"What?"

"Nothing. It's just—my thoughts are a bit muddled." He lifted his head and stared at the wall. "I'll be fine once we leave."

While she waited, he stripped and wiped his body with a dry cloth, knocking away the dust and cleaning off as much of the blood as he could. He changed back into his slacks and button-down, unwilling to wear a ridiculous costume any longer. And then he walked by Aislin's side toward the throne room, hope growing with every step.

Baheera's subjects were huddled around her chaise, one oiling and braiding her hair, another feeding her bits of pineapple from a skewer, a third offering sips of wine. The rest were chattering among themselves. A hum of unhappiness and anxiety filled the air. Magda and Cavan, standing at the edge of the entourage, were the first to notice Aislin and Moros as they entered. Zayed sat in a chair nearby, the serious wounds he'd sustained in the battle now completely healed. He'd fought gallantly, actually, and for as long as he could, until Moros had shoved him toward the water. He was lucky to be alive. His gaze streaked over Aislin and then he looked away, as if ashamed.

Brave or not, you aren't worthy of her, Moros thought, pleased that the boy had finally realized it. He glanced at the woman next to him and then looked away just as quickly as Zayed had. She was blinding, almost too beautiful to look at. Perhaps no one was worthy of her.

They reached the base of the dais where Baheera sat, and Aislin bowed. Moros inclined his head. He was afraid that if he tried to bow, he might fall over.

Baheera held up a hand, refusing a piece of offered pineapple. "Charon. Welcome." Her yellow eyes strayed to Moros. "And Lord of the Kere."

"We'll be taking our leave of you soon," said Aislin. "I know you all will need time to recover from this tragedy."

"We'll be moving the realm," Baheera replied. "I don't feel safe here anymore."

Aislin nodded. "I understand completely."

Baheera waved her hand. "You may go."

Moros's stomach lurched. "We'll be happy to," he said. "But before we do, perhaps you could give us the blades. We need them to fight the Shade-Kere—and their masters—in the real world and the Veil. It's the best way to destroy them." And the only way to destroy Chaos.

Baheera gave him a wide-eyed look. "But by all reports, you easily destroyed at least fifty of those monsters yourself. It hardly seems like you need a blade to kill. Aren't you Death himself?"

"I have an enemy that is immune to my touch. And if he rises, no one will be safe."

Baheera's lip curled. "Am I safe now, my lord?" She gestured toward her subjects. "We've never been attacked in our realm. And now, the very day we welcome Death as a guest, the beasts invade. Coincidence?"

"Maybe not," said Aislin, "but they hunted and killed your Mother earlier today—it's more likely that they followed her body back here."

The new Mother's palm slapped down onto her bare thigh, and her cheeks went pink with rage. "How dare you blame this on my people, especially after everything we've been through!"

Moros's vision flashed red, and he closed his eyes. "I am terribly sorry for what you've been through, but I daresay it would have been much worse if the Charon and I hadn't been here."

"Small comfort," snapped Baheera. "We have nearly a hundred dead. I'm afraid that I cannot give you any weapons. To offer you instruments of death would be like spitting on their memories."

"What?" Fiery hatred coursed over Moros's skin. "I saved you. If it weren't for me, those Shades would have torn you and your lover apart."

Aislin cleared her throat. "I think what the Lord of the Kere is trying to say, Mother, is that he is honored to have been of service to you, and wishes he could have done more to save your people."

Moros's mouth clamped shut. He could feel the sharp edges of his fangs lengthening in his anger. At this moment, he craved Baheera's blood. But when Aislin's fingers touched his shoulder, so lightly, so gently, it cooled his temper momentarily. "Well said, Charon," he murmured. "I wish I could have done more."

Aislin laid her palm on his upper arm, just above the wound he'd sustained from the Blade of Life. "Both of us are eager to eliminate this threat and ensure that the Lucinae realm is never violated again. Our request for the weapons imbued with water from the lake is for that purpose only. It will benefit the Lucinae to give them to us."

"Will it?" Baheera asked. "Or will it only make your enemy more desperate to destroy us? Why must I take sides?"

"Mother," said Magda, her voice even, tightly controlled. "There are things worse than death."

Baheera's eyebrows nearly rose to her hairline. "Are you suggesting I accept this-this-this *thing* as an ally?" She waved her hand at Moros with clear disgust.

"This thing saved your life," he mumbled, his voice a little slurred. Suddenly his head felt too heavy for his shoulders.

Aislin's grip on his arm tightened, and she moved closer to him, as if afraid he would collapse, which left him feeling more pathetic than ever. And more vulnerable. He had to get out of this realm or he was going to fall on his face, right at Baheera's feet. He was sure it would give her great pleasure.

Magda was arguing in favor of giving Moros the blades now, but before she'd finished her sentence, Baheera shot to her feet, pointing a finger at her. "Sister, I think you've been corrupted," she said loudly. She gave Cavan a hurt look. "And I think our ambassador might be the source of this corruption. Perhaps I have been blind. Maybe we do need a new emissary. Or no emissary at all."

Magda shrank back at the threat as Cavan stood next to her, stone-faced. Moros was fairly sure that the man was boiling inside, but he'd learned long ago to remain stoic.

"I don't think it's fair to blame Cavan," Magda said.

"Oh, don't worry. I don't." Baheera's gaze swung to Aislin. "Look at his mistress, practically hanging on the Lord of Death like a pining lover. No wonder everyone's confused."

Suddenly, *every* gaze in the throne room was on Moros and Aislin, but her hand did not fall from his arm like he expected. "We are servants of fate," Aislin said steadily. "We are devoted to the same cause and fight the same enemy. We need those blades. Please, Mother. In the name of fate, in the name of our alliance and the help we provided tonight, give them to us. Even one would be a priceless gift and a source of eternal goodwill."

"I'm afraid I can't," said Baheera, sinking back onto her chaise. The Lucinae around her looked back and forth between their Mother and Moros, frowning. Of course, Moros thought, they had a different perspective. While Baheera had been quaking inside her hut, the rest of them had watched from the safety of the lake as Moros took on the Shade-Kere who had attacked them. But all remained silent and watchful as Baheera continued. "I will reconsider your request once our realm is safely moved and my traumatized subjects have recovered. Until then, I have too many concerns to spend another minute arguing with you." She turned to Zayed. "Escort them to the edge of the realm, please. The sooner they're out of our land, the better."

CHAPTER TWENTY-FOUR

They passed through the barrier between the Lucinae realm and the Veil, and as soon as they did, Moros gulped at the frigid air as if surfacing from underwater. Before her eyes, the wound at his temple began to heal, his skin knitting together neatly, leaving only blood-streaked skin. His slumped shoulders straightened, and he threw his head back, his gorgeous face emanating pure relief. She'd never been repulsed by his fangs or his claws, his fierce appearance in the Veil. But right now, he was so beautiful that her throat tightened. She'd been so worried.

But when he spoke, his voice was flat with despair. "Only a few hours until our summit with the Keepers."

She shifted her garment bag on her shoulder. Zayed had been courteous enough to collect it for her before escorting them off the premises. "What should we do?"

He stared at her for a moment, and then he ran his hands over his face and through his ebony hair, which fell across his brow a moment later. "At the risk of sounding like Declan, I think we're fucked." He let out a weary chuckle. "It sounds slightly less ridiculous when he says it."

She touched his elbow. "Take us back to your penthouse. You need to wash off and change, and then we'll talk."

"All right," he murmured, and then he pulled them through space and worlds, materializing in his living room. He walked away from her briskly, and a moment later she heard the water in his shower switch on.

She sank onto his couch, her iridescent skirt fluttering in the breeze from his open patio door. After a few minutes staring into space, she pulled her phone from her bag and made a few calls, surmising that the world hadn't fallen apart just yet. And that was good, because she sensed that the Lord of the Kere was about to. She'd never imagined anyone as strong and confident could look so completely defeated, but after what he'd endured in the Lucinae realm, there was no other way to describe him. His body was healing, but his mood . . . it was as if the fight had been drained from him. Like he was giving up. And that was unacceptable.

Moros finished his shower and went into his closet to change, then emerged barefoot, smelling faintly of sandalwood, wearing slacks and an undershirt. He sat down next to her on the couch. "Any brilliant ideas?"

The nonchalance in his tone elicited her fury. "Stop it," she snapped. "Stop sounding so detached. I know you care what happens."

He sighed. "If you think Baheera despises me, that's nothing compared to the Keeper of Hell. I believe he's reserved a special torture chamber in the fiery pits, just waiting for my arrival. He's probably sharpening his knives as we speak."

"So fight," she said. "Stop acting like it's a foregone conclusion."

"Nothing lasts forever," he said wearily. "Even order. Even fate."

"But it doesn't have to end today!"

His eyes closed. "I never said I wouldn't fight, Aislin. But if I let myself fade to abstraction, not only would it make a lot of people very happy, it would cut my siblings off at the pass. Without me, there would be no point to their efforts, no common enemy."

She rose to her knees on the couch and took his face in her hands. "Stop this."

When he opened his eyes, the sorrow there was a sword through her heart. "It might be best for everyone."

"What about your Kere?"

"They'll be free. I'll return their souls, and they can move on to meet their final fate, whatever they've reaped. Again, don't you think that would be best?"

"No." It was so wrong that she could barely breathe. Cacia might never recover from the loss of Eli, and that was just the start of it.

His gaze traced her brow, her cheeks. His fingers rose to caress her face. "Why, my dear? Would you miss me?"

She put her hand over his, holding it to her skin. "I would. But I won't be here, remember?" She swallowed the lump in her throat. "And I was hoping . . ." She gritted her teeth and willed tears away. "I was hoping I could depend on you to be an ally to my family when I'm gone."

"I'm not so sure they'd want me as an ally." His voice was gentle, but he had looked away.

It was as if he'd built a wall around himself and she was banging her fists against it, unable to get through. This wasn't working. She needed a new strategy. *You have nothing to lose, so tell him the truth.*

"I'm scared," she whispered. "And I don't want to spend the last hours of my life feeling this way."

His gaze returned to hers.

"I need you, Jason," she said. "I know you want to let go, but I need you to hold on to me until the end comes." She didn't try to keep the tears inside this time. "You're the only one who can do this for me." The only true partner she'd ever had. The only man who had ever matched her in every way. "I know I've only been a part of a moment of your existence, but somehow you've become the center of mine."

Something in his fathomless eyes shifted, like a diamond turning in the light. Slowly, he drew her face to his, and the touch of his lips made her heart speed. The kiss was tender, fragile, and precious, like a question instead of a demand. Aislin's fingers slid into his hair, her need for him growing by the second. The mountain of lost plans and wishes, all the years she'd thought she had, faded into the background as she anchored herself entirely to the now. She was with him now. They were together now. No matter how he felt, he was willing to soothe this ache. Her silent wish was that, in doing so, he would remember his will to win, his hunger for life.

She slid her leg over his, straddling him, deepening their kiss as her body pressed him into the couch. His fingertips traced her curves, traveling along her back until he undid the buttons holding her shirt closed. He tugged the flimsy fabric from her shoulders and down her arms, baring her breasts. And then he broke their kiss, his tongue hot as it trailed along her throat, across her collarbone. She gasped as she felt his teeth against her skin, and arched her back as he took one of her breasts in his mouth. His hands closed over her hips and pushed her down against the hard length of his erection. She ground against it as he sucked and teased, kindling an inferno inside her.

Her desperation growing, she tugged at the voluminous fabric of her skirt, which was folded around her legs. Jason sensed her urgency, and his warm hand skimmed under the cloth, caressing her thigh, inching upward with agonizing slowness. His fingertips patiently stroked and swirled, making her squirm. When he realized she wasn't wearing anything under the skirt, his breath fanned hot against her chest. He cursed quietly and pulled her mouth to his as his fingers slid along the seam of her body.

Their tongues tangled while she pushed her hands under his shirt, eager to feel the heat of his skin against hers once more. This was so unlike their first encounter, which had felt full of anger and defiant challenge. She didn't want to punish him for imagined crimes, for her vulnerability, for her fear of her fascination with him—now she wanted him to crave life again, to take what he needed from her. He raised his arms so she could pull his shirt over his head, and his eyes fell shut as her palms stroked down his chest.

His touch was tender as he slid his fingers into her, making her whimper. Her hands dropped to his waist, and she unfastened his belt, his button, his zipper, releasing his hot, silky cock from the confines of his pants. He groaned as she lowered her hips, as her slick, tender flesh slid over his, coating him with her desire. His eyes opened, and his forehead touched hers, his thumb stroking her cheekbone. Though he looked about to speak, instead, he took hold of his shaft and guided it into her.

She sank onto him, biting her lip at the feeling of intense fullness that only made her want more. Their eyes met as they began to move together, a deep, unhurried rhythm. Part of her wanted to cry, knowing this was probably the last time, and part of her wanted to rejoice, because it felt so essential. That elation overcame her, and she wrapped her arms around his neck, bowing her head over his to kiss his brow, his temple, his closed eyelids—each touch of her lips an offering, a plea. Her fingers tangled in his black hair when his hands closed over her breasts, possessive and firm. He pressed his face to her neck, his breath wafting across her collarbone, his arm looping around her waist as she took all of him inside. She could feel him pushing at her boundaries, owning every inch of her. She was panting, sweat beaded across her skin, but it still wasn't enough.

Perhaps he sensed it, too, because he twisted with her in his arms, laying her back on the couch. She hooked her toes in the waist of his slacks and skimmed them off his legs. Her gaze was full of wonder as she stared at him, naked and perfect above her.

Braced on one hand, he hooked his arm under her leg and thrust so deep that she cried out, pleasure skating along the delicious edge of pain. Her skirt spread along the cushions, she wrapped her legs around his hips as he bucked against her, a frenzied need sweeping through her body. Jason's head dipped low to claim her mouth again, and she moaned as his tongue thrust in time with his body. Each time he buried himself inside her, his grip on her tightened, as if he needed more.

Her hands stroked along his back, pulling him in, offering him everything she was, everything she had, as long as he kept up this sweet assault. When he pulled away to nuzzle her throat, she whispered his first name. "I never should have let you call me that," he said as he grabbed her hair and drove himself deeper inside her, making her whimper. "Now I'll crave the sound of it forever."

She held him close as a tear slipped from her eye. "I'm glad," she whispered. "It means you'll remember me."

He took her face in his hands. "Aislin." He was deep inside her, the center of her awareness. She stared up at him as he brushed his lips over hers. "I couldn't forget you if I wanted to. You are a part of me."

He leaned down and kissed the salty tear from her cheek, then began to move again, slow at first, then long, hard thrusts, each one more fierce than the last. Aislin lifted her hips to greet each incursion, to feel the slide of his shaft into her aching, taut body. The pleasure spiraled higher with each collision, each grind, and when he nipped at the junction of her neck and shoulder, she held his head there, craving his teeth as he rocked against her. He was everywhere, unrelentingly hot, his weight pushing her into the couch, his mouth claiming her skin, his body unwinding her. His heart thundered against her chest, and she knew hers held the same beat, ferocious and defiant. Unwilling to stop or fall silent.

He'd awakened something ravenous in her, but it was too intense to last. Every muscle was straining for him, tight and pleading, demanding more. She shattered all at once, the ecstasy raising her up and sending her falling as she cried out his name again, this time in complete surrender.

CHAPTER TWENTY-FIVE

Aislin was gorgeous as she came, her eyes shut but her lips parted. She was emitting the most irresistible moans as he continued to pump his hips. His jaw was clenched—he wasn't ready for this to end.

It doesn't have to end today, she'd said. How right she had been, but it had taken her touch to remind him of the truth. The weakness and pain that had become his constant companion in the last few days fell away when he was inside her. It was as if her body had been made to undo him, her mind to challenge him, her will to inspire him, her spirit to strengthen him. And he couldn't help the thought that he was meant to do the same for her.

I know I've only been a part of a moment of your existence, but somehow you've become the center of mine.

She'd unraveled him with those words. He'd been on the verge of letting go, of bowing to time and the weight of others' hatred, of disappearing just so he didn't have to deal with any of it ever again. And then she'd said that to him, and made his existence worth fighting for.

I'm going to save you.

That was what he wanted to say. But simple words spoken aloud didn't seem like enough, so instead that promise drenched every kiss as he made love to her, echoing through every breath and moan, every thrust of his body into hers. No matter what he had to sacrifice, or what pain he had to endure, he would make sure Aislin was safe and whole.

She spasmed around him, letting out soft cries as his own plea-sure hunted him down and stole his rhythm and sanity. He fought it hard, lost in the relentless clutch of her body, the sweet scent of her arousal. If he held her any tighter, he'd damage her. As it was, he was probably hurting her, but her hands were woven into his hair, and her mouth was pressed against his ear, keeping him close. The need for release grew inside him like a living thing, taking control, until his body was moving on its own, unable to slow or stop even if he'd commanded it to. Aislin was clinging to him, still shuddering in the aftershocks of her own orgasm, when he lost his grip. The feeling crashed over him, so sudden and consuming that he was blind to everything else. *Of course* he would save her. The two of them would go on forever, just like this, and no one would be strong enough to stop them. No one could defy fate, and this could be nothing else.

He let go inside her, and she wound herself around him, sob-bing as she felt him come. His eyes burned with the absolute per-fection of the moment. He buried his face in her hair and held on as all his muscles contracted and then began to loosen. And as they did, just like before, that sense of well-being slipped away with it, as did the confidence that had made him so sure he could protect her. Now, as he stroked her hair and panted against her skin, it was replaced with desperation, a raw determination held together at the edges by his adoration of this woman, the only one who had ever touched his heart, who had ever understood him for what he was, who had ever stood by him as an equal—despite the cost.

He brushed his lips over the beating pulse on the side of her neck and pressed his fingers over the spot, feeling her warm blood just beneath the surface. "I'm not going to let you go," he murmured.

He lifted his head to find her smiling, though her pale eyes were shiny with tears. "I was hoping you'd say that," she said quietly.

He arched an eyebrow. "Was this all part of your master plan?"

She grinned. "Of course."

He laughed, astounded at the bright happiness he felt at the sight of her smile. "Well played, my dear."

Her fingertips slid down his cheek and traced along his jaw. "Never has the prize been more compelling," she said.

Her tone was light, but her gaze said everything. *She loves me.* She didn't have to say it out loud for him to know in his bones that it was true. He kissed her tenderly, lost in an ocean of gratitude and wonder. They stayed like that for seconds, minutes, unwilling to relinquish the closeness.

Aislin's phone buzzed from somewhere on the floor. She groaned and pressed her face to his chest. "No."

He shifted, sliding out of her as he turned to look at the device. "It's Declan."

Her fingers dug into his skin as he tried to pull away. "We can't hide here forever," he said gently, even as he relished her resistance. "Not if we want to experience anything like the last hour ever again." He ducked his head, finding her mouth and kissing her deeply. "And I, for one, want to make sure that happens." Even the thought was making him hard again.

"Me too," she said with a sigh as he shoved himself up, needing to get away from her before he bowed to the temptation. Her gaze moved down his body like a caress, and it nearly broke his will—but then her phone began to buzz again.

She answered it as Moros went down the hall to clean himself up and change his clothes. The summit was less than two hours away. The odds were stacked against them—with the string of catastrophes over the last day, the anger of the Keepers would be kindled, ready to burn. His only hope was to direct it at the right source, to enlist their help in defeating the enemies of fate. They hated to interfere with earthly matters, but perhaps they hated disorder even more. Two thousand years ago, it had led them to make concessions, but with the forging of that treaty had come a resentment that had smoldered ever since. Maybe his sisters would be willing to appear at his side, to show the Keepers the damage Eris and Apate had done. They'd never left the weaving room, so dedicated were they to their work, but now they might have no choice.

Besides, he'd been gone for nearly a day, and he'd left them in bad shape. He was eager to check on them, to make sure they were all right. He went back out to his living room to find, sadly, Aislin was clothed once more, this time in the black pantsuit she'd worn to the Lucinae realm. She looked temptingly disheveled, her normally neat hair mussed and her lips still swollen and flushed.

"I need to go back to Psychopomps before the summit," she said. "I want to let the board know about the Shade-Kere attack on the Lucinae—they need to hear it from me and not Baheera."

He nodded. "And I need to check on my sisters. Shall we meet in the Veil? Your Scope will take you to the entrance to the Keepers' earthly meeting place."

She looked up at him and placed her hands on his chest. "Which compels me to mention, is it possible one of the Fates is helping Eris?"

"The thought has occurred to me. But they risk their own existence by doing so. None of us can survive if the fabric of fate is completely destroyed."

She frowned. "Could Eris or Apate affect them like they affect the rest of us?"

"No, it wouldn't work like that."

She looked unconvinced. "Grudge and resentment are powerful, though."

Moros thought of Atropos, how her love had slowly turned to hate. "Perhaps you're right," he murmured. "I don't want to believe it, but maybe that has blinded me to the truth."

"Could one of them have removed souls from your trunk, allowing Eris to influence the chosen Ker? Eli was under Eris's influence—and then, very suddenly, was not."

Moros remembered Eli contorting in midair and falling to the ground at his feet. One moment, he'd been free of Moros's influence and ready to kill, and the next, he'd been at Moros's mercy. "I assumed it was one of my other siblings."

"Assuming they could somehow enter your domain without being noticed by at least one of the Fates, would Eris, Apate, or Nemesis have recognized which soul belonged to which Ker?"

Moros gritted his teeth. "No. Probably not." Aislin was asking all the questions he had skimmed over in his mind, but it was time for him to drill down to the truth. "Atropos has made it clear how deeply she resents me." He shook his head. "I just never believed she would destroy herself—and her sisters—to get to me." It made his heart hurt, and his blood boil. "But if she has, I think she'll be coming with me to our summit." He would throw her down before the Keeper of Hell, let her get a taste of the Keeper's blades.

Aislin laid her cool palm on his cheek. "Be careful." She gave him a small smile. "I need you."

He laid his forehead on hers and pulled them through the Veil, reappearing in her living room. "I'll see you in an hour?"

She rose on her tiptoes and kissed him. "I'll be there."

He closed his eyes, drinking in the feel and scent of her for one more precious moment. And then he willed himself back into the cold gray world where he was born, preparing himself to face yet another betrayal.

CHAPTER TWENTY-SIX

A islin showered and changed quickly, her thoughts abuzz with plans and worries. Declan had called to tell her that Shade-Kere had been spotted within Boston again. Not en masse, just random sightings in the area around Psychopomps, followed by quick disappearances. It made her wonder what they would do next. Declan wasn't wondering—he was certain they planned to attack Galena, and he was back at her lab just in case. Aislin hadn't mentioned the appearance of the Shade-Kere to Moros, because she'd wanted him to be focused as he went to check on his sisters. She had a bad feeling that yet another person he should have been able to trust had turned against him. She would make sure Galena was safe.

In fact, she planned to make sure all of them were safe, no matter who she had to piss off to do it. She placed a call and left a voice mail, providing very clear instructions for what she wanted, and then broke the time-honored rules and used her Scope to travel quickly through the Veil, stepping through a portal into the fifteenth floor of Psychopomps. The usually bustling building was running on a skeleton crew—all the human employees had been told to stay home, as they were the most vulnerable to attack.

Family members were staffing the main desks and monitoring the markets in addition to ferrying souls as necessary.

Aislin watched from the Veil as Galena Margolis hunched over a screen in her new lab, her long dark-blonde hair pulled up into a sloppy ponytail. She absently toyed with the Scope around her neck as she tapped at the display. Tamasin and Nader stood nearby, their red eyes zeroing in on Aislin the moment she appeared. "Anything unusual?" she asked.

Tamasin, her mass of braids pulled back from her face, her brown eyes intense, shook her head. "She's been extremely happy ever since they got that interface up and running for her this afternoon. It's kept her busy."

Aislin read Tamasin easily: she was glad Galena was back in the lab instead of on the street, risking her safety to deal with the Shade-Kere.

Aislin looked around Galena's new lab, all gray in the Veil. It was cluttered with boxes large and small, and a few pieces of equipment the purpose of which she could only guess. "It's coming together quickly."

"Declan is quite determined," said Nader, his olive skin a shade paler than usual. He'd seemed subdued and anxious since he had lost control of himself and attacked his partner—and Galena herself. "Dr. Margolis has been very restless—she hadn't been able to work in days."

"Declan seems to understand the way her mind works," Tamasin said quietly, looking toward the elevator bays, where Aislin's brother stood, a tablet in his hand, apparently checking through an inventory of recently delivered supplies. "He also believes in what she's doing."

"We all should," Aislin muttered, guilt slicing through her once more as she watched Galena use her fingertip to scrawl something on the screen. "Thank you for guarding her."

Tamasin and Nader each took a step closer to Galena as the renewed weight of their responsibility seemed to hit them once more. "No one will harm her," said Nader.

Aislin gave him a smile and stepped through her Scope, entering the real world right behind Galena's desk. The woman spun around as she heard Aislin's heels hit the floor. "I thought you might be Cacy."

"Why?" Aislin asked as she clipped her Scope to the chain around her neck.

"She and Eli are coming over here. With the Shade sightings, they're feeling a little overprotective."

Aislin pulled her phone from her pocket and fired off a text to her guards, telling them to come to the fifteenth floor as soon as they were able. "It seems wise. I'd like you to be safe."

Galena gave her a flickering, fragile smile. "I'm grateful that you're protecting my ability to work."

Aislin met her eyes. "It's not just that. My brother loves you. You're part of my family now. And I'm sorry I didn't provide you with more protection from the very beginning. It's a mistake for which I will never forgive myself."

"But I forgive you," Declan said quietly from behind her.

Aislin turned to see him leaning against a pile of plastic crates containing various lab equipment. "You do?"

He nodded as he moved to stand by Galena's side. She leaned back against him and smiled at Aislin. "I do, too. I know you were under tremendous pressure, and in the end you made the right decision."

Aislin folded her arms over her middle and looked at the floor, wrestling her feelings back into order. "Thank you both. It means a lot." She was going to do her best to return from this summit, but it seemed entirely possible she might not, and she wanted to leave with things resolved between herself and her siblings.

She also planned to leave them with the means to survive.

Declan put his hand on her shoulder and squeezed. "You all right?"

She nodded. "I need to leave for the summit in a few minutes. I just wanted to check with Rosaleen and fill her in on a few things."

Eli and Cacia appeared in the center of the lab, both wearing their uniforms. Cacia grinned when she saw Aislin and Declan standing together. "How was the Lucinae realm?"

Aislin offered a tight smile in return. "The new Mother has much to learn."

Cacia tilted her head. "That good, huh?"

"That good." Aislin looked back and forth between her brother and sister. They were so strong-willed, so powerful in their own right, and she was ashamed not to have told them how proud she was of them before now. As she saw them standing with their chosen mates, who were just as strong and brave, she felt a spark of hope light in her chest. "It's part of the reason I'm here, actually. If, for any reason, I don't return from my summit with the Keepers tonight, I need you to do something for me."

CHAPTER TWENTY-SEVEN

Moros braced himself as he watched Atropos limping back and forth under the unraveled tapestry. She had her sickle in her hand and was swishing it through the air. She was barefoot, and her black hair hung in tangled waves down her back. Her eyes glowed red as she looked up at the frayed, holey cloth.

She had tended the threads of destiny, the fabric of fate, for millennia. She'd had all that time to nurture a grudge against Moros, too. And now they would have a reckoning. Gathering his determination and shoring up his aching heart, he stepped through the Veil into the weaving room.

Atropos spun around as soon as she heard his soft footfalls on the travertine floor. "Empty-handed again," she said hoarsely. "I should have known."

"*Did* you know?" he asked quietly as he approached.

Her brows lowered. "I knew I couldn't rely on you."

"When did you decide I was your enemy, Atropos? I saw you as my sister."

Her face twisted with anger. "Are you really so blind? Two thousand years ago, you made a decision that hurt us. You refused to Mark the doomed, and you Marked for death those who should have lived. You frayed this fabric intentionally, all because you wanted freedom and status in this world."

He spread his arms. "It was a last resort after centuries of pleading with the Keepers. I told you of my plan from the start—including the promise that I would never push it past the point of no return. And I offered to share any wealth I gained with you!"

"I have no use for gold! We're trapped here by our duties."

He sighed. "Where are the others?" It was eerily silent here under the permanent stars, when usually he could hear the sounds of Lachesis working the loom, measuring out the thread as she wove it into the fabric, the clicks of the spinning wheel as Clotho spun the thread of life from the shimmering wool that rose up from her bottomless basket.

"How would I know?" Atropos snapped, folding an arm over her middle and wincing as a few shimmering threads of the fabric—vibrant lives ended far too soon—unraveled above her head. Moros felt the pain, too. Somewhere out in the world, the Shade-Kere had taken a few more victims. He pushed his worry for Aislin aside for the moment—she had more than proven that she knew how to take care of herself.

His eyes met his sister's. "Have you done something to Clotho and Lachesis?"

Atropos's gaze flared with rage. "Have *I* done something to them? Have you lost your mind?"

He began to walk toward the loom, his heart stirring with fear for the other two. He called their names but received only silence in return. "You had me fooled for so long," he said.

"I have never hidden my anger for you. I have never pretended you were anything other than a selfish bastard. And now I will meet my end hating you with even more passion than I do now!"

"Have you done this?" he roared, gesturing at the fabric, the gray threads scattered across the floor, the silent loom. His claws grew from his fingertips, sharp and brutal. "Have you been my enemy this whole time?"

He stalked toward Atropos, who widened her stance and raised her sickle. "Come any closer and I swear I'll strike."

"Please do," he said, baring his fangs. His thoughts were bloody crimson, so full of betrayal and rage that he had room for nothing else. "You've been helping Eris and Apate. You stole the souls of my Kere so they could influence them. You warned them that I was going after the Blade so they could get there first. You hurt all of us just to spite me."

She swung her sickle at his face, but he caught her wrist and twisted it out of her grip, hurling it far out of her reach before kicking her back. She fell and skidded across the floor, arms and legs sprawled. Her arms shaking, she sat up to face him again. "You are such a fool," she said quietly, a tear slipping from her eye. "But I've been a fool as well."

"Agreed," said a voice behind him.

Before he had a chance to turn, blazing agony seared through his chest. His breath burst from him in a spray of blood, and he raked helplessly at the air as he fell to his knees. His head lolled as his strength failed, and he opened his eyes to see a shining blade protruding from his chest. Thin and glowing and unmistakable—the Blade of Life.

Someone planted a foot onto his back and wrenched the sword from his body. He fell forward, his head slamming into the tile. His faltering heart thundered in his ears as his vision blurred. And then fingers curled into his hair and wrenched his head up.

"Thanks for disarming Atropos," Clotho said, her soft, round face in front of his. She was deeply pale, with dark circles beneath her eyes, but her mouth was set as she pressed the Blade beneath his chin. "How does it feel?" she whispered, her voice a broken thread of pain.

His breath wheezed from his throat, which burned as blood filled his lungs. His mind throbbed with disbelief. "You . . . ," he managed to moan. She was the gentlest. The most loving. The one who had believed in him.

Her eyes narrowed. "Thousands of years in slavery changes a person," she said quietly.

"Lachesis," he whispered, worry surfacing within the bloody ocean of his pain.

"What's going on?" At the sound of Lachesis's voice, Clotho released Moros's hair and he fell to the tile again, staring as his frail blonde sister appeared next to Atropos.

Run, he thought, willing her to flee as Clotho approached her, the Blade of Life in her grip. His blood slid in rivers down its thin blade, spattering the floor with fat drops. Clotho's steps were unsteady; she might have betrayed them, but her plotting had weakened her, too, and if Lachesis and Atropos were determined enough, they could escape.

As Clotho's arm rose, bearing that deadly blade, Moros dragged himself forward, reaching for the dirty hem of her gown, desperate to protect the others.

But then Lachesis smiled. "You got started without me."

Atropos moaned and tried to scramble back as Lachesis accepted the Blade from Clotho. With it hanging from her grasp, she turned to her black-haired sister. "You could have joined us," she said. "It didn't have to end this way."

And then she lifted the Blade with both hands and drove it into Atropos's chest. Moros cried out with grief and pain as Atropos screamed, writhing beneath the shredded, shimmering fabric she'd dedicated her existence to preserving. Tears stung his eyes as he watched Lachesis twist the Blade, knowing he could do nothing to help Atropos, knowing he had failed her one final time.

Clotho sank down next to him, swaying with weakness. Her hand rubbed along his back, deceptively loving—yet another betrayal. "It will be over soon," she murmured. "It's going to happen any minute." Her gaze strayed along the sagging tapestry. "I want to watch it fall apart."

Lachesis ripped the sword from Atropos's twitching body, and Moros jerked with the molten agony of watching her suffer.

Lachesis's eyes met his. "Eris wanted to be here for this, but she's hard at work in Boston, I'm afraid." She took a faltering step toward him, her smile ghostly. "Once she's done, she'll return to retrieve the Blade. But we wanted Chaos to feel welcome in the world, so she's going to send a message that he can feel as he regains awareness."

Moros swiped weakly at her as she and Clotho turned him onto his back. His body slid through the growing pool of his blood. He was drowning in it.

"Look up at it," Clotho crooned. "You can watch with us. My children have almost completed their task."

Dread welled up, only enhancing his pain and weakness. "You created the Shade-Kere," he breathed.

Clotho smiled. "Rylan Ferry was my first creation. Eris brought him to us as a present for our cooperation, and I couldn't resist." Her brown eyes shone with victory. "And the Shade-Kere were actually his idea. He and Eris have been capturing Shades and bringing them to me for days. They really helped speed this process along. Much more efficient than focusing solely on Galena Margolis."

"You're killing yourselves," he said, blood trickling from his mouth.

"Yes," Lachesis said gently, falling to her knees, the Blade of Life held in her trembling hand. "There was no other way to be free. You were too dedicated to the treaty, to your freedom, to your own life, to notice the pain we were in." She gestured clumsily at Atropos, who'd gone still now, her eyes open and empty. "It's really for the best. She was so miserable. We all were. Except for you."

Lachesis leaned down and kissed his clammy forehead, her soft touch more painful than anything he'd yet experienced. Her platinum hair was the exact color of Aislin's, and Moros thought of the Charon, wishing he could have held her one more time, hoping she understood how hard he'd tried.

Lachesis's gaze traced his face, and a half smile pulled at her lips. "You're thinking of Aislin Ferry, aren't you? Of course you are. At a time like this, how could you not?" He shuddered as her hand stroked through his hair. "The agony of knowing you'll never be with her must be truly terrible." Her smile grew. "And it's a punishment you've more than earned."

He blinked up at her in shock. His chest heaved as he tried in vain to move his limbs, but they defiantly refused to obey. His sister's eyes glinted with malice. "Oh, yes. I know something you don't. I've known it for a century, ever since she was born."

Known what? If he could have, he would have begged her to tell him. But all he could do was stare. His blood was on fire, burning him from the inside out, turning his thoughts black.

Lachesis laid her hand along the side of his face, and he wished he had the power to destroy her. Hatred surged along his bones as she said, "Should I tell you? I don't want to increase your pain."

She already had. The pressure inside his chest was immense and jagged, carving panic and fear along his ribs. *Aislin.*

Lachesis patted his cheek. "I think I'll wait for the right moment. I don't want us to be interrupted." She glanced up at the tapestry. "I've been waiting so long for this. I wouldn't miss it for the world."

Horror choked Moros. He couldn't disappear, couldn't get up, couldn't breathe. Something was going to happen in Boston. Something devastating.

And he was going to be forced to watch.

CHAPTER TWENTY-EIGHT

Aislin had just gone over her plan with Declan, Cacia, Eli, and Galena when Rylan appeared in the center of the lab. Nader and Tamasin materialized on either side of him instantly, ready to leap, but Rylan raised his arms. "Hear me out," he shouted. "You'll regret it forever if you don't."

Normally, the Kere would look to Moros for leadership, but as he wasn't here, their warrior gazes found Aislin. "Keep an eye on him," she said quietly as her heart pounded. "But let him speak."

The last time she'd seen Rylan, he was giving her up to be tortured. Bile rose in her throat at the memory of what had happened next. "I'm surprised you're brave enough to come here," she said.

Rylan, his dark hair disheveled and his suit coat unbuttoned, opened his mouth to reply but seemed to choke on his words.

Eli moved between Galena and Aislin. "Say the word," he muttered to Aislin. "One word is all it takes." Heat and violence poured from him in waves.

"Tamasin, enter the Veil to make sure we're not being stalked," Aislin said. "Stay close to Galena."

The Ker disappeared, and Rylan focused on Aislin. "You think I'm here for Galena."

"No, I think you're here as a distraction," Aislin replied.

"You're wrong," he said in a low voice. "I'm here to help you."

"Fuck off," said Declan, his fists clenched as he took a protective half step in front of his wife.

Rylan grimaced. "I know you have zero reason to believe me, but it's true."

"After everything you've done, why would you help us?" snapped Cacia. "You don't care whether we live or die."

Rylan's forehead glistened with sweat. He was leaning forward, and his broad shoulders were hunched with tension. "I need . . . to tell you . . ."

Every cell of Aislin's body was on high alert. "Something you've been told not to tell us?"

He let out an agonized breath and nodded. "It's . . ." He shook his head.

"Something's going to happen," Aislin said, looking at Declan and Cacia.

Declan's ice-blue glare didn't soften. "He's the ultimate gameplayer, Aislin. Have Nader and Eli take him out before he can spring whatever trap he's set."

Rylan's eyes glowed red. "That would be a mistake."

"It was a mistake to ever trust you in the first place," Cacia spat out. Rylan had filled the role Aislin had always wanted to play in Cacia's life, and his betrayal had probably hurt their youngest sister the most.

"I want to atone for that," Rylan said, his tone pleading.

"Bullshit," shouted Declan. "You've already sold your dark, twisted soul, Ry. You can't get it back now."

"Stop arguing and let him talk," Aislin barked, throwing her arms out to keep Eli and Declan from moving any closer to Rylan.

"You believe me," Rylan said, his voice raspy. "I can tell that you do."

"Are you here to warn us?" she asked him.

He looked like he was straining against invisible bonds. "They made me promises when I said I'd help them destroy Moros," he finally said, every word an effort. "They promised!"

"Let me guess," Aislin said quietly. "They lied?"

He nodded, his handsome face a mask of agony. "They said we would be left alone."

"The Ferrys?" Cold dread crept along her skin, making her shiver.

Rylan nodded again, his cheek twitching. "They promised to leave us alone!"

"Is it an attack?" Aislin's voice was ringing and sharp. "Are the Shade-Kere coming?"

Rylan opened his mouth to speak, but all that came out was a choked groan. He let out a roar of frustration, his fingers curling into claws.

"Is it about to happen?" she asked. "How much time do we have?"

Rylan's eyes were bulging, and his face was turning red.

Declan looked around as if he expected Shades to materialize in the lab.

"Can they enter buildings?" Galena asked in a small voice. "Regular Shades don't, right?"

"These can show up anywhere," said Aislin, watching her eldest brother wrestle with his own words. It seemed like an unseen hand had closed over his throat, silencing him. "Is that it, Rylan? Are they about to attack?"

"We have to get you out of here," Declan muttered to Galena.

"I'm okay with that," she whispered. "It sounds like everyone might be safer if I weren't here."

"Agreed," said Aislin. "Go."

The two of them quickly stepped through their Scopes as Rylan's face contorted. "The Shades aren't the threat," he finally managed to say.

"What's going to happen, Ry?" yelled Cacia. "Come on!"

"He can't," said Aislin.

"His master has commanded him to keep his mouth shut," said Eli. "Whoever took his soul told him he couldn't tell us."

Rylan closed his eyes in obvious relief, but it only scared Aislin more. "But whatever it is, it was heinous enough that even Rylan couldn't stomach it."

His eyes opened, and he stared at her. "Please," he whispered. "I can't say more. Please."

Aislin bowed her head and stared at the floor, her thoughts whirling. Rylan was trying to warn them, and his continued presence now that Galena had disappeared made her think the scientist wasn't the target this time. Rylan's conscience was black, and yet he was risking everything to be here. "It's Psychopomps," she said suddenly, taking a step back and looking around. "Something's going to—"

The entire building shuddered as a muted explosion went off below their feet. Her eyes met Rylan's. "I'm sorry," he whispered, then disappeared.

Aislin felt a wave of dizziness as the world swayed in front of her. "They're bringing down the building," she yelped. "We have to get people out!"

Another explosion knocked her feet out from under her, and a roaring filled her ears. With fumbling fingers, she reached for her Scope, and turned to see Cacia doing the same. Eli was already gone. "Can you take the top floors?" Aislin asked. "I'll evacuate the lower ones."

Cacia's eyes were round with terror, but she nodded and stepped through her Scope. Aislin pulled wide her own window to the Veil a second later and stepped into the cold gray faltering world. Even here, they weren't safe. She opened a portal down to the executive floor and stepped through. The ceiling rained plaster as she ran down the hall screaming, "Go through your Scope now! Get to safety!"

Hugh poked his head out of his office. "What happened? It felt like an earthquake."

"It's the building. Don't bother to take the stairs—go through your Scope. Is Rosaleen here?"

Hugh already had his window to the Veil open—it was clear he had no intention of helping to warn anyone. "She said she had a meeting on the eighth floor," he mumbled just before he pulled the Scope over his head and disappeared.

Aislin entered the Veil again and then opened a portal to the eighth floor, the home of their domestic banking operation. And as soon as she pulled open her Scope to step into the real world, she had to close her eyes against the roiling heat that greeted her. The air was hazy with smoke despite the spray of the sprinkler system, and the cold droplets rained on her skin as she closed the window to the Veil. "Anyone here?"

She covered her mouth with her sleeve as she started to cough. The smoke became thicker and the heat became searing as she jogged past cubicle after cubicle. The lights flickered and then went off. In the darkness, Aislin fumbled toward the conference room, and then her toe hit something and she tripped, crashing to her knees. Her hand shot out and found the obstacle—a body. It took only a moment to find the Scope attached to the person's neck. Holding her breath, Aislin wrenched her own Scope wide and wrestled the person's legs, hips, torso, and head into the Veil.

It was Rosaleen, her nose and mouth smudged with soot, her silver hair soaked with sweat, her eyes swollen red and streaming. But she was a Ferry, and so she was alive. Aislin opened an intra-Veil portal to an apartment she owned in New York City, the safest place she could think of, and yanked Rosaleen through. She kissed her aunt's forehead and willed her to live, and then she returned to Psychopomps. Rosaleen had gone for a meeting, and so she couldn't have been alone on the eighth floor.

This time, she stayed in the Veil, searching for shadowy silhouettes as the ground shuddered beneath her feet. After a few minutes, she found two more people who had been overcome by smoke, in the hallway near the conference room. By the time she'd gotten them to safety, she was drenched with sweat and her lungs were burning, but she couldn't stop herself from going back in. This was her empire, and anyone inside this building was her responsibility. Satisfied that she'd cleared the banking floor, she flipped her Scope and opened another portal, this time to the finance floor just above it. She stepped through to the real world once more, relieved that the smoke wasn't nearly as thick. But as soon as she began to walk up the hallway, a massive explosion caused the floor to heave. Aislin collided with a wall and fell backward, smacking her head against the hardwood floor. Her world spun as deafening crashes filled her ears. Huge chunks of the ceiling tumbled down around her, and she threw an arm up to shield her head as a light fixture hit the floor next to her, the bulbs shattering on impact.

Wincing with pain, glass crunching beneath her, she rolled to her side. Then the floor tilted, and she lurched forward with a scream. As she clawed for purchase, her Scope slipped from between her sweaty fingers and slid out of her reach. She lunged to her hands and knees, shards of glass cutting at her palms and slicing through her pant legs while she crawled frantically after it. The building was coming apart, and she would be crushed if she couldn't get out. Just as she was about to reach the Scope, the floor tilted again, and she toppled forward and smashed into the elevator door, the impact ringing in her ears and fogging her vision. The air was filled with dust and the bitter scent of smoke. Bracing herself against the wall, she pushed herself up once more—but then the floor dropped out from under her completely, a roar filling the air as the building began to implode. She looked around desperately for her Scope, her only chance of escaping intact.

It was across the hallway, against the crumbling wall. But as she dove for it, falling through space, surrounded by the debris of her shattered empire, she knew it was already too late.

CHAPTER TWENTY-NINE

Moros arched back as a new, raw agony took control, blinding him to his surroundings. Nearby, he could hear Clotho and Lachesis shrieking. Something soft and warm and suffocating covered his face, and he realized it was the fabric of fate, falling apart completely, unraveling the threads of lives still meant to be lived—threads of heroism and betrayal, of love and lust, of deaths foretold. His teeth clenched against the screams as he felt his ribs breaking, his muscles pulling loose from his bones, his physical form coming undone. The wound in his chest was a vortex of pain, sucking his awareness down into a bottomless abyss. His thoughts exploded into a storm of hopeless confusion.

A shadow passed through his mind, a dark silhouette striding toward him, malice in every step. Chaos was rising. But Moros was helpless, beyond fighting, as his arms and legs flopped uselessly. The torment went on and on, but his sisters' voices faded. He was alone in this, like he had always been, with no one to fight by his side.

Aislin was the one person who might have. He was leaving her alone to face the demon god who even now was coming for her and everyone she loved. There was nothing he could do to protect her.

He had lost.

. . .

Pain. That feeling that had been so foreign to him only days ago was the first thing that entered his awareness.

The second thing was laughter. Deep and rumbling. And despite its volume, it held no humor or joy. Moros fought to open his eyes but found he barely had the strength.

"You're early," said a voice that was devastatingly familiar, even though he hadn't heard it in two thousand years.

Groaning, Moros forced his head up. He was in a mostly empty room, smooth marble beneath his palms. Cold air lay heavy on his skin, the brutal chill penetrating his bones. In front of him was a dais upon which sat two thrones: one made of light, and the other of darkness. He squinted, just able to make out the shape of the beings who occupied them.

"I have to go back," he said in a weak, rasping voice. "Chaos is rising."

The figure on the dark throne rose. "You're never going back, my friend. You're mine now." The Keeper of Hell slowly descended the steps toward him, his black cloak flowing behind him as he threw back his hood. His body was roped with muscle, and his face was youthful, with a blade of a nose and a prominent brow. His hair was golden, but his eyes were pure darkness, pits of dense, inky black that regarded Moros like one might a rat or a cockroach. "You've destroyed everything," the Keeper growled. "What you did two thousand years ago is nothing compared to what you've done now."

"My love," said a lilting voice from the throne of light. "That's not really fair."

The Keeper of Hell grunted. "Fairness is a vastly overrated concept," he said, but his voice had gentled at the sound of his eternal lover's.

The Keeper of Heaven slid gracefully from her throne, her skin shimmering as she moved. Her long black hair was the only part of her not made of light. "He didn't do this on purpose," she said quietly.

"It doesn't matter. He violated the treaty. Under his watch, the entire fabric has fallen apart."

"Lachesis and Clotho," Moros said with a gasp, looking around as he tried in vain to get his eyes to focus.

"Are guests of mine now," said the Keeper of Hell, leaning down to glare at Moros. "Who said I wasn't fair?" He gestured toward the stone wall behind the dais, and Lachesis and Clotho chained to it. "They thought they'd be allowed to truly die, or perhaps just fade into abstraction, but I think that's too generous. For *all* of you."

"He's the reason we're here!" shouted Lachesis. Her arms were shackled above her head, and there was an iron cuff around her throat. "If you punish anyone, punish him."

"I intend to," the Keeper of Hell said softly. "I've been waiting for this moment for a very long time."

"Send me back," Moros said as he tried to rise to his hands and knees. "Even as we speak, Chaos is about to plunge the world into mayhem. You don't want that. Send me to fight him."

"You've already lost!" the Keeper hissed at him, his impossibly long forked tongue darting out from between his lips.

Moros turned his face away just as that tongue lashed at his cheek, and a few drops of blood splattered onto the stones beneath him. "I was betrayed," he said through clenched teeth. He couldn't bring himself to look at the two who had done this to him, so he turned toward the Keeper of Heaven instead.

Her prismatic eyes glittered with light as she regarded him. "Atropos is safe," she said gently. "She's not in pain anymore, and she never will be again." She opened her fingers, and in her palm sat a ball of glowing light. "But she gave me this. Inevitability. Her divinity, and part of fate itself."

Moros felt himself sag. "Will she forgive me?" he asked, his throat tight. He had blamed her for everything, simply because she was the only one who had been honest about hating him. Instead, he had believed in the love of his other sisters, and that had turned out to be a wretched lie.

The Keeper of Heaven gave him a sad smile. "Perhaps. With time. But you don't have to worry about her anymore. She's safe. Always."

"I hope that will comfort you as I unravel your intestines," said the Keeper of Hell with a nasty grin.

"You value order." Moros heaved himself up to a sitting position. His muscles were weak and twitching, not fully under his control. His skin was almost translucent, and the blood that ran through his veins was black. "You know the souls who come to you—I know you have a place prepared for each. With fate and destiny destroyed, all of that will be ruined."

The Keeper of Hell clenched his fists. "Chaos cannot reach us here."

"Are you sure?" the Keeper of Heaven asked, misgiving in her voice. "I'm not."

The Keeper of Hell turned his ebony eyes to the one being who seemed to quell the hatred and bloodlust inside him. "What do you mean?"

"There are countless windows into our domains. We made sure of it when we signed the treaty that created the Ferrys." She approached her lover, her gossamer gown floating around her legs. "We were so confident of the order of things, so sure we had hit upon a permanent solution that we may have made ourselves vulnerable."

The Keeper of Hell glowered at Moros. "Chaos cannot be in more than one place at once."

Moros refused to look away from the Keeper's gaze. "But he has helpers. My sister and brother will be at his side. The Ferrys and their Scopes are woefully vulnerable." Especially if Aislin wasn't there to lead them.

"We'll void the treaty!" the Keeper of Hell bellowed.

"But the Scopes will still exist," the Keeper of Heaven reminded him. "They would all have to be destroyed for us to be certain."

"And how will the dead reach you?" asked Moros. "My Kere used to lay them at your feet, before you banished us from your throne room. And with me gone, they'll be masterless."

"I can bend them to my will," rumbled the Keeper of Hell.

"To what end? There is no fate, not anymore!" Moros felt a flash of strength as his rage surged to the surface. "This will be the beginning of your end. Don't fool yourself into believing Chaos will be satisfied with the earthly realm alone."

"We prize order, but we can survive without it, as long as the sanctity of our realm remains intact," the Keeper of Heaven said calmly.

"Then you'd better hope the Ferrys are strong enough to survive Chaos's reign," Moros said.

"The Ferrys exist only because we bowed to *your* demands!" shouted the Keeper of Hell.

"The Ferrys exist only because you didn't trust me," Moros corrected.

The Keeper of Hell reached down and grabbed Moros by the throat, hoisting him up and yanking him close. "And I will deal with them directly." He grinned as his fingers sank into Moros's skin, filling his nose with the scent of burning flesh. "Starting with their Charon."

CHAPTER THIRTY

Aislin grasped at her surroundings, but everything was falling—there was nothing to hold on to. The air was choking her. Her eyes were squeezed shut. She was about to be torn apart, left in pieces, unable to heal or help her family meet the oncoming threat.

Something hot wrapped around her waist, and she was yanked through space, completely unsure which way was up as her world spun.

And then her feet were on spongy, not-quite-steady ground. Her eyes popped open as the chill of the Veil crept across her skin. Trevor looked down at her, his red eyes glowing. "Dec told me to come get you. He knew I'd be able to find you." He released her arms. They were on the patio of Moros's penthouse. Aislin looked toward the Psychopomps tower and gasped.

It wasn't there anymore. Only a massive pile of debris clogged the space between the buildings around it. "Oh my God," she sobbed, her chest convulsing as her hand rose to her mouth. Cold tears streaked down her face. How many of her family members were buried in that rubble? "Cacia."

"Hang on." Trevor disappeared.

Aislin swayed, trying to regain control of her body as the knowledge sank in—everything else had been destroyed.

Trevor reappeared. "Cacy's fine. Eli got her out. She said she warned as many people as she could." He rubbed the back of his neck with his large hand as he looked down at the catastrophe. "This is bad," he said quietly.

"Can you help with a rescue effort?" Aislin said, her breath puffing out in front of her. "There might be humans trapped in the rubble. If they weren't Marked . . ."

Aislin froze as a terrible realization hit her. Declan had said Shades had been appearing around Psychopomps and disappearing just as quickly without attacking. "They were Marking people," she whispered. "We have no way of knowing how many they got to."

Trevor grimaced, his fangs glinting dully. "But all of them would be unsanctioned kills."

"Moros," she said softly. What if this had been enough to destroy the fabric of fate? Would it kill him? "I have to go."

Trevor's eyebrows rose. "But the rescue efforts—"

"You and Declan can coordinate." Her eyes met Trevor's. "Warn him that worse is probably coming. Tell him to follow through with my plan immediately."

"Plan?"

"He'll know," she said, reaching for her Scope. Her heart nearly stopped as she realized it wasn't attached to her necklace.

Trevor smiled. "Looking for this?" He opened his fingers and revealed the ornately stamped platinum disk, the raven surface upturned: *Fatum Nos Vocat.*

Fate calls us.

She plucked it from his palm. "I owe you."

"No, you don't," he replied. "I'm at your service until the end of my existence."

She reached out and gave his massive forearm an affectionate squeeze. "Then please help Declan."

Trevor grinned. "No problem."

"And please protect him. He's human. We all are. And I'm afraid—" Her throat tightened, making it impossible to speak. The memory of her brother, torn raw and bloody by Eli's claws, stole her breath.

"No one's gonna touch him, Aislin," Trevor said, his determination showing in the flex of his jaw.

She nodded. "Thank you," she said, her voice strained. "Be sure to warn him and Cacia about Apate and Eris. I have a feeling they're nearby. I'm going to go to the summit with the Keepers now."

"Have you heard from Moros?" Trevor asked.

She stared up at the big Ker, wishing she could confide her fears, but there was no time left. "I'm meeting him there." She needed to see his face right now. She needed to know he was alive. More than anything, she wanted to be in his arms, letting his heat and strength wrap around her.

As Trevor disappeared, Aislin looked down at her Scope. She flipped it over so the scales were up, the symbol of justice and judgment. Closing her eyes, she whispered the ancient incantation all Charons knew from the moment they accepted the Scope. It was imprinted into her thoughts, each word a small, cold comfort.

The Scope grew warm and then hot beneath the pad of her thumb, and just as it became unbearable, she pulled it wide to reveal a stone wall. Cautiously, she stepped through the portal before compacting the disk and clipping it to her necklace once more. She was standing in a small windowless chamber. "I request audience with the Keepers," she said, focused on making her voice low and steady, even as her heart kicked frantically against her breastbone.

The rocks directly in front of her shifted backward and slid out of the way, revealing another chamber, this one cavernous and cold, with a dais at the front. Aislin shuddered as she realized it was identical to the visions she'd had while in the grip of Apate's lies. Two women were chained to the wall behind the dark throne, their faces twisted into pained grimaces. But the thrones were empty, and two people stood together in the center of the room.

The first, a black-robed man with blond hair and obsidian eyes, looked up as she approached. "Welcome, Charon," he said, his voice as deep as an abyss.

"Welcome," echoed the second, a woman with black hair and eyes that looked like diamond chips, making it hard to meet her gaze. In her hand she held a small glowing globe.

Aislin clasped her hands in front of her. "I'm here for our summit. The Lord of the Kere and I require your assistance in meeting a dire threat to the earthly realm."

The black-eyed man, who could only be the Keeper of Hell, smirked. "This one has a nice turn of phrase, don't you think?"

"Lovely," said the Keeper of Heaven, her diamond eyes glinting as she gave Aislin a once-over. "In every way."

"But I'm afraid you're too late," the Keeper of Hell said to her. And then he stepped aside.

Moros lay crumpled on the floor behind them, and Aislin gasped as she saw his face, ghastly pale and lined with black veins. His throat was striped with dark bruises. "What have you done to him?" she asked, unable to keep her voice from breaking as Moros stirred, his eyelids fluttering.

The Keeper of Hell folded his thickly muscled arms over his chest. "Very little as of yet. He's just more dead than usual."

Moros made a choked sound and raised his head. *Aislin,* he mouthed. His eyes had clouded over, and he was squinting as if trying to bring her into focus.

She couldn't stop the tears. "The fabric."

"It is completely destroyed," said the Keeper of Heaven.

"And now Chaos has risen," said the Keeper of Hell. "It will be your job to stop him if you'd like to continue to exist."

He wanted *her* to fight Chaos? "My family is scattered and hurt. Our headquarters has just been destroyed. And only Moros can summon his army of Kere." It would take all of them to destroy the Shade-Kere. And as for Chaos himself . . .

Aislin looked back and forth between the Keepers and Moros as a sudden peace settled inside her. She sought Moros's gaze and found it riveted on her. "You were right," she said quietly.

Moros's brow furrowed.

"About how this would end."

The Keeper of Hell chuckled. "Only we decide how it ends."

Aislin inclined her head respectfully. "Of course. But I have been aware for the last few days that my death was drawing near." She looked up at the Keeper of Hell. "And everything is suddenly clear."

Moros was struggling to rise to his knees. "No," he said, his voice little more than a rasp.

She ignored him. "I assume the Lord of the Kere has requested permission to return to the earthly realm to fight Chaos."

The Keeper of Hell let out a snort of laughter. "Demanded, more like."

She pressed her lips shut. No surprise there. He'd have been desperate to make things right. Affection and exasperation coursed inside her. "And I further assume you refused." She gestured to the two women in chains on the dais. "Because you believe he has earned an eternity of punishment."

The Keeper of Hell regarded her steadily but said nothing.

"Would you consider accepting a substitute?"

"No," Moros barked, finally gathering the strength to kneel.

She looked at his face, contorted with horror, and gave him an apologetic smile before saying, "Take me instead."

"No!" shouted Moros, glaring at the Keeper of Hell with murder in his cloudy eyes. His arms trembled as he braced his palms on his knees and swayed unsteadily.

Aislin took a few steps forward, forcing herself to look directly into the eyes of the Keeper of Heaven. "This is just and right. And it will get you the results you want."

"Order restored," murmured the Keeper of Heaven.

"Chaos in his grave once more," said the Keeper of Hell, giving Aislin a speculative look. "But Moros is weak. He cannot take on this enemy alone. He's already been defeated."

"Give him one more chance. Let him take physical form in the earthly realm once again." She held out her arms. "And give him my life to use as his own."

"No!" Moros tried to get to his feet but failed. "Aislin, stop." His voice was guttural and harsh.

She slowly walked forward. "If this is what was meant to be, Jason, you have no right to refuse."

"It was *not* meant to be!" he cried. "I will not let you sacrifice your life for mine."

"You can't stop her," said the Keeper of Heaven. "That is her choice." She turned to the Keeper of Hell and placed her hand on his arm. "You can't deny her that, not even if the person she's saving is the Lord of the Kere."

A vein throbbed at the Keeper of Hell's temple, and his black eyes glittered with fury. "This is a dirty trick."

"Agreed," said Moros.

Aislin pushed away a surge of fear and knelt next to Moros. "I need you to do this," she said quietly. "This is your fight." She met his eyes. "But you won't be alone."

"It can't happen this way," he whispered. "You will not die for my sake."

"It's not just for you," she murmured. "But if it frees you, that only makes it easier for me."

He squeezed his eyes shut, his expression crumpling with pain. And then he clumsily pulled her into his arms, his mouth pressed to her ear. "I will never forgive you for this."

"Another sacrifice I'm willing to make."

His limbs trembled with weakness, and for once, his body was cold instead of hot. It felt wrong. But the embrace didn't last long, because a moment later, she was yanked away from him. The Keeper of Hell had wrapped his thick fingers around her throat. "Any last words?"

She began to shake as his grip tightened, as her mind began to scream for oxygen. She had to tell Moros her plan, what she'd asked Declan and Cacia to do, but she couldn't hold on to the thought. The Keeper of Hell held Moros in a similar position on his other side, but the Lord of the Kere was struggling feebly, clawing the air as he tried to get to Aislin.

"Jason," she managed to say as her fingers rose from her side.

"Interesting choice." The Keeper jerked her off her feet, his fingers closing around her windpipe. "And now . . . a life for a life."

CHAPTER THIRTY-ONE

Moros was forced to watch as Aislin's skin paled, as her blood ran black, as her blue eyes clouded over. He had never found death anything but natural and satisfying, but this . . .

"Stop struggling," the Keeper of Hell said in an annoyed voice. "Accept the gift that the Charon offers you. It is only because of her that you live."

It is only because of her that I love. He closed his eyes as he felt his heart begin to beat, warmth radiating outward along his limbs, filling his muscles with strength. Her strength.

"It's done. Now go and fight." And with those words, the Keeper released him.

Moros dove for Aislin as she fell, lifeless, from the Keeper's grasp, and he caught her just before she hit the marble at their feet. Her body was as cold as his had been a moment ago. His chest tightened, and he gritted his teeth. "I'll fight. But when I return, you will undo this."

The Keeper looked down at him. "Perhaps." His lips curled into an amused smile as he watched Moros fold Aislin against his chest. "But on the other hand, I want you to suffer. And I wonder if it wouldn't be worse for you, knowing she is here in my care."

Moros turned to the Keeper of Heaven. "You know this isn't just. This woman is innocent."

The Keeper of Heaven was looking down at the glowing ball in her palm, all that was left of Atropos, as if in deep thought. Then she raised her head. "Be fair," she said to her mate. "If he wins this battle, the choice should be his." She turned her diamond gaze to Moros. "You can live without her, or die to take her place. But if you lose, you forfeit the choice." She smiled. "I would think you'd find that quite motivating."

His fingers wove into Aislin's platinum hair as he held her. The sound of clanking chains on the dais drew his gaze to his sisters. Lachesis was staring at him, a look of intense satisfaction on her black-veined face.

"Is this what you knew?" His voice echoed in the massive hall. "Is this the secret you kept, that she would make this choice?"

She gave him a defiant smile and shook her head.

"But you removed her thread from the tapestry," he said. "And you did it to keep *something* from me."

Her eyes glittered with hatred as she nodded.

He looked down at Aislin. Spidery black veins traced across her white eyelids and crisscrossed her delicate cheekbones. If she hadn't been doomed to die, he'd never have been able to touch her like he had. They had been the happiest moments of his existence, but he'd give them all up to see her alive again.

His fingers stroked down her soft, chilled skin to the Scope at her throat. Determination grew with every beat of his awakened heart. "I told you I wouldn't let you go," he whispered to her, pressing his lips to her brow. "And I meant it." Gently, he laid her down, brushing her hair back from her face and kissing her lips tenderly before rising to his feet.

He turned to the Keeper of Hell, every muscle pulsing with rage and love and war. "Do not touch her until I return," he said.

"Save your bloodlust for more worthy victims." He gestured at his sisters.

The Keeper of Hell arched an eyebrow. "Fair enough."

The Keeper of Heaven was staring down at Aislin, the glowing globe still cradled in her palm. "Fair," she murmured.

Moros allowed himself one final glance at Aislin before willing himself back into the Veil. But instead of going straight to the battleground of Boston, he traveled to his own domain, the first place he had kissed Aislin—and the home of the souls of all his Kere. He appeared in the chamber and spread his arms, and the walls moved back, stretching the space until it was a vast hall. He was surprised at how strong he felt; ever since the fabric had begun to fray, he'd forgotten what it felt like to have this much energy flowing through his body. It was Aislin, he knew. Her vitality, her strength. And her love for him. He could feel it with every breath he took. It was a gift he couldn't keep—but for now he would make the most of it.

He strode to his trunk and opened it, gazing down upon the wriggling, colorful mass of souls within. "Come to me. All of you," he said quietly.

He turned as they began to obey, appearing instantly in the huge space, looking around with confusion before approaching him warily. Each of their gazes held a question, and as more and more of them materialized, their surprise grew. Luke appeared in the middle of the crowd. "Boston is in chaos," he announced. "Shade-Kere everywhere."

Hai popped into the space right in front of Moros, followed by Parinda. "There are too many of them," Hai said, breathing hard.

"That is why I am gathering everyone," Moros replied. "It will take all of us to beat them."

Parinda looked him over. "You look stronger than when you left for the realm of the Lucinae."

Moros ran his hand over his chest. All his wounds were gone. "That had nothing to do with the Lucinae themselves."

"What about the Charon?" she asked, her tone defiant.

He met her gaze. "Without her, this fight would already be lost."

Trevor and Eli appeared right next to Parinda. "Something bad is going down," Trevor said between heavy breaths. "The Shade-Kere are massing around Psychopomps."

"What's left of it, you mean," said Eli, his jaw tense. "It's been completely destroyed. A bunch of Ferrys were buried in the rubble, but we haven't been able to get to them because of all the Shades in the area."

Moros closed his eyes and focused on sensing Declan and Cacia, knowing Aislin would want them to be safe. He relaxed a little when he felt them both, pushing them out of his mind for the moment. "Eris and Apate—have you seen either of them?"

"Not yet, but we've been on the lookout. I figured they'd enjoy watching the chaos they've caused." Trevor looked around the room. "Where's Aislin? What happened at the summit with the Keepers?"

Moros swallowed hard. "It's not over yet." He met Trevor's gaze. "Aislin is still there."

"But you're going back for her," Trevor said slowly.

"Nothing could stop me."

Trevor nodded. "Then tell us how to help."

Moros turned to address all his Kere, for the hall was now filled to the brim. "The fabric of fate has been destroyed," he said in a loud voice. "I am here on borrowed time."

There was complete silence as shock pervaded the room. Moros let it sink in for a moment before continuing. "I have called you here to offer you a choice." He stepped aside and gestured at the open trunk of souls, and every gaze in the room focused on it like a beacon. "Any of you who would like to collect your soul and exit my service are welcome to do so. You will appear before the Keepers to meet your final fate."

He looked over the crowd. He'd given each of them a chance after their deaths, knowing them to be capable of taking lives, but now he was thinking of what Clotho had said to him just before the end: two thousand years as a slave changes a person. "I am offering you your freedom."

"But only if we're ready to go to Hell," Luke shouted. Many of his brethren grumbled their agreement.

Moros stared Luke down. "Yes. You will reap the reward that you have *earned*. You have all had the freedom to decide how to carry out your duties."

Luke looked away from his gaze, and the irritable muttering stopped. But no Kere came forward to claim their souls.

Moros looked at Eli, who shook his head. "I won't leave Cacy. Ever," Eli said quietly.

"Very well then," Moros said as he closed the lid. "Then listen closely, for this is your final choice. I am going into battle, and I need allies by my side. You can join me, or you can choose not to. I will not decide for you. If I win, I will find a way to restore fate. And if I lose, Chaos will reign on Earth, and you can take your chances."

He took a step back. "Those of you who choose to fight, follow me."

His heart beat hard against his ribs as he willed himself into the Veil. The very air seemed to shudder around him, a sensation he'd only felt once before—when he'd gone to retrieve the Blade from Chaos's tomb. The creature was loose in the world, and Moros had the feeling that all he needed to do was follow the trail of mayhem to find him.

Given what Eli and Trevor had just told him, Boston seemed like the epicenter. He materialized on the patio of his penthouse to get a view of the battlefield. Screams and sirens filled the night air, along with a haze of smoke. The magnificent Psychopomps tower was gone. He wondered if Aislin had been in it as it fell, if that was the reason for her bloody pants and the soot smeared across her shirt when she'd arrived at the summit. It must have sliced right through her heart, seeing it fall, and the knowledge only stoked his desire to fight. The tremors he felt in the Veil were here, too, like the monster was thriving on the catastrophe unfolding below. Moros knew the only reason he was able to withstand it was that he wasn't powered by his own strength now—Aislin had enabled him to fight this final battle. He had insisted it wasn't meant to be . . . but had he been wrong? Would he be able to face Chaos because she'd sacrificed herself?

Trevor and Eli appeared on either side of him, and Moros stepped back from the edge of the patio, steeling himself. "Just as before," he said. "Bring them to me and I'll destroy them."

Trevor gave him a knowing look. "I think you'd better brace yourself, then. You're gonna be busy." He pointed down at the city.

The sidewalks were packed; tiny figures with glowing red eyes were everywhere. Moros's heart leaped at the sight. His Kere had followed him.

Eli smiled. "We're all with you. Let's get this done." He vanished. So did Trevor.

Moros gritted his teeth as he felt another vibration beneath his feet, like the earth was beginning to shake itself apart. "Let's get this done," he echoed quietly, then willed himself onto the streets below to destroy the enemies of fate his sisters had created.

His world became a blur of killing as his Kere brought him offering after offering, and each time a Shade-Ker exploded into dust, he felt himself growing more confident. Clotho might have created a horde of monsters, but with fifty thousand Kere on the streets, they didn't stand much of a chance. The servants of fate pursued them in and out of the Veil—there was nowhere they could hide that they couldn't be followed. One by one, Moros destroyed them, his hands blazing. He knew it couldn't possibly be this easy, but for now he would slaughter with joy in his heart. Every kill brought him closer to victory, closer to the moment when he would see Aislin's skin regain its color, when her eyes would open, full of that cleverness and graceful strength that had earned his devotion.

He would submit to the Keeper of Hell gladly, as long as he knew she was alive and well, and he would fight for that moment. The streets and canals of Boston were cluttered with debris and wreckage, with the bodies of innocent victims who had not been able to escape the evil that had descended upon the city. The Shade-Kere might be dwindling in number, but they were still trying to kill as many as they could.

Hai appeared at his side, offering up yet another struggling monster for Moros to destroy. As soon as he did, Hai grinned. "We're getting there, I think. I—" His eyes went wide as a deep rumbling filled the air.

Moros spun around to follow the direction of Hai's startled gaze in time to witness two skyscrapers crumbling about ten blocks to their east, close to the waterfront. The ground bucked as two more, this time a block closer, began to fall. Moros's stomach turned as a wave of weakness rolled through him. "He's here," he said as he and Hai steadied themselves.

The battle in the street had spread throughout the city, and his Kere were hard at work to quell the marauding Shade-Kere. He turned to Hai. "Continue to disable as many of the Shades as you can. Do whatever you can to eliminate any enemy of fate."

For the first time since Moros had claimed his soul, Hai looked frightened. "What is that?" he asked as two more buildings disappeared into a cloud of dust and smoke.

"That's Chaos," Moros said. "And he is mine to deal with." He willed himself into the Veil and appeared four blocks to the east, squinting to see his enemy through the haze. His brow furrowed as he struggled to focus on the lone figure walking along the side-walk next to the canal, steps unhurried, pulling down the buildings behind him with casual flicks of his fingers.

Wait—*were* they fingers? The more Moros stared, the more he wondered if they were tentacles, the way they stretched and shrank, curving in the air like snakes. His head swam with dizziness as he tried to focus on just one part of Chaos's body, but every time he did, the being's appearance shifted and changed, becoming something else.

He knew the moment Chaos saw him, because he stopped walking, and for a second, he took the form of an ordinary man. One who wore Moros's own face. "Did you come to fight me?" he asked in an impossibly deep voice. His countenance began to shift, then, changing to take on Apate's face, then Eris's, then Clotho's, then Lachesis's.

"No," said Moros, fighting nausea as he tried to focus on Chaos's ever-changing features. "I came to kill you."

The air around the creature warped as he grew and twisted, arms and legs sprouting from his back, his chest. "You can try," he rumbled as his face became that of Nyx, as dark and beautiful as Moros remembered her. "But you will fail."

And then Chaos disappeared. Moros's heart thundered as he whirled around, looking for his enemy. But no sooner had he closed his eyes to try to sense him than his head exploded with pain and he found himself being lifted into the air, his wrists and ankles held in the grip of his enemy's ever-shifting arms. The being looked up at him and suddenly his countenance changed again, creasing and folding in on itself to form a monstrous calamity of a face, with six black eyes and a gaping mouth. "This world is mine now, servant of fate," the creature said as massive horns sprouted from his head.

Moros struggled in vain—his strength was nothing compared to this god, fueled by all the destruction brought about by the Fates themselves. He fought with all his might, but Chaos had no trouble controlling him. Hot frustration roared through him as he tried to concentrate on summoning his Kere, on disappearing into the Veil, but Chaos merely shook him, rattling his bones and scattering his thoughts. "I'm not going to kill you," Chaos said, his voice so ominous and deep that Moros felt it vibrating along his bones. He yanked Moros close to his rancid mouth, his black tongue swirling. "I have to reward the ones who raised me from the dead."

Chaos hurled Moros into the air. He collided with the side of a building a block away, glass windows shattering on impact as he fell to the ground two stories below. His head slammed into the sidewalk, and he gulped at the air, trying to gather the energy to rise, but his arms and legs wouldn't obey. Blood trickled along the side of his head; the wound was already healing, but his mind was still a frenzy of scattered images and plans. Gritting his teeth, he focused on pulling himself back together, thought by thought. He wasn't beaten yet.

But as he began to push himself unsteadily to his hands and knees, he heard a familiar laugh.

Eris and Apate stood only ten feet away, looking gleeful. "I don't know how you survived the destruction of the fabric when none of the Fates did," Eris said, twirling one finger in her long hair.

Apate leaned against the wall that separated the sidewalk from the canal. "I'm glad you did." The malice in his gray eyes suggested the opposite, but Moros would have expected no less.

Eris gave Apate an affectionate slap. "I actually *am* glad." Her hand disappeared behind her back, and she drew forth a thin glowing blade. "Because that means I get to shove this right through your chest."

CHAPTER THIRTY-TWO

Aislin opened her eyes and saw a face above hers, too blurry to make out. "Am I dead?" she asked.

"Extremely," said a deep voice she recognized as belonging to the Keeper of Hell.

Fear sliced along Aislin's spine as the Keeper took her hand and guided her to her feet. She looked down at herself, still clad in her torn, bloody suit, her ashen skin a maze of black veins. Swallowing back nausea, she reminded herself why she had done this. "Did you keep your promise?" she asked, wishing her voice weren't so unsteady.

"The Lord of the Kere is fighting the battle even as we speak," said the Keeper of Heaven, moving gracefully to Aislin's other side. The glowing ball she held in her hand pulsed, going dim before lighting up bright once more. "The odds are against him." Her diamond eyes rose to Aislin's face. "But he is very determined."

Aislin smiled, even as her silent heart ached for him. "He fights for all of us."

The Keeper of Hell grunted. "He fights for himself. He always has."

"Not true," said the Keeper of Heaven, her voice like a bell.

The Keeper of Hell rolled his eyes. "You can't stop me from punishing him. If it weren't for his rebellion all those centuries ago, none of this would have happened. He sowed the seeds of this disaster."

"Because he demanded payment for the work he and his Kere were doing," Aislin said.

"Work he was created to do," snapped the Keeper, his black eyes narrowing.

"And how long had he existed before he rebelled?" she asked.

"Thousands of years!" The Keeper of Hell threw his arms up. "But then all of a sudden, it wasn't enough for him."

"How many Kere did he have in the thousands of years before he rebelled?" Aislin was careful to keep her voice even.

The Keeper of Heaven nodded knowingly. "He built the numbers slowly over the years. By that time, he had nearly a hundred."

Aislin looked up at the Keeper of Hell. "Is it possible he did it for them?"

His mouth tightened, and he didn't answer.

"He certainly never did it for us," said a voice from the dais. Aislin's gaze shifted to the women chained there. One was blonde and thin, and the other curvier, with thick brown hair. Both were glaring at her. "His rebellion weakened the fabric, so he has no right to fault us for doing the same," the blonde one continued. "He wanted to be free, and so did we."

"You did a little more than weaken the fabric," said the Keeper of Heaven.

"You're his sisters," Aislin said.

"Lachesis," the Keeper of Heaven murmured, pointing at the blonde. She moved her finger to the brunette. "And Clotho."

Aislin blew out a breath as cold fury pulsed inside her. "He didn't want to believe you'd betray him."

"He deserves everything he's getting," said Lachesis, her smile sharp as a knife despite the fact that her arms and neck were shackled to the wall. "It's worth whatever we have to go through to see him suffer." Her malevolent gaze was riveted to Aislin. "And you are a huge part of that."

Aislin's brow furrowed. "I would never be a part of his suffering." She pushed the heartbreaking image of his face from her mind, how he had looked as she died right in front of him.

"You're the dagger between his ribs," Clotho said quietly. "You're the twist of the blade."

"Explain," said the Keeper of Heaven.

"Her fate was to be with him," Lachesis replied. "Clotho and I knew it as soon as we first touched the thread of her life. Neither of us could believe it at first, but as the years went on, the sense only became stronger."

Aislin felt like the floor had dropped out from under her. "I was fated to be with him?" she asked, her voice breaking as she realized the absolute truth of it—and that she'd sensed it herself, vaguely, so many times before. It was the feeling of rightness when he was inside her, the sense of inevitability between them. "Does he know?"

Clotho shook her head, then winced as the metal cuff around her neck rubbed beneath her chin. "He is blind to those whose fates are entwined with his Kere—or with his own. He's never sensed it. And when he first touched you, he assumed his lack of future-sight was because of your impending doom."

Aislin gestured at her body. "Was he wrong?"

Lachesis nodded. "He was *always* able to touch you. He could have done it at any time, and the result would have been the same." She grinned. "You doomed yourself because you believed your death was a foregone conclusion, but you were wrong. It was perfect."

"I would have done it anyway," Aislin murmured.

The Keeper of Heaven made a soft, surprised noise as her fingers tightened around the glowing orb in her palm. "Even the Lord of Death was subject to the threads of fate, as it turns out."

"And the manipulation of his sisters," Aislin added bitterly.

"Ask me if I was ever fated to love someone," Lachesis blurted out, her smile gone. "Ask me if I ever even had a chance."

"Ask me the same," snapped Clotho.

Aislin tilted her head. "I can guess the answer. And I can tell that you're not happy with it."

Clotho's eyes were wide. "So why did *he* have the chance to fall in love, when we were denied such things?"

"It was the last straw," Lachesis said in a low voice. "It was then we decided to bring him down."

"You didn't think he should have happiness after thousands of years of being alone?" Aislin asked, stepping toward them on unsteady feet. "After millennia of being unable to touch another person without hurting them? This was the reason you chose to destroy him?" Her breath rasped as she mounted the first step on the dais. She wasn't sure if she had the strength to get up the stairs, but, God, how she wanted to. "You begrudge your own brother the right to love and be loved?"

"Why did he get it when we didn't?" shrieked Lachesis.

Aislin stared at her. "Can you see the entire future?"

"Only what the threads tell us," Clotho said.

"Then how do you know it never would have happened? How do you know you weren't a decade, a year, a *day* away from a love of your own?"

Clotho's mouth opened and closed, then clamped shut. Lachesis's eyes were bulging. Disgusted, Aislin turned to find the Keeper of Hell stifling a smile. "I'm trying not to like this Charon," he said to the Keeper of Heaven.

The Keeper of Heaven chuckled. "But you're failing."

He grunted as he started up the steps toward Clotho and Lachesis, his black robe billowing. As he moved to stand in front of them, his large hands rose from his sides. "Since you were so eager to shed your responsibilities, ladies, I think it's time to hand over your divine mandates."

He plunged his fists into Clotho and Lachesis, whose mouths dropped open in agony as he yanked a glowing ball from each of their chests. He opened his fingers to reveal the one he'd pulled from Clotho. "Birth and Mortality." He did the same with the globe he'd wrenched from Lachesis. "Destiny."

He strolled down the stairs and handed them to the Keeper of Heaven, who cooed to the three globes in her hands as if they were infants. "In addition to Moros, who carries Doom inside him, this is the totality of fate," she said. "We have the means to build it again."

Lachesis and Clotho had both gone ashen as the gaping holes in their chests slowly knitted together again. "But only if Moros wins," croaked Lachesis. "And he won't."

"Moros will lose!" Clotho said in a shrill voice. "He's fighting a battle he can't win. I'm certain of it."

Aislin looked up at the women, hope stirring weakly inside her as she pictured Jason, his fangs bared and his claws out, tearing through his enemies with fire in his eyes. "You destroyed the fabric of fate and what was meant to be. Right now, certainty seems like a rather foolish notion."

CHAPTER THIRTY-THREE

Eris stalked toward Moros as he got his legs underneath himself. He was still woozy and unsteady, but if he didn't challenge her, that cursed blade would be between his ribs in a matter of seconds.

"Hold him, Apate," she said, her breaths coming quickly as the roar of destruction in the city rose to new levels, making it hard to hear. Her excitement was sickening.

And stupid. "Yes," hissed Moros, spreading his fingers on the concrete. Pain rocketed up his spine, but his defiance held him together. "Come here, brother. Try to put your hands on me."

Apate froze where he was. "Cut him first," he said to Eris. "Make him bleed."

With a feral snarl, Eris lunged, and Moros threw himself out of the way. She let out a frustrated shout. "Rylan, hold him!"

Rylan Ferry stepped from the Veil, and the mere sight of him made Moros's thoughts turn red. The former Ferry looked cautious. "What happens if he touches me?" Rylan asked.

"Come and find out," Moros said as he slowly got to his feet.

Rylan's eyes met his. "Aislin wouldn't want you to kill me."

"You have no right to say her name," Moros roared, diving for Rylan. He dodged, and the distraction was just enough to allow Eris to strike. The Blade of Life pierced Moros's thigh, sending a bolt of searing pain through his leg. Apate laughed as Moros hit the sidewalk again, his blood smearing the concrete. He had to get ahold of the Blade—it was the one weapon that would give him a chance against Chaos, who was still pulling buildings down only blocks away. But his injured leg trembled uncontrollably as he tried to stand again, and he wasn't fast enough to move out of the way when Apate kicked him in the chest, knocking him backward into Rylan's waiting grasp. The Ker looped his arms under Moros's, controlling the swipes of his hands. Still trying to heal from his hard collision with the building, Moros didn't have the strength to will himself into the Veil.

Eris blew a few loose strands of her dark hair off her forehead and walked forward with Apate at her side. Moros arched and twisted, but Rylan held him fast as Eris looked him over and gave him a small smile. "I used to worship you. I would have done anything for you. Did you know that?"

"Not anything. You couldn't allow the world to have peace. Your thirst for conflict was too strong." He glanced around as she advanced, working to gather enough strength to summon one of his Kere, but Chaos was so near that Moros's thoughts of them kept fluttering and fading.

Apate drew back and punched Moros in the side of the head. "When you got what you wanted, you tossed us away," Apate said.

Moros spat blood on the pavement. "I couldn't trust you. You would have ruined everything I'd fought for."

Eris jabbed the Blade at him. "We fought at your side!"

"But I was fighting for freedom, for better treatment for my Kere—and you were fighting for the sake of fighting!" He was running out of time—he saw his end reflected in her eyes. "Look at what you've done, Eris. Do you think Chaos won't destroy you, too?"

She laughed. "Do you have any idea how good this feels to me? I've never felt stronger." She raised the hilt of the Blade of Life with both hands. Moros tried to maneuver out of the way, but Rylan wouldn't yield.

"This is for Nemesis," Apate hissed as he glared at Moros. "Revenge for revenge."

Moros's breaths burst from his throat in agonized wheezes as his sister tensed to strike. He watched helplessly as the Blade sliced toward his chest, the seconds like hours, all spent thinking of Aislin, how she would be trapped because he hadn't been strong enough or fast enough.

It didn't matter what the Keeper of Hell did to him—knowing he hadn't been able to save her would be the ultimate torture.

But before the Blade could touch him, Eris's mouth dropped open and her fingers spasmed. She arched back, and the weapon fell from her grip. Next to her, Apate cried out in pain and jerked forward—enough to reveal Eli standing right behind him. Then Rylan Ferry screamed and released Moros, sending him to the ground in a shocked heap.

"Sorry, Ry," Declan said softly. He was standing over his fallen brother, a glowing knife in his hands. Rylan's wide, empty eyes were riveted on Eris, but when Moros turned to look at her, he realized Cacia Ferry had just buried a different glowing blade in her back. Eris writhed on the ground next to Apate, who'd been stabbed by Eli with yet another blade.

Declan's ice-blue eyes flicked over to Moros, and he held up his glowing knife, his brother's blood dripping from its edge. "Aislin sent us on a little errand before she left."

Cacia looked down at Eris, who was flailing in a growing pool of crimson. It streamed from her lips as she gasped for air. "The new Mother sends her regards," Cacia said quietly.

"But . . . but Baheera refused to give us weapons," Moros said as Eli stepped forward and helped him to his feet. His leg was unsteady beneath him, and his chest felt like it had been stuffed with broken glass, but he was able to stay upright.

"Baheera's not in charge anymore," said Declan. "Apparently a bunch of the Lucinae watched you risking your existence to protect hers, and they didn't take well to her sending you away empty-handed. Aislin noticed and didn't think it would take much to push them over the edge, so she put Cavan to work. Magda was crowned as the new Mother a few hours ago." He wiped the blade of the knife on his pants and pointed toward the wreckage of Psychopomps. "She was pretty generous."

Moros squinted up the block, where he could just make out the blur of glowing blades, wielded by at least twenty Ferrys who had joined the fight, along with several Lucinae. "All of the weapons have been dipped in the Spring?" he asked weakly as he watched Cavan plunge a dagger into the chest of a Shade-Ker, which fell to the ground instantly.

Eli offered Moros the dagger he had used to kill Apate, its blade curved and wickedly sharp. "This one's for you."

The hilt had been wrapped in leather to form a protective barrier between his hand and the metal. Moros took it with disbelief pulsing in his chest. Aislin was responsible for this. She wasn't even with him, and yet she'd somehow managed to put the weapon he needed right in his hand. His fingers coiled around the hilt, and he raised his head. The noise of battle was rising to an incessant roar as the enemy closed in. Chaos was only a block away, bringing devastation in his wake.

Moros aimed the tip of his dagger toward the god who was coming for them all. "These blades are the only thing that can destroy him."

Declan, Cacia, and Eli narrowed their eyes as they tried to see through the dust and destruction. "Is he a man?" Eli asked.

"I can't tell what I'm looking at," said Cacia, rubbing her eyes.

But just as she said it, Chaos walked from a cloud of debris, and she gasped.

He looked exactly like Patrick Ferry.

"Father?" Declan asked quietly. He gave Moros an uncertain look.

"It's an illusion," Moros said, limping forward as his old friend smiled and beckoned to him. "Go gather the others. If I fall, it will be up to you to destroy him." Without waiting for them to obey, he pushed off, determined to bury the dagger in Chaos's chest.

"Patrick Ferry" shook his head as he saw Moros coming for him. "Know your enemy," he said in an eerily deep, wrong voice that carried easily over the crashes and screams and sirens. He spread his arms. Moros skidded to a stop as dark shapes peeled themselves off the being's arms, spiraling to the ground and sprouting upward, growing instantly into thick-bodied, hunched creatures, each with four muscular arms. Their faces were covered with slitted eyes and a few gaping mouths. Within seconds, there were dozens of them, and Moros was surrounded. He lashed out with the blade, slicing off an arm, which turned to ash before it hit the ground. As one of the creatures grabbed for his wounded leg, he struck again. He stabbed it in the neck, and its eyes bulged before it exploded into dust. As he fought to keep the creatures off him, Moros glanced toward the Patrick Ferry version of Chaos, who stood with his arms outstretched, watching with amusement. The minions were still flying from his hands, and now some of them were running down the block toward Psychopomps, where all the Ferrys and their Lucinae allies were fighting.

Leaving Moros here, alone. He stabbed and slashed, afraid to stop moving or attacking lest they overcome him with their sheer numbers and weight. The air filled with the rotten-egg smell of brimstone as he cut through arms and legs and throats, ignoring the pain in his chest and leg. He'd fight until the absolute end.

But there were too many, and they began to land blows, their fingers tearing at his sleeves and raking down his back, their teeth snapping near his face. The distance between him and his enemy was growing—they were pushing him back, trying to hem him in against a building. Just as he felt his back hit a wall, though, some of the creatures shrieked and fell as Eli, Trevor, Hai, Parinda, and a horde of his Kere materialized around him. Reading his need, they grabbed creatures and held them so Moros could deliver the deathblow. "The others are coming this way," Trevor shouted.

The Ferrys and the Lucinae. None of them were really warriors, but all of them were armed with deadly glowing blades that might easily destroy a Ker. "Help them kill these things," Moros commanded. "But be careful of the blades."

Trevor vanished as the fight continued, and Moros began to cut a path toward Chaos, whose appearance had begun to shift again. He undulated in the flashing lights of hovering drone cams that had begun to gather over the catastrophe, capturing images of unimaginable carnage. As one of them swooped low, Chaos looked up at it, then waved his hand through the air as if swatting a fly.

The machines began to fall from the sky, crashing down onto the sidewalks, colliding with buildings, falling into the canals, some of them sparking and catching fire. Moros shielded his face as one shattered at his feet, and continued to slice his way toward Chaos. The Ferrys and Kere were fighting all around him, but with every second, the number of minions was growing. He had to get to the source, or they would be overwhelmed. Meanwhile, the buildings on either side of them swayed precariously, bowing to the disorienting, scattering vibrations emanating from the being who stood calmly on the corner, watching the mayhem with a pleased smile on his ever-shifting face.

As Moros fought his way forward, paying for inches with his own sweat and blood, the creature was hidden behind the wall of his minions. Pushing his growing exhaustion aside, Moros lunged through them, desperate not to lose sight of his foe. But when he managed to thin the group, he blinked in confusion and horror.

Patrick Ferry stood before him—holding Aislin by the throat. Moros froze in confusion as the battle raged behind him. Patrick had his struggling daughter against his chest, his other arm wrapped around her waist. Aislin's feet were bare and bleeding, kicking frantically inches from the pavement.

"Is this what you're fighting for?" Chaos asked, staring out at him through Patrick's blue eyes. His fingers tightened over Aislin's throat. She was staring at Moros, her expression pleading. "I've been informed that she's important to you."

Moros's hand tightened on the hilt of his blade. "This is an illusion," he muttered. But just as he raised his arm to attack, he was hit from behind. Declan and Cacia had fought their way to the front, aided by Trevor and Eli.

"Aislin!" shouted Cacia, her turquoise eyes full of horror as she watched her father jerk her sister back a few feet.

Moros tried to shove Cacia away, but Declan grabbed him as he charged forward. "He'll break her neck if you don't stop," Declan yelled, and when Moros tried to shake him off, the Ferry raised the knife he'd been using to cut through the minions. "Don't you fucking dare do anything to endanger my sister."

Aislin's arm rose from her side, reaching for Moros, and as her fingers grasped at the air, it felt like she'd closed them around his heart. She looked exactly as she had in those last moments of her life, as the Keeper of Hell had drained the vitality from her limbs and the spark from her eyes. "Moros," she said in a choked voice.

Patrick smiled in triumph as he began to squeeze the life out of her. Declan and Cacia screamed her name and lunged forward. "Trevor and Eli, hold them back," Moros shouted as he raised his blade. The two younger Ferrys cried out in horror as he plunged it into Aislin's chest, twisting as Patrick fell backward, a look of shock on his face. Moros landed on top of Aislin as her body convulsed, blood streaming from her nose and mouth. He watched her, expecting her to change shape, to reveal the true face of Chaos, but she remained beautiful and dying beneath him.

Eli fell back, hissing in pain, his arm bleeding, as Cacia stalked forward with murder in her eyes. Moros barely had time to flip onto his back and catch her before she tried to plunge her blade through his chest. Her face was contorted with rage and grief as she screamed, "You bastard! You killed her!"

"It wasn't her!" shouted Moros, but he could hear the choked gurgles as Aislin tried to draw breath, and it sent doubt and fear and confusion coursing through him. Had the Keepers betrayed him somehow? Had Chaos managed to get to her? As he wrestled with Cacia, the thoughts flew through his mind like a sandstorm, scraping the inside of his head raw, blurring his vision. With a forceful push, he threw Cacia to the side just in time to roll away as Declan attacked him, his arm arcing back and his blade flashing. Trevor, hard on his heels, managed to grab Declan just in time to prevent him from burying his blade in Moros's gut, but the movements of both men were growing uncoordinated and jerky.

Moros swiped at a trickle of liquid on his upper lip and found his fingers smeared with blood. It felt like the storm in his mind was tearing his brain apart, and by the look of Cacia and Declan, it was doing the same to them. They'd all gotten close enough to stop Chaos, but his mere presence was going to kill them quickly at this rate. Dizzy and weakening, Moros spun around to where Patrick had been, only to find him shifting and growing, sprouting arms and eyes as he loomed over the battle. Scrambling away from the clumsy slash of Declan's blade, Moros gripped his own dagger and lunged, but the creature kicked him in the chest, sending him flying. His panic grew as he watched Cacia and Declan collapse, twitching on the pavement. Aislin's beloved siblings were suffering and dying because their love for her had been used against them. Moros summoned all his strength.

Her strength. Theirs. He couldn't tell where she ended and he began, but knowing she was with him pulled him from the ground. Chaos stomped toward him, his many arms reaching, and Moros jabbed and parried, chopping off a few. For the first time, the monster's face twisted in clear frustration. He tried to kick Moros again, but Moros dove between his tree-trunk legs and sliced at his calves before rolling away in time to avoid Chaos's feet. Then the monster turned, with surprising quickness for something so huge, and before Moros could escape, the god had him in his grip. Moros's fingers clutched at his dagger, barely able to hold on as Chaos lifted him into the air.

The monster pulled him toward his gaping mouth. "You can't destroy me," he rumbled. "Everything falls apart. No order lasts forever."

At those words, Moros's thoughts suddenly cleared, and Aislin's face appeared in his memory. "But it doesn't have to end today," he said.

Then he shoved the blade upward, the point penetrating one of the creature's armpits. With a shrieking howl, he released Moros, but instead of letting himself fall, Moros looped his arm around one of Chaos's flailing limbs and plunged the dagger into the god's flesh again. Black blood spurted from the wound, a bitter-smelling liquid that burned as it splashed over Moros's legs.

Not today. Not today. Aislin's voice powered every thrust of his blade until the creature fell, landing with Moros's dagger buried in his chest. His massive arms twitched as his six eyes sought Moros's. "Someday," he rasped before going still.

Moros scrambled back as the beast began to crumble, and he turned to see the minions doing the same, collapsing in on themselves as shocked Ferrys and Kere watched. The air around him swirled with cinders and dust as he got to his feet. It was more destruction than he'd witnessed in millennia. The dead and injured were everywhere. The Veil would be crowded with souls waiting for their eternal reward—or punishment. The city was in ruins. But the survivors were looking around as if their thoughts had suddenly cleared. It gave Moros hope.

Cacia was stirring weakly in Eli's arms. The Ker looked up at him as he held his beloved close. "She was ready to stab me to get to Aislin," he said, nodding toward the false version of the Charon that lay crumbling on the sidewalk a few feet away. "So was Dec. How did you know it wasn't actually her?"

Moros glanced at Declan, who was leaning against Trevor, looking like he had a massive headache. "I'd like to know that, too," Declan muttered.

Moros tossed his blade to the ground and began to dust himself off. "She never calls me Moros."

Declan's eyebrows rose. "Okay," he said slowly. "Do you happen to know where the real deal is, then?"

Moros nodded, his heart taking on a new, urgent beat. He'd won. And that meant these were his last moments on Earth. "I'm going to get her now." He met Declan's eyes. "She'll be with you soon."

CHAPTER THIRTY-FOUR

The Keeper of Heaven looked down at the three glowing balls that floated an inch or so above her upturned palm. She'd been staring at them as she awaited the outcome of the great battle being waged in the earthly realm. The Keeper of Hell stood at her side. Their murmured conversation was so quiet that Aislin couldn't catch what they were saying.

She'd long since sunk to the floor, too tired to hold herself up. It was better than being chained to the wall, though, so she didn't bother asking for a chair. Clotho and Lachesis had gone quiet, but Aislin knew they expected good news soon.

Not if she had anything to do with it. She'd been very specific in the voice mail she'd left for Cavan before she'd headed for the summit. The Ferrys would double the quarterly gold allowance for the Lucinae, if only they put Magda on the throne. She'd basically incited a coup, but she'd known the Lucinae were on the verge of rejecting Baheera anyway. Aislin had simply wanted to speed the process along, because Moros needed those blades.

· She hoped the plan had worked, that Cavan had succeeded and Declan and Cacia had made it to the realm before it moved to another hidden location. Misgiving pricked at her silent heart. Even if everything went perfectly, Moros was going to come back and try to give himself up. His reward for victory would be eternal torture. The more she pondered that, the more insane it seemed, and the more determined she was not to let it happen. Slowly, she rose to her feet, shuddering as she caught sight of the black veins spidering across the back of her hands. "I'd like to discuss what happens next," she said to the Keepers.

The two of them turned to look at her. "Funnily enough, that's what we were just doing," the Keeper of Hell said to her. He gave her a speculative look. "Let me guess. You're about to offer yourself permanently, to save the Lord of the Kere from eternal torment." He yawned, an exaggerated, teasingly human affectation. "Mortals are so predictable. And selfish. We have bigger things to worry about, Charon."

"Really?" Aislin gestured toward the glowing orbs. "You seem eager to restore order, but isn't Moros a fairly important part of that? Punishing him to repay a two-thousand-year-old grudge seems rather *small* in that context."

The Keeper of Heaven stifled a giggle and poked the Keeper of Hell in his bulging biceps. "Do you still like her?"

The Keeper of Hell grumbled under his breath. "A little less than I did."

"Liar," said his mate. "She's perfect for what we need."

Aislin blinked at them. "Perfect for what?"

The Keeper of Heaven tilted her head, sending a sheet of shining black hair sliding over her shoulder. "You seem eager to save him. Is it because you were fated to be with him, do you think? Like a compulsion?"

"Are you implying I didn't make a conscious choice?"

"Your heart used to beat without you thinking about it. Is that what this is?"

"I don't think so," said Aislin. "I've watched him for as long as I can remember, and I know he's brave and he's determined and there is no better ally. If you want to repair the damage Chaos has done, you would have no stronger or more dedicated servant of fate than him. I am replaceable. He is not."

Something flared in the Keeper of Hell's eyes as he snatched one of the silvery balls from the Keeper of Heaven's protective grip. "Wrong. You think I can't reach into his chest and yank out one of these?" He inclined his head toward Clotho and Lachesis, who had sagged in their shackles, all their energy and divinity gone.

"Who is better suited than Jason Moros to bear its weight, though?" Aislin asked, her throat tightening as she thought of the way her entire family looked at him, the way the Lucinae openly loathed him, the way his own siblings had betrayed him. He'd borne it all with such strength. He deserved better than he'd gotten. It crushed her that she wouldn't be able to offer him everything she wanted to. But she could offer him this. "If he wins this battle, you should allow him to remain free."

"And what price would you be willing to pay for that freedom?" the Keeper of Heaven asked.

Aislin looked at the Keeper of Hell, at his ebony eyes and massive hands, remembering how his thick fingers had plunged into the chests of Clotho and Lachesis as if their breastbones were cobwebs. She wasn't arrogant enough to believe that centuries of torture wouldn't destroy her love for Jason Moros, but perhaps knowing he loved her, too, would sustain her. The alternative—seeing him in chains, brought to his knees, hurting and defeated after he'd fought so hard—was unthinkable. "Everything," she said. "Anything you ask."

The Keepers grinned and advanced on her as one. "I'm so glad you said that," the Keeper of Heaven said as the Keeper of Hell tossed the third glowing orb at his lover. It flew onto her palm and floated there with the other two.

Aislin took a reflexive step back but gasped as she collided with a hard chest. The Keeper of Hell had appeared behind her.

His hands covered her shoulders, holding her still. His midnight gaze moved from her face to his mate's. "This will be interesting."

The Keeper of Heaven nodded as she approached Aislin. The orbs in her hands were bright and pristine. They swirled in a circle as if they were magnetized. Aislin stared at them. "What are you—?"

"Birth and Mortality," the Keeper of Heaven said quietly as she plucked one of the orbs and examined it.

And then her fingers closed around the orb, and she slammed her fist into Aislin's chest. Aislin's mouth dropped open as her vision went blinding white. Her body filled with a pressure so intense that she was sure her rib cage would explode outward, scattering the wreckage of her heart across the throne room. But just as she felt herself cracking and breaking, the pressure eased for a moment.

"Destiny," she heard the Keeper say.

The agony doubled as she felt herself collide with the Keeper of Hell's chest, as his hands held her mercilessly tight, as she lost control of her limbs and thoughts and self.

"Inevitability," a voice echoed far away, and then Aislin was falling, flailing and screaming and unable to slow herself down as she plunged into a shimmering white abyss. Her only thought was that she had to stop her fall and climb back up, but bits of her were breaking off as she bounced against diamond walls—her fingers and toes, her arms, her legs, her skull. She was losing herself, and the further she descended, the less of her there was. Her loved ones' faces passed through her mind and fluttered away like butterflies, too quick and fragile to hold on to. Her understanding of herself, her pride in her work and everything she had built over the years, her fear that she would disappoint her family . . . gone. The more she tried to cling to herself, the more she was lost. So she held on to the one thing that comforted her—she might be gone, but Jason would be free.

She hit bottom, shattering into a million glittering shards that pinged off the walls and floor of a wide white room before coming together once again, splinters of flesh and bone wedging themselves back into place. Panting, she rose and looked around. She was wearing a gossamer white dress, and her skin was smooth. Her hands ran down her body as she looked around in confusion. This room had no ceiling, and the walls rose so high that all she could see was endless white for miles. The chamber was empty—except for a large basket sitting a few feet away. With faltering steps, she shuffled over and looked inside.

It was full of glinting threads. Mesmerized, she reached down to touch them, but as soon as her fingers sank in, her mind filled with images, people she'd never seen before in places she'd never been, so many at once that the shock drove her to her knees. She grabbed the edges of the basket to keep from falling.

When she'd caught her breath, she reached in again, but this time she was careful to only brush a fingertip over the end of one thread. A vision of an old man rose before her, with a bulbous nose and a kindly smile. When she pulled her hand away, the image disappeared. Her heart kicking against the walls of her chest, she touched another, and another, and another as realization loomed. These were the threads of people's lives, all tangled together in this basket. The torn, jumbled remnants of the fabric of fate.

And it was her job to put it back together.

CHAPTER THIRTY-FIVE

Moros appeared in the throne room of the Keepers, his stomach tight with dread and eagerness, loathing and love, extremes that could barely be contained as he braced himself for what he would find.

"You did it," said the Keeper of Heaven, who had her back to him. She was facing the Keeper of Hell, and whatever was between them glowed with an eerie light.

"I did," said Moros. He hobbled forward. Most of his injuries had healed rapidly, but the wound in his thigh, delivered by the Blade of Life, remained. He would have preferred to appear before the Keeper of Hell strong and unbowed, but getting Aislin out of here was far more important. "As promised, I'm here to give myself up."

"And to liberate Aislin Ferry from my diabolical clutches." The Keeper of Hell smirked. "Very moving. But there's no need."

Moros froze. "What?" He looked around for Aislin, but she was nowhere to be found. Worry and need twisted together inside him. "Where is she?"

"Right here." The Keeper of Heaven stepped to the side, revealing the source of the eerie glow.

Aislin was limp in the Keeper of Hell's grasp, her platinum hair hanging in waves over her face. Moros cried out as he rushed forward.

"She's free to go," the Keeper of Hell said as he released her, allowing Moros to scoop her into his arms.

Her head lolled against his throat, and her breath was warm against his skin. "She's alive again," Moros said quietly.

"She's more than alive," said the Keeper of Heaven.

"Aislin," he whispered, kissing her forehead. "Wake up, darling." He needed her to look at him, to smile at him. He needed to feel her arms around him.

The Keeper of Hell laughed. "You didn't think it would be that easy, did you?"

Moros's gaze traced over Aislin's face. Her skin was luminous, her lips soft and pink. She looked perfect. But the Keeper's laugh sent a chill down his spine. Something was very wrong. "Wake her up. I want to say good-bye to her."

"Like I told you, I'm not keeping you here. You can take her and go." The Keeper turned his back and strode away, heading for his dark throne.

Moros held Aislin tighter and looked at the Keeper of Heaven. "What's wrong with her? What did you do?"

The Keeper shrugged her slender shoulders. "We asked a lot of her. But we needed someone to bear the burden of order, now that your sisters have given up their duties. And she really was perfect."

Moros looked up at Clotho and Lachesis, still chained to the wall. They were staring at Aislin with an odd yearning in their eyes, and their chests were concave. Hollow. "No," he murmured, looking back down at Aislin with horror taking root in his heart.

"She agreed to it," said the Keeper.

"She did it for you, brother," said Clotho, her voice a mere whisper.

The Keeper of Hell reached his throne. "Shut up," he said in an annoyed voice. He looked over his shoulder at the Keeper of Heaven. "I'm off to reunite these two with their sisters and brother. Their screams will echo for an eternity. " His ebony eyes were wistful.

The Keeper of Heaven blew him a kiss. "Until next time."

The Keeper of Hell made a catching gesture, his large fist closing over empty air. And then he turned to Clotho and Lachesis, whose chains dissolved. But before they could flee or fall, he grabbed them by the throats and dragged them toward his throne. They began to shriek as he pulled them into the black and disappeared into the inky darkness.

Moros felt his wounded leg begin to shake beneath him as he returned his attention to the woman in his arms. His strength was fading, grief filling him up. "You destroyed her," he said in a low voice.

"I remade her," said the Keeper of Heaven. "She is Fate now." Her smile was bright. "She'll be amazing."

"She is mortal," Moros shouted. "Her mind and body weren't made for this!"

"Well, she's immortal now," said the Keeper of Heaven. She reached out and touched Aislin's hair. "We decided to place the whole of Fate in her hands—and in her body, where it will be safer than a realm within the Veil. But I'm sure it's overwhelming for her."

Moros's world was bleeding crimson. "Overwhelming? You've given her the burden of every fate, of every living human. A responsibility three immortals used to bear. And you've forced it upon her. You forced it *inside* her." He could barely breathe as he imagined what they'd done, jamming those glowing orbs of divinity into Aislin's precious chest.

"She was willing. She said she would do anything to set you free."

It felt like Chaos's hands were locked around his windpipe again. "She should never have had the choice," he whispered.

"Her body will go on forever," the Keeper said. "That should console you." She turned to walk up to her throne. "And as long as she does her job, I'm not really concerned either way." She lifted the hem of her gown and strutted up the stairs of the dais. "Nice seeing you again, Moros. I'm glad you defeated Chaos." She disappeared into the glittering light of her throne.

Leaving Moros alone with the woman he loved in his arms. He'd expected a tragic good-bye. He'd expected her to cling to him before he was taken away. He'd expected to send her off, back into the earthly realm, with her taste on his lips and her scent in his nose, the things he would carry with him into Hell.

He hadn't expected this.

With leaden footsteps, he walked to the edge of the Keeper's throne room and willed himself back into the real world, to his penthouse, his refuge. The building was still standing, as it was a few blocks to the west of Psychopomps, but he had a clear view of the devastation. Aislin would have been horrified—but then she would have set to work overseeing the salvage and rebuilding. But now, as he laid her on his bed and brushed her platinum hair from her brow, she'd been given an infinitely larger responsibility, one she might not be strong enough to bear, one that had driven her so deep inside herself that her mind was unreachable.

He squeezed his eyes shut as he sank to his knees. His sisters had taken their revenge, and so had the Keeper of Hell.

Moros had Aislin back. They were both alive. But he'd lost her all the same.

CHAPTER THIRTY-SIX

The threads were a mess, and the basket seemed bottomless. The more she pulled, the more came up. The pile of them, taller than she was, filled the room. She'd been tugging and yanking, blowing her hair off her sweaty forehead as she worked without stopping. No one else was here to do the job, and she couldn't help the sense that these people needed her. Every time she touched a thread, she could see their lives stretching before them. At first it had been incapacitating—she could touch only one at a time or she would get dizzy and end up on the floor. But now she could grab a handful and manage the flickering flashes of lives that needed living. She'd found she could separate and sort each image as it appeared before her eyes, but now she had to do the same with the actual threads.

She straightened up and set another bunch of tangled strands on the pile, rubbing her back and looking around at the hills of shimmering filaments around her. "This is going to take a while," she said quietly.

It didn't matter how long it took—she would find a way to reassemble the fabric. Because she was Fate, and she knew that now. She couldn't believe she'd ever forgotten it.

An echo of a voice reached her, and she stopped as she leaned over the basket again, listening. It wasn't coming from the threads—she wasn't touching any of them at the moment. The murmured words were too quiet to understand, but the voice sounded familiar and filled her chest with unexpected longing. "Hello?" she called.

The voice went quiet, and she began to work on separating each thread from the next, laying them out along the infinite floor of her domain. If she was supposed to rebuild the tapestry, she'd have to examine each strand individually. She pulled at one, the life of a woman, now in her thirties, with years and years stretching ahead of her. But as she tried to tug the woman's thread, she found it was knotted with another. As she ran her fingers over those tangles, planning to unknot them, she let out a surprised cry at what she saw, the woman in a man's arms, him offering her an umbrella in a downpour, her shopping for his favorite kind of candy. Fate stopped trying to untangle them, and instead laid them out together. A strange yearning came over her, and she fought the urge to return to those knots, to watch and watch as the couple made love and fought and forgave and fell asleep together.

She pushed it out of her mind and refocused on her task, separating threads and organizing them. As she pulled a new thread from the pile, she noticed it was still knotted with several others but had gone gray and dull. That wasn't right. Something had to be done about it.

She frowned and reached out, pulling a pair of scissors from the air.

She blinked down at her hand. She had needed this tool, and it had appeared from nowhere. Biting her lip, she raised the scissors and peered at herself reflected in the metal blade. Ice-blue eyes looked back at her. She lowered her hand and looked down at the gray thread. Though she'd been working for . . . really, she had no idea how long she'd been working, but it seemed like a while . . .

this was the first gray thread she'd noticed, and it felt important. Her thumb ran over the dull strand, but she couldn't see much, just a fog. With a trembling hand, she followed the path of the thread, right to where it tangled with several others.

She lowered the scissors, positioning them over the thread at the place that felt right. Then she snipped it away and watched it float to the floor.

CHAPTER THIRTY-SEVEN

Moros jerked as he felt the sting in his chest, making his chair rattle against the hardwood floor. He hadn't felt that sensation in days, but he knew exactly what it was.

Cacia looked over from her spot at Aislin's bedside. "You okay?"

Moros stood up and slowly walked over to the woman he loved, who lay still and unmoving on his bed. It had been ten days. Ten agonizing days. And Aislin hadn't so much as twitched. But . . . now a face rose in his mind, one with a beaky nose and prematurely receding hair. Antoni Banach, thirty-four, resident of Warsaw. His time had come.

Moros let out a bemused laugh. "I'll be right back."

He followed his sense of the young man through the Veil and found him sitting at a long table in a crowded refugee center, eating synthesized protein from a tin. Slipping into the real world, Moros walked by, touching Antoni on the shoulder as he passed, Marking him for death.

He waited impatiently in the Veil as Antoni choked to death, then watched as his soul rose from his body in the cold gray world. Almost immediately, a portal opened, and Rosaleen Ferry stepped through. "Moros," she said in surprise.

Moros gestured at Antoni. "Do the honors, if you please."

Rosaleen's fingers rose to the Charon's Scope at her throat, maybe wondering if this was a trap. "I just want you to know—Aislin's will made it clear that she wanted me to be the Charon if—"

"She's not dead."

Rosaleen bowed her head. "Of course not. But she wanted me to take the role if she . . . couldn't."

"I know," Moros said quietly, staring at Antoni, who waited passively to meet his final fate. "And she's busy anyway." He wasn't sure if he wanted to shout with rage or laugh out loud. Maybe both. Aislin had figured it out. She'd cut her first thread.

Rosaleen guided the young man to Heaven, but when she looked into the portal she'd opened with her Scope, waiting for her coin to emerge, she jumped back in surprise. Moros leaned over to see the Keeper of Heaven herself standing in the opening. Her diamond gaze was triumphant. "She did it," the Keeper said happily. "Now we're in business again."

She tossed a coin out of her realm, and it hit Moros in the chest and landed on the ground between him and Rosaleen, who closed her Scope quickly and snapped it to the chain around her neck. "Was that—?"

"The Keeper of Heaven herself. Yes."

Rosaleen gave him a cautious look as she scooped the coin from the ground. "So it's true, what you've told us about Aislin."

Moros was already impatient to get back to her. He waved dismissively as Rosaleen offered him the coin to split with his teeth. "My dear woman, did you really think I had made up that outrageous story just to entertain myself?"

The woman's chin lifted in defiance. "I'm not sure what to think about you yet."

Moros grinned, giving her a nice view of his fangs. "Likewise. And keep the change." He willed himself back to his penthouse.

Cacia was still there, but she'd gathered her things and was preparing to leave. "Aislin looked better today, I think. I swear she thought my story about nearly losing my Scope in the canal was funny. Her lip kind of twitched."

Moros ran his hands over his face, wishing Cacia weren't so sunny and optimistic all the time. She'd been here every single day for hours, talking to Aislin nonstop. *She can't hear you,* he wanted to shout. But he'd managed not to, for Aislin's sake. She loved Cacia. She wouldn't want her to despair. "How encouraging," he murmured as he saw her to the door. "I suppose I'll see you tomorrow?"

Cacia stopped and turned to him. "You don't believe she's going to wake up, do you?"

He sighed. "You have to understand the magnitude of the task she's been given." And she was doing it. She'd figured out how to cut the threads, and that meant she must be hard at work. Somewhere in the realm of her mind, Aislin was puzzling out her new responsibilities.

It made him miss her more than ever.

Cacia's eyes met his. "Do you remember the things you saw when you touched me?"

Guilt pulsed inside him. "Yes."

"I do, too." Her voice was level, but the note of sadness was impossible to miss. "I was destined to be with Eli all along. We were going to have kids. It was going to be messy and awesome and heartbreaking and beautiful."

He looked away. "That's true."

"We'll never have those kids now. We'll never have that life, because his was interrupted." Cacia poked Moros's arm to draw his gaze back to hers. "But we're still together. And it's messy and awesome and heartbreaking and beautiful. I'm still me, and he's still him, just dealing with different stuff. But even when his thread was cut, or however that works, it didn't keep us apart."

Moros shivered as he felt Aislin cut another thread. He pushed the sensation out into the Veil, assigning one of his Kere to do the honors. "I'm glad the two of you are finding your way."

She put her hands on her hips. "I'm not telling you this so you can be condescending."

"Then please tell me what you do want, Cacia, and I'll do my best to provide it."

She rolled her eyes. "I guess the condescension is just a built-in perk." She adjusted the strap of her bag on her shoulder. "I'm telling you this because, after you touched me, you told Eli that I belonged to him, and you were right. And as traumatic as that whole experience was, knowing that I was meant to be with him helped me stick it out, even when things got really bad. I wouldn't give up. I won't *ever* give up." She leaned forward. "You shouldn't either."

"But Aislin and I aren't—"

"She belongs to you," Cacia said quietly. "Right?" She scuffed her foot along his floor. "It makes sense, to me at least. I can't really picture her with anyone else."

"Does it matter? She's *gone*. She was never meant to play the role of Fate, and it's too much for her."

"Then help her."

"I can't reach her," he said from between clenched teeth.

"Find a way! I want her back, and I'm doing my part. I come here every day and make sure she hears my voice. I make sure she knows what she's missing." Her voice had gone tight, and her eyes were shining. "I tell her how much I want to talk to her again, and how I'm so sorry I was such a bitch to her. I promise her that the next gala we go to, I'll wear an *appropriate* dress." She angrily swiped at a tear. "But I don't think she'll come back until you do the same."

"I'm not partial to wearing dresses."

"Goddammit, you know what I mean!"

"She has enough to do!" he said, his voice rising along with his frustration. He was by Aislin's side night and day, the shadow in the corner as her family visited, the ghost watching over her all night, pacing the floor and listening to her heart beat. He would protect her and take care of her until the end, but that was as far as it went. "I refuse to add to her burden."

"But she needs to come back!" Cacia's cheeks were suffused with pink, and her hands were balled in fists. "And she needs *you* to remind her why she should." She took a step toward the door, tightening her ponytail and letting out a deep breath. "See you tomorrow." She turned on her heel and headed for the elevator.

Moros watched her disappear inside, his heart pounding. None of them understood. They'd never seen the weaving room, or how hard his sisters worked. And the Keepers had made Aislin like him, carrying all that responsibility inside her mind and body.

She hadn't been made to handle it.

He closed his front door and walked back to his bedroom, pausing in the doorway. Aislin was as beautiful as ever, her skin smooth and luminous, her face peaceful.

His want of her was slowly crumbling his heart, and suddenly it was too much.

He kicked off his shoes and crawled onto the bed, pressing his face to her hair and wrapping his arm over her body. He had been trying to keep his distance, not wanting to distract her from her duties, not wanting to drive her further into the realm of her mind where she'd been banished, but now he was certain his chest was going to cave in if he didn't hold her.

His throat was impossibly tight as he kissed her temple. "Your sister is a fierce little creature," he said quietly. "I think she almost punched me just now." He laid his head on the pillow, inhaling Aislin's clean violet scent. "She believes I should be telling you all the wonderful things you're missing." His thumb stroked her cheek. There was no momentary blindness when he touched her anymore. Now it was simply skin on skin, him and her.

"I can't do that," he continued. "Because very truthfully, the world is a mess, and slightly messier than it should be right now. You're not the Charon anymore, and Psychopomps will suffer for it. I certainly won't stand in Rosaleen's way, but she's not you. She can't read a room like you can. She can't tell within an instant what each person wants, and she's not as clever about making people feel like they're getting exactly what they crave when all the while you're pushing them into place, getting them to follow your agenda." He chuckled quietly. "What you did with the Lucinae . . . brilliant. I was so determined to save you, but you saved me instead. You saved us all."

He propped himself on an elbow and skimmed his fingertips across her brow, over her cheekbones, each touch an act of worship. And as he gazed at her, he thought about everything he'd just said, and everything he knew about the woman he adored. "Actually, I'm not sure why I didn't believe you could manage this. You're in there, setting things right, aren't you? You're organizing and innovating, and you're going to make it better than it ever was." He caressed her pale cheek, a desperate hope sinking its fingers into his marrow. "Once you've turned that mess of thread into a tapestry, once you've figured it out—come back."

His eyes burned, and he swallowed hard as he gave in to the pull of all his wishes, as he surrendered his pride and his distance, as he stripped away the armor that had held him together ever since he'd returned from the Keepers' throne room. "Please come back, Aislin. I'm here, and I need you. I can't be happy until you're by my side. I was alone for thousands of years, but that loneliness was nothing . . ." His voice had faded to a rasp, and he cleared his throat. "That was *nothing* compared to having you with me but not really having you here. So do what you must do, but then come back. Come back to me."

He nestled in close to her, her hand in his, and lay awake all night, whispering his plea into her ear, even as he felt the sting and prick of Aislin, deaf to his words and hard at work, snipping away the threads of lives and loves that had come to an end.

CHAPTER THIRTY-EIGHT

Fate was happily digging in her basket as the magnificent loom behind her did its work. When she'd discovered that she could pull what she needed out of thin air, she'd set herself to the task of building the most efficient machine possible.

This was her job, after all, and it was her mind, her realm. She made the rules. As soon as she'd discovered that, things had begun to really move. The knowledge of what needed to be done came to her intuitively, as if she'd been meant to do it. Despite that, the task had been all-consuming. The only time she had been distracted was when she heard the faint, echoing voices, the ones that filled her with quiet longing. Every time she heard them, she hummed loudly until they stopped, because straining to listen only made the feeling worse and slowed her down.

She had finally reached the last of the threads in the basket, and one final strand lay coiled, all alone and untangled, atop a swell of unprocessed wool. She could only assume the wool was the raw material for new lives, whose threads had to be created, whose paths had to be set. Once she got this final thread into the tapestry, she could begin to spin new strands. Surely there was a way to automate that, too. She reached into the basket and scooped up the last remaining thread. Images flooded her mind as it coiled around her fingers.

It was Aislin Ferry, gazing out over the city she loved before turning to look at the man standing in her office. He had olive skin and gray eyes, ebony hair and an impeccable sense of style. His smile was dangerous and inviting at the same time. And his face . . . she could have stared forever. She'd memorized all his expressions but still didn't know what all of them meant. She wanted to, though. God, how she wanted to.

"Jason," she murmured, then jerked with surprise as she heard his name come off her tongue. "Jason Moros."

She held the thread tightly, her fingers dancing along the length of it, reliving nearly a hundred years of victories and failures, frustrations and joys. And then she slid her fingertip along to the end, when it cut off abruptly—the last thing she saw was his face, decorated with a smile that took her breath away. She was in his arms, and that was where she belonged.

Come back, Aislin, he whispered, the sound reaching out to her, slipping around her, holding her still. *Come back, and we'll have forever together.*

Aislin. That name, *his* voice . . .

"I'm Aislin Ferry," she said quietly, looking around at her loom and her basket and the brilliant order she had brought to this previously chaotic room. The thread fell from her fingers as confusion and memory battled. "I wasn't always here, and this isn't everything I am."

As soon as she said it, a ladder appeared, rising from the floor up into the white sky. She walked over to it and began to climb.

CHAPTER THIRTY-NINE

He was telling her about Santa Maddalena, a beautiful little village in Italy where he longed to take her, when he heard her heartbeat accelerate, tapping fiercely within her chest. He held his breath, refusing to allow hope to take root. It had been nearly three months now, and she was unmoving, unchanging. The only thing that had kept him going was the sting when she sliced through the threads—it told him she was in there, working tirelessly. Order was being restored, driving Chaos deeper and deeper into eternal slumber, never completely dead, but no longer an immediate threat. All the Shade-Kere had been killed, all his Kere were loyal, and the Ferrys had already rented new office space while construction began on their new headquarters.

Cacia and Declan came to visit every day, sometimes bringing Eli and Galena along. Declan always glared at Moros with quiet suspicion and wouldn't say a word until he gave them privacy. So Moros would sit out on his patio and pretend he couldn't hear, drinking Scotch and listening to Declan telling his sister how he meant it when he said he forgave her, how he'd made mistakes, too, but what he really wanted was for her to come back. She was missed. She was loved.

It was hard to listen to. Harder every day.

Moros turned to Aislin, placing his hand on her chest, over her heart, which was pounding. "What's going on in there, darling?" He said it gently, mostly to himself.

But at the sound of his voice, her eyelids fluttered. He propped himself on his elbow, his own heart crashing in time with hers. "Aislin?"

Her fingers twitched.

"I'm here," he said to her, his voice breaking. "Come back, Aislin. Come back, and we'll have forever together."

"Jason," she whispered.

One word that shattered him. He let out a choked sound and laid his forehead on hers. "Yes. Come back now. Open your beautiful eyes."

She obeyed, and he tensed. Her eyes were solid white. "Jason?"

"I'm right here." He lifted her hand and placed it on his cheek.

She blinked rapidly, and suddenly the white cleared, and her blue eyes focused on him. She gave him a wistful smile. "Hello."

"Hello," he said in a strained voice.

"I remembered who I was."

"I've never forgotten, even for a moment."

Her face fell. "Have I been gone a long time?"

He shook his head, eager to bring the smile back to her face. But then her eyes went white again, making his heart stop. He felt the familiar sting in his chest just as she focused on him again, and the miracle of it settled on him so heavily that he nearly collapsed on top of her. Instead, he pushed the face and name outward to one of his Kere, and then tenderly kissed Aislin's palm. "You amaze me," he murmured. She had remained conscious, here with him, and still managed to attend to the threads of fate.

"I take it you defeated Chaos."

He laughed. "Thanks to you."

"And that the Keeper of Hell let you go."

"Again, thanks to you."

Her gaze traced over his face, and she sighed happily. "Are you all right?" she asked.

He closed his eyes as she slid her fingers into his hair. "I am now. I've never missed anyone or anything as much as I've missed you."

"That's because we were meant to be together," she said simply. His brow furrowed, and she stroked her fingertips over it, smoothing it out. "Your sisters told me. They wanted to use it against you." She drew him down, and he brushed his lips across hers, scared to give in to the overwhelming relief and passion winding along his bones. "But when they told me, I knew they were right."

"I don't see how it's possible." He was outside of fate and always had been. But he thought back, how he'd watched her grow, how she'd always been the first person he noticed in a room, how hers was the heartbeat he found himself tapping his fingers in time with, the face that made him smile . . . and then there were the times they'd been together, when everything had become startlingly clear. "Never mind," he said with a chuckle. "They were right."

She stroked her hands along his shoulders and chest. "What now?"

"Now we make sure you don't try to do too much too soon. You are bearing a huge responsibility, and it's still very new." He drew his thumb along the edge of her jaw. "But there are a few people who will be desperately happy to see you awake, and we should probably go see them in the morning."

Her eyes flashed white again, and Moros felt the result, another soul to be reaped. Then she blinked, and her fingers strayed to her throat. "I'm not the Charon anymore."

His stomach tensed. He hadn't anticipated having to talk to her about this. "No, and you're not a Ferry anymore, either." Her raven mark had disappeared; he'd spent a few evenings holding her to his chest, tracing his fingers over her back, following the lines that used to be there.

Her eyes filled with tears, and he waited, his chest aching, while she fought to control them. "Rosaleen could use your guidance, I'm sure," he said. "And if she's not wise enough to accept it . . ."

Her eyebrows rose as she swept a stray tear from her cheek. "Yes?"

"If being in control of the fate of every living human isn't quite enough to keep you busy, I may have a job for you. I do happen to own a number of businesses myself, all of which would benefit from your leadership and brilliant management."

She sniffled and laughed. "You want me to work for you?"

He leaned down and nudged her nose with his. "Not *for* me. With me. And if we are together, no one else stands a chance."

The intrigued, triumphant spark in her eyes was too much, and he captured her mouth, unable to resist for another second. Her arms wound around his neck, and she moaned. It was so devastatingly right that he wanted to roar with satisfaction. They were equals in every way now. Immortal and timeless, servants of fate who were fated to be together.

It had been worth the long, lonely wait, worth the fight, worth every moment when he thought he'd lost everything. As Aislin arched up, seeking the weight and heat of his body, seeking *him*, he couldn't help the joy that burned through him.

The future stretched long and beautiful in front of them, and it was time to get it started.

ACKNOWLEDGMENTS

My endless thanks to the publishing team at 47North, including and especially Jason Kirk, Britt Rogers, Ben Smith, and Alex Carr, for their tireless dedication to making sure the Servants of Fate series had the visibility it needed to reach its readers. Thank you for your confidence in me, your patience, and your creativity. My books could not be in better hands. And a special thanks goes to Cliff Nielsen, for designing my incredibly beautiful covers.

To Leslie "Lam" Miller, my developmental editor: you have spoiled me rotten. Thank you for carving out the time to work with me on this book, and for the honesty, encouragement, questioning, and "benevolent butchery" that made it better. And once again, thank you to Elizabeth Johnson, my copyeditor, for patiently fixing all my little writing foibles—and for letting me know that, despite them, the story touched you.

My agent, Kathleen Ortiz, has been an unparalleled partner in this journey. It's been over four years, lady, and a dozen books, with no end in sight. Thank you. This time around, Danielle Barthel and Joanna Volpe filled in all the gaps and held me together during some critical times. More thanks goes to the rest of the New Leaf team, including Jaida Temperly, Jess Dallow, Suzie Townsend, Dave Caccavo, and Pouya Shahbazian. You guys are simply awesome.

To my dear friends Lydia Kang and Brigid Kemmerer: whether I'm ecstatic or in despair, I know you'll be there to share it with me. Your wisdom and empathy have kept me going on days when it has felt like the fabric of my own life was unraveling; your beautiful, intense stories have made the rest of the world drop away right when I needed it to; and your keen eyes and astute feedback have steered me in the right direction every time. I am so lucky to have you.

I am fortunate to have colleagues who make this double life I lead not only tolerable but fun. Catherine, your wit and warmth makes me look forward to work. And to the rest of the CCBS leadership team—Chris, Casey, Kristal, Bethany, and Erica—you are inspiring. I am so proud of you, and so thankful for the work we've done together.

Paul, I could not ask for a better mentor or friend. Thank you for everything. And more gratitude to Liz, for offering your friendship and your home as a refuge, and to Jim, for unwavering support.

To my parents: thank you for your faith in me and your unconditional love. To my children: you are my loves. Thank you for being your adorable selves.

And to my readers: thank you for coming on this ride with me.

ABOUT THE AUTHOR

Sarah Fine is a clinical psychologist and the author of the Guards of the Shadowlands series—*Sanctum, Fractured,* and *Chaos*—as well as other young adult novels. She was born on the West Coast, raised in the Midwest, and is now firmly entrenched on the East Coast.